PRAISE FOR
VIOLENT ENDS

☆ "The storytelling is wonderfully intense and distinctive on such a difficult, tragic topic. Readers will be captivated, not wanting to put the book down, but also needing a break due to the extremely engaging, emotionally charged content of characters' feelings and thoughts."—*VOYA*, starred review

"A fresh and thought-provoking take on a disturbing but relevant topic."—*School Library Journal*

"Provocatively and effectively illustrates the multidimensionality of someone considered to be a monster."—*Kirkus Reviews*

Shaun David Hutchinson · Neal Shusterman and Brendan Shusterman ·
Beth Revis · Cynthia Leitich Smith · Courtney Summers ·
Kendare Blake · Delilah S. Dawson · Steve Brezenoff · Tom Leveen ·
Hannah Moskowitz · Blythe Woolston · Trish Doller · Mindi Scott ·
Margie Gelbwasser · Christine Johnson · E. M. Kokie · Elisa Nader

VIOLENT ENDS

Simon Pulse
New York London Toronto Sydney New Delhi

SIMON PULSE

An imprint of Simon & Schuster Children's Publishing Division

1230 Avenue of the Americas, New York, NY 10020

First Simon Pulse paperback edition December 2016

Compilation copyright © 2015 by Shaun David Hutchinson

"Miss Susie" copyright © 2015 by Steve Brezenoff • "Violent Beginnings" copyright © 2015 by Beth Revis • "Survival Instinct" copyright © 2015 by Tom Leveen • "The Greenest Grass" copyright © 2015 by Delilah S. Dawson • "Feet First" copyright © 2015 by Margie Gelbwasser • "The Perfect Shot" copyright © 2015 by Shaun David Hutchinson • "The Girl Who Said No" copyright © 2015 by Trish Doller • "Pop" copyright © 2015 by Christine Johnson • "Presumed Destroyed" copyright © 2015 by Neal and Brendan Shusterman • "The Second" copyright © 2015 by Blythe Woolston • "Astroturf" copyright © 2015 by E. M. Kokie • "Grooming Habits" copyright © 2015 by Elisa Nader • "Hypothetical Time Travel" copyright © 2015 by Mindi Scott • "All's Well" copyright © 2015 by Cynthia Leitich Smith • "Burning Effigies" copyright © 2015 by Kendare Blake • "Holes" copyright © 2015 by Hannah Moskowitz • "History Lessons" copyright © 2015 by Courtney Summers

Cover photograph copyright © 2015 by Getty Images

Also available in a Simon Pulse hardcover edition.

All rights reserved, including the right of reproduction in whole or in part in any form.

SIMON PULSE and colophon are registered trademarks of Simon & Schuster, Inc.

For information about special discounts for bulk purchases, please contact Simon & Schuster Special Sales at 1-866-506-1949 or business@simonandschuster.com.

The Simon & Schuster Speakers Bureau can bring authors to your live event. For more information or to book an event contact the Simon & Schuster Speakers Bureau at 1-866-248-3049 or visit our website at www.simonspeakers.com.

Jacket designed by Jessica Handelman

Interior designed by Mike Rosamilia

The text of this book was set in Adobe Garamond Pro.

Manufactured in the United States of America

2 4 6 8 10 9 7 5 3 1

The Library of Congress has cataloged the hardcover edition as follows:

Violent ends / Shaun David Hutchinson, Neal Shusterman and Brendan Shusterman, Beth Revis, Cynthia Leitich Smith, Courtney Summers, Kendare Blake, Delilah S. Dawson, Steve Brezenoff, Tom Leveen, Hannah Moskowitz, Blythe Woolston, Trish Doller, Mindi Scott, Margie Gelbwasser, Christine Johnson, E. M. Kokie, Elisa Nader.

p. cm.

Summary: Relates how one boy—who had friends, enjoyed reading, played saxophone in the band, and had never been in trouble before—became a monster capable of entering his high school with a loaded gun and firing on his classmates, as told from the viewpoints of several victims. Each perspective is written by a different writer of young adult fiction.

[1. School shootings—Fiction. 2. High schools—Fiction. 3. Schools—Fiction.
4. Perspective (Philosophy)—Fiction.] I. Hutchinson, Shaun David.

PZ5.V468 2015   [Fic]—dc23   2015010653

ISBN 978-1-4814-3745-5 (hc)

ISBN 978-1-4814-3746-2 (pbk)

ISBN 978-1-4814-3747-9 (eBook)

VIOLENT
ENDS

"MISS SUSIE"

Susanna Byrd turned nine that Thursday morning at 7:17 a.m. She kept her eyes on the digital clock on the stove, the spoon of Cream of Wheat with a swirl of clover honey halfway to her mouth, and when it flickered from :16 to :17, she grinned and chomped that spoonful.

Miss Susie had a steamboat.
The steamboat had a bell.

No gifts at breakfast—that'd been the rule forever. But there were three cards under her bowl of Cream of Wheat when she came to the table, and there was her mother, standing behind her chair, smiling.

"Did Dad leave already?"

Mom frowned and nodded, her head cocked at a sympathetic angle. "And Byron, too."

Susanna's big brother—the high schooler. He was never around and Susanna didn't care, anyway.

She'd saved the cards till 7:17, of course, and then she pushed aside her barely eaten bowl of Cream of Wheat with a swirl of clover honey. The top card was from Byron. Susanna tore the envelope (and a little of the card in the process) and scanned his scrawled note that might as well have said, "You suck and I hope you die," even if it actually said, "Happy birthday, Sis. Love, Byron."

The next card on the stack was from her grandmother in New York, Susanna's only living grandparent. That one had a check in it. Susanna adored checks. She pulled it out—it was a pink one—and folded it once and then once again and shoved it into her back pocket.

"Do you want me to bring that to the bank for you today?" Mom asked.

Susanna shook her head. "I wanna go with you. Wait for me to get home."

The bottom card was from Mom and Dad, with a message from each inside, their handwriting as different as a hammer and a nail.

After breakfast—Susanna ate every last speck of Cream of Wheat with a swirl of clover honey—her mother tied three silver ribbons into her hair, which was the color of buckwheat honey, and she said, "Happy birthday, Susanna. I hope you have a perfect day."

It was three blocks south and three blocks east to the bus stop. Susanna would rather walk diagonally, but the streets weren't made that way. Sometimes she fantasized about soaring like a crow straight from the top of her house to the bus stop, over the other houses and fenced-in yards and other kids. Sometimes she imagined tunneling way down deep, under the basements and sewers and electric cables.

Sometimes she just slipped out the front door and waved to her mom and set her eyes on the road ahead till the door closed behind her. Then she skirted the homes and pranced across the grass and cut across backyards and front yards and went diagonally anyway.

Miss Susie went to Heaven
And the steamboat went to Hell—

"I like the ribbons in your hair." Susanna stopped at the words and let her backpack drop down her arm so the strap settled into her hand. She found Ella standing there, right smack in the middle of a backyard that rightfully shouldn't have held either of the girls. Ella Stone was the tallest in her grade—but only eight for another six weeks. That gave Susanna seniority.

Ella had hair the color of starflower honey. So rare and desirable.

"Why do you have ribbons in your hair?"

"It's my birthday," Susanna said. She didn't add, "I'm nine." She hoped Ella would ask.

Ella didn't.

"Are you going to school today?" Susanna asked.

Ella coughed twice into her elbow—the Dracula; that's what Susanna's teachers called it since preschool—and then shook her head. The waves of starflower-honey hair—such a prettier and gentler honey than Susanna's honey hair—caught the morning sunlight and made Susanna shiver.

"Not ever? You're skipping school?"

Ella coughed like Dracula again. "I'm going to the doctor. I have pneumonia, Mom says."

Susanna took a step backward and lifted her bag onto her shoulder again. "Bye."

-O! operator
Please give me number nine

Susanna crossed Cassowary Lane. She didn't look both ways. In fact, she closed her eyes as she crossed diagonally through its intersection with Heron Lane, and she listened. She listened and she listened hard, and she didn't hear a thing. She knew it was safe. The whole time she knew it was safe, but she wasn't sure she was alive till she felt the grass beneath her feet on the far corner. Then she opened her eyes, and above her a crow croaked and cawed. Susanna had to squint to find it against the sun, still low over the houses of Birdland. It landed at the very top of a fir tree in the nearest backyard.

"I'm nine," she said to the crow in a quiet, private voice. "Today's my birthday."

The crow heard her—she was sure of that. It cocked its head just like Mom.

Crows recognize faces. She saw that on PBS, and PBS only tells the truth. Dad told her that. Susanna couldn't tell one crow from another, but at least all the crows in Birdland would know her.

She was still looking at the black bird—it shined under the cloudless blue sky, and if its feathers were black (and they were), then its eyes were blacker still, deeper than onyx, deeper than the peak of the night sky if stars didn't exist—when there came a *crack*, another *crack*, and the bird seemed to puff into its own feathers, feathers that fluttered too slowly and fell out of view. The bird was gone.

4

Susanna dropped her eyes and found three boys. They stood in the backyard two over from that fir tree, and the middle boy—he stood in the center, and was taller than the shorter boy and shorter than the taller boy—held a little rifle. Susanna hurried to the fence and stood there, glaring at them through the chain-link.

"What do *you* want?" said one—the shortest one. His hair was sandy—barberry honey—and close cut, and his eyes were the color of celery and set far apart. His ears stuck out quite a bit, and the whole package made his face—especially once he grinned, revealing his braces—look like the front view of a family car. He was thirteen, she guessed, because he looked particularly mean, and Susanna set her mind again never to kiss a boy, never to marry one, and never to have babies.

The boy with the gun brought it down from his shoulder and held it by the butt, letting the nozzle bounce along the grass as he walked to the fence. "We shot that bird," he said. "Are you going to cry about it?"

Susanna shook her head. "Why'd you shoot it?"

"We're allowed," the middle boy said. His hair was shaggy and thick, and Susanna imagined putting her fingers in it. She thought they might get stuck. His eyes were like hot chocolate with a single black mini marshmallow in the middle. There's no such thing as black marshmallows, though. "It's October. We're allowed to shoot crows this whole month."

Susanna didn't know if this was true. It didn't seem to make sense that it would be okay to kill a bird in October. Why October? Would it be okay to kill the same bird in November if you shot at it in October and missed? If you went hunting for crows on Halloween, did you have to stop at midnight?

5

Still, the boy didn't answer her question, and Susanna didn't push it. She turned her back on the fence and hitched up her bag and kept on toward the bus stop.

And if you disconnect me
I'll chop off your behind—

The next street—through two more yards—was Egret Lane, and Susanna stopped again. She was early anyway. Ten more minutes till the bus would get there, and it usually sat for five at the corner since it was the last pickup before the school. She stopped this time because she found another boy.

He was twelve, and he sat in a front yard, wearing his St. Luke's school uniform and reading a superhero comic book. Susanna didn't care for superheroes. Byron did, or he used to. Susanna had no idea what he cared for nowadays, but his disposition in favor of super-heroes had turned her off from them forever. Forever and ever, amen.

His hair was no honey color. It was shiny and black and wet or greasy, like the crow that got shot. His eyes were red at the edges and his nose was peppered with freckles. She didn't have to get close to know those things because he was Kirby Matheson and he lived in that house. The house with a pine tree in the front yard whose lower branches reached wide and close to the ground and made a little hideout beneath them. He said to her when he saw her staring, "What do you want?"

"Nothing," Susanna said, but she walked across his yard and stooped under the low-hanging pine branches and sat down with him on the bed of brown needles and dirt and sparse grass.

"So get out of here."

Susanna didn't, though. She brought her bag around and put it on her lap and said, "It's my birthday today. I'm nine."

"Good for you." He breathed in through his nose and let it out through pursed lips. "Happy birthday."

"Thank you. Where's Carah?" That was Kirby's eleven-year-old sister. She and Kirby were usually outside together in the morning.

"She has a doctor appointment."

"Is she sick?" Susanna thought about Ella and her pneumonia.

"I don't know."

The Mathesons still felt new in Birdland to Susanna because she could remember when they moved in. She couldn't remember when anyone else in the neighborhood moved in—at least anyone with kids.

"You shouldn't wear shiny ribbons in your hair and then sit under a tree."

"Why shouldn't I?" Susanna reached up and found the end of each ribbon with her fingertips. They were all still there, all still in place.

"You'll attract crows. They like shiny things."

"That's magpies," Susanna said. "And it's a myth, anyway."

"Like you know anything," said Kirby. "You're nine."

Susanna let him sulk a minute and decided to poke at him. She asked, "Were you crying?" It made her feel older for that instant, but also a bit worse. It hurt her heart.

"Get out of here, okay?" Kirby said.

Susanna didn't. She picked up a pinecone—a dry and brown and open one—and ran her fingers along its teeth. She doubted those flaps of stiff plant matter were really called teeth, but she liked the notion of pine trees dropping hundreds of thousands of brown, sticky teeth. "Did you hear the gunshots?" she asked him, but she didn't take her eyes off the pinecone.

"Yes." He grabbed his own pinecone now—Susanna caught him with the corner of her eye—and started pulling the teeth off. "They shot a crow."

"Did you see it?"

He shook his head. "They do it all the time."

"Are they in your grade?"

"Yeah. I don't like those guys, though."

Susanna watched the bus stop—she could just make it out through the branches and down the block. Kids gathered, most of them with chins down, kicking at curbs, swinging around the stop sign at the corner by one hand, with feet together against the base of the sign like dancers without partners. "They're mean, right?" Susanna said. "They seem mean to me."

"I guess," Kirby said.

Susanna spoke over him. "You look like a crow to me," she said. "Because you have shiny black hair and black eyes."

"I have brown eyes."

"They look black."

"Because it's dark under here."

Susanna leaned forward and squinted at him. "They look black to me."

"They're not."

Susanna tossed her pinecone and pressed her sappy forefinger against her sappy thumb, hard enough and long enough so they stuck for a moment when she pulled them apart, and the skin of both fingers stretched a bit as she did. "You look like a crow."

8

"Why are you even here? Go wait for the bus like a normal person."

Susanna stuck and unstuck her fingers four more times and then grabbed a handful of needles and stood up. She let the needles rain down on his slacks.

"What are you doing?" he snapped, brushing the needles away more violently than necessary. "Get out of here!"

This time, Susanna did.

—the 'frigerator
There was a piece of glass

"Hi, Susanna," said Henrietta Waters at the bus stop. "Happy birthday."

"Thanks," Susanna said, because it was polite and decent to say thanks, but she still thought about Kirby Matheson under his tree and wondered if he'd get up and climb out from under that pine tree to wait for the bus to St. Luke's, which should be rumbling up Egret Lane any moment now. The boys—the three boys with the rifle—cut across Kirby's lawn as she watched from the stop sign with one hand on the smooth green stop-sign pole. They didn't have the rifle anymore. They didn't see Kirby, either.

"I like your ribbons," Henrietta said, and Susanna thanked her again. She held on to the pole and let herself swing around it, all the way around—once, twice, three times.

"Did you get any good presents?"

"Not till I get home," Susanna said, and quickly corrected herself. "Not till my dad gets home from work. But I'm getting a scooter. I think."

"Ooh, I have a scooter."

9

Susanna knew that and she didn't care, and at that instant she hoped for anything *but* a scooter. She didn't like Henrietta Waters, whose hair was nothing like honey as much as Kirby's hair was nothing like honey, but instead of crow black it was too-bright yellow, like a dandelion head. Dandelion *honey* was a pretty color, but this wasn't it. This was sickening.

A silver sedan slid around the corner from Cardinal and slowed as it passed the bus stop. "There goes Ella Stone," said Henrietta as she gave Susanna a little shove in the arm, meant to get her attention, but rougher.

It was Ella Stone. She sat in the backseat next to the window and looked at her classmates on the curb, coughing into her elbow as they passed.

"She's dying, you know," Henrietta said. "My mom told me."

"No, she's not." But Susanna believed her. She even wanted to believe her.

The bus coughed and rumbled up Cardinal Lane and turned wide and rude onto Egret to stop with a hiss for the riders. Susanna watched the pine tree across the street, catching glimpses of it between heads as she moved up the dark, green aisle of the bus. She sat down toward the middle, as usual, next to Andrea Birch, second grader and renowned tattletale. Susanna stretched her neck and looked out the window, and she saw Kirby Matheson, out from his conifer hiding place, and plodding to his bus stop, his shoulders high and his eyelids low, dragging his bag behind him like the dregs of his morning.

Miss Susie sat upon it
And broke her little—

It was a school day like any other for Susanna, inasmuch as a day is like any other when the whole of Mr. Welkin's third-grade class sings "Happy Birthday" to you and you walk up and down the room passing out erasers with cartoony drawings of frogs and penguins and hippos and unicorns.

"These are dumb."

Susanna stood next to the Bald Eagle table—they were all named for animals native to the state—and looked down at Simon Loam and his blackberry-honey hair that made her hungry.

"They're not dumb."

Simon said it again. "Because those three"—he gestured at the erasers still in her bag—"are real, but this"—he held up his eraser, a unicorn—"is fake-believe."

"It's *make*-believe," Susanna said. "And if you don't like it, put it back."

"I didn't say I don't like it." He shoved the favor onto the back of his crayon. "I just said it's dumb."

Ask me no more questions
I'll tell you no more lies.

Henrietta Waters wasn't on the bus home. Neither were two of the boys who shoot birds. One of them was—the tallest one. Susanna didn't know his name.

None of this was odd. Plenty of kids stayed after school or went home with other kids for playdates in the afternoon. Susanna pulled her book from her bag and flipped through the pages till a chapter title caught her eye—the place where she'd left off or close to it. She didn't use bookmarks. The sight of a bookmark sticking out from the pages of a book depressed her.

Susanna didn't walk diagonal from the bus stop to her house. Crossing yards in the afternoon meant dogs off their leashes and parents in kitchens looking out back windows and seeing children not their own traipsing through. They didn't like that. In the morning they were drowsy and pleased to have their children out of the house, but by late afternoon, with dinner to make, they were grumpy and run-down. So Susanna stuck to the streets, walking with one foot on the grass and the other on the pavement.

When she was half a block from her house, she spotted the black coupe in the driveway beside Mom's van, and she smiled with her mouth open wide and ran, letting her backpack bounce up and down without a care in the world about how she must have looked to everyone peeking out their front-room windows and the rest of the kids from the bus somewhere behind her.

"Dad!" she shouted as she pushed in through the front door. "You're home early!"

He stood back from the door, clear across their modest entryway, and crouched with his arms wide. "Here's the birthday girl."

She ran to him and smirked at his *humph* as she collided with his body. She closed her eyes as his arms fell around her.

The boys are in the bathroom
Zipping up their—

Dinner was fish sticks and sweet potato fries with as much ketchup as she could fit on her plate, in spite of Byron's wailing and moaning on the subject, and in spite of Mom's head shaking and tongue clucking with every last fart-sounding squirt. Dessert was medovnik—a Czech honey cake of paper-thin layers that took Mom three days to make. Susanna could have melted with every forkful. She could have collapsed to a puddle of honey goo and slid to the dining room floor.

The gifts came at the end, when the dishes were cleared and the table was wiped down and Dad had carried Susanna like a queen from her seat at the table to the very middle of the deep pillows of the living room couch. Byron's was first: a hardcover copy of *Anne of Green Gables*, her favorite book, which she only had in paperback.

"Thank you," she said after a squeal for the book. It had to have been Mom's idea, because the gift was much too thoughtful for Byron alone.

Mom and Dad each got her a gift of their own choosing in addition to the big gift that leaned against the coffee table in its awkward wrapping, about as clearly a scooter as a scooter could be. First, though, from Mom, was a helmet in golden yellow with a smiling bee on each side, and from Dad, an electric rainbow to shine in her room.

She thanked them both and then grabbed the big present. Byron rolled his eyes, but Mom and Dad laughed as she tore off the paper and there it sat: her scooter, all put together, shiny metal without a speck of color, just like she asked for.

"Do I have to wear the helmet *every time*?" she said, knowing full well the answer.

"You still have a little light," Dad said as he dropped the helmet down on her head and fiddled with the straps.

"Be back in fifteen minutes," Mom added.

Dad clicked the clasp under her chin.

"Fifteen minutes," she said, and she dragged the thing behind her toward the front door.

Flies are in the meadow
Bees are in the park.

Birdland was blessed with gentle slopes and curves and streets almost entirely devoid of traffic. Cars that passed—when they did, which was rare—rolled slowly, the drivers smiling and waving, their faces as familiar as the fronts of their homes.

Susanna rode her scooter like she'd done it a thousand times before, but she hadn't. She'd ridden Ella Stone's three times, only for a few moments each time because Ella wasn't fond of sharing. Susanna wondered briefly who would get Ella's scooter when she died, if she really was dying.

Evening crept in, and the sun was low over the park at the bottom of Cassowary Lane. From the top of the hill, Susanna could see ten or more kids in the park, standing in little clusters or running across the ball field or climbing on the monkey bars. She pushed off lightly and let gravity pull her to the park. If Henrietta was there, she'd show off her birthday scooter. If not, all the better.

"O! Susanna!" sang a boy's voice as she got close to the park. "O! Don't you cry for me!"

Miss Susie and her boyfriend
Are kissing in the—

She tried to find the voice and the pair of laughs that followed, but the light was dim and she was moving faster now. She hit the curb and tumbled from the scooter onto the grass. She heard the three boys' collective teeth-suck and, when she sat up and made it clear she wasn't seriously hurt, their laughter again.

"Shut up," she said as she stood. She went to her scooter, which lay in the gutter, and dragged it up onto the grass and into the park, where the clusters of kids had all stopped, had all froze to watch her recuperate from her crash.

"Yeah, guys," said the middle boy, the gun boy, the boy with thick hair and eyes like black marshmallows. "Shut up. She probably broke her scooter."

"I didn't." She turned her back on them and pushed it farther along, deeper into the park, where she hoped she might find Ella if she was still alive, or Henrietta if she'd forgiven her for her mean thoughts about her. They were her friends, after all. She could sit with them or stand with them or climb with them and then the gun boys would leave her alone.

She reached the sand of the playground and the scooter's wheels became useless, so she let it fall and sat on the rim of the playground, her helmet in her lap, watching the kids on the monkey bars, all younger than her, and all boys. She felt the gun boys behind her before they spoke. They seemed to heat the air around her.

"She's still crying about the crow you shot."

Susanna wasn't crying.

"She's a baby."

"Babies can't ride scooters."

"She can't ride a scooter. She crashed, remember?"

Susanna sniffed and wished she hadn't. "Go away," she said, and she lifted her chin in time to see Kirby Matheson on the far side of the playground walking slowly, and stopping to watch her and the gun boys.

"No, no," said the middle boy as he crouched beside her. "Because we can't just let a baby be alone with a scooter. It's a safety issue."

He took it by the handles out of the sand and before she could grab for him—the other gun boys held her wrists anyway—he was off on a joyride.

"Give it back!" she shouted, but he kicked and kicked, and he circled around the playground in a wide loop, even passing right by Kirby Matheson.

He said something then, that boy who looked like a crow, but Susanna didn't hear what. She only heard the laughter of the tall gun boy and the short gun boy and she only felt their hands on her arms. She did hear the middle boy—the boy who'd stolen her scooter—snap back at Kirby, "Shut up, Matheson. Don't be such a baby."

Then he rode that scooter at top speed toward her, shouting to his friends, "Hold her there. Hold her right there."

They did—they stretched her out by the arms as the boy sped toward them, and now Susanna cried. She cried because she couldn't break free. She cried because her wrists hurt. She cried because this was her birthday. She cried because the gun boy was going to kill her.

"Oh my God," whispered the boy on her left wrist, scared.

"He's going to do it," said the boy on her right, afraid.

And like that, they let go, and Susanna dove onto the sand, and the middle gun boy zipped by, shouting at his friends, "What the hell?"

He stopped and stepped off the scooter and picked it up by the post. "Why am I surrounded by a bunch of frightened *babies*?"

Susanna sat up on the sand. The boys who'd been playing on the monkey bars were gone now. The sky was dark. It had been fifteen minutes. Dad would probably come marching down Cassowary Lane any minute. She squinted into the early evening, praying for his ambling figure at the top of the hill, but all she saw were amber streetlamps and parked cars and the darkest bit of sky close to the horizon.

"You want your scooter back, baby?"

Susanna didn't answer. Why should she? He knew she did. She wouldn't say it to please him. And she was no baby. Especially not today.

"Fine." He held the scooter off the ground by its post, like a stiff corpse by its throat, but he didn't drop it at her feet. He didn't even roughly toss it into her lap, which would probably hurt. He strode right past her, raised the scooter like a baseball bat, and swung it into the steel frame of the monkey bars. It clanged and echoed, and he cursed and did it again. And again. And again.

Susanna shrieked at him to stop. She shrieked and cried and pleaded, but he didn't stop till the post bent and a wheel fell off and the footboard cracked. Then he tossed it into the sand at her feet, his face as red as hers, and stomped out of the playground while his two friends stood there gaping at her till she screamed at them. "Go away!"

They did. Slowly and casually they turned around and followed their huffing friend away from the playground and into the amber light of the street.

"Are you okay?"

Kirby Matheson stood ten feet away, his hands in his pockets and his chin down and his face as flat and bored-looking as Tall's and Short's had been.

Darker than the ocean
Darker than the sea

"What do you think?" She stood up and kicked her helmet and carried the scooter to the big plastic garbage can colored green and lifted the lid and dropped it in.

Kirby followed her.

"Leave me alone."

"Those guys do stuff like that to me all the time," he said.

"I don't care."

"I'm just saying you shouldn't feel bad about it," Kirby went on, walking beside her out of the park. "They're jerks. They deserve to die."

"I don't feel *bad*," she said, talking over him. "I feel *mad*. And you're not helping."

Kirby sniffed and stayed beside her, but he didn't say anything more, so Susanna did.

"You *are* like that dumb crow." She stopped and he stopped and she clenched her teeth hard and went on. "I'm nothing like you, because you're a *loser* and that's why those boys pick on you."

Kirby stared back at her, his black eyes shining and his flopping black hair catching the wind.

"I wish you'd stay away from me," Susanna said, her chest getting hot and her eyes stinging and her temples hurting from clenching her jaw so hard and so long. "They probably did that because they saw me with you."

"Stop."

"Make me," Susanna said. "Loser. *Make* me stop. I bet you can't. I bet you can't make me stop. You didn't stop those boys"—screaming now, screaming as loud and violently as she could—"from torturing me and breaking my birthday present."

"Stop."

She closed her fists at her side and stomped at him, raised her fists like hammers, and brought them down on his chest, and with the pound of each fist she snapped, like two gunshots, "Make! Me!"

So he did. He shoved her once, hard, and she fell on her butt to the pavement. She looked up through her tears at him, bending over her and blurry and reaching for her, so she kicked his ankle and scrambled to her feet and ran up Cassowary Lane. Kirby's sneakers slapped the street behind her. He chased her because she'd said awful things to him. Stupid things. So she prayed again in a whisper and found her father at the top of the hill.

Darker than the boy in black
Who's chasing after me.

VIOLENT BEGINNINGS

Despite speeding on the bypass and cutting through the middle school parking lot, Teddy is still almost late to his first-period class at East Monroe High School. He slides into the art room seconds after the bell. His English teacher, Ms. Reaver, would have counted him tardy, but Ms. Albans doesn't care.

The art room is one of Teddy's favorite places in school. It's not like he's any good at art. He can do the assignments, but he's really just . . . passable. It's obvious that Charlotte and Bucky have all the art skills—they always find a way to make whatever the assignment is into something else. Something wonderful. Like when Teddy did his self-portrait last month, he just looked at a mirror and drew himself. And it was kind of okay. You could tell it was a picture of him, at least. But Bucky drew himself as an animal, sort of, a weird mytho-logical chimera mishmash—and it didn't really look like him, but if you squinted, you could totally tell it *was* him, on a different level;

it showed who he was. And Charlotte did a sculpture that was so lifelike it looked real. It was good enough to be in a museum. It's obvious that Charlotte has true talent, and it's sort of ridiculous that she's still in high school.

Teddy's nowhere near as good as either of them, but he still likes art. It's a nice contrast to math and science and all the other classes where he has to bust his balls to get straight As. His only real shot at college is a scholarship, and his only real chance to get one is through his grades. At least in art he can relax.

Teddy throws his backpack down by his table. In the art room, there aren't desks. There are mismatched paint-splattered tables with random chairs culled from various different eras of the school. Some of them are wooden from way back, some are blue plastic, and some are green from when the school changed its official colors. Teddy has a wooden one, so carved with different names and hearts and daggers from years past that Teddy thinks he could tell his chair apart from any other just by the way those engravings feel on his butt.

Every morning, each class is required to watch some stupid news show that's supposed to make current events look cool by having teenagers report them, but thankfully Ms. Albans always turns it off. Today she claps her hands and moves to the front of the room.

"The assignments I have given you previously have been rather specific," Ms. Albans says, a gleam in her eye. "Art is not about assignments, though. For the next two weeks—and note that I'm giving you two weeks, so you'd better create something worthwhile—you have free rein. You may use any of the materials in the class, or let me know if you want to work with alternate materials. You may paint or sculpt or make collages or mixed media or anything at all."

Ms. Albans stops speaking abruptly, then nods to herself, as if satisfied that she's said all that needed saying.

Madison, a preppy girl who is always complaining when she doesn't get high marks on her art despite the fact that she can barely color, raises her hand, her fingers stretching toward the ceiling. Ms. Albans nods at her. "But what are we supposed to make art of?" Madison asks.

"Anything." Ms. Albans sits back down at her desk.

Madison looks around the room, confused. Several of the other students look eager at the prospect, but quite a few are as bewildered as Madison to be given such an open-ended assignment.

"You have two weeks," Ms. Albans adds as an afterthought. "You don't have to start now. You can just spend today thinking."

If anything, this confuses Madison even more.

If another teacher had given an assignment to just create something in two weeks, it would have been the perfect excuse to spend half a month goofing off and slapping together some shit at the last minute. But Ms. Albans holds everyone to a higher standard, and that should make the students much more willing to actually do something with the time and materials she's given them.

But no one really knows how to begin either.

Teddy spends the rest of the morning doodling in his art notepad, vaguely trying out ideas on paper. He draws a car, and considers trying to make an actual model of it, maybe out of old soda cans. He sketches some ideas he'd considered turning into a tattoo. He tries to do something like M.C. Escher, but it looks like shit.

Just before the bell rings, an announcement blares over the loudspeaker, instructing all teachers to read their e-mail. Ms. Albans was listening to Madison run ideas past her, and looks relieved at the possible escape.

Teddy closes his notebook with a sigh. None of his ideas were bad, but none of them were good, either.

The bell rings. Everyone moves to pack their things and leave, but Ms. Albans rushes to the door, standing in front of it. "We're staying in first period for now," she says gravely. "Everyone, stay in your seats."

"Why?" Bucky asks.

"Just stay in your seats." Ms. Albans looks sick, like she's about to throw up.

The room erupts in whispers and conjecture, but Ms. Albans stays silent. Teddy has never seen her so serious before.

Outside, the halls are supposed to be filled with the sounds of students rushing to their next classes, of locker doors slamming and people talking. But now they hear nothing but silence.

After a moment, the principal's solemn voice fills the loudspeaker. "Attention, all students and staff of East Monroe High School. A terrible tragedy has occurred at our neighboring school, Middleborough High. All students should be held in their first-period classes. Teachers: We are in Code Yellow. Repeat: We are in Code Yellow."

Ms. Albans tests the knob at the door, ensuring that it's locked, and places a laminated green placard over the little glass window in the door. She takes more green placards and puts them in the windows of the classroom, checking each one to ensure that it's locked; then she lowers all the blinds.

"What's going on?" Madison whispers loudly.

"Oh my God." It's Charlotte. She has her phone out.

"What? What is it?" Madison asks, craning her neck around.

"Holy shit," Bucky says.

Teddy pulls his own phone out of his pocket.

"Everyone, stay calm," Ms. Albans says in a serious voice. Her voice breaks over the last word.

Teddy's phone buzzes before he can bring a web browser up. It's his mom. *Are you okay???* she's texted.

Yeah, Teddy texts back. Another buzz. His father. Then his best friend, Saul. *Did u see?*

Finally the headline loads on his screen.

SEVEN DEAD, FIVE WOUNDED IN LOCAL SCHOOL SHOOTING

Ms. Albans turns the class television to the news. Cameras are already all over Middleborough High, less than ten miles away from East Monroe. Madison's crying. Her cousin goes there. She keeps saying, over and over again, "What if Sydney's dead?" No one knows what to say to her.

No one can leave, not even to use the restroom. The school's in a precautionary lockdown. Bucky says he thinks everyone will be heading home as soon as the lockdown's lifted, that school will be canceled at least for the day. A couple of the kids are excited about this, but no one's really feeling like they can say anything in front of Madison.

The art room is one of the biggest classrooms in the whole school; only orchestra and band are larger. For the first time in his life, Teddy wishes that the room were a little smaller, that they could all be a little closer.

Saul keeps texting Teddy. He's stuck in English class, and Ms. Reaver is forcing them all to read silently. Ms. Albans doesn't bother trying to make the kids work. It's lockdown, so everyone's supposed to be quiet, but she keeps the news playing on low.

She doesn't have to tell the kids to hush. Aside from hurried whispers and Madison's silent sobs, nearly everyone's focused on the news.

"I was just there for a game," the girl next to Teddy, Juliana, says in a low undertone. She's on the basketball team. "I was just there."

On the screen, a line of kids rushes from the gym at Middleborough. Men dressed in black SWAT outfits have guns trained on the doors of the school as they hurry the kids to the parking lot and to safety. Teddy scans their faces, looking for someone he knows. From the relieved sighs or the terrified gasps from his fellow classmates, he knows they are all doing the same. He doesn't have any relatives at Middleborough, but he's been to some of the games there, and he went to summer camp with kids from that area before.

But he doesn't recognize any of the faces.

A news reporter comes on. She looks professional, but there's a hollowness in her eyes, as if she is trying to stay detached from the story, but the way her brows furrow shows she can't. "We have confirmed that the total number of fatalities remains at seven, including the shooter, although three of the five wounded are in critical condition. All area schools are currently locked down. Parents, please keep phone lines and traffic clear. No other school has been attacked, and authorities confirm that Middleborough's shooting is an isolated event and has been contained."

The reporter pauses, her head tilted. Listening to someone in her earpiece.

"And we have confirmed that the shooter is high school junior Kirby Matheson." A school picture of Kirby fills the screen. He's wearing a black T-shirt and his hair is combed. He stares straight ahead, no smile on his face. Even though the background is obviously for a yearbook photo, it almost looks like a mug shot.

"Jesus fucking Christ," Teddy says, throwing back his chair and standing up. "I know that kid."

"Approximately fifteen minutes after the shooting began, Matheson took his own life," the reporter continues.

Teddy falls back into his seat. Every single person, from teary-eyed Madison to stoic Ms. Albans, has turned to stare at Teddy.

"I went to summer camp with him when we were kids," Teddy says. He doesn't know where to look, but finally his eyes fall on the sculpture Charlotte made of herself two weeks ago. He talks to the plaster eyes instead of any of the real ones.

"What was he like?" Bucky asks at the same time Charlotte says, "Holy shit." But before Teddy can answer, Madison's teary voice pipes up: "Did you know he was a killer?"

That one question brings everyone up short. No one speaks. They just stare and wait for Teddy to answer.

"I mean," he says, "we were young. It was freaking summer camp. Do you expect someone you went to summer camp with to be a killer?"

"You really had no idea?" Bucky asks, his voice lower. Respectful, maybe, or doubtful.

All Teddy can think about is the first time he met Kirby. The summer camp had been a solid week of pure hell for Teddy before he met Kirby. It was a sort of pseudo–Boy Scout, super-high-activity camp. It was all about surviving outdoors. Everyone slept in tents. You had to carry your food for the day with you in your backpack as you ventured farther into the woods. It was supposed to stress teamwork as everyone worked together to build rope ladders and shit, but all it had really done for Teddy was stress how much of a lard-ass he was, and how no one wanted to team up with him, and how he would rather be literally anywhere else than stuck at this summer camp that seemed bent on leaving him dead in the woods while a group of boys his age from the tri-county area pointed and laughed.

There was one asshole—his name was Rick—and he made it his personal mission to destroy Teddy. The first night, he slipped rocks in the back of Teddy's pack so that the next morning it was twice as heavy. When Teddy complained to the camp leader that his pack was too heavy, the camp leader mocked him. Everyone started calling him "Teddy Bear" and the older boys started to poke Teddy in the stomach to see if he'd giggle like the Pillsbury Doughboy.

And then Rick was assigned to be the leader of digging latrines for the night. He enlisted Teddy to dig. And Teddy, apparently, wasn't digging fast enough, because Rick started to unzip his pants and piss in the hole while Teddy was still digging. Teddy remembers the moment vividly—the smell of the dirt, the bile rising up in his throat as he realized he was about to be pissed on, the sense of inevitable dread as he realized he wasn't strong enough to fight back, that he would just take the humiliation and hope it didn't get worse.

And Kirby came out of nowhere and rammed himself into Rick.

He was an animal. He didn't even say anything, he just knocked Rick over so hard that he was breathless, and he stood up and stared at him. Just stared at him. And Rick zipped his pants back up silently and left.

"I hate that asshole," Kirby had said, watching as Rick sauntered away. "You know, one time I saw him kill a crow in front of a little girl, just because he wanted to. Bam, and it was dead. What a dick."

Kirby wasn't one of the popular kids, but he was tall, and there was something fierce about him, something that none of the other boys wanted to mess with. They still called Teddy "Teddy Bear" and they were still snide, but they let up after that. And if they got too rough, Kirby would just stand up and walk over to Teddy. He didn't have to say anything. His presence was enough to make the other boys shut the hell up.

The next week of camp was . . . better. It was rough, but it was livable. Kirby started talking to Teddy. They became friends, or at least summer-camp friends, much like friends among prisoners, trapped together for a time and making the best of it. Teddy had never been good with kids his age before that. He had moved around a lot because his dad's job kept transferring him, and he had always been pudgy and never into the popular stuff. He had dreaded going to camp—his parents' way of trying to get him to make friends before starting another new school—and it hadn't worked. Not until Kirby.

Kirby was his first friend. The first person to show the fat kid compassion. The first one to treat Teddy like a human.

"No," Teddy says now. "I had no idea that Kirby could . . . could kill like that."

* * *

Bucky was right—they closed school early that day. Middleborough was too close to home. There were grief counselors available for students, but a lot of the teachers and counselors from East Monroe were going up to Middleborough to help with grief counseling there. There were a few news reporters gathered outside of East Monroe, looking for reactions from students about the shooting. They didn't seem human to Teddy; they looked like emotionless androids thrusting microphones at students until the principal forced them off of school grounds.

Teddy drives straight home. It just feels . . . right. Something tragic happens in the world every minute of every day, and nowhere is really safe, but home is the only place we really have to go back to in the end.

It makes Teddy wonder if Kirby had a home he wanted to go to or not. If maybe that was why . . .

When he walks in the door, his mother rushes at him, wrapping him in a tight hug. She doesn't let go until Teddy pushes her away, protesting.

"Are you okay?" she asks immediately.

"Mom, I'm fine," he says. "The shooting wasn't at my school."

"But so close." Her voice cracks. "So close to here. Oh, God. It could have been you." She grabs him again, squeezing hard.

Teddy gives in and hugs her back.

His mother finally leans away. "Did you know any of them?" she asks.

Teddy freezes.

"The victims?" she presses.

Teddy shakes his head. Before school let out, the news had flashed six photographs on the screen. Billie Palermo, a pretty-looking girl. Sydney Kemble, Madison's cousin. She had been right to be so scared and upset. Tyler Bower. Mia Kim. A teacher. And Jackson Parker.

Teddy stares at the last picture. Jackson had been to one of the summer camps too, the first one, when Rick had been such a jackass. He'd egged him on and laughed at Teddy. He'd laughed at everyone. And now he was dead.

As soon as Teddy opens his laptop, Saul pings him with a chat. **Holy shit, dude,** he types. **What a day.**

Teddy types, **Yeah.**

Bucky says you knew that killer.

Teddy frowns at the screen. "Why don't you get right to the point," he mutters, but all he types is: **Yeah.**

Daaaaaaaaammmmmmmmm.

"Damn" has an "N" on the end, dude.

Like that matters.

Teddy shrugs, even though Saul can't see it. He considers logging off. He doesn't want to chat.

He wants to find out more about the shooting. About *why*. He brings up all the local news sites. He scans CNN and MSNBC. They give him the statistics over and over again. Six dead. Five wounded. Two in critical condition. And the shooter. Kirby Matheson. Suicide.

What was he like? Saul asks.

Shut up, Teddy types. He finds an article describing the events at Middleborough High minute by minute. It's hard to believe that everything happened in less than a quarter of an hour.

8:03 a.m.: School security cameras catch Kirby driving into the school parking lot in his beat-up blue Ford Focus.

8:06 a.m.: Kirby exits the car, a coat slung over his arm. The coat's slung over his gun, too, but you can't see that from the grainy black-and-white photo from the security camera.

8:10 a.m.: Kirby enters the school. He heads straight to the gym, where there is a pep rally going on for an upcoming basketball game.

8:11 a.m.: The first shot happened before he gets to the gym. And just like that, Billie Palermo and Sydney Kemble are gone. Poor Madison.

8:22 a.m.: The last shot. The shot Kirby fired into his own head.

The article is vague on most of the shootings, but specific on Kirby's death. The bullet traveled through the bottom of his chin into his brain. He was killed instantly, and messily. There were witnesses to the suicide. CNN says that their description of Kirby's death was "too graphic to share with the public" and that "school counselors will be providing aid to the students who witnessed this and the other deaths."

That phrasing sticks out to Kirby. "Other deaths." All the reports talk about is the six people killed, but it was seven, wasn't it? The six victims . . . and Kirby. He was killed too. By the same gun that killed the others.

Teddy swallows down the sour taste rising in his mouth. Can he really feel sympathy for a guy who *slaughtered* five innocent students and a teacher? He forces himself to stare at the pictures of the dead until he can't see Kirby in his mind's eye anymore.

There's a difference, he tells himself, *between the killer and the victims, even if in the end, they're all the same kind of dead.*

Come on, dude. Saul's chat message pops back up on the screen. **Tell me about him.**

I don't want to talk about it, Teddy types. His eyes feel tired, drinking up the images on the screen.

Just tell me one thing, and I promise I'll leave u alone, Saul types.

Teddy sighs angrily. **What.**

Did you know that he was like this, dude? When you knew him, did you know that he was such a messed-up monster?

Teddy immediately pounds two letters on the keyboard: **N-O.**

But he doesn't hit send.

The second year he went to the outdoor summer camp, he was actually kind of looking forward to it. A year of being away from that shit—plus a year of getting taller but not wider—had given him some confidence, and he planned to show the dicks just how much he wasn't what they thought he was. Turned out that hardly anyone from his school had attended summer camp, so no one knew him as "Teddy Bear" at East Monroe Middle School. It was eighth grade, and most of the kids had already made friends, but there was one more new kid that year, Saul Hutchinson. Teddy and Saul had become friends quickly and easily. Saul was into wrestling, so Teddy got into wrestling, and even though he didn't lose much weight, he got a lot more toned. He towered over the sixth graders. He was never as good as Saul was at sports, but he didn't suck quite so hard. He did a good job of fitting in. He never stood out one way or another, and it was . . . good. Easy. Nice.

So summer camp didn't seem like such a big deal. He didn't

think Rick Harris could pick on him anymore, and he knew from practice that he wouldn't have as much trouble carrying his pack, with or without rocks in it. He had changed in a year.

So had Kirby.

Kirby was still one of the tallest boys in their camp group, but also one of the skinniest. He kept to himself—even more so than before.

But he was still friends with Teddy.

It didn't take long for Teddy to realize that something was going on between Kirby and some of the other boys, the ones from Middleborough. Kirby had been attending a private middle school—he never told Teddy why—but he wasn't going back next year. He was going to Middleborough High. Sometimes he seemed happy about that. Sometimes . . . not so much. The boys who were going to Middleborough High in the camp group were mostly okay—people like John. But Rick was also going to be there.

On one of the first days of camp, some of the boys were playing flag football. Teddy and Kirby sat on the sidelines, sharing a can of Pringles. Teddy was being stupid, sticking two chips in his mouth upside down so he looked like a duck. Kirby was staring at some of the kids, just staring. He'd take a chip and snap it in half, then crush it in his fist, letting the crumbs drop down. Teddy spit out his duck-lip chips and ate them properly, then watched Kirby. Kirby's entire focus would be on one kid, his eyes following every move. Stare. Take a chip. Stare. Snap the chip in half. Stare. Crumble.

Smile.

When the next game started, Kirby stood up.

"Where are you going?" Teddy asked.

Kirby didn't answer. He bounded down the bleachers, two at a time, and snatched a thin yellow banner, attaching it to his shorts. As he joined the other players, Rick had said something to Kirby. Teddy watched as Kirby didn't answer, but the second the whistle blew to start the game, Kirby ran at Rick like a wild animal, throwing him to the ground so hard that Rick's breath was knocked out of him and Kirby was kicked out of the game.

Later that week, Teddy had confronted Kirby right-out. "What's your problem?" he said. "You're so effing angry. All the time."

"I don't want to go to public school," he said, not looking him in the eyes.

"So don't," Teddy had said. "Stay at St. Luke's or whatever that place is."

Kirby scowled. "Who's going to pay for it? You?"

"It may not be so bad."

Kirby gave Teddy the most incredulous look he'd ever seen. "I went to elementary school with those losers. I know exactly how bad it's going to be."

Teddy half shrugged. "People change." He was proof of that. No one, not once, had called him Teddy Bear that year.

Kirby turned his full attention to Teddy. He looked him up and down, slowly, from the bottom of his boots to the cap on top of his head. "Yeah," he finally said. "People change. Not always for the better."

And he walked away.

Come on, man, tell me. The words flash in Saul's chat box on Teddy's screen. **Did you know he was such a cold-blooded killah?**

Teddy deletes the **N** and the **O** from his text box.

Yeah, he types. And then he turns off the computer and walks away.

Teddy's dad comes home early with a box of pizza from Brothers, his favorite Italian place. Teddy's dad works close to Middleborough High School, as a city manager.

Teddy's dad goes straight to him, doesn't say a word, just drops the pizza on the counter and wraps Teddy up in a tight hug. It's only then that Teddy starts to think about how his dad almost bought a house in the Middleborough district. It would have looked better for his job, but Teddy had liked this house more than the one on Egret Lane. That if they'd ignored Teddy and bought the other house, he would have gone to Middleborough High School. Where Kirby went. Where the shooting happened.

He might have been one of the victims. He might have died.

He hugs his dad back as hard he can. They just stand there, clinging to each other. They don't cry. They don't talk about what might have been. They just hold each other so tight that nothing else exists between them, not the fear, the doubt, the worry.

Teddy and his parents eat pizza while gathered around the television, watching the news. Teddy's dad talks about what a bitch traffic was, how the roads around the school are all closed and clogged with media vans. Everyone's at Middleborough—all the big news stations, some of the celebrity reporters Teddy's mom watches daily.

There's a candlelight vigil. People are cramming flowers and ribbons and stuffed animals and photos and cards into the holes of the chain-link fence around the track, the closest area to the gym that they can get to without crossing the police tape that surrounds the area. There are so, so many pictures of people crying. They keep replaying that one image, where the kids stream out of the gym with their arms raised on their heads as black-jacketed SWAT teams move in.

The news reporters are uncharacteristically quiet as the hundreds of people gathered for the candlelight vigil start singing "Amazing Grace." Teddy's dad puts down his pizza slice. His mother bows her head. Teddy stares silently, grease and cheese dripping off his pizza, a lump in his throat as the camera scans the crowd gathered at the fence. He sees Madison there, her eyes red and her cheeks tearstained, clutching a framed photograph of her cousin, the second person shot and killed by Kirby Matheson.

Almost as if reading his dark thoughts, the news flicks from the vigil to another analysis of Kirby. Flashy text flies across the screen. WHY DID HE DO IT? it says in bold letters. Underneath that, beside a picture of Kirby, there's a caption: KIRBY MATHESON, PORTRAIT OF A KILLER.

"Kirby Matheson seemed like a classic American boy," the reporter says in a calm voice, like she's narrating a documentary or something. "But beneath his gentle exterior lay a monster." The image of Kirby's school photograph flips to a negative, making him look monstrous.

The image flies off the screen, replaced by a woman walking across the front lawn of Middleborough High School. It's still daylight; this must have been filmed earlier. "Matheson had few friends, but showed no real tendency for violence, officials say. Unlike the shooters at Columbine or Virginia Tech, Matheson was not considered an outsider. An active member of the school's band, Matheson seemed, if anything, a bit of a loner. But not someone others considered dangerous."

The reporter paused in front of the sign for Middleborough High. "One counselor at the school, who wishes to remain nameless, suggested that Matheson suffered from an anxiety disorder. Prior to attending Middleborough High, Matheson was enrolled at St. Luke's Academy, where he excelled academically in the smaller classroom setting and was a favorite among the staff."

Another image of Kirby flashes on the screen. He's younger here. In front of some trees, with a pack on his shoulders. Teddy sits up straighter. This is Kirby the first year at summer camp. Another image. Kirby in front of a campfire with a group of boys—their camp group. Another image. Kirby, with his arm slung over Teddy's shoulder. He remembers this picture. Kirby's mom took it the last day of camp, just before Kirby went home. The boys look happy. Kirby had promised to text Teddy every day, and to help him escape if he hated East Monroe Middle School.

Teddy's parents turn to Teddy. His mother has her hand over her face; his father is pale.

"That summer camp you sent me to in middle school," Teddy says lamely.

"Oh, my baby," his mother cries, reaching for him. He thinks for a minute that she's going to hug him again, and he hopes that she won't. He can't handle more hugging. But she only grabs his arm, squeezing his elbow, as if affirming to herself that he's still there.

"I don't remember that kid," his dad says, pausing the TV and squinting at the picture.

"He was . . . nice," Teddy says. "He was really nice to me. Remember Rick?"

His dad nods, frowning. "That kid was a dick."

"Well, Kirby stopped him from being a dick to me."

Something passes over his dad's face. Conflicting emotions Teddy can't read.

"You knew this boy, this boy who killed those other kids?" his mother says, as if she still can't believe it.

Teddy nods. "We shared a tent at night."

His mother's eyes are wide and watery.

"Look," Teddy says, pointing at the television screen and the paused picture of him and Kirby. "I didn't know he was a killer. He was nice to me. He didn't seem like . . . like the kind of guy who would . . . who could . . ." His voice trails off.

"It's not your fault," his mother says, patting his arm, but it wasn't until she said that that Teddy had even considered the possibility of that being true.

"So he didn't seem . . . strange?" Teddy's dad asks. "He didn't seem like the kind of kid who could grow up and become a monster?"

Teddy casts his eyes down. Everyone keeps asking the same question. Everyone wants to know—needs to know—if there was some sign of something broken inside of Kirby. They want proof that he was a monster from the start. They want to take comfort in the idea that it takes a special kind of evil inside a person to kill like that.

But . . . there is no proof. Teddy never would have thought that the Kirby he knew would grow up to become the Kirby that killed. If he had had to guess, he would have said that Rick would have become a murderer. Not Kirby.

But there's no comfort in that truth. There's no way to make his parents less worried about the evil hidden inside the heart of someone who doesn't look like a monster. Who never really acted like one.

Looking back now, he sees the shadow of the monster. He sees the hatred in Kirby's eyes as he watched the boys from Middleborough play during camp. He remembers how quick Kirby was to anger. He recalls the way Kirby's first instinct was to withdraw into himself. He wonders if Kirby saved him from Rick to be nice to him, or to hurt Rick.

Now he can guess at what went wrong. How things could have been different. If Kirby's parents had known how vital it was for him to stay away from Middleborough High, for whatever reason, they could have found the money to keep him at St. Luke's. If Rick had known his antics would feed the monster inside of Kirby, maybe he would have pulled back. If Teddy had known that the boy who was kind to him would one day kill others, maybe he could have been more kind to him back. Maybe he could have made sure that Kirby still had a friend, even if he lived almost an hour away. If Teddy had moved to Middleborough rather than stayed at East Monroe, maybe he could have stopped Kirby from becoming what he became.

Maybe, maybe, maybe. All he has are possibilities, and none of them are real.

His dad unpauses the television. "So what," the reporter says over the image of Teddy and Kirby as kids, "turned this sweet young man into this murderer?"

Another image fills the screen, one that must surely be the last image of Kirby alive. The image of Kirby here is perfectly lit, beautifully illuminating the gleam of metal around the gun barrel, the hint of a smile playing on Kirby's lips.

"This is the last image of Kirby Matheson, taken by his first victim, photography student Billie Palermo, moments before she was shot and killed."

It's the smile that slices into Teddy, the smile and the smoke and the way one caused the other.

Teddy's mother reaches over and touches his fingers, reminding him that she's there. He grabs her hand, holding it, and she pulls him down to her shoulder, resting her forehead on the top of his head.

"Maybe," Teddy says quietly, "if I'd stayed in touch with him. If I'd talked to him more. We weren't really friends after the second year of camp. I could tell he wasn't happy. I could have reached out. If I had . . ."

"Shh," his mother whispers into his hair. "There's nothing you could have done."

But Teddy's not so sure.

When East Monroe returns to normal operations, there is a solemnity in the air. The halls are quiet. The classrooms are in mourning. Many of the kids wear black armbands. There's a fund-raiser going around to help the families of the victims with funeral costs and hospital bills. Madison's friends are gathering money to send her flowers. She's still not back in school.

Word spread quickly that Teddy had been friends with the killer. People quit talking when he walks by. They move out of his way. Some cast him angry looks, as if the shootings are partly his fault.

Some reach out, try to engage him in conversation so they can pick out the morbid details.

Teddy ignores them all. He goes straight to the art room and, before the bell even rings, selects a canvas and sets it up on his desk. He gathers together paints. He's focused. Ms. Albans said they had two weeks to create anything they want. Teddy squeezes the black tube of paint across the palette, and the red. A lot of the red. But he also smears on unexpected colors. Purple. Yellow. A dash of silver.

He knows exactly what he wants to paint.

SURVIVAL INSTINCT

1

You take off your belt.

And it happens again.

2

I'm going to kill you.

I watch cop shows like they're televangelists, promising me the *how*s and *where*s of murder. They testify to my salvation, and my salvation is your end. I watch lawyer shows to see how best to get away with it. I am on a first-name basis with Mariska Hargitay. She tells me, "Zach, you better do it before you're eighteen."

I tell her, "Mariska, I will if I live that long."

She tells me, "No girl should put up with what you put up with."

I tell her, "Easy to say when you carry a gun."

I wish you would drink, like Mom. I wish you did drugs. I wish there were something else I could blame this on.

You shout my name from your office down the hall. One loud, growly bark, like a mastiff.

Zach!

Why did you name me that? Why would you give a girl a boy's name? Before one of us dies, I need to find out. I won't ask you, though. I can't. I don't know if it would make you mad. And I don't want you to get mad.

Zachary!

You must've wanted a boy. And was Mom even sober during my birth? You probably got to choose my name because she was too hammered to speak coherently. Just like the good old days.

I curl up tighter under my blanket, drawing my legs to my chest and squeezing tight. I'm a python, constricting myself to death. I shiver.

When's dinner? you shout.

I manage to stick my mouth out from between the blanket and mattress and say the word *Soon,* but I don't move. It hurts too much.

Maybe someday I'll cry again. Maybe that would help. I haven't cried since I was fourteen. Or thirteen. It's like a word problem: If Mom left when I was ten, and you first hurt me when I was eleven, which train will take me as far away from you as possible?

I'm really hungry, you say from your office, like you're singing it. Like a little boy.

I get up.

3

Kirby calls the house after dinner. You answer the phone, because only you are allowed to answer the phone. You tell me it's some boy. You make me ask you if I can talk to him. You nod. Magnanimous. You bequeath unto me the right to speak to a friend for five minutes on a corded landline. A short cord. Oh, my unending graciousness, mighty liege. Mine is but to serve.

What I say is, "Thank you very much." And you smile. It's not the way Kirby's dad smiles. Like he loves his kid. You smile like you're the smartest man on Earth.

"How's it going?" Kirby asks.

"Okay." This is our liturgy. Holy Mary, Mother of God, How's it going, It's going okay, Amen.

"Is he there? Close by?" There's a snarl in Kirby's voice.

"Uh-huh," I say, mustering a grin from some dark place inside so you won't know what I'm talking about.

You're not nearly as smart as you think you are.

"So I'll just have to ask you a bunch of questions and you're going to just have to say yes or no?" Kirby says.

"Pretty much," I say through another smile. If I looked in a mirror, I would see a shark. All teeth and black, lifeless eyes.

"Can you make it tonight?" Kirby says. "I can drive."

"Mmm . . . I don't know. Maybe."

Your eyes flick toward me. I look away.

"Well, we'll be there," Kirby says. "John's bringing all the stuff. Ten o'clock. But, listen, don't do it if you think your dad'll catch you."

"I know. I won't."

"I'll wait at the end of the street," Kirby says.

"I know."

"I really wish you had a cell."

"Yeah. Trust me, me too."

"Maybe we could just get you one of those throwaways," Kirby says. "I could pay for it."

"No, no. Don't do that."

"It might not be a bad idea," Kirby says, pretending not to have heard me. "You might need it someday."

"How is John?" I ask, because I can't bear how the hope cuts through my stomach like a laser. With a cell, I could say anything I wanted, under the covers or in my closet after you are asleep. I could text.

I could call the police.

Kirby sighs at me. "He's fine. He's breaking up with Samantha. Just in case you're interested."

Samantha. Sam. Another boy name. Maybe there was a sale. And I am interested. But not enough to do anything about it.

"You could run off to Tahiti together or something," Kirby says. "Open up a coed naked Twister gym or something."

Kirby is the only person, the only thing, on planet Earth that makes me laugh. And I laugh when he says that. But my laugh is a closed-mouth sort of thing, a series of rapid hums only. I hate my laugh.

No. No, I *miss* my real laugh, that's more accurate. When I was little, I laughed all the time. Cackled, really.

Time's up, you say.

"Gotta go," I say. "Talk to you later."

I hang up before Kirby can say anything else. He's used to it.

How is old Kirb doing these days? you say as I limp toward my room.

"He's fine," I say. You've never met him in person.

You didn't have much to talk about, you say to me.

"No," I say. "Just gossip about John."

I wait to see if you'll keep talking. You hate when I walk away before you're done talking. Except you never indicate when that is, so I have to guess. You like that, don't you? You like that I wait.

So I keep waiting.

Time for bed? you say at last.

"Yes," I say. "Good night."

Good night, Zach, you say. **Sleep well.**

"Thank you very much," I say, because you like it when I say that, and go on to my room. Easy to find; it's the one without the door.

4

My heart clenches when I see the kitchen lights go out. I start to shake with anticipation. I hear you yawn. You sound like a lion.

It's almost time. Sweet relief, so close, so soon.

From under my blanket, I listen to you walk down the hall to your bedroom. I want a snorkel to pipe in fresh air from outside the blanket, like a cartoon I saw once. *The Far Side.* A little boy with a monster snorkel hides under the covers while giant, rabid beasts wait beyond his blanket, but they can't get him because a blanket protects us from everything.

Almost everything.

Your door closes. Clicks. I wait. Listen to the blood pulsing rhythmically in my ears. It sounds like footsteps that aren't getting nearer or farther: *thub, thub, thub.*

I pull down the edge of the blanket just far enough that I can see my clock: 9:15. Good.

To pass the time, I think about Mom. I make up a new story for her. Tonight, she's in Nepal, hiking the Himalayas. That's why she hasn't written or called. If I had a TV, I could watch a TLC special on her exploits: *The first woman to get to the top of Mount Everest with nothing but rum and Cokes to sustain her!* Or maybe she could become a spokeswoman: *When climbing Mount Everest, try . . . Everclear!*

I very nearly laugh. But that would mean I am awake, and you can't think I am anything but asleep.

The radio is on low in your room. I think it's NPR.

At 9:50, I crawl out of bed and walk cautiously to your door. I listen carefully, but there's no real reason to. Your snores are so loud, I could hear them by the time I reached the hall. Excellent. I race—

I *slowly edge* back to my room.

In the movies, people wear their sneaking-out clothes to bed and just hide under the covers. I can't take that risk with you. I have to get dressed instead. My legs are stiffening up and it's a challenge to bend and flex and slide them into jeans, but I do it. I do it because I need this tonight. I need my fix.

My black hoodie is easier to pull on. Most of the real damage is below my waist. A moment later, I slide my window open, take off the screen, rest it on the ground, and stand on my bed for leverage as I hoist myself through.

I push the window nearly shut and bolt across the brown grass in our backyard. I'm through the side gate and down onto the street in just a couple of breaths. It is only at these times I'm glad we do not have a dog. Usually, I want one terribly—some other living thing to hold.

I race to the end of the street. It's only one minute before Kirby pulls up to the sidewalk in his blue Ford. It needs a bath. I get into the passenger seat and, at last, breathe.

"I knew you could do it," Kirby says, driving away from the sidewalk.

I only lean back in the seat, eyes closed, and nod.

"What would he do to you if he found—"

"No. Don't talk about it."

"I'm worried about you."

"Don't."

"Zach, I'm serious."

I shake my head. I need to get into character.

"You should write everything down," Kirby says.

"Like what?"

"Everything. Anything. Anything he does to you. Keep a record of it. It might be important. Later. If you ever tell anyone."

I cringe inside at the reproach in his voice.

"Why don't you?" he adds. As if he's never brought it up before. We've been over it. And over it. And—

"You don't understand," I say.

"*Make* me."

"I'll leave. It'll end. I'll go to college or something."

"Plan on paying for that yourself?"

He's got a point. I've never talked about school. Neither have you. Maybe Kirby's right: maybe you are planning on keeping me at home. Forever.

We pull into a parking lot. I see Meiko's car already there in front of the shop. Kirby parks, shuts off the engine. We get out and walk together into Pulp Fiction, a small, struggling, but beautiful bookstore at the edge of Little Mexico.

Pulp Fiction stays open all night. They have a coffee and wine bar, which I believe is why they are still open. On Wednesday nights, they let Kirby, John, Meiko, and a few others use a table in the back. I play when I can, which isn't much. But I try. I do.

John and Meiko are already there when Kirby and I come in. The maps are out. The figures are set. The adventure can begin.

"Hey," Meiko says, smiling at me.

John gives me a nod. Kirby and I sit down.

"Just us?" Kirby asks.

"Think so," John says. "I asked that new girl, Billie, but she didn't answer. I mean, like, literally. Girl never talks. Whatever."

John is hot. Like, should-be-on-TV-shows hot. But then, so is Meiko. Some girls try to dress up, and it looks trashy at worst, or trying too hard at best. Meiko makes it work. She's stylish in a casual way. In a mail-order-catalog way, not a *Playboy* or MTV-reality-show way.

So I'm a little envious. I don't look like either of them. I think I look Midwestern. That's a synonym for *plain*. Plain, like a wheat field. In Little Mexico, Dad and I are in the minority. Maybe I'm a charity case to John and Meiko and Kirby. If so—that's fine. They talk to me. They love me.

"Let's roll," John says.

I pick up my dice, which are borrowed from Meiko, who has a wooden cigar box full of them. The dice fit beautifully in my hand. I cradle them like jewels. Or keys. There's magic in them, transformative and transportive—turning me into something else and taking me somewhere else.

"The orc camp is getting ready to break and start traveling again," John describes for us. "The chest is being held in the chieftain's wagon. You guys are still stationed in the forest about fifty yards off the road. You notice Aurorian and Malice start to fade, then disappear, and of course you have no idea when or if they'll return. That leaves Murron, Corwin, and Aphex to plan the attack. What do you do?"

John is a brilliant game master. Knowing that not everyone could play each week, the first time we all gathered together, he created an in-game curse that could cause any member of the party to mysteriously vanish. That way, a group could still play any time, even if it was only a couple of people. Since John is the game master, he is here every week. And almost always Meiko, too. Kirby is here only once in a while. Lately he's seemed distracted at school, and I don't know what's bothering him. Since he's my ride to the game, Murron is never around without Aphex, Kirby's dragonborn warrior.

I am Murron. I am a male dwarf. I carry a dozen daggers spread across two bandoliers criss-crossed over my chest. Murron is brave but not tactical. He's better at following directions than coming up with his own plan of action.

You'd probably approve of that, wouldn't you?

This game is the only secret I have anymore. You've seen too much of me. You know too much of me. You own too much of me.

But not Murron.

"I say we attack," Kirby says. "Full frontal assault."

"That could result in casualties," Meiko—or Corwin the half-elf—says. She's already in character. Her voice changes when she speaks as Corwin.

"I *want* casualties," Kirby says. "The more the better."

"I meant us," Meiko says.

"Obviously not us," Kirby says. "I would never hurt you. Them—them I would hurt."

"The orcs," I say, to clarify.

Kirby glances at me. I feel like he hesitates for just a second.

"Sure. The orcs."

5

We play until midnight. I play well: Murron decimates three orcs on his own with his daggers, disemboweling two and cutting the throat of another. The team cheers me in real life while the characters in-game grimly fight on around me. Our party is successful at reclaiming the magic chest from the orcs. We don't have time to celebrate, though. A white dragon flies at us after we've taken an extended rest to heal up, and that's where John stops it for the night.

Kirby drives me home. We talk about the adventure. About the fun. There's no question that pretending to hack up bad guys feels good.

"You going to be okay?" Kirby asks as I open the passenger door.

"Sure."

"I don't believe you."

"Okay."

"Zach, dammit . . ."

"I'll see you tomorrow," I say, and get out. I close the door before he can say anything else.

Kirby waits at the curb until I reach my house. I appreciate that. Lots of people think my neighborhood is dangerous, but it's not. Not really. My neighborhood is safer than my own room. You moved us here after Mom left. I haven't heard from her since. I think she's forgotten me.

I climb slowly through my window. My legs ache, but it's getting better. My room is dark, dark like some of the caverns our adventuring party has crept through, hunting for evil to conquer and treasure to hoard.

I replace the screen gingerly, taking my time, then close the window. Safe.

Safe until you grab my neck from behind.

Bitch.

I have no time to gasp, to scream. You pull me backward. You shove me forward. I'm facedown against the mattress. Murron would never let this happen—

Thought you could just slip in and out whenever you wanted, huh?

"No," I say, hoping, praying, wishing. Not again. Not so soon. "No, no, no, I—"

Shut up. You shut up and don't move.

I shut up.

I don't move.

I also do not go to school the next day because I can barely walk by the time you're done.

6

Someone knocks on the front door at 7:34 the next night. You've already finished dinner—steaks and canned corn, which I cooked. Now you are in the living room to watch football per usual.

The knock punctuates Pachelbel's *Canon*, which is playing softly on my radio, an old Scotch-taped-together thing that you let me keep in my room. Who on Earth could it be? No one ever comes over here.

Who the hell is that? you shout.

"I don't know. Want me to go—"

Go see, for Christ's sake!

I pick myself up from my desk chair and hobble to the door. I don't know who I'm expecting, but it's definitely not Kirby.

"Oh! Hey."

He grins but doesn't seem to want to. "Hey, bud. Can I come in?"

I don't know the answer to this. I don't know what you will do.

But I open the door and shut it quickly as soon as Kirby is past the threshold.

"What're you doing here?" I say, glancing behind me toward the living room. You can't see us from there.

"I know it's after Christmas, but I wanted to give you something. Hey, can you show me your room? I've always wondered what it looks like."

He's lying. But I don't know about what. And I don't know the rules. No boy has come over here, ever.

"You should meet my dad first."

Kirby grins that same non-grin. "Won't that be fun."

Nervous now, I take him into the living room. You barely glance up as I introduce Kirby. The only thing you say after Kirby says hello is, **Don't stay too long—it's a school night.**

"Of course, sir," Kirby says.

You glance again, like you don't know how to react. And I think . . . I think for just one fast moment . . . he scares you.

I take Kirby back to my room.

"Where's your door?"

"It, um, broke."

He knows I'm not being honest. But he doesn't push. We go in together. Kirby scans the room carefully, and I see him eyeing the pillow on my desk chair with distaste.

Kirby takes his backpack off and sets it on the desk. For some reason, the last thing I want to know is the reason for Kirby's sudden visit. He fixes me with a friendly but determined stare.

"Missed you at school today."

"I was sick. I am sick, I mean."

"You sound okay."

I don't answer.

"Anything happen when you got home last night?"

I shrink under Kirby's gaze. His words automatically bring up a replay of last night and make me feel like I'm six years old.

Nothing, I almost say. *Nothing happened. I was bad, I got what I had coming, end of story. Happens to everyone.*

But it doesn't. It doesn't happen to everyone, and I know that.

Kirby's chin drops, adding a degree of severity to his already serious expression. "Let me help you."

I look at the floor and count bits of fuzz that dot the cream-colored carpet.

Kirby steps up to me. He keeps his voice low so you won't hear. "He's killing you. Don't you see that?"

"You can't help."

I'm still counting bits of carpet fuzz when from the corner of my eye, I see Kirby go into his bag. He unzips it, then turns toward me, his arm raised. When I look up, my heart seizes and my vision goes cross-eyed.

In the middle of the blur is the matte black barrel of a pistol.

"Oh yes I can," Kirby says, and lowers the gun to his side.

"*Are you out of your mind?*" My voice is a clenched fist. "Do you know what would happen if he came in here and saw you with that thing?"

"Yes. I know exactly what he'd do." Kirby moves a step closer. "Don't I?"

"That's a *gun*."

Kirby nods easily. "Yeah. And I know how to use it. Want to see?"

I try not to, but my eyes drift down to the pistol still hanging in Kirby's right hand. It looks heavy and deadly.

"It's a nine-millimeter Glock nineteen," Kirby says. I'm grateful he's still keeping his voice down. "It'll stop a person. You know?"

I actually laugh. This scene must be fictitious. Sixteen-year-old Kirby, sax player, dragonborn warrior, standing in my room and giving me lectures on firearms.

"You are not serious," I say.

Kirby plops down on the edge of my bed. "Zach, look. I love you, okay? I'm not going to explain that any further because you know what I mean. I know what he's doing, and I know it hurts because you can barely walk. But can you guess how much it hurts to know that it's happening and I can't do a damn thing about it? People shouldn't be able to do that. He shouldn't be allowed to hurt you. I'm sick of it. I'm sick of—"

He clenches his jaw shut, eyes glistening like Murron's daggers. I sink into my pillow-softened chair, gripping the back with small, dry hands. I know he's right. Kirby scoots toward me, still seated on the very edge of my mattress.

"Do you know how much Meiko hates watching you sit in the bleachers during gym? She told me you tell Coach Thomas that you hurt your knees, and that you can't dress out because you keep losing your gym clothes. You're going to be the first person on Earth to fail P.E. Because of *him*."

My voice barely carries. "When I'm eighteen, I'm moving out. Maybe I'll go to New York or Seattle or Canada or something."

"That's two years away. You can't wait that long. You have to do something."

"I will. Someday."

A shadow in the hall. I gasp and stand up, then bite my lip to stifle a groan. My legs and back are knotted.

You stand in the doorway. Kirby has slipped the gun under his leg. **You're done in here,** you say. **Time to go.**

I nod. Fast. Urge Kirby to leave without a word. You sneer at him and go down the hall to the bathroom.

Kirby gets up and slips the gun into his bag. "You're sure you won't take it?"

"No. I mean, yes, I'm sure. I'm sorry."

"Don't apologize to *me*." He puts the bag over his shoulders. "Take care, okay?"

"I will."

Another lie.

We walk to the front door. I open it for him. He steps out onto the porch, and turns back to me.

"Doesn't it make you mad?"

Back in the hall, the toilet flushes. I hear you go into your office. I don't say anything to Kirby. But maybe I nod a little.

"Doesn't it make you want to do something about it?"

I nod a little more.

"Yeah, well. Just saying. I know the feeling."

He goes out to his car and gets in. I watch him drive away and don't close the door until I can't see him anymore. I wonder what he means. His family is nice, as far as I know.

Get me some ice cream!

I shudder. You sound like a child. I waddle into the kitchen and make the bowl for you, bringing it down the hallway to your office.

60

You are seated at a long brown desk. Your computer screen displays some sort of accounting program. I wonder how I will manage my own finances without you when the time comes.

What if it doesn't come? What if you never let me go?

Can you do that? Is it legal?

Does it *matter* if it is or isn't?

Is that Birdland bastard finally gone?

I turn to go back to my room. "He's my friend."

Didn't ask, don't care. He's a Birdland bastard. All those Birdland assholes think they're hot shit.

"He's not like that." I am almost out the door.

I didn't ask for your opinion. That better be the last thing I hear out of your mouth.

Kirby's voice rings inside me. Not in my ears, not my brain—my entire body. *Doesn't it make you mad? Doesn't it make you mad?*

I'm so tired. Exhausted. I'm sick of it too, Kirby. I'm sick of it too.

"Fuck you."

This is what it's like to fall into a black hole. My body stretches, time stops, infinite blackness ahead and the real world left behind.

The metal prong of your belt buckle clinks as you slide the leather out of its loops. It slithers like a snake.

I run.

7

Your heavy, thumping, maddened footsteps shake the ground behind me. I turn the hallway corner, aiming for the front door.

Locked.

Screeching, I duck and spin. The muscles in my legs cry from the torque. You crash into the door above me, bellowing, swinging. The tip of your belt lands across my shoulders as I race for the kitchen. The door in there leads to the garage. Maybe I can get out that way, call for help.

—say that to ME in MY HOUSE?!

I am either screaming or crying or laughing because terror makes my brain mushy. I can hear myself apologizing, as if that will stop you. I scramble for the kitchen door, past the counter where the remains of our dinner sit in a domestic pile by the sink. The plates clatter as you bear down on me, and the butcher knife bounces in the frying pan where it's soaking in soapy water. I grasp the doorknob for the merest of moments before your weight crashes into me, expelling my breath out in one near-fatal cough.

Your arms circle my midsection. My ribs bend and threaten to snap. You sling me easily to one side. I smash into the edge of the Formica countertop, head tapping painlessly against the faucet above the sink. The counter is less forgiving: the edge cracks into my hip, sending a pistol shot of agony down my leg. The grease-stained plates shift uneasily nearby.

You swing me around again to face you. Your eyes are demonic with rage. I don't see the first blow coming, and don't register the pain in my face until a half second later. My head bounces the opposite way beneath your returning backhand.

What did you say to me? WHAT DID YOU SAY?

"Nothing."

I really say this. Because, as my brain settles down in its case, I assume you mean, what did I say just *now*. Recently. A moment ago. In which case, the answer is truly nothing.

It occurs to me, dimly, that you're probably talking about what I said in the office. Oh, that. Yes . . . yes, maybe that was not a good choice.

You slam a fist into my belly. I stop breathing.

You spin me fully around with one hand and force my head into the stainless steel sink. My breath backs up as you push me against the counter's edge. The air in my lungs can't get past it as it drills unmercifully into my belly.

You are either muttering or screaming. I can't tell. I can only try to maintain both consciousness and sanity.

I realize Kirby might have been right. Whatever else you've done to me these past years, it wasn't like this. Right now, my life is in literal, mortal danger. Your powerful fist sinks deep into my kidney area, making flames lick the inside of my throat and lift my feet inches off the fake tile floor. My hands hang loose and numb beside my head in the sink. It's like being in a colonial pillory, arms and head secured. I stare with absurd fascination at how close I am to the sink drain. Such vivid detail up close like this . . .

You've dropped your belt. You don't bother to go back and get it. Instead of your usual weapon, you rain blows into my entire back side with alternating slaps and hammer fists, deadening my already bruised flesh. My breath chokes in and out in a painful wheeze.

Bitch! Show you what HAPPENS when you—

I go numb. This is what it's like to die.

I twist my head. What will be the last thing I see? The dirty dishes. Wonderful. The frying pan. The cracked wooden handle of the old butcher knife, sticking out from the rim of the pan.

My right hand, oddly steady, reaches toward that handle. I pull the knife out of the pan. Watch its dull edge drip thick gobs of water. I wrap my fingers around the handle tightly and stare at it for eternity.

How's that FEEL? Huh? Talk like that to ME in my own—

In one heartbeat of time between blows, I throw myself upward out of the sink and twist my hips around to face you. My right hand shoots out like it's got a mind of its own. I feel a sickening moment of resistance before the blade plunges into your midsection.

You are paralyzed, one arm upraised in a fist that slowly relaxes. Your face contorts, red, screwed into what a moment ago had been mad rage and is now clearly pain. You look down at the handle protruding from just below your rib cage.

And stumble backward.

I am motionless against the counter, watching with total clarity as you cup your hands beneath the knife, but do not touch it.

Oh, shit.

You state it, and it almost makes me laugh. It's like you forgot to start a load of laundry or missed a TV show.

Oh . . . shit.

I slide along the length of the counter toward the doorway to the living room.

You collapse.

One arm stretches out, trying to find something to grab against the wall to slow your descent. You find nothing and slip to the floor. Your head angles down, staring incredulously at the knife.

That's when thick crimson fluid seeps through your shirt. At the sight of it, I try to rush for the doorway, but the knots in my muscles drop me to the floor. I pull myself toward the front door with one hand. I manage only to crawl. It's a lifetime before I can pull myself up enough to unlock the front door. I stumble through it and out onto the lawn. It is brown and brittle in the January chill.

I fall to the ground just as a Ford LTD drives past, thumping its bass for the world to hear. There are no clouds overhead. Just pinprick stars. My right side is a cauldron of ice spikes and fire. I try to find a comfortable position in which to pass out.

A face suddenly hovers over mine. A boy. A man. Some mix between the two. I've seen him around school. He's a superstar. Gabriel. An angel.

"You okay?" he says, like it's not something he says very often.

I open my mouth. It's so dry in there. Can't speak.

"You all right?"

Someone behind my eyes pulls gray drapes over my vision. That's it.

I'm alive, and I think it is spring.

Spring begins in March, doesn't it?

It . . . *is* March, right? No. January, I think. It was January when—

9

Mourning doves pipe outside my window: *who-whoooo, who-whoooo.*
I know they are mourning doves only because I specifically learned
about them at a botanical garden on a field trip, and they had one of
those listening stations where I could press a button and hear a bird's
call. I don't remember the other birds.

But that's not where my window is supposed to be. My window is—
I'm not in my room.

I close my eyes. You've taken me somewhere. Taken me.

"Baby? You awake?"

It's not your voice.

It's Mom.

I open my eyes and turn my head and there she is, standing
beside the bed and holding my right hand. Beyond her, I see a very
wide door, open to a hall. A smell like rubbing alcohol invades my
nose. Something sticks in my left hand.

Hospital. I'm in a hospital.

"Mom?"

She touches my face. Tears pool in her eyes. "I'm here, Zach. I'm here."

"Are you drunk?" It occurs to me that I'm on some kind of medication, because while I recognize I'm in pain, I don't actually feel it. Very odd. My back feels thick and bumpy, as if I'm lying on a series of racquetballs.

"No, sweetheart. Not for a couple of years now. I tried to find you, but your dad kept moving and the courts would only do so much. . . . I'm so glad you're here instead of . . ."

Before she can finish, a man walks in. Not you. He wears dark dress pants and a blue button-up, no tie. There're a gun and badge on his belt.

"Hi, Zachary," he says, coming to the foot of the bed. "I'm Detective Kiernan. How are you feeling?"

"Hurt. Sleepy."

"Well, that's fair. You've taken some damage to your liver, it sounds like. Nothing serious at the moment. Doctor said they want to keep you here for a while, see how the rest of your tests come out."

"Okay. Where is he?"

"Who? You mean your dad?"

"Yeah."

"Stable now. And in custody. You're safe. All right, Zachary? You're safe. You need to know that."

I nod. My eyes start drooping like those old night-night dolls whose eyelids raise or lower depending on how you hold them.

"Can you answer a few questions for me?" he says.

"Okay. Um—"

What happens is, I tell him everything. He doesn't need to ask a question. I leave nothing out. I hear Kirby's voice somewhere in my brain, hiding behind a corner, telling me to be brave and not hold back. Mom being here, holding my hand, clear-eyed and smelling of lavender instead of alcohol—that helps too. She breaks down sobbing less than a minute into everything I say.

But I don't. I don't cry. Not one bit. I just tell the cop everything.

He seems satisfied by the time I'm done. He talks half to me, half to Mom. "That's all consistent. I don't think you have anything to worry about."

"I wanted to kill him."

Detective Kiernan frowns. "Ah . . . that's the kind of thing you shouldn't say to people, Zachary. All right? This looks to me like self-defense and that's how I'm reporting it."

But I don't care. I look at Mom. "If I'd had Kirby's gun, I would have shot my dad. I would have. I wish I had, I wish I'd—"

"Excuse me."

The detective's voice is sharp. Louder now, suddenly.

"Did you say 'Kirby's gun'? Kirby Matheson?"

I face the cop again. "Yes. But it's okay, he was just trying to help. Really. Please, I don't want to get him in trouble."

My mother wails and almost smothers me, lying across my body, wracked with great sobs. The cop stares—glares?—down at me. Not nearly as friendly as two minutes ago.

"You knew Kirby Matheson, and you saw him with a gun."

"Yes. A Gleek, or Gremlin, or . . . something with *G*. He was worried about me, and wanted me to be able to defend myself."

Mom won't stop crying. I wish she would. Detective Kiernan won't stop staring.

"Okay," he says finally, like a little sigh. "I'm going to send someone else in here to talk to you about that, all right? It'll just be a few minutes."

"Please," I say, as loud as I can, which isn't very loud. The effort almost puts me back to sleep. "He's a good guy. He was trying to do the right thing."

The cop clears his throat, gives me a professional little nod, and walks very fast out of the room.

"Mom? What's going on?"

"Zachary, Zach, thank God, I just, I can't believe you're here . . ."

"Mom, what are you talking about? Mom?"

I don't know if she answers because it gets dark and I fall back to sleep.

10

When I wake up again, the mourning doves are gone. So is Mom. The wide door is closed. It's quiet outside my window. A bush of some kind, with tiny pale green leaves, gently scrapes and taps against the glass. I must be on the first floor. It's not a great view from here in my hospital bed, but it's something. It's the sun. It's plants. Life.

I can't wait to see Kirby again. Thank him. I don't think I could have gotten out if he hadn't come over that night. I hope he's not in too much trouble because of the gun.

Plants around here have amazing recuperative properties. Bushes that look long dead can suddenly sprout to life with brilliant reds or yellows or greens. They are hardy things, living things that don't give up easily.

You have to be strong to live here.

You have to be just a little immortal to survive.

THE GREENEST GRASS

I do what I do for one reason: because I love flying. The less I weigh, the higher I go. I love the feel of my shoe perfectly placed in someone's palm, that little down-pull before I'm launched in the air. I love twisting, flipping, feeling my skirt twirl. Time seems to stop, and I'm perfectly weightless. I don't like the catches so much, especially when they bruise. But the flying? Makes everything worth it.

But the only way I get prime placement in every stunt is to eat less than everyone else, which means my entire life revolves around moments like this one. Somebody brought donuts to first period, and *ugh*. When the box hovers over my desk, I just wave a hand.

"I'm allergic, but thanks."

"I got this box just for you, Lauren. No nuts. I remembered."

I take a deep breath, and the oily, sugary, fatty, disgustingly yummy scent squirms into my body, so unwelcome and yet so wanted. My stomach is hollow just like my smile, all bone and acid.

"Oh, that's so sweet!" I say, touching his hand for just a second. "But the last time I had a donut I almost died. I can't take that chance, not with the game tomorrow. But really, that's so nice of you to think of me!"

"No, thank you. I mean, you're welcome." He stares at his hand with a goofy grin and steps to the side, holding out the box to Tyler Bower, who grabs three in a gorilla fist.

"I'll take Lauren's and Elsa's. You don't want yours, right, babe?"

On his other side, Elsa purses her lips and shakes her head. "A moment on the lips, a lifetime on the hips," she says.

We stick to our mantras, and that's why we're always at the top of the pyramid. It only took one politely formal letter home from Coach Castle about how my skirt button needed to be resewn, and I learned my lesson. It's easier to say no to donuts than it is to go home and explain to my mom why I look puffy. For me, it's the flying, but for her, looking good is a religion.

Beside me, Tyler has already finished all three donuts and is dusting flakes of sugar off his varsity jacket. Mrs. Johansen goes into something or other about *Hamlet*, and I tune out. I'm so hungry that I almost float away. I don't remember anything she said.

After flying, my next favorite part is what happens between classes. At the door, Tyler drapes his arms over Elsa's shoulder and mine, and he knows he has to be gentle or we'll bruise like dropped apples. We smile and swing our hips to make our skirts flip up as we sashay down the hall. He high-fives the other guys on the team. Every boy looks at us with unstoppable hunger and yearning, and every single girl we pass is filled with jealousy and hope. This is what they all wish they were, where they want to be. They think I'm Tyra Banks in a Middleborough Muskrats cheerleading uniform, tall and fierce and flawless. And for just a moment, I believe it too.

I flick my hair, and it swirls around me like a shampoo commercial, a perfect sheet of golden-brown silk. They don't know it's a weave—my mom pays extra to make sure. There was a picture of the three of us just like this in last year's yearbook, and it's a far cry from the pic of me in my sixth-grade yearbook: pudgy and shy with glasses and braces and frizzy hair, playing my nicked-up oboe between Kirby Matheson and Jenny Bernard like a nobody. That was before my mama married into money and everything changed.

Tyler sweeps us down the hall at a swagger, just slow enough so that everyone has to stop and stare. He's so well trained that he even knows which bathroom we prefer to use in between first and second period.

"I'll be right here, ladies." By which he means he'll keep the teachers and other girls from interrupting us.

Mia's already at the middle mirror, as if that actually means something. I head for the last stall and try to pull something up, but I'm empty and just make myself cough.

"You okay, Lore?" Mia's white Keds line up outside my stall. It's a worry and a dare, all at once.

I fling the door open just to watch her step back to avoid getting hit. "I'm awesome."

"Must be that darn tree nut allergy again. Always making you gag."

I smile and nod, sweet as pie. "Must be."

"As long as you don't pass out during practice again." Her shoulder lifts in a shrug. "I worry about you. We all do."

She wants to be head cheerleader so bad she once switched out my chocolate protein powder with vanilla almond. I couldn't prove she did it, but I knew. The entire week I was in the hospital, she took my place on top of the pyramid, got to do all the best stunts. I use a bigger lock on my locker now and pretend she's my second-best friend.

"My only worry is that my winter formal dress has to be taken in again," I say, walking to the mirror. "My mom's taking me back to the tailor today." And I say this because I know her winter formal dress is a size three. If she gains any weight, Mia will be back on the bottom of the pyramid instead of right under my foot. Coach can't officially weigh us, but she watches like a hawk. There's no worse punishment than standing on the ground.

"We're going to have the best time," Elsa says, joining me at the mirrors while Mia inspects her peeling nails behind us. "I love that they got a white limo to match all our dresses. You're a shoo-in for Snow Queen, Lore. I mean it."

Behind us, Mia snorts, but I know well enough that the only way to respond is to shrug and look down. "Oh, I don't know. I mean, it could be any of us."

"But it won't be," Mia says. "It'll be you. It's always you. You're always perfect."

"You kind of are," Elsa says.

I give a little shrug and curl my hair around my finger. "Yeah, I guess I am." But they don't know what it costs me. They don't know it's my only choice.

Second period is a bore. I used to get good grades, but the less I eat, the less I can concentrate. I'm so polished that numbers and letters won't stick anymore. But I'm the head cheerleader and my mom is terrifying, so I get Cs that become As as if by magic. I look out the window and watch the drizzle fall, light and transparent, just like me.

Third period is group work, and I smile and nod while my group argues.

"What do you think, Lauren?" asks the kid with thick glasses.

I beam at him. "Let's just do what'll get an A."

"Ryan says we should do a conversation in a restaurant, and I think we should do a protest," the other kid says. "Like they're having in Mexico City. It's more exciting. Topical." They both stare at me, waiting.

I know them, but I don't *know* them. Before ninth grade, I knew everybody, knew their histories and where they sat on the bus and who was cool and who wasn't. But now I don't waste energy caring. There's the cheerleading squad, the football players, and the basketball and soccer teams, if you're desperate. And everyone else is nobody.

What are we studying again? I look down at my pristine book. Spanish.

"Let's do a restaurant," I say. "We can pretend we're eating."

The first kid cackles in triumph; the other one looks embarrassed and angry. But what could they expect? I never protest anything, and I'm great at pretending to eat.

All day long, I look forward to lunch. Or, more accurately, the walk to the cafeteria. I used to dream of this moment back in middle school. I pack up my stuff slowly, giving all the other kids in fourth-period physics time to get out the door. By the time I'm primed and standing, Tyler and Elsa are waiting by the lockers. Tyler's arm is back over my shoulders, and we're parading in slow motion down the hall. Mia joins us from calculus, her ink-black hair in bouncing pigtails and her lips a flat cherry red. Patrick and Chung flank us at the next hallway. Kelli and Calli step from the bathroom in unison, their freshly brushed hair in flawless red ponytails. Javier rounds the corner with his arms over Bella and Mary-Catherine, while Kelso and Nate stomp behind them like bouncers. At each intersection, we pick up more of our clique until we reach the cafeteria doorway with half the football team, half the cheerleaders, and every single eye in the caf staring at us like we're royalty.

"I wish I had her hair."

"I heard her winter formal dress cost a thousand dollars. Her stepdad's, like, a bajillionaire."

"She's going with Javier. He's so hot."

"I would give every piece of tech I own for three minutes with her lips."

I smile and remember to thank my mom for the new lip gloss. It's working. It means they don't notice my crumbling teeth.

The guys head to the lunch line as the girls sit down at our empty table. Everyone knows their place, and I take my seat in the middle, tucking my skirt under my butt so I won't have to feel the plastic chair against the backs of my thighs. I'm always cold, even with leg warmers and my cheerleading jacket. Elsa is on my left, Mia is across from me, and the other girls surround us, chattering. But the three of us are silent as we unfold our brown bags and inspect what the others have brought. I have a Diet Coke, celery, mustard, carrots, a hard-boiled egg, and a tin of tuna. Mia has a bento box of sushi made with brown rice. Elsa has tonic water, a low-calorie protein bar, and the unthinkable: a chocolate bar.

"Suicide?" Mia says, gently prying a piece of raw fish from its log of rice and placing it carefully on her little pink tongue.

"You're not eating that. Right, Elsa?" I say, because I have to.

The rest of the table goes silent and stares, waiting. No one will say it, but Elsa . . . She's not being as careful as she should be lately. Mia's dress is a three, but Elsa's is a five.

"I don't know. I mean, I'll get rid of it. But . . . I guess my dad's worried about me. He keeps trying to take me out to fast-food places."

Mia snorts. "That's not suicide. It's sabotage."

"I can handle this," I say. I turn to the table behind us and tap the closest kid on the shoulder. "Hey. Want some chocolate?" I hold out Elsa's bar and give him my sweetest smile.

The kid looks at me nervously, licks his lips. It's Kirby Matheson. Nice guy, kinda quiet, used to sit next to me in band in middle school. We were friends back then, and we were conversational partners in Spanish when I used to pay attention in class. He was pretty funny, once you got past the shyness. I guess if I'm going to be giving anybody candy in public, it might as well be him.

This weird, bemused smile passes over his face. "Uh. Okay. Sure. Why?"

"No reason. Elsa doesn't want it."

"Did you do something to it?"

I shake my head and laugh. "Kirby, come on. What am I going to do to a chocolate bar? It's just a gift, okay?"

He takes it like I'm handing him a bomb. "It's just that you don't talk to me anymore. You don't talk to anybody."

"I'm talking to you now. Enjoy."

I turn back to my table. "See, Elsa? It's gone."

Someone taps on my shoulder, and I spin. "What?"

Kirby's face is bright red. "I just forgot to thank you. So . . . thanks, Lauren."

A shadow looms over me. Javier. "What did that guy say to you?" He drops his tray with a bang. "Is he bothering you, Lore?"

I glance at Kirby, and he's all hunched over as the entire caf whispers about how he's about to get his ass kicked.

"It's fine. He's an old friend. I gave him a chocolate bar. No big deal."

Javier shakes his head, narrows his eyes. He's the biggest, hottest guy in school, my date and my boyfriend, supposedly; whatever that means. We don't talk much. It's mostly macking and watching him shoot people in Call of Duty. But he doesn't ask me tough questions, and he's gentle and sweet after, so I guess it's as good as any relationship. But I do know one thing: when he's getting ready for a game, you don't mess with him. He didn't get that huge by being nice and taking vitamins.

He grabs Kirby by the shoulder, his fingers digging dents into Kirby's black T-shirt. "Look, you little turd. You don't talk to her. You get it?"

"I didn't. She talked to me first," Kirby mutters.

Javier's fingers dig deeper, and I wince on Kirby's behalf. "Seriously, Javier, it's cool. Just leave him alone," I say.

My boyfriend snorts. "He can't touch you."

"He didn't."

"Tell him, Lore. Tell him he's nothing."

Kirby hunches deeper as he waits. His face and neck turn red.

"You're . . ." I look down, shake my head.

"Tell him he's nothing. Tell him he's a crappy little turd. Tell him if he ever touches you again, I'll pound his face in, and nobody will care, because he's a nothing little pussy."

"I'm not saying that," I say quietly, because now the entire caf is silent, staring, waiting.

Javier's face swivels from Kirby to me, staring daggers.

"Kirby." My mouth is dry, all acid and bile. "Don't touch me."

"Tell him he's nothing!"

"I . . . You're nothing." I put my head down, and Javier releases Kirby and sits beside me.

But I'm the one who feels like nothing. More than usual.

What's the point of being at the top if you still feel like nothing?

Kirby gets up and leaves. The chocolate bar is still on his table. No one touches it. Tyler smacks Javier on the back, and they bump fists and laugh and laugh and laugh.

I drink my Diet Coke and eat my tuna because Mia is right: if I pass out again, Coach won't let me fly. I don't eat the egg because farting is social death. I save the celery and carrots for later, just to have something in my stomach for practice. It's funny how throwing up because you want to and throwing up because you're scared are entirely different. I have to stay on top, for me and for my mom.

Next period is my only class that doesn't include a single

cheerleader or football player: Art. I love it and I hate it. I love it because I get to be myself. I hate it because I always worry that myself isn't who I'm supposed to be. It's easier with Elsa and Mia and Javier and Tyler around, reminding me how to act.

I sit on a low stool between an emo girl named Kat and a pretty girl named Morgan. Mrs. Recupido hurries between the tables, handing out paper towels and lumps of clay. A chunk lands in front of me with a splat.

"That wasn't nice, what you said to Kirby," Morgan says under her breath as she rolls up her sleeves.

I ignore her, like she's not even there.

"Today we're merging current technology with one of mankind's oldest forms of self-expression. Take a selfie. It's up to you whether you smile or scream, but use it to express who you are in a photo of just your face. Then e-mail it to me. I'm going to print them out, and you're going to sculpt what you see into a mask."

I take and discard several images before settling on my most practiced smile, the one that will win Best Smile in my senior year-book. My mom taught me how to plaster it on until I didn't need the mirror anymore. I dutifully e-mail it to Mrs. Recupido and quickly check my texts.

MOM (10:55 a.m.): *Appt. at tailor 5 p.m. Hurry home after practice. Prom pictures are 4ever!*

MOM (11:32 a.m.): *Remembr to smile at practice. Top of the pyramid is top of life!*

Javier (1:15 p.m.): *Cum over tonite? DTF? Basement door. Don't let my folks c u.*

I delete them all.

Mrs. Recupido slides a piece of paper in front of me, and I'm staring at a beauty pageant contestant. My lips are smiling and wide, carefully covering my teeth. My cheeks are sucked in, my head cocked at the right angle to make me seem both innocent and sexy. It's perfect. Perfectly pretty, perfectly posed, perfectly empty. I want to wad it up and throw it in the trash.

As everyone goes quiet and starts working, Mrs. Recupido turns on her boom box, some band from Norway that sounds like snow and ice. All her music is in another language. She says it's to help open up our creativity, but it just makes me feel strange, like the singers are talking about me behind my back, too low for me to hear.

The directions are on the whiteboard, the supplies on the table. I hang my jacket up and put a towel over my uniform skirt. Only then can I touch the chocolate-brown clay, and I immediately hate it. How it's cold and slick, then dries to powder. How my gelled nails make half-moons in the places I've smoothed again and again with wet fingers. I glance from the printed photo to the clay, trying to make a piece of mud match what I see. But no matter what I do, it's monstrous. Wide clown lips, a bulbous nose, perfect swoops of hair that coil at the end like Medusa's snakes. And the eyes—the eyes are dead.

But the eyes are dead in the photo, aren't they?

I end up using a clay knife to cut them out. Because isn't that what you do with a mask? You cut eyeholes so you can see.

So you don't bump into anything and get bruised.

Practice is wonderful. I'm flying. Coach is happy. All the stunts are flawless. Everyone tells me I'm amazing. Some senior asks if I lost weight.

The only thing I know about the future is that we're going to rock tomorrow's pep rally.

"Right there. Smooth that line."

My mom's long, rhinestone nail points to a wrinkle at the curve of my back, and Mrs. Cho hovers, pins in her mouth. She shakes her gray bob. "I can't. Need room to move. Room to dance, yes?"

She does a little shimmy and flaps a hand at me. I try to imitate her, but I can barely move. I'm all butt and no hips, and the dress is a cage. If she takes it in any more, I'll have to walk with my legs pinned together, my posture flawless. I would walk like a doll.

"It's pretty tight," I say, breathless.

"You try sit down," the tailor says, and I tiptoe to the bench and lower myself down. I can feel the pins tugging, the fabric taut.

"I have to be able to get into the limo." I look to my mom, pleading. "And we're doing dinner at the fondue place."

"I bet they use peanut oil, and that's always got traces of tree nuts. You can't—"

"I'm not going to eat. Obviously. But I have to be able to sit in the booth and drink water, at least."

My mom taps her chin, turns to the mirror, and smooths her hair. Her weave is the same color as mine. My stepdad prefers blondes. "Fine. But no tuna tomorrow, right?"

"Right."

Mrs. Cho snaps her fingers and holds out her hand, and I turn my back to my mom, who unzips the beaded white sheath. It's almost heavier than I am and thumps when it hits the ground. I wobble out, and my mom hands it to the tailor.

Mrs. Cho frowns, her mouth turned down as she looks at me. "She need a nice meal. Look hungry."

"Damn right she looks hungry," my mom says, a mixture of pride and irritation.

When Mrs. Cho leaves, my mom stands behind me and pulls back my shoulders to inspect my body, hunting for fat. I feel small and wrong and awkward, both proud and embarrassed in my sagging panties and a strapless push-up bra. "You can't listen to people like her. They don't know what it's like. Being special. She's never been beautiful, never stood on a stage in a tiara. She didn't have what it takes. Most people don't." She strokes my hair, gives me her pageant smile. "I did, and you do. Because we take care of ourselves." She steps beside me and puts her arm around my bare waist. With her size-two jeans and boob job, she looks more like a fellow cheerleader than a former Miss South Carolina who keeps her tiara in a glass box in the den.

"Mrs. Cho seems pretty happy," I venture, gesturing to a line of photos tacked to the wall. Mrs. Cho with her husband, grand-children, a fluffy white dog. She's always laughing, her chubby cheeks pink and her eyes wrinkled.

My mom snorts and shakes her head. "You know what they say. The grass is always greener on the other side of the fence. You want to aim low, you go on and eat everything you want and pop out a bunch of children and live in a single-wide like my mama did. You think Mrs. Cho's ever going to live on a golf course in a house with six bedrooms? You don't know where I came from. What it's like. I've done my best to make sure of that. You've got to fight for what you want. You've got to fight to keep it."

I shrug away and pull on my oversize sweater and size-zero skinny jeans.

"Baby girl, trust me. You don't want to be on the bottom of the pyramid."

"I'll never be on the bottom of the pyramid," I say, stepping into the front room of the dry cleaner among a forest of white wedding dresses.

I'm not strong enough to hold anyone else up.

I text Javier that I'm going to Elsa's. I text Elsa that I'm going to Javier's. But I don't want to do either of those things, and I don't want to go home. I wish I were still at practice. The thing about flying is that you can't do cheerleading alone—you need a team. I need something else that makes me feel that good, that free.

I pull down my mirror to check my makeup. It's dark out, and I'm all strange angles. I don't recognize myself sometimes. Something about that stupid clay mask really got to me. It felt good cutting out the eyes. When I held it up and looked out through the holes, breathing in the clay, I wondered if that was what it's like to be a ghost, surrounded by grave dirt and seeing everyone around you clearly, everyone who can't see you.

I liked it.

I mean, I like when people look at me, when the crowd is cheering and the kids in the hall stare. But it seems like if everyone stopped staring, if they couldn't see me, everything would be better. I think . . . I might like to be a ghost.

And ghosts get to fly all the time, don't they?

No one has to hold them up.

86

Being hungry has become a part of me. Being empty. I wonder what it would be like to be completely full. We used to have pizza parties after band practice in middle school, and I would eat slice after slice until I couldn't eat any more, laughing with Kirby and Jenny. They probably still do that. They're probably at Brothers Pizza tonight, gorging before the big game. Band uniforms are a lot more forgiving than cheerleading uniforms. That's why they sell chocolate to raise money and we sell kisses in a kissing booth.

I love being a cheerleader, but I miss being in band. Back then, I only wanted this, and now it's like I'm clutching it so tight that it doesn't mean anything.

I feel like two people who don't add up to one. Is that nuts?

An idea comes to me then—a horrible, wonderful, insane idea. I've got to be smiling like a lunatic. I screech into a convenience store before I lose my nerve. Inside I walk to the candy aisle, inhaling deeply. So much forbidden treasure that I've never even tasted. All chocolate is made in factories with tree nuts, and that means that even before I started watching my weight, I couldn't eat chocolate. I get a basket and grab Reese's Peanut Butter Cups, a Hershey's bar with almonds, a Baby Ruth, a Snickers. Standing in front of the cash register, I feel more alive than I've felt in years.

"You're Lauren Hamby, right?" the guy behind the counter says. He looks familiar, like maybe he was one of the football guys who couldn't get a scholarship after graduation.

"Yeah."

"I didn't know cheerleaders could eat like this."

I hand him cash, and he hands me a bag. "Oh, it's not for me. It's for my boyfriend."

"Of course," he says. "I mean, I know."

Outside in my car I crank up the heat and breathe in the chocolate. I know where I want to go. Where no one will find me until it's too late to stop me.

The school parking lot is almost empty, but not quite. The asphalt is wet and sparkly, the oil slicks reflecting the Christmas lights they've strung up around the streetlights for the dance. It reminds me of Mrs. Recupido's music from art class today. I grab my paper bag, tuck it under my arm, and hold my face up to the soft patter of drizzle, letting the rain settle into my brittle bones and drop onto my eyelids. I blink a few times, reach up, and rip off the fake eyelashes and throw them in the gutter.

The doors are open to accommodate all the work that goes into winter formal weekend. I pass the basketball guys running drills and blow them a kiss. From the hall, I see a dozen kids decorating the cafeteria with cut snowflakes and twinkling white lights as Mrs. Recupido looks on. The band door opens, and kids hurry out carrying beat-up instrument cases and uniforms in plastic bags. They're so easygoing, laughing and elbowing each other. One of them carries a pizza box. Another has a liter of Coke and a bag of red plastic cups.

"Hey, Lauren!" says some stranger, and I smile and wave like a robot.

Everyone knows me. I don't know anyone.

None of us know anyone, not really.

Once they turn the corner, the hall goes eerily silent. The art room is dark but the door is unlocked, and I slip in and find the light switch. The fluorescents flicker on, washing everything in a cold bluish white. I close the door, place my bag on my usual table, and head for the plywood board in the back, where all our masks are drying on piles of rolled-up newspaper.

It's kind of amazing, how different they all are. You can tell which ones belong to guys—they have jagged scars and pointy teeth like wild animals. The girls' masks are smooth, small features and lots of eyelashes, like they're afraid to mess up or take up space. Mine is . . . kind of terrifying. Scarier than I remember making it. The lips are too big, the eyes gaping holes, the eyelashes spearpoints, the hair curling up like snakes poised to strike.

It's like nothing I've ever made before, and I slip it out from under the plastic and take it to my seat. Pulling the candy out of the bag, I line up the bright paper wrappers in alphabetical order beside the mask.

I've always wondered what chocolate with peanut butter tastes like. But considering that even a touch of almond flour can send me to my EpiPen and the hospital, a Reese's Peanut Butter Cup is suicide.

That's why I'm going to eat that one first.

But it doesn't feel right yet. Something's missing. I go to Mrs. Recupido's boom box and hit play. The sound of sparkling snow fills the room, and I turn it down to background noise.

Back on my stool, I pick up the mask and hold it over my face, letting the clay settle and stick to my skin. I can't breathe, but that doesn't really matter. Through the eyes, the room is different, the lights brighter and framed in black. With my fingernails, I rip off the clay lips and open up a gash where my mouth is. Fingers wet and sticky, I pick up the orange wrapper and open it slowly, salivating when I smell the chocolate and peanut butter.

"What are you doing?"

I drop the mask and plaster on a smile.

"Nothing."

Kirby Matheson stands in the doorway holding his sax case. His eyes—God, they remind me of a beaten dog, scared and angry but still hopeful.

"Uh, aren't you allergic to nuts?" He gestures at the exhibit of candy on the table.

"How did you know that?"

He puts down the sax case and ventures into the room, leaning his butt against a table and crossing his arms. "Everybody knows that. Everybody knows everything about you."

I shake my head and my eyes start to burn. "Not everything."

"I thought that was why you gave me that chocolate today." He looks down and swallows hard. "Because you couldn't eat it."

Shame rushes back to me. I stare at the candy, at the mask, now twisted from when I dropped it. "Look, Kirby. I'm sorry about that. I really am. I didn't mean it. But you know Javier . . ."

"Yeah, everybody knows Javier." There's a broken pencil on the floor, and he moves it around with his white Chucks. "Why do you do it?"

"Do what?"

"Whatever Javier says. And Elsa and Mia and Coach Castle and . . . whoever. You used to be fun. And nice."

"I *am* nice."

His eyes meet mine. "You're nice when they let you be nice."

I roll my eyes. "You don't know what it's like. Being popular. It's this thing you want, and once you get it, you can't go back. It's social suicide."

Kirby laughs, kinda crazy. "Yeah, I don't know what that's like." He steps closer, picks up the Baby Ruth. "So what's this, then? *Un*-social suicide?"

My mouth is dry now, and my stomach roars so loud that Kirby looks at my torso with concern. "I just wanted to try it," I say softly. "I just wanted to . . . know what I was missing, you know?"

"Do you at least have an EpiPen?"

I shake my head.

"That's so stupid. Everybody wants to be you, and you're just going to eat yourself to death? And be found on the art room floor, all swollen and purple and gross?"

The way he's looking at me . . . with pity? Does he pity me? Does Kirby freaking Matheson pity *me*?

"Don't do this. I hear anaphylaxis hurts. Like you suffocate, and no matter how hard you try, you can't get enough air. That doesn't sound like Lauren Hamby's style."

I laugh, but it's half a sob. When he puts it that way, it's so horrible. "So what *is* Lauren Hamby's style?"

His eyes burn. "If you're going to go, go out with fireworks. With a bang. Make them see who you really are. You don't need some dumb clay mask to do that. You don't have to do this. Just . . . say no. Be a rebel. You don't have to do what they tell you to do. Do you even play oboe anymore? I bet you don't."

I shake my head again. Kirby grunts, opens his sax case, and slides all my candy bars into it. "This is my fee," he says. "For today in the cafeteria."

Tears are pouring out of my eyes now but he won't look away, and I'm sick of looking down, so I just nod. "Are we even?" I ask softly.

"We're even. Just . . . look, will you do me a favor?"

"If I can."

"Just don't come to school tomorrow, okay? Tell your mom you're sick and eat something nut-free and sit in bed and watch bad movies all day. Order pizza. Pick up your oboe. Play 'Memory' like we used to in sixth grade. Will you do that for me?"

He picks up his sax case and leans against the door, waiting. Staring at me like I matter, like I'm not Lauren Hamby, cheerleader and winter formal queen, but an actual person. Like he needs me to say yes.

I have to look down. "I don't even know why you care. I've been a bitch to you for years."

"No, you haven't. Not really. Plenty of people have been a lot worse."

He's still waiting for an answer, so I give him my old smile, the real one, the one with teeth. "Okay, Kirby. I really am sorry, you know."

"Yeah, I know."

"Are you going to the dance?" I ask.

Kirby shakes his head. "I might have, but . . . I don't think so."

"Maybe I won't either. They're kind of miserable, aren't they?"

"That's putting it lightly," he says.

And then he's gone.

The next morning I bite into an almond from my stepdad's office kitchen, stick the EpiPen in my thigh before my throat can close up, and go to bed. He's still at his office in New York, and mom's hysterical about me missing the pep rally, maybe even the game.

I point to my swollen lips and eyelids as she looms over me, arms crossed. "Can't be at the top of the pyramid looking like a pig, Mama. Must've been that new lip balm Mia gave me."

As I lounge in bed, my mom tears my backpack apart, looking for the potentially murderous lip balm that doesn't exist and cussing at me for letting it touch my mouth. When she doesn't find it, she screams at me for a few minutes before excusing herself to fix her makeup and go to a charity luncheon at the country club.

"You take care of yourself. Answer my texts. Let me know the moment the swelling goes down. And don't eat a damn thing! You could still make the game tonight, if you're careful. Remember, sugar: the grass is always greener on our side of the fence. You don't want to miss that. Don't you let anybody steal the top of your pyramid."

"Yes, Mama," I say obediently.

As soon as her Mercedes pulls out of the driveway, I'm raiding my stepdad's office cabinet for his hidden private snack-food stash, Nilla Wafers and potato chips and Coke that my mom would never let into her kitchen. My belly sloshes contentedly as I wait for my phone to start buzzing, as I know it will. It's not like me to rebel.

ELSA (7:31 a.m.): *OMG COACH IS GOING TO KILL U WHERE R U*

MIA (7:48 a.m.): *Guess who's on the top of the pyramid, bitch?*

JAVIER (7:49 a.m.): *where were u last night babe? u sick again?*

MIDDLEBOROUGH HIGH SCHOOL (8:20 a.m.): *WEAPON ON CAMPUS. SHELTER IN PLACE.*

There are more texts. Dozens. From my mom, my stepdad, Javier. No more from Elsa or Mia.

None of it makes sense.

I gave him chocolate. I gave him hell.

He gave me a second chance.

I'm going to start by ordering a pizza. I dig through my closet until I find my oboe case. It's stumbling and awkward, but I play "Memory" and cry as I watch the TV footage of what Kirby Matheson did to my friends. And then to himself. What he could've done to me.

I wish I could go back. Back to sixth grade. Back to last night.

I wish I could ask Kirby Matheson what it's like to be a ghost.

I wonder if he can fly now, all by himself.

FEET FIRST

Day of

I stood in the parking lot of Munson's with two coffee cups in my hands. The cups had sleeves but were still too hot. I put one on the curb and texted Kirby. When he didn't text back, I called. He didn't pick up.

After fifteen minutes, I realized he wasn't coming back and threw his coffee in the trash. Why did he bother choosing a coffee shop five miles from school if he was going to ditch me? If this was his way of teaching me to "gradually" fend for myself, it was crap. I started the long walk to school, getting angrier with each step. Truth be told, I was madder at myself. I followed Kirby. Again. Why didn't I have the guts to be my own leader? I promised myself this was the last time. Kirby was right about one thing that morning: we were even now, and I didn't owe him anything.

Before

Sometimes I think if I had been more coordinated or less scared things would have turned out differently. I wouldn't have needed Kirby, and I wouldn't have owed him. It's not even Kirby I started off needing. It was his feet. His sneakers, actually. White Converse with a treble clef on the side. Clarinet in my hands, heart pounding, I sought them out every band practice. When they came into view, I relaxed and did what I did best—played. If I could just follow those shoes, I didn't need to remember the marching band formations. All I had to do was let the music guide me. It was two weeks into band camp before I matched a name to the Converse.

"Kirby," said Joe, our drill instructor, "you'll lead the saxes."

My head snapped up to see who he was talking to, and it was Converse kid. That's when I noticed his dark hair and brown eyes. And the whispers and giggles from the girls. I guess he was good-looking, but the whole thing was jarring. It was weird connecting a person to those shoes. I now felt obligated to thank him for the use of his feet.

I tried to get him alone for a week, but he was always surrounded by moon-faced majorettes. They were like a mini harem, and he was an unwilling sultan, looking like he wanted to get away from the attention but wasn't really sure how. Finally, right when we were about to break for lunch, I rushed up to him.

"Your shoes are a lifesaver," I blurted, feeling like a moron.

Kirby ran his hand through his hair and smiled a lopsided grin. He did this a lot when dealing with the harem girls, like he didn't know what else to do. But I wasn't a flirt. I didn't want him. Not then. Then, it was really all about those Converse sneakers.

"Yeah?" he said, wiggling his eyebrows. "How's that?"

My face reddened. All I had wanted to do was thank him. I hadn't expected he'd want to talk. I had expected the same pained look he wore when surrounded by majorettes.

"I—I follow them," I stammered. "My parents are banking on a music scholarship." Ever since I first picked up the clarinet at age ten, and it became the third hand I never knew I needed, college became a real possibility—as long as I earned a music scholarship. In high school, you couldn't do band without marching band, so here I was.

He laughed. "That's a new one."

"It's the truth."

"What if I get sick?" Kirby asked.

"Not an option."

Kirby let out a low whistle. "Is that so?"

"We're talking about my future here!" I tried to look serious.

"Well then," he said, "I'll do everything in my power to make sure you have one."

After

First, I was the girl Mr. Daniels saved. I mean, Kirby needed coffee to stay awake for his midterm, which is how I ended up at Munson's. Only when I told the police my story, I left out the part about going with Kirby. I made it all about me. How I needed the coffee for midterms. And, in the wake of the deaths, no one bothered to further question the hiccupping, shocked, freaked-out girl. No one asked me why I chose Munson's, which was five miles from school, when I didn't have a car. Instead, reporters ran with the miracle angle. How the smallest decisions can make a difference. People wanted to find meaning in a senseless tragedy. And I let them.

But then a go-getter detective realized it was downright crazy to walk five miles for coffee, no matter how good that coffee might have been. So the cops questioned me again. This time I told them the truth. Only then did I realize what sitting on the facts looked like to the police. The newspapers and blogs grabbed hold of the story through a leak in the police department, and sensationalized headlines followed. From the straightforward "Kirby Matheson's Accomplice?" to the oh-so-witty "It Takes Two."

I wanted to throw up. We got death threats. Police raided my room. They took my phone and laptop. Finally they realized that I wasn't a mastermind, just a clueless idiot. New headlines followed: "Survivor's Guilt: Coping with the Aftermath." They found a picture where I looked like death, my hair unwashed, my face pinched, my eyes lost. I don't know where they got it. Maybe they hid out in the bushes beside my apartment building snapping photos of me falling apart. People apologized. Someone sent a cake. My parents breathed easier now that they had confirmation that their daughter wasn't a mass murderer in training.

Throughout the emotional strip search, I let them see everything. I even told them about playing for Kirby on our balcony. But there was one question I never answered. One answer I kept hidden from their probing mics and tape recorders. "Why do you think Kirby abandoned you that day?"

I said I didn't know. I said he looked stressed and frazzled. Mr. D's midterms were killer. He probably panicked and split without thinking. I never told them what I knew to be the truth. That he meant to save me.

Before

In October, after three months of being at the mercy of Kirby's Converses, I began to wonder about the guy behind the shoes. Like why did he care about me? There was one time Joe wanted to change the instrument order. While I sat on the side playing with my clarinet keys, my hands getting clammy at the prospect of trying to follow someone else, Kirby stood up in the middle of the field to deliver a three-minute soliloquy against moving the saxes. Something about the pitch and being drowned out by the percussion.

Joe shrugged. "You raise good points, Mr. Matheson. I'd still like to try it my way and see how it goes."

How it went was disastrous. The saxes *were* drowned out. I tried to remember where I was going but couldn't do that and play at the same time. So I did neither. I kept the clarinet in my mouth but didn't blow, then proceeded to trip over my own feet. Kirby went the wrong way, and the saxes collided. Joe sighed.

"Today is not a good day for change," he said.

When practice ended, I retreated to an empty corner of the field. As much as I loved playing, I hated marching. Maybe if I'd tried harder to learn the steps, it would have been a different story, but I had already decided I couldn't do it.

I could never tell my parents. They loved going to the football games and competitions and determining which blue-and-white uniform was me among the rest of the marchers. I watched them on the bleachers, clutching each other, probably the only people in the stands who didn't give a damn about whether our football team scored. After the games or competitions, we'd move the performance to the balcony of our apartment. I'd play *Flight of the Bumblebee* or Jean Françaix's Theme and Variations—the kind of soul-stirring music I adored but couldn't play in marching band. Usually our neighbors opened their windows to listen too.

"Jenny's concerts are almost like being at the Philharmonic," my parents said, eyes shining with pride and hope. Always the Hope. We lived in a two-bedroom apartment in Little Mexico, the poor side of town. In a section where all the streets were named after rodents. Ours was called Gopher Lane. I was not only my ticket out, I was theirs, too.

The day that Joe created the new formations, I put away my clarinet and lay on the grass, feeling both annoyed and sorry for myself. Suddenly, I felt a tap on my toe. It was Kirby.

I sat up. "Thanks for today," I said.

"It's all for the good of the band." He smiled that lopsided smile that I thought might actually be real.

"Just the band?" I said. This boy saved me from embarrassment. I was starting to like him.

He looked me in the eyes. "Not just the band." He extended his hand to me. "If I'm going to keep saving you, we should get to know each other." I took his hand and let him pull me up.

We hung out a lot that month. He lived in Birdland, in one of the many white-picket-fenced houses on streets named after birds. Egret, Cassowary, Dove. That threw me because he didn't act or dress like a Birdland kid. He didn't have that Birdland stench of entitlement. I told him where I lived. I searched his face for the ever-present disgust that appeared on Birdland kids' faces when they came in contact with Little Mexico kids. Especially when they found out which section of Little Mexico. They went out of their way not to touch us, saying rodents carried fleas and diseases. But I couldn't read his face.

I liked the posters in his room. Instead of half-naked center-folds, Kirby's posters were of books. I recognized them from the list Mr. D gave us in the beginning of the year, but I hadn't read them yet. *Catch-22, Lord of the Flies, Brave New World, The Once and Future King*. The last one was on his ceiling. We were scheduled to start it in Mr. D's class in January, after midterms and holiday break. I wasn't a big reader, but I was excited about it. Mr. D told us it was a retelling of King Arthur, based on *Le Morte d'Arthur*. He said we'd create our own kingdoms, with the opportunity to throw social order on its head. Serfs could be rulers and kings could be peasants.

"What kind of world did you create when you had Mr. D freshman year?" I asked.

"No knights. No kings or queens or princesses needing rescue." He talked like he'd given it a lot of thought, like I'd find a blueprint of his world in a dresser drawer if I looked hard enough.

"No damsels needing rescue from marching-band fiascos," I added.

He cocked his head and studied me to the point that I became uncomfortable. All I was trying to do was flirt. Kirby, though, seemed to want to see inside me. Before the shootings, I was pretty boring. I had no deep secrets or tragedies. Then he smiled a smile I hadn't seen yet. It was wide and toothy, and I remember thinking, "This is the real Kirby." Later, reporters would write he rarely smiled. A few majorettes said he'd had a lopsided smile. Not their fault. I once thought that was a special smile too. Looking back, I think it was a grimace. Then there'd come the photo. The one where he's smiling that same toothy smile. The one where he seems truly happy. The one where he's pointing a gun.

He kicked me lightly with his toe. "Marching-band damsels are okay."

Then he got close. He put his hand on my cheek, and I didn't pull away. His lips brushed mine, and I leaned in, wanting more. He stroked my hair. "Marching-band damsels are definitely okay."

We hung out after band almost daily. Checking out local parks, climbing rocks, grabbing food from food trucks. Each time out felt like an adventure. There was never talk of what we were or what we were doing in the romantic sense. I liked not being one of those couples that sucked face at each other's lockers or laid claim to the other's time. My life was "Twinkle, Twinkle, Little Star" and being with Kirby was like Debussy's *Rhapsodie*. I'd follow those Converse anywhere.

One night, a week before Halloween, we heard music coming from behind a park we were exploring.

"Let's follow it," I said, and we crossed over railroad tracks trying to find the source of the jazz.

Kirby squeezed my hand as the music reached a crescendo, but when we finally spotted the source, he deflated. "It's a country club," he said.

It wasn't just a country club. It was the country club owned by Nate Fiorello's parents. Nate hadn't bothered me in years. I was old news, and he preferred fresh victims. But I still hated him for leaving dead rodents on our balcony, his disgusting laugh echoing through the night as my dad scrubbed at the metal slats to remove the blood and guts.

"Let's crash it," I said.

Kirby laughed. "I like how you think, but we'd be thrown out in two seconds flat. My parents don't need the drama today."

Instead we climbed behind the gazebo and lay flat on the grass, part of the celebration but not really. Strung-up tiny lights twinkled like stars, and the air was laced with the smell of roses. I wondered if it was a wedding, sweet sixteen, or an anniversary party. My family never threw parties like that. We decorated our paltry balcony and ate our cake while we watched the people below. It never bothered me. I never wanted fancy. The balcony felt special and different, and I thought my parents were cool for creating something pretty out of the dark and broken. But that night, I wanted to dance on the mirrored floor of the country-club hall.

"What do you think they're eating in there?" I asked.

"Pretentious finger sandwiches, twice-killed meat."

"Twice-killed meat?"

"Yeah," said Kirby, "they kill it once, cook it, and then spear it again with a skewer."

I knew he was trying to make me laugh, but it sounded so good. "Why does everything taste better on a stick?"

Kirby rolled his eyes. "Be right back."

He was gone so long, I was beginning to think he'd ditched me. I closed my eyes and let the orchestra music wash over me. I imagined joining in with my clarinet. If I had to march and play right then, I could have done it.

"Hey," said Kirby, beside me again. "I brought you something."

He carried three plates of appetizers. Chicken skewers, sushi, mini empanadas. "How?"

"I have my ways," he said.

For a second I wondered if there was a country club girl he'd sweet-talked into giving him food, but I decided it didn't matter. He'd done it for me.

After we finished eating, after our lips danced to the sounds of slow jazz, he pulled me to him and said, "Saved the damsel once again, huh?"

It was another thing to add to the list. Something else I owed him for. And I wondered if that's what he wanted. For me to feel forever in his debt. But that night, it seemed like a small price to pay.

After

The *We Go There* interview is when it all fell apart. The title alone should have warned me, but I was still paying penance, still thinking that the more they gutted me, the more the world could make sense of Kirby Matheson. I owed it to the dead I didn't know, but whose screams still ricocheted off the hallway walls. To Mr. D. To the families who were now less well off than mine.

The interview began like the others. Carrie Conlan, interviewer extraordinaire, showing the many faces of Kirby, ending with that notorious image Billie Palermo took. Billie, who was a junior, who struggled with who she was, keeping her secrets inside. Whose name I didn't know until the photo came out.

Carrie's voice was soothing, lulling me into submission. I had done so many of these chats, I thought I knew what came next. I made the mistake of letting my guard down.

"Jenny," she said, brushing her Barbie dream-girl locks behind her ear, leaning in, "you bought Kirby's coffee that day."

"He paid for it." I don't know why I thought this was important to add. To show that I wasn't helping a killer?

She handed me a tissue as my eyes teared up.

"What amazes me about this story," Connie continued, "is that everyone tiptoes around the obvious."

I felt tingles in my spine. I knew then where she was going, but I was hoping I was wrong.

"Kirby obviously knew what was going to happen that day," said Carrie.

I nodded.

"This has been traumatic for you, so I'm sure when the police realized you weren't involved, they didn't want to upset you. They chose not to push the issue. But on this show"—she turned to face the camera full-on, not even pretending to care about me anymore—"we do go there."

I shifted in my seat. "I—I really didn't know what was going to happen." My voice came out small.

"Of course you didn't," said Connie. "No one's questioning that."

My mother squeezed my hand and pulled me to her. She sensed something was off too. "Maybe this is enough. My daughter was a victim too."

Carrie softened. "Of course, of course. I was only wondering why Kirby chose to save her."

My mother's eyes narrowed. "What do you mean? There were many survivors that day."

"True," said Carrie, "but he went out of his way to keep your daughter away from the school."

"Who knew what was going through that boy's head?" my mother sputtered.

"He knew what he was doing, didn't he, Jenny?" Connie pressed, talking over my mother. "He drove five miles to get coffee and left you stranded, knowing there was no way you would make it to school on time. Why would he do that?"

"Stop!" my mother yelled, and someone was screaming and sobbing, and I don't know if Connie stopped talking.

Cameramen raced as the screaming continued.

I heard my voice yelling something about damsels who needed saving. I felt myself being carried off the stage as I cried about kingdoms and knights and princes. Later my mom told me the network refused to air the episode because it was too disturbing and they feared backlash. That was my last interview.

Before

In November, Kirby and I lay on the cold metal slats of my balcony. Wrapped in heavy sweaters, we held hands as music played from my phone.

The star-filled sky made me think of our marching-band show, "A Salute to the Stars," a tribute to musicians past and present, everything from jazz to classic rock to hip-hop. I loved the change in styles as my fingers played furiously, trying to keep up with the transitions of beats.

"Want to hang out after tomorrow's competition?" I asked.

"Oh right, the competition," he said.

I wanted to laugh except that it sounded like he really did forget. "We have one every weekend. How do you not remember?"

"I have a lot going on," he said. But in all the times we hung out, we never talked about our lives. Not really. When I was with Kirby, we only lived in that moment. "I have to study."

"For what? Midterms are months away." I rested my head on his shoulder and closed my eyes, letting the music fill me, just like the night at the country club.

He rubbed his temples. "It's not just that. I'm a junior. I'll be looking at colleges soon. I need to focus."

I heard it in his voice, but I didn't want to believe it. I opened my eyes, and it was in his face, too.

"It's all too much now," he said.

"So you're quitting band?"

He looked surprised. "No, I'm staying in band."

I replayed the words in my head, trying to make sense of them. He's staying in band, but things were too much. No, not things. Me. *I* had gotten to be too much.

"I can't focus on school and band and making sure you know where you're going."

His words stung. Letting me follow him was that much of a burden?

I felt the tears running down my cheeks and didn't bother wiping them away. "I thought you said marching-band damsels were okay," I mumbled.

He took my hands in his and kissed me longer and deeper than he ever had. This wasn't the kiss of someone wanting to get away. It was a needy kiss. "You're not a damsel, Jenny."

The next day, we lined up in our formations. Joe said that once this competition was over, he was shaking things up. I followed Kirby's treble clef as I had for months, knowing this would be the last time. My clarinet stayed silent, the notes choked back by silent sobs. I kept wondering what I'd do when there would be new shoes to follow, new shoes that didn't know they were my ticket out of Little Mexico. I was mad that he was abandoning me, and madder still that I owed him for the past, for keeping me afloat for so long. Because even with him leaving me then, the score was nowhere near even. It was Jenny owes Kirby a hundred times, Kirby owes Jenny one.

After

My parents sent me to a shrink after the interview freak-out. I told her I knew he saved me, but I didn't know why. She had no answers, so I stopped going. I made a habit of staying late after school and roaming the halls, specifically the spots where the bodies were found. I changed up my route in case the school cameras took note. I didn't want the administrators thinking I was casing out the area, ready for a copycat crime. I just wanted to know why. It seemed wrong to be handpicked for salvation.

Before the *We Go There* interview, the reporters always asked if I felt lucky to be alive, and I always said yes. No one wanted to know the truth. They didn't want to hear that I left pieces of myself behind in those halls too. That each time I passed my locker, I bled. That I wasn't anything special before I met Kirby, and I felt even emptier after he was gone. I tried explaining this to the shrink, and she called it "survivor's guilt." It's not that. Not only that, anyway. The words are wrong. To have survivor's guilt, you need to have survived. How can I explain that Jenny no longer exists? How can I explain why I stopped performing on our balcony? How can I explain that, even though they scrubbed and bleached the cement to erase the blood, I still see it everywhere? How can anyone understand that even though I should feel grateful to be alive, I feel dead?

Before

After the competition, Joe moved the saxes three rows behind the clarinets. There were trumpets in front of me now, and none of them slowed down enough for me to catch up. I resorted to holding the clarinet by my mouth and not playing. It killed me, but it was either that or ruin the whole formation, and I wasn't selfish enough to trample over others' futures.

I wondered if Kirby still kept an eye on me, checking to see if I could survive the kingdom on my own. He made it clear I was weighing him down, but pathetically, I texted him anyway. He never texted back. Then two months after the breakup, I heard jazz coming from the country club again. I ran to the gazebo. I hoped to find Kirby there, and he was. He looked off. His hair was greasy, his face thinner. He sat on the grass, knees hugged to his chest, staring at the strung-up lights. Beside him was an empty bottle of wine. The good kind, and I wondered if he'd gotten it from the same benefactor who'd given him the appetizers.

"I've been working on my kingdom again," he told me, like us being together was totally normal.

I sat beside him. "Oh yeah? Still no knights?"

He laughed this barking laugh I'd never heard before. "Most definitely not. My kingdom is ruled by the little people."

I smiled. "Like the damsels?"

"That's right, Jenny. Like the damsels."

I thought of something. "But how can it? I mean, the damsels are used to being saved. The little people are used to fighting for something. Take away the baddies, and it messes with the rules of survival." I didn't really know what I was talking about, but I missed him. I just wanted to keep listening to his words. If he kept speaking, he couldn't disappear again.

He nodded, like he'd thought of this too. "They have to learn to survive on their own. They have to be better. March to the beat of their own drummer, so to speak."

"And if they can't?" My weakness disgusted me. Before he'd ditched me, he told me I wasn't a damsel. Yet since Joe changed the formations, I hadn't played a note.

"They die too," he said.

I snorted. "You paint a pretty world."

He shrugged. "It is what it is." He got up to leave and started to walk away.

"Later," I called after him.

Then I closed my eyes and imagined playing the country-club music. I imagined marching to the music too. But each time I tried to picture doing both together, the image shattered.

That was the last time Kirby and I hung out until the day of the shootings, two weeks later. Afterward I replayed the conversation in my head, trying to read between the lines, trying to see how I could have changed my words to produce a different result. Trying to see how I could have saved everyone instead of being the damsel. The day of, I was thinking about Kirby. I wanted us to be friends, or whatever we were, again. And that's when he pulled up beside me, window rolled down.

His face appeared more drawn than the last time I saw him, but his hair looked clean.

"Good luck on your midterms," I said.

"I need coffee," he said, unwrapping a chocolate bar. "No way can I pass Mr. D's test without it."

I looked at my watch. We had a half hour before school started. "You better hurry, then."

"Come with me. I need the company."

Two weeks of calling with no response. I should have walked away. Instead, I felt myself thawing and desperately tried to stop from melting. "Doesn't your sister usually ride with you?"

"Not today," he said.

I tried to hold my ground. I wanted to be the kind of damsel who could rule Kirby's kingdom, not the one who needed to be saved. "You'll be fine on your own. It's just coffee." I peered inside the car. The cupholders were brimming with chocolate bars. "Chocolate has caffeine too."

He cocked his head and went for the jugular. "You owe me."

He had me, and he knew it.

"Fine," I said, getting into his car and slamming the door.

"Munson's?"

"Are you kidding me? That's on the totally opposite end of town!"

His eye twitched. "No other coffee does it for me."

"We'll be late," I whined.

"We have a pep rally. They won't even notice."

I still had my hand on the door handle. He squeezed my knee. The cold left my body. I turned my head to the window so he wouldn't see.

"After this, we're even, okay?" he said.

"Even," I said.

The lot was full when we reached Munson's, and Kirby let me out. "Here's a five. Can you just run in? If I park, we'll definitely be late."

I sighed and got out of the car, and Kirby idled illegally in the middle of the lot.

I was almost inside Munson's when he called after me. "I meant to tell you, you were right," he said.

I stopped, shielding the sun from my eyes. "About what?"

"My world. I can't just let a damsel fend for herself if she's used to being saved," he said. "It's a gradual process."

The minutes were ticking away, and we had to go, but he got my hopes up. "Does this mean you'll talk to Joe about moving the saxes?" I asked.

He shook his head no. "It means, some point soon, you'll have to be responsible for your own ticket out. But maybe not today."

After

It's been five months since the shooting, and I quit band shortly after. My parents didn't try to convince me to stay, but my mom did bring it up with my shrink, who said I'd go back if and when I was ready.

Some days I picked up my clarinet and even tried to blow, but the music never made it past my lips. I heard the results of competitions. Sometimes our band placed first, sometimes second. I couldn't help thinking I'd bring them down if I returned.

My mom says I should do something. Anything. I don't tell her about my hobby of roaming the halls. We got a new English teacher. She has us reading a lot of Dickens. We never did read *The Once and Future King*, and I'm not sure I want to anymore anyway.

At lunch today, I walk to the band room. Joe is there drawing formations. He sees me and motions for me to come over.

"Look at these with me," he says.

My heart beats quickly and my palms start sweating. "I can't."

"We miss you," he says.

"I heard you guys have been doing well."

"Yeah. The band has." He looks at me. "He was a good kid."

I nod. No one has said that. We're not allowed. We're not allowed to say we miss him. I wipe my eyes. I want to say I miss him. Instead I say, "I don't know how to march and play at the same time."

"I know," Joe says. "But I can help you."

I move closer to him and look at the formations. "No more 'Salute to the Stars'?"

"No. I tried reworking the shapes but decided to start fresh. There's room for you."

I use my index finger to trace the shapes he created. Circles, rectangles, a flag. I stand up, and Joe starts the music.

I put one foot in front of the other, close my eyes, and follow the beat.

THE PERFECT SHOT

I wait for the perfect shot.

Mrs. Recupido says that patience is more important for a great photographer to master than proper use of lighting, exposure, or framing. Good photographers, she says, take thousands of pictures hoping they'll be lucky enough to capture just one beautiful frozen moment in time. But great photographers are willing to hunch down in the heat—their backs aching, sweat pooling in the uncomfortable folds of their skin, while mosquitos suck their blood or bullets explode around them—for that one perfect shot.

I don't know his name or why I chose him as the subject of my photography project. There are more interesting students at Middleborough High. Quite a few who are better-looking. I've passed him in the hallway before and never noticed anything particularly special about him.

And yet . . .

Cameras never lie. When I view him through the lens of my camera—the Nikon D810 I splurged on with the money Nona left me when she died—I don't see a boy who sometimes sits alone at lunch and sometimes eats a bologna and mustard sandwich. I see the boy I might have been.

"My name is Billie Palermo."

"My *name* is Billie Palermo."

"My name *is* Billie Palermo."

I repeat it like a mantra as I stand in the shower washing my hair, letting the hot water run down my back and over my chest. As I carefully choose the perfect outfit for school. As I apply my makeup and gather my unfinished homework and eat my breakfast apple.

Papa sits across from me at the kitchen table and reads work e-mails on his phone while he shovels cereal into his mouth. Listening to him grind and crunch his Oatholes makes me want to flip the table and beat him with his spoon.

"You remember to take your pills this morning?" he asks.

"Yes."

"How's the new school?" Papa's gun and badge rest on the counter behind him, though they look out of place now that he wears a suit instead of a uniform. His new job with the Middleborough Police Department may have included a promotion, but we're both rookies in this town.

"Fine. It's fine."

"Kids giving you any grief?"

I shake my head.

He eats his cereal. *Crunch, crunch, grind.* "You'll tell me if anyone messes with you, right? I can talk to your principal and—"

"It's good. Everything's good."

Worry lines crease Papa's forehead, which grows longer each year as his hair retreats farther back. I've tried telling him he'd look younger if he shaved his head, that he's lost the battle and no longer looks like the young father in that old picture of us at the Jets game he keeps trapped on the fridge with a magnet, but he never listens.

"I don't want this to be like your last school, Billie."

"It's not," I say. "It won't be. I'm different. Everything's different here."

I sit on a bench in front of the library, waiting for him after the last bell. He has Spanish with Ms. Fernandez seventh period. Students at Middleborough are required to take two years of a foreign language. Papa wouldn't let me sign up for Spanish and pretend I hadn't grown up speaking it with Nona, even though it would have guaranteed me at least one easy A on my report card. I opted for French instead. *Ce n'est pas ma classe préférée.*

My skirt rides up. I tug it down and cross my legs. I keep my camera beside me, resting my hand on top of it while I pretend to read an interesting message on my phone. The last ten texts I received were from Papa. Two telling me he was going to be home late, three reminding me to stop at the store after school, and the rest just checking up on me. I used to receive hundreds of text messages from kids at my last school, which is why I changed my number when we moved.

A mob of shadows darkens the bench, and I look up. His name

is Nate Fiorello. He's with another boy—Jackson, I think—and his girlfriend, Katy.

"Chin up," Nate says. This earns him laughter from the others. I don't mind the chin jokes so much. After seven years, I'm numb to them. My braces fixed most of my underbite, but my chin still juts out. Fixing it is considered cosmetic, and Papa's insurance won't cover it.

Katy slaps Nate's shoulder. She looks like the weight of her breasts might cause her to topple over at any moment. It would be comical if I weren't so envious. "Don't be a jerk, baby. She can't help it if her face is fucked up."

"Seriously, though, New Girl," Nate says. "You should get that thing taken care of before you put out someone's eye."

They laugh as if they think they're the first people to ever make that joke about me. I'm trying so hard to avoid looking at them and praying that they grow bored and leave me alone that I almost miss my subject leaving his Spanish class. I grab my camera and stand. Nate, Jackson, and Katy block my path.

"Excuse me." I brush past them, folding in on myself, willing my body to be narrow and small.

"You should smile more, New Girl," Nate calls after me. "Nobody wants to fuck a girl who doesn't smile."

My subject's name is Kirby Matheson. I found this out by digging up last year's yearbook in the library and scanning every face until his leapt out at me. Everyone hates school photos, but Kirby was grimacing in his like he was being forced to sit for it at gunpoint.

Most days after school, he practices with the marching band. He plays the sax, though I get the impression he'd rather be on drums. It's the way he walks. Each step sharp, every turn precise, always in time with the other members. The way his red cheeks puff when he plays. The way he wears his blue-and-white uniform like a straight-jacket. When I watch him, I imagine him tearing it off, running around the field screaming at the top of his lungs, his feet—wearing the Chucks with a treble clef drawn on the side that I only ever see him wear for band—banging out a tune only he can hear.

It's hot out today sitting on the bleachers on the west side of the football field under the afternoon sun. Through my telephoto lens, I can see each bead of sweat that rolls down his smooth cheeks, collecting in the stiff collar of his uniform. I wonder what he's thinking about as he plays the theme to *Star Trek*, the notes rising and falling, swooping through the air, the drum line rumbling. Is he focused on the music, stressing about screwing up, or does he know it by heart? Does he have a girlfriend his mind wanders to? A boyfriend? Any friends at all? There's one girl in band—a clarinet player—that he hangs around with. Some days he eats lunch with a group of kids. One girl has a boy's name, I think, which I found interesting. Mostly, though, he's alone.

Sometimes I think about talking to him, but I don't want to ruin my objectivity. Mrs. Recupido says keeping a professional distance from our subjects is important so that we don't allow our personal feelings to influence our work. I get her point, but I can't help wondering what Kirby dreams about at night. What he wants to do with his life when he graduates and leaves Middleborough behind. I doubt knowing those things will help me take a better photograph, but I want to know them anyway.

* * *

Kirby sits at a table in Brothers Pizza with his parents and sister. I overheard their server call her Carah. Kirby's tapping the screen of his phone as if he's totally alone. I followed him after band practice and waited until he went inside before I hurried in. A perky girl with cool hair dyed purple on the ends led me to a booth in the back.

Kirby's parents share a bottle of red wine and chat while they wait for their food. They seem like normal parents. Kirby's father wears jeans and a plaid shirt, his mother a smart black dress. Carah dresses preppy and cute. They order a large antipasto before their meal, which is two pizzas—one mushroom and sausage, and one that might be a margherita.

I didn't dare sit near enough to hear their conversation, but I imagine them discussing how their days went and what they did at work. I imagine them asking their kids about school. About their plans for the winter formal. About whether Kirby's started thinking about college even though he's still got another year and a half before he graduates. Kirby hardly glances up from his phone.

The same server who took the Mathesons' order approaches my table. His name tag says RAY. He's plain and a little goofy-looking. I order a cheese calzone and a water. Coke makes my skin break out. He nods at Kirby when he walks by their table, like they know each other. I wish I'd had my camera ready. That might have been a good picture.

I showed Mrs. Recupido a few of my early photographs. When she asked me why I'd chosen Kirby as my subject, I lied and told her he was in my anatomy class. I doubt she'd approve of me taking his pictures without his permission. Though, and I can't exactly explain it, I get the impression that *he* wouldn't mind so much. That the idea of someone peeling back his layers one shot at a time would appeal to him.

I've already learned so much. He doesn't visit his locker often—once in the morning and once at lunch. And he reads more than anyone I've ever known. I don't think they're books for class, either. Last week he was reading *East of Eden.* Yesterday, *Slaughterhouse-Five.* I checked *East of Eden* out from the library and tried to read it, but the wall of text lulled me to sleep.

He plays Dungeons & Dragons. I know that because at lunch one of the boys he sometimes eats with asked me if I wanted to play. They meet up at a coffee shop called Pulp Fiction in a part of town the locals refer to as Little Mexico, though I'm not exactly sure why. The boy, the one who asked me, said his name was John. He was good-looking—pretty, almost—with one of those smiles that make him seem like he's in on a joke that no one else is aware of. I tried to answer him when he asked me if I wanted to join their game some night, but the words got lodged in my throat like a fish bone I couldn't cough up. He shook his head and went back to his table. I wanted to say yes. I wish I'd said yes.

I keep my camera on the seat so that I don't give myself away. Anyway, the lighting here is terrible. There are too many shadows. Even if I did manage to fire off a shot or two, they wouldn't develop well.

Ray drops off my calzone and tells me to let him know if I need anything. I cut into it and the gooey cheese leaks out and begins to congeal into a rubbery blob, killing my appetite. Still, I should try to eat. Papa's working the late shift and won't be home until after midnight, and there's nothing at the house but frozen dinners and a box of day-old donuts. Papa's such a cop cliché sometimes.

I cut off a corner of the calzone and dip it into the cup of marinara sauce on the plate. It's not too bad. Not that I really taste it. My eyes are focused on Kirby, and I can't help thinking about Mrs. Recupido's question. If I'm being honest, I'd have to say I chose Kirby as the subject of my project because, when I look at him through the lens of my camera, I feel as if I'm seeing the parts of him he doesn't show the world. Everything he keeps hidden. All his secrets.

I can't help thinking that if I learn his secrets, they'll give me the courage to tell him mine.

After band practice, I follow Kirby to his car in the school parking lot. He drives a beat-up blue Ford Focus. The paint is peeling off the hood. Ours are the only cars left in the lot. Papa lets me drive his Civic most days because he's got his nondescript undercover sedan that everyone knows is really a cop car.

I don't actually plan on following Kirby home until it's time for me to turn left toward my house. I signal with my blinker and get into the turn lane, but when the light changes to green, I don't move. The truck behind me honks, but I wait for an opening and veer right, drive straight through the light, two cars behind Kirby.

He lives in an area of Middleborough called Birdland. All the streets are named after birds. Real imaginative. He pulls into the driveway of a house on Egret Lane, and parks. The word *egret* comes from the French word *aigrette*, which can mean either "silver heron" or "brush," in case anyone cares.

There's nothing special about Kirby's house. Nice, neat yard, white fence, pine tree in the front. If I hadn't caught the numbers on the side of his mailbox—1184—I might not have been able to distinguish it from the other houses if I'd driven by again.

I park down the street on the side of the road and watch him drag his backpack from the passenger seat and trudge into the house through the garage. A dog barks from inside, so loud that I can hear it in my car.

I hope Kirby will come back outside so that I can snap a picture of him in the right light. Photographers call it the "golden hour." There are two of them—sunrise and sunset—when the sun is just below the horizon and the light is indirect rather than direct, giving the world a soft, reddish glow. Mrs. Recupido says all serious photographers should become intimately familiar with sunrise and sunset.

The "golden hour" is also used by doctors to describe the period of time after a person is traumatically injured, during which prompt treatment results in the highest probability of preventing death. Papa taught me that one.

After twenty minutes, I get bored and look up Kirby's Facebook profile on my phone. He's posted a couple of pictures of movies he wants to see—mostly superhero stuff—and made a few comments on his friends' posts about their D&D games. That boy John tagged Kirby in a couple of cartoons that I think are supposed to be funny, and a girl named Meiko posted some stuff, but she seems to speak exclusively in emo song lyrics. Sometimes what a person doesn't say gives away more than what they do, but I don't think that's true in Kirby's case. Maybe he just doesn't post often. I don't have a Facebook profile at all. I deleted it last year. I don't miss it.

I consider creating a new profile. Middleborough is my fresh start. I could send Kirby a friend request and we could write messages back and forth. Since all our interactions would be online, I wouldn't technically be violating Mrs. Recupido's rule on maintaining artistic objectivity. Kirby might be more willing to open up with a digital buffer between us.

I end up putting my phone away without creating the profile. The memories of last year are still too fresh, and I don't want to risk kids from my old school finding it.

Carah strolls out the front door with the dog I heard barking earlier. I slide down in my seat as she crosses the street and disappears. Kirby doesn't come outside again. When the golden hour ends, the last of the sun's light dead and gone, I start the car and drive home.

Mrs. Recupido liked a picture I took of Kirby on the football field. Said it was a good use of lighting and negative space. She specifically mentioned the way the other members of the marching band were cut off made it appear that they were walking out of the picture, leaving Kirby alone, and she suggested I use it for my project. It's a good photo, but not perfect. It doesn't capture the soul of Kirby Matheson, and I won't be satisfied until I snap one that does.

I was late getting to school and forgot to pack a lunch. Nothing I put on this morning fit right. The asymmetrical top I bought from H&M made my shoulders look too square. Even my favorite white tank top betrayed me. I didn't recognize my own body in it. I tore it off, ripped it down the seams, and left it shredded on my floor. I probably would have skipped school, but I had an exam second period. I ended up throwing on a pair of jeans and an oversize black T-shirt.

At lunch I grab a tray and slide into the line. If the smells hadn't driven my hunger away, the sight of the slop in the metal chafing dishes would have. It all looks like wet dog food. Chunks of unidentifiable meat (God, I hope it's meat) float in red or brown sauce. The kid in front of me orders by color. "Gimme the brown," he says. I wind up with an apple, a water, and a tray of fries. Papa would not approve.

Usually I get to lunch early enough to grab the end of a table to myself, but my options are limited today. I spy a boy sitting by himself and ask if I can join him. He barely looks up from the notebook he's writing in, but he waves at me to sit.

"My name is Billie Palermo," I say.

"Ruben."

"I'm new here."

"One second, I'm almost done."

Ruben continues writing, his hand flying over the page, the letters boyish and cramped. Which is fine. I pull my camera out of my backpack and scan the cafeteria for Kirby. He's sitting with his friends today. John keeps slapping his arm, laughing at something. The girl with the boy's name—Joe? Zach? I can't remember—looks more uncomfortable than Kirby. I snap a picture of her, covertly. Then one of Kirby. I'm sure the lighting in the cafeteria will wash them out.

"You on yearbook or something?"

I'd almost forgotten Ruben was there. I shake my head, ashamed of being caught. "It's for an art project."

"So you secretly take pictures of random people for fun? Creepy. I like it."

Ruben returns to his writing. I want to ask him what he's writing about, but Kirby stands up. My fingers tighten on my camera, waiting to see what he's doing. He walks across the lunch room to a table full of girls. They're on the soccer team, I think. He stops in front of a girl with dark hair. She's beautiful and tough. Cuban? It's difficult to tell from so far away. One of her friends—a blond girl—watches them. Her nose is turned up and her lips turned down.

Kirby's hands are in his pockets. He says something; I wish I could hear what. I lift my camera to my eye and capture the scene. I twist the lens to bring them into focus. The dark-haired girl's mouth hangs slightly open. She blinks and blinks and blinks. Kirby stands and stands and stands. I press the shutter button once. Twice. The girl hasn't replied to whatever Kirby said, and for a second, the whole of Kirby expands and becomes the universe. The planets and stars swirling around him, the supermassive black hole at the center.

And then the girl speaks, and Kirby collapses back in on himself. He nods. His shoulders fall. The dark-haired girl says something else. Kirby replies and walks back to his table. I keep snapping pictures.

Kirby shakes his head at his friends when he reaches his table. The blond girl next to the girl Kirby talked to laughs.

"What do you think that was about?" Ruben asks.

I set my camera on the table again. "I don't know."

"You friends with Kirby?"

For a brief moment, I consider running up to Kirby and introducing myself. He'd look at me like I was crazy until I disarmed him with my smile. We'd talk for a few minutes and agree to meet up after school for pizza at Brothers, where I'd admit to being the new girl, and he'd entertain me with stories about his life that would have me holding my sides from laughing so hard. I'd mention that I was reading *Slaughterhouse-Five* and he'd tell me he'd also read it. We'd discuss the meaning of the Tralfamadorians and forget to eat. We'd lose track of the hours. Somewhere during our meandering conversation, Kirby would tell me I'm beautiful, and I'd blush and tell him he needs glasses. But I'd believe him because he isn't the type to lie. Eventually, I'd have to go home, but Kirby would type his number into my phone and call me that night. We'd stay up talking until dawn.

I practically live an entire life with Kirby while Ruben waits for me to answer his question.

"No. But I think we could be."

Economics is my least favorite class of the day. Not just because it's last period and feels like it drags on forever, and not because Mr. Weatherdon walks and talks like a slo-mo marionette. I hate econ because of Nate Fiorello.

Every school has a Nate Fiorello. Popular, hot, psychopath-in-training. He's going to grow up to be a lawyer or a politician or the CEO of a wildly successful hedge fund. He usually passes time in class by throwing wadded-up bits of paper at me or whispering insults in my direction just loud enough for me to hear.

I know I'm not like other girls. When I was in fifth grade and I'd see the girls in eighth grade beginning to develop breasts and curves, I couldn't wait for those changes to begin for me. I envied their hips and their long lashes and their soft skin. I wanted to be pretty and popular and for the boys to want me and the girls to want to be me. I still do. But I was always weird. An easy target. Most likely to be punched in the hallway. I still am.

Toward the end of class, Nate raises his hand, interrupting Mr. Weatherdon's snooze-fest lecture, for a restroom pass. He bumps into me on his way out, and apparently it's hilarious, because everyone behind me laughs. Their snickering continues while he's gone, when he returns, and they follow me into the hallway when the bell finally rings.

One thing being bullied at my old school taught me was how to tune out laughter. I memorized "The Arrival of the Bee Box" by Sylvia Plath, and I recited it to myself over and over until the taunts and snorts and snickers became but a buzz. I recite it now.

The box is only temporary.

By the time I reach my car, I have to force myself not to scream because I refuse to let them win.

The box is only temporary.

I slam the door behind me and pull my seat belt across my chest.

The box is only temporary.

I turn the rearview mirror toward me to make sure I'm not crying. To make sure I haven't let them win.

The box is only temporary.

That's when I see the gum. The wad of pink gum tangled in my hair. I pick at it, pull at it, try to tear it out, but it's superglue. It has made a rat king of my hair.

The box is only temporary.

I'm shaking as I drive to my doctor's appointment. I'm crying by the time I reach the office. Papa is standing beside his cop car in the parking lot, waiting for me in his crisp suit and violet tie. I scream in the confines of my car. Papa is running toward me. The door is opening. He's kneeling.

The box is only temporary.

"Billie? Billie, what happened?"

I show him my hair.

He says, "It's not bad. We can cut it out."

The box is only temporary.

It took me two years to grow my hair this long. Two fucking years! I can't remove the gum without cutting off pieces of me.

The box is only temporary.

"I can't do it anymore, Papa! I can't."

He guides me out of the car and into Dr. Thermin's office. I barely hear anything she has to say. I don't feel the needle when a nurse draws my blood. "Don't cry," she says. "It's only a little prick."

"It's not the needle," I tell her, and I show her the gum.

"We'll cut it out, Billie," Papa says. "No one will notice."

The nurse fills a vial with my blood and smiles. "I've got a daughter about your age. Rub peanut butter into it, and the gum will slide right out." She removes the needle, packs up her equipment, and leaves.

"See, Billie. We'll stop at the store on the way home for peanut butter. Everything's going to be all right."

The box is only temporary.

I follow Kirby home again, and this time, rather than hiding in my car, I wait until dark and sneak around the side of his house to peek through his bedroom window. The blinds are down, but the slats are open enough for me to see through. His back is to me, though if he turns suddenly, I'll be caught. I'm fascinated by his bedroom. So tidy. And where other boys might have posters of busty women in wet T-shirts, Kirby has posters of books. *Brave New World*, *Lord of the Flies*. Is that what turns him on?

I snap a couple of pictures even though the lighting is all wrong. I hope his sister doesn't come into his room. She'd see me for sure.

He stands. I move to the side and watch him. He moves to his dresser and opens the top drawer. He stares at whatever is inside. I wonder what it might be. Porn? A love letter? A book of poetry he's afraid his mom or sister will find? With Kirby, the possibilities seem endless.

As I stand there, my legs trembling, I imagine what would happen if he caught me peeping. Would he invite me in? Show me what he's working on? Tell me how lonely he is in school and how he wishes he had a friend?

I could be his friend.

A woman's voice—most likely his mother—calls him from another part of the house. He shoves the dresser drawer shut, grabs a shirt off the floor, pulls it on, and stomps out of his bedroom.

On the drive home, a memory pops into my head. Something I haven't thought about in a while. When I was fourteen and the bullying was so bad I wanted to drop out of school, Papa took me to see our church pastor.

Father Mike was different. Open-minded. When I asked if God had made a mistake with me—how it was possible that he'd created me so wrong—Father Mike told me that God didn't make mistakes. That God had a purpose for everything, and that he gave us challenges to teach us lessons about how to be better human beings.

What lesson could God have possibly wanted me to learn? How could being a freak teach me about being a better person?

Father Mike replied that God hadn't created me to teach *me* acceptance, but to help those around me learn it.

I held on to Father Mike's words for a long time. It helped me get through some of the roughest patches. And as I drive home, I can't help wondering what lesson God put Kirby on Earth to teach all of us.

We have a pep rally tomorrow. Go Muskrats! Or something.

I stay late to watch for Kirby. Band practice must be running long because of the big game tomorrow. I'm not a fan of football. Football players, yes. Football, not so much.

When he leaves, I follow. He doesn't walk toward the parking lot, though. He walks toward Mrs. Recupido's classroom. Thank heavens I didn't let her hang the photo of Kirby on the field on her wall like she wanted to. I'd die if he saw that.

The lights in the classroom are on, which is weird since Mrs. Recupido hardly ever stays late. Kirby walks into the classroom; I wait a minute before sneaking up to the door and peeking inside.

He's in there with a girl. Lauren . . . something. She's a cheerleader. Beautiful and tall and thin, with the smoothest skin. If I could have any body, I'd want hers. I bet Kirby wishes the same. I've wondered what kind of girls he likes. Light-skinned girls, or dark? Blondes or redheads or girls with short, kinky hair? Do breasts turn him on, or nice round asses?

No, Kirby likes smart girls. Anyone who says physical appearances don't matter is lying, but Kirby is more attracted to girls he can talk books with, to girls who can make him laugh. What's on the inside is more important than what's on the outside.

I wish I could hear Kirby and Lauren's conversation. She looked like she was going to cry earlier, but now she's smiling. He made her smile the way I think he'd make me smile.

Kirby opens his sax case and sweeps a bunch of candy bars into it. Was Lauren going to eat all of that? I can't imagine she stays so skinny eating candy. If I looked like her, I could be on the cheerleading squad. I tried out at my old school, but the girls on the team laughed me out of auditions. I cried for a week.

I leave before Kirby does and hurry back toward the parking lot and sit on a bench in the hallway in front of the bus loop. A couple of days ago, I saw him reading *Something Wicked This Way Comes*, so I bought a copy. It's a strange book about two boys and a traveling carnival. Admittedly I haven't read much of it, but it's interesting. I dig it out of my purse and pretend to read while I wait for Kirby to pass me on the way to his car.

I spent hours last night deciding on the perfect outfit. A charcoal-gray circle-skirt dress that makes my hips look fuller and my shoulders narrower. I cross my left leg over my right and lean back slightly while holding my book in front of me, trying to appear thoroughly engrossed in the story.

I have this fantasy that Kirby will see me reading it. That he'll ask me out to a movie and we'll hold hands through the film. At the end he'll kiss me before he drops me off at home. In ninth grade I had the biggest crush on Joey Mancuso, who had eyebrows like two furry caterpillars. I even wrote him a five-page note telling him how I felt, but I never gave it to him. It's different with Kirby, though. It's more than a silly crush. I feel like I already know him and that if we talked, he'd want to get to know me, too.

When I hear the heavy echo of approaching footsteps, I shake my head, straighten my dress—making sure I look perfect—and angle the book so that he'll see the cover when he passes. Then I wait.

I glance up from reading when Kirby is directly in front of me, but he stares at the ground and never at me. I clear my throat. He keeps walking. He turns the corner and is gone.

Papa is watching TV when I get home. I flop down beside him and rest my head on his shoulder.

"How was school, Billie?"

"Okay, I guess."

"Anyone giving you trouble?"

"No, sir."

"Make any new friends?" Papa stops flipping through the channels and turns toward me.

I told him that the gum was an accident, but I don't think he believed me.

"There's a boy."

"A boy?" Papa's voice deepens when he says it.

"Not like that," I say. "He's just . . . I don't know what he is."

Papa eases my head off his shoulder. "Does this boy have a name?"

"Kirby Matheson."

"Is he the reason you've been coming home late so often?"

The answer sticks in my throat. I thought I was careful, only following Kirby home on the nights Papa was working. When I don't respond, he says, "I drove past the house a couple of times to check on you. It's all right. I'm not mad. I'm happy you're making friends."

"I'm sorry," I say, my voice barely a whisper. "I'll call if I'm not going to come right home from now on."

Papa nods. "Tell me about this boy."

"He's sweet," I say. "Kind of a loner. Shy, you know? He plays the sax in the marching band and he loves to read."

"Sounds like you've got a crush."

"Seriously?" I say, exasperated. "I'm not twelve anymore."

"No. No, you're not."

"I think I want to tell him the truth. About me, I mean."

"Do you think that's wise after what happened at Jupiter?"

The last thing I want to do is dredge up *those* memories. "It's not like that. Kirby's different."

Papa frowns. Worry lines form canyons across his forehead and around his eyes. I'm his daughter, and he takes his job protecting me from the evils of the world seriously. "I trust your judgment, Billie. I just don't want you to get hurt."

The idea that Kirby would ever hurt me is preposterous. He's so gentle and kind. Like he was with Lauren earlier. I can't imagine Kirby hurting anyone.

"I won't, Papa."

He nods. "Now, what should we do about dinner? I'm thinking steak."

I wake up in the middle of the night. I fell asleep thinking about Kirby. Papa is right to be concerned. If I'm wrong about Kirby I'll become the joke of Middleborough High.

I need to see his soul.

I spread all the photos I've taken of him out on my bedroom floor. I have hundreds. Kirby at band practice, Kirby in his car. At home in his bedroom, wandering the school halls. None of them are perfect. They're all missing something. Each is a clue to who Kirby is, but none of them tell the whole story.

Because no single picture could capture a boy like Kirby.

I sneak into the kitchen for scissors. I stay awake all night cutting up the photographs. I stitch together bits and pieces of many photos into one perfect picture. The real Kirby Matheson.

My alarm goes off as I stand back and stare at what I've created. Almost finished. All that's missing is a smile. Kirby isn't smiling in any of the pictures I took, and it doesn't seem right to leave him without a smile. I need one more shot to complete my project.

Exhausted, but more awake than I've ever been, I drive to school and stake out a bench on the main hallway leading from the parking lot so that I can catch Kirby on his way to class. All the students will be gathered in the gym this morning for the pep rally.

Usually, Kirby is early to school. He gathers his books from his locker and arrives at class before anyone else. This morning, he's late. The hallways are filled with students, all babbling excitedly to each other; all ignoring me. I take a couple of shots to make sure the lighting is good. It's not golden-hour great, but it's not bad. When the warning bell rings and he still hasn't shown up, I begin to worry that he's not going to be in school. Maybe he took a different route to his locker. But no. Kirby is a creature of habit. He rarely deviates from his schedule.

He'll come.

I'll wave at him. Tell him everything.

I rehearse what I'm going to say.

"Hi, Kirby. You don't really know me, but I feel like I know you. I've been following you around for a few weeks, taking pictures of you for a photography project, which sounds creepier than it is. Since I know your name, it's only fair you know mine. My name is Billie Palermo."

It sounds dumb in my head, but the more I practice, the more my stomach does flips. Backflips and front flips and those side flips that I could never master without falling over. Kirby will probably be confused at first, but eventually he'll understand. He'll see me for who I really am, and smile. I'll take a picture of that smile, cut it out, and paste it with the rest. My project might be complete, but our story—mine and Kirby's—will only just be starting.

The last bell rings. A few stragglers run to the gym. I wait.

I hear Kirby approaching before I see him. I recognize the heavy stomp of his feet on the concrete. My hands are shaking and bile rises into my throat. He rounds the corner.

This time, he's not going to walk past. This time, he's going to see me.

I can do this. I'm *going* to do this. It's going to be brilliant.

I peer through the eyepiece. I turn the lens to bring Kirby into focus. His arm is raised toward me, his lips raised in a smile. I rest my index finger on the shutter.

And I take the perfect shot.

THE GIRL WHO SAID NO

Senior year

Weeds have sprouted at the base of the Japanese red maple sapling planted near the gym, tiny green shoots pushing through the circle of dark mulch. The groundskeeper on staff at Middleborough High School usually handles such things, but Morgan notices the weeds in a way only someone who looks at the tree every day would notice, caring as only the person who planted the tree would care. Students stream out around her as they leave campus in all directions, to busses, cars, after-school activities. Morgan is in no hurry to suffer the indignity of being the only senior on the school bus, so she stops to pull the weeds.

The task takes only a minute, but painful thoughts don't need much time to take root in her brain. This was supposed to be their year: Morgan Castro and Sydney Kemble. Seniors. Cocaptains of the girls' soccer team. They were going to apply to the same colleges and had *Bend it Like Beckham* dreams of soccer scholarships.

She misses the two of them kicking the ball around her front yard, making the Border collie next door go crazy. He could easily hurdle the four-foot chain-link fence between yards, but he wasn't allowed, so he'd balance all four feet at the top of the fence like a tightrope walker before dropping back into his own yard. It cracked Syd up every time. Morgan remembers how they'd sit at the breakfast bar as Morgan's dad prepared test recipes for the restaurant—*cherry clafoutis, poireaux vinaigrette, homard en croûte*—the way other people's parents made macaroni and cheese. Watching *Doctor Who* at Syd's house on Saturday nights, making up crazy dances to the old rhumba records Morgan's grandma brought with her when she fled Cuba in the sixties, going along with the Kembles on their yearly trip to Disney. A tear tracks down Morgan's cheek and she pushes it away with the back of her hand.

Caleb Graham finds her clutching a handful of weeds. Today his otter-brown hair is loose and Morgan's heart turns a little cartwheel in her chest when he tucks a bit behind his left ear. Caleb always looks a little sleepy, like his mind is elsewhere, and when he talks, it's like coming back to reality surprises him. Syd called it his stoner face—even though he is not a stoner—and perfected an impression that would crack up the whole girls' locker room after practice.

Last year (and the year before that) she would have given anything for Caleb to have asked her to a Middleborough dance, but this year . . .

It's not that Morgan doesn't like him anymore. She does. She always has. His smile makes her insides go twisty and she loves the way his hair is long enough to pull into a little knot at the back of his head. *Man bun* is what Syd called it, which sometimes made Morgan snort when she giggled. She also likes the way his butt looks in varsity blue soccer shorts. It's not a skinny white-boy butt, even though Caleb is about as white as it gets.

"Hey." He sounds surprised now as he greets Morgan, and she holds back a laugh that manifests itself as a smile that makes him respond in kind. Excitement, sadness, attraction, and regret form a knot in her stomach. "I've been trying to track you down all day. What, um—what are you doing?"

Morgan unfurls her palm. Dirt clings to the roots of the weeds. "Just—nothing." She drops them on the grass and wipes off her hand on the thigh of her jeans. "It's stupid."

Caleb squats beside her, his threadbare jeans drawing tight at the knees. He uses the side of his fist to brush the dirt off the plaque in front of the tree.

IN LOVING MEMORY OF SYDNEY ROSE KEMBLE.

Morgan's heart feels so big when he does that, like it could crack right through her chest. If Caleb understands how much the gesture means to her, he pretends not to know. "Feels like people are forgetting, huh?"

"Sometimes."

The school enacted a policy of kindness after the shooting, and for several months it was easy to follow. Middleborough was bound by loss, the belief that *something like this could never happen here* ripped away. Candlelight vigils for the victims were held at school, at churches, and in the park. Memorial trees planted around town. Casseroles cooked for the families of the dead. People *were* nicer to each other because they were all united by fear. Until, invariably, the weeds began to sprout. Kindness is impossible to sustain.

Morgan and Caleb stand at the same time. He clears his throat. "Um—"

"Hey, G. Hi, Morgan." Chris Buzzeo, a.k.a. Buzz, interrupts, offering up his fist for Caleb to bump as he passes. They play varsity soccer together, Buzz at defense, Caleb at midfield. They'll be cocaptains this coming season, the way Morgan and Syd would have been. The way Morgan would have been if she hadn't quit the team.

"Bunch of us are going to the football game tonight," Buzz tells Caleb. "You in?"

"Maybe," Caleb says, as his friend keeps walking. "I'll text you later." Then, when Buzz is out of earshot, to Morgan he says, "You and Sydney used to come to our matches."

Her face gets warm. "We didn't think you noticed."

He laughs, but not in a mean way. "Usually only our families show up, so trust me, we noticed. We spent the entire season arguing about who you were coming to see."

"Who did you think we were there for?"

"Luna."

Gabriel Luna is Middleborough's superstar. He lives in Morgan's neighborhood, the one everyone calls Little Mexico, even though not everyone who lives there is Mexican. Gabriel is from Argentina. Morgan and Syd used to joke about how much work it would be to date him. Gabriel is painfully good-looking and his ego is bloated from being the leading goal scorer in the league last year.

"Ew. No." She shakes her head and crinkles her nose. "We were there to see you."

"For real?" Caleb sounds more surprised than usual. Morgan and Syd used to drive past his house over in Birdland all the time, sometimes when he was outside shooting baskets in the driveway or washing his old Cherokee. They screamed their heads off at games whenever he did anything good. How could he not have known?

"For real."

He jams his hands in his pockets and looks down at his Sambas. "So, um—was it *you* who came to see me, or Sydney?"

Now it is Morgan's turn to look at her shoes, her cheeks pink. "It was me."

"Oh, man." Caleb runs a hand up through his hair and shakes his head. "All this time I thought—well, every time I saw you and Syd in the hall or wherever, you were looking at me and laughing, so I thought—"

"We were just being stupid about your hair."

"Do you hate it?"

"Oh my God, no," Morgan says. "I love your hair."

Her brown eyes meet his brown eyes and Caleb finally poses the question he has come to ask. "Will you go to homecoming with me?"

A moment like this one lived in her daydreams for two years. She and Syd spun up elaborate fairy tales about the Middleborough winter formal in which Morgan and Caleb double-dated with Syd and whichever boy she liked at the time. In the deluxe edition, a black stretch limo was rented and a hotel room booked for after the dance. In more realistic versions, they all rode together in Caleb's Jeep Cherokee and barely made it home in time for curfew. At least a hundred times in her imagination Morgan has kissed Caleb on her front porch while wearing her mom's cool prom dress from 1987 and Caleb with his hair bound up in a knot.

But now that the moment is actually here, Syd is not. Sydney's boyfriend has a new girlfriend. And the dance she and Syd dreamed about no longer exists, discontinued for being tied so closely to the shooting. Morgan doesn't really want to go to homecoming anyway—not even with Caleb Graham. It isn't fair that they get to move on while Sydney Kemble was buried with her hopes and fears, dreams and secrets. How can Morgan say yes? But after what happened the last time someone asked her to a formal dance, how can she say no?

Junior year

"Will you go to winter formal with me?"

The cafeteria was so loud that Morgan almost missed the question. She sized up the black-haired boy standing in front of her and wasn't sure how to answer. Over his shoulder, Sydney was spreading out her lunch at their regular table, giving Morgan a *What the heck are you doing?* look. The boy's name was Kirby and he was in her first-period World Lit class. She couldn't remember his last name and didn't think she had ever heard his voice—at least not directed at her.

"I, um—" Her brain tumbled over itself trying to figure out how to handle this with grace. Kirby was kind of cute in a skinny, scruffy way. She felt shallow judging him by the way he looked, but she was drawing a blank on who his friends were or what he did for fun. Middleborough was big enough that it wasn't unusual for classmates to be strangers, but Morgan felt weird for not knowing anything about this boy.

Winter formal was a week away and nearly everyone she knew already had a date. Her friends were making plans for dinner before the dance, and most of them had already gone dress shopping. Morgan had been holding out hope that Caleb Graham might ask her, but was beginning to think he didn't know she existed, even though she and Syd had gone to all of his soccer games.

"Ask him." Syd made it sound simple. But someone tall and blond like Sydney Kemble could get away with it—David Ackerman had said yes to Syd in a heartbeat—while Morgan would probably die of embarrassment before the words even left her mouth. What if Caleb turned her down? What if he looked at her and had no idea who she was? What if she was the Kirby? The thought made her a little sick with hopelessness.

Kirby was still there, waiting for her answer, and in the middle of her swirling thoughts was the idea that she could say yes. Except she didn't know Kirby. He seemed nice enough, but was *nice* enough? A war waged in her brain and the question grew in enormity until Morgan was surprised the whole cafeteria wasn't waiting to hear her answer.

"I know it's kind of last-minute," Kirby offered. "But I, um—I guess I was waiting for the perfect opportunity."

"I'm sorry, but I can't."

His face didn't collapse in bitter disappointment, but she noticed the way his smile melted into a straight line. He nodded like everything was cool. "Okay."

"I'm sorry," she repeated, but it didn't feel like it was enough. She almost changed her answer. If he hadn't walked away, she might have said yes.

"Who was that?" Syd asked as Morgan opened her lunch bag. Her dad had packed school lunches that morning, so there was no telling what she might find. Once, he gave her a *tartine* with onion marmalade, which she didn't eat because she didn't want bad breath. To her relief, it was a standard-issue ham and cheese sandwich.

"Kirby something," Morgan said. "He just asked me to formal."

Her eyes tracked Kirby across the cafeteria to a table where he dropped into a seat, shaking his head. A girl at the table patted his back and Morgan suffered another pang of guilt for saying no, especially when she looked at the table where some of the soccer players were sitting and watched Caleb laugh at some highly animated story Lauren Hamby was telling. She envied Lauren's ability to drop in on any table and be instantly adored, but even more, she envied that Lauren had Caleb's undivided attention.

Syd groaned. "Please tell me you did not say yes."

"Don't be like that."

"Like what?"

"Like Kirby is an outcast or something. He might be really nice."

"What does that even mean?" Syd pointed her plastic fork in Kirby's direction. "Who does he hang out with? What does he do for fun? What kind of music does he like? What's his favorite movie? Do you have anything in common? These are the things you should be asking yourself, Morgan. Nice means nothing."

"Maybe I would have found all that out if I said yes."

Syd rolled her eyes. "Look, I'm not trying to be a bitch, but do you see yourself kissing *him* at the end of the night?"

Morgan looked again at Kirby—eating lunch in silence while his friends laughed and talked—and shook her head. "I guess not."

That night after dinner, she unearthed her yearbooks from a box in the back of her closet and scoured the pages until she found him. Kirby Matheson. His dark hair fell past his eyebrows in his freshman class picture and a subtle bulge behind his unsmiling mouth suggested he wore braces. On one of the marching band pages she discovered a candid shot of a smiling Kirby, dressed in his uniform, which proved Morgan's braces theory correct. By his sophomore portrait, his orthodontia had been replaced by the hint of a smile. The activities listed below his name—office aide, marching band—did nothing to help color in a more complete picture.

She sat cross-legged on the closet floor as her dad came into the room, still wearing his L'Aigre Doux chef's whites and weird clogs. "Your mom said you were pretty quiet at dinner tonight. Everything okay?"

"This guy asked me to formal today." Morgan put the yearbook aside. "I feel kind of bad for saying no."

"Were you mean to him?"

"No."

"Okay, so." He scratched his head just above his ear and Morgan noticed that a few more strands of gray had started to show. He always joked that working in kitchens should have given him a whole headful already. "Did you *want* to go to the dance with him?"

"No."

"Then don't sweat it, *mija*." He bent over and kissed the top of her head. She caught a whiff of cooking oil and onions, the distinct scent of her dad. It should have been gross, but after so many years the scent was familiar and comforting. "He'll get over it."

Despite her dad's advice, Morgan became hyperaware of Kirby

Matheson as the week progressed. She had gone two and a half years without seeing him, but now he was everywhere. She passed him near the portables on her way to soccer practice on Wednesday and stood two places behind him in the lunch line on Thursday. And when Carah Matheson gave him a dollar, Morgan felt so stupid that she hadn't made the connection between them sooner. She avoided making eye contact with Kirby, but she couldn't help wondering if he was going to winter formal with some other girl. She imagined him feeling smug that Morgan didn't have a date. She wished he had never asked because now she felt this weird responsibility to him, to acknowledge him, to include him. By Friday morning, when Syd's lime-green Beetle pulled into the driveway before school, Morgan was sick of herself and sick of obsessing over a stupid school dance.

Syd handed her a to-go cup of coffee from the coffeehouse near downtown as Morgan slid into the passenger seat. The girls were dressed to match in their soccer jerseys—number eight for Sydney Kemble and number two for Morgan Castro—with thick blue ribbons tied in their hair. They were both secretly thrilled that they'd each been assigned one of Clint Dempsey's numbers. He was one of their favorite players from the U.S. men's national team.

"We're going to be late."

"It's pep rally day, so whatever." Syd waved her cup at Morgan as she drove. "Listen, I've been thinking—I know for a fact that Caleb hasn't asked anyone to formal, so *you* are going to ask *him*."

"I can't."

"Of course you can, because you have absolutely nothing to lose."

Except Syd was wrong. The truth was that as long as Morgan

didn't know exactly how Caleb felt about her, there was a possibility he might like her back someday. If he turned her down for the dance, both her crush and that possibility would die. Morgan would be left with a big empty space where her crush used to be, and she couldn't bear the thought of that. She knew she was being ridiculous and that even best friends don't always understand. "I just—I'll think about it."

The student parking lot was nearly full when the Beetle came to a stop in a space near the back. First bell had already rung, and they were later than normal stragglers, but Syd was right—with the pep rally underway no one would notice them sneak in late.

"Don't think about it, Morgan. Do it. Ask him. Promise me."

"Okay." Morgan didn't bother to cross her fingers behind her back as she and Syd weaved their way between parked cars toward campus. She would look for a loophole later. "I promise."

They were cutting between J Building and the cafeteria when Morgan heard a sharp pop, like the report of a gun. Her neighborhood was not as violent as it was when her dad was her age—before gentrification, as they liked to call it in the Middleborough newspaper—but once in a while gunshots could still be heard coming from the south edge of Little Mexico. As they neared the gym, the sounds from inside spilled out. The band was playing the school fight song to kick off the pep rally.

Morgan and Syd reached the building at the same time as Kirby Matheson. Morgan barely had time to register how strange it was that their paths were crossing yet again when she saw the gun.

She was knocked off her feet by the force of a bullet slamming into her shoulder. The pain was searing and she felt like she had been hit by a baseball bat. Kirby looked down and their eyes locked for a beat, the gun in his hand still pointed at her.

And then he went inside.

Morgan crawled to Sydney, wetting her palms and knees in the puddle of her best friend's blood. The front of Syd's jersey was stained, the circles inside the number eight filled in red. Her blue eyes were open to the sky overhead, but as Morgan collapsed beside her, she couldn't tell if Syd was breathing. Blood dripped down Morgan's arm from the wound in her shoulder and the edges of her world grew fuzzy and dark.

"It's going to be okay," she said against Syd's hair. Morgan smelled Sydney's melon shampoo mixed with blood scented like a handful of old pennies, and the blue ribbon rubbed softly against her cheek. "Stay with me, okay? You have to be here when we get our scholarship letters, Syd. And I'm going to ask Caleb to winter formal, remember? I promise."

Senior year

Morgan is haunted by the way Kirby looked at her after he shot her best friend. Did he kill Sydney as a punishment? Did he spare Morgan's life so she would never forget? Or did he simply decide she wasn't worth a second bullet?

She is haunted by the memory of Sydney Kemble's soft yellow hair against her lips, the feel of her blood on Morgan's skin. Syd died in her arms in the grass outside the gym, just a few feet from where Morgan stands now. Would Sydney still be alive if they'd made it into the gym? Or if Morgan had given Kirby a chance?

She is haunted by her own inability to move forward. Her therapist suggested she do her senior year at St. Luke's Academy, the Catholic school on the other side of town. Some students transferred there, others to East Monroe, after the shooting because using the gym where their classmates were murdered, where Kirby Matheson took his own life, was too painful. Morgan's parents can't afford the tuition at St. Luke's and she doesn't want to put them in debt when the ghosts of Middleborough follow her everywhere.

Death was the terrible epicenter of the shooting, but the aftershocks rippled out far and wide. He robbed Middleborough of its sense of security. Planted seeds of fear. Erased a long-standing high school tradition, replacing it with a day that can never be erased from history. He changed everything and Morgan doesn't know how to set her life right again.

She feels like a mechanical girl, wound up in the morning and ticking her way through the days, but she remembers the girl she used to be. One who liked going to the farmer's market with her family on Saturday mornings. One who believed buying new socks at the beginning of each season and touching the Jozy Altidore poster in her gym locker would bring her good luck on the soccer field. One who had a ridiculously huge crush on the boy standing right in front of her now, looking as unbearably cute as ever, asking her to go to a dance with him.

"What is going on in your brain?" Caleb's voice brings her back to reality, and when his fingers touch her cheek, Morgan realizes another tear has escaped.

"I'm sorry," she says. "I just—I feel like I've been in a fog since the shooting. How are we supposed to go on? How do we play and sing and *dance* when Syd will never get to do any of those things again?"

"I don't know." Caleb shrugs. "I guess we just decide we're not going to let a fucked-up kid with a gun choose how we live."

Kirby Matheson's sister walks past, holding hands with Bobby Avalos. She smiles at him the same way she smiled last year when he gave her a plush black Lab as an invitation to the winter formal. Carah looks happy, and anger licks up inside Morgan like a flame. Guilt snuffs out the anger when she reminds herself that Carah was a victim too. She lost her brother long before the day of the shooting. Carah deserves to be happy.

So why is it so difficult for Morgan to accept the same kind of happiness for herself? Why can't she decide that a fucked-up kid with a gun is no longer allowed to decide her future?

Morgan reaches across the space that separates her from Caleb, takes hold of the front of his T-shirt, and pulls him toward her. She has never been so bold, done something so impulsive, but she can't help thinking that Sydney would approve. Caleb's lips are, at first, confused as she presses her mouth against his, but then Morgan feels the warmth of his hands on her back and the subtle tilt of his head that turns the touch of their lips into a *kiss*. Her arms encircle his neck and she dares herself to sink her fingers into his hair.

Oh my God, Syd, she thinks. *I am touching glory.*

The laughter that wells up from inside her vibrates against Caleb's mouth and when he pulls back, he looks more surprised than she's ever seen him. And a little dazed. "I didn't expect that," he says.

She smiles. "Neither did I."

"So, um—was that an answer?" Caleb slides his fingers between hers, their palms pressed together. Holding his hand feels every bit as good as she imagined, and she pushes back against the small voice that says it shouldn't. "Will you go to homecoming with me?"

She pushes back against her promise to Sydney too.

The world is irrevocably changed, torn and patched, but for the first time since her best friend died, Morgan feels awakened. She is not ready for pep rallies or school dances, but she might just be ready to be happy, to find a new place for herself in this changed world. Tomorrow she will ask the soccer coach if she can rejoin the team. Tomorrow she will go to the farmer's market with her family. She'll ask Caleb to come with her.

But right now she says the word she needs to say because in this new world she can't be afraid to say it.

"No."

POP

Last week, Katelyn had strep throat. That's all Mark can think, lying crammed into the space between two bleachers. She missed three days of school, and he brought her soup and tea and her homework. He'd give anything for her to be home in bed today instead.

He squeezes his eyes shut and hopes so deep that it hurts that she hadn't slipped in without him noticing. She'd never responded to his text about meeting up—sitting together. Maybe she'd ditched the pep rally and gone to Starbucks. Maybe she wasn't one of the ones he'd seen . . . Maybe she wasn't . . .

The thought makes him gag, and he struggles to stay still. Quiet. Wishes it were a normal morning, that they were meeting at his locker. But then they'd pulled so much crap with Kirby's locker this year. What if that's what made him snap? What if Mark had caused this? The thought of that makes Mark even sicker. It had all started so innocently . . .

* * *

"What's up with the Pop-Tarts?" Katelyn had asked one day, just a couple of weeks into the school year. It was right before first period, and Kirby had just slammed his locker door and slouched down the hall, his backpack dangling from one shoulder.

"What Pop-Tarts?" Mark asked, shoving his trig textbook into his bag. He'd forgotten to take it home, which meant he hadn't done the assignment, which meant he was already behind. And he did *not* want to get grounded. It wasn't that long until the winter formal, and he would die if he couldn't take Katelyn.

"You seriously haven't noticed?" Katelyn's blue eyes were even wider than usual. Something about her—her hair, or maybe her lip gloss—smelled like strawberry, and it made him want to sneak her out to the unused shed behind the football field and pretend first period didn't exist. "Every morning!"

"Every morning what?" Mark asked, shaking off his foggy-headedness.

"Every morning he pulls two packages of Pop-Tarts out of his bag, squishes them, and throws them in his locker."

"Huh," Mark said. "Yeah. I guess that's kind of weird. I hadn't noticed."

"Obviously." Katelyn rolled her eyes at him, but she was smiling all the same. "I mean, seriously, Mark . . . half the time an elephant could walk past you and you wouldn't notice."

Mark cocked an eyebrow at her. "I noticed that you smell like strawberries," he said. He took a step closer to her.

"You like the way strawberries smell?" she asked.

"I never thought about it much before, but now?" He brushed

his lips against hers. "It's definitely my favorite." He kissed her—not the kind of kiss that would draw attention, but one that promised. It promised more, later. Soon.

She made a happy little noise and rested her forehead against his chest, just for a moment.

"It's my—" she began.

"Lip gloss," Mark finished, before she could. "Your lip gloss tastes like strawberry."

The warning bell rang, and the two of them headed in opposite directions toward their first classes of the day. After their kiss, Mark's own lips tasted faintly of strawberry, and he spent most of trig distracted by the thought of Katelyn. He didn't have a completed assignment to turn in, and when the final bell rang, he realized he couldn't remember a single thing that Mrs. Alvarez had said during class.

He had it bad for Katelyn and he knew it. Now he just had to keep it from ruining him.

The next day he'd made a point of noticing the Pop-Tarts so that he could prove to Katelyn that he wasn't *always* missing things. It was true. In the bottom of Kirby's locker was a silvery pile of Pop-Tart packets, like a tiny pyramid devoted to some god of the lower middle class. There was other weird stuff in there too. Neat piles of—index cards, maybe? And receipts and—

Kirby slammed his locker shut before Mark could get a better look. Mark pulled his phone out of his pocket and texted Katelyn.

Saw the Pop-Tarts! That's so fucked up. Also now I'm hungry for Pop-Tarts.

Katelyn didn't text him back until the end of first period, but the long string of smiley faces thrilled him.

You noticed!!!!!! she texted him.

Yeah, he texted back. *That's me. I'm a noticer.*

"Yo, MB!" Mark looked up to see Jason Price eyeing him from the doorway of the chemistry lab. "What you grinnin' at like that?"

"Nothing," Mark said, tucking his phone back into his pocket. "You wanna eat lunch with us today or what?"

"Us?" Jason folded his arms.

"Yeah, me and Katelyn."

"Oh, it's like that now, is it?" Jason said.

Mark touched the phone in his pocket. "Yeah," he said. "It's like that."

"Fine," Jason huffed. "I'll meet you in the cafeteria."

Jason and Mark were already hunched over a couple of slices of greasy, terrible school lunch pizza when Katelyn slid into the empty seat next to Mark. She eyed his tray. "No Pop-Tarts?" she teased.

Mark grinned at her. "Not on the menu today," he said, "but that's okay. I know where I can score some later if I need to."

"What the fuck are you two talking about?" Jason asked.

"You know that weird kid Kirby Matheson?" Mark asked.

Jason thought for a minute. "The one who plays the saxophone?"

"That's the one. It turns out he has, like, a prepping-for-the-apocalypse-style stash of Pop-Tarts in his locker," Mark said.

"SMASHED Pop-Tarts," Katelyn added. She sounded amused and amazed at the same time. "He crunches up the packages before he tosses them in there. I don't get it. Why wouldn't he just throw them away?"

Jason rolled his eyes. "Y'all have too much time on your hands, and since you're *together*, that says some pretty sad stuff about both of you." He had a slice of pizza in his hand, and he pointed it at each of them in turn. "I'm just sayin'."

"Dude. There is *no reason*—" Mark started, but Katelyn put a hand on his leg.

"Wow, Jason. Since you're not dating anyone at all, I can't *begin* to think what that says about your free time."

Jason's mouth dropped open. "Daaaaaaaaaamn."

With a tiny, satisfied grin on her face, Katelyn pulled a carton of yogurt out of her lunch bag. That was the first time Mark thought that maybe, just maybe, he was in love.

As the weeks went on, the Pop-Tarts became an in-joke between the two of them. Katelyn left a packet of them on his seat in history. He put one, unwrapped, beneath each of her windshield wipers. Mark asked her to the winter formal, officially, and brought her a box of them when he picked her up. Her eyes lit up and she laughed, hard, in that whole-body way that he adored. She doubled over, ribs shaking and completely unself-conscious about it.

He'd practically forgotten how the joke started. Kirby wasn't at his locker at the same time in the morning anymore, but it didn't matter. The entire thing had taken on a life of its own, far beyond the initial amusement they'd gotten from one weird kid's odd habits.

Then, on Tuesday, Mark started the day by his locker, just like usual. He was dawdling, waiting for Katelyn, idly wondering if he should put his lit binder in his bag, even though Mrs. Johansen never said anything worth taking notes about. The sudden presence at his shoulder startled him, and he looked up with a goofy smile on his face, expecting to see Katelyn.

Except it was Kirby. He eyed Mark and smirked as the smile fell from Mark's face.

"Sorry," Mark said. "I thought you were someone else."

"Clearly," Kirby said. He spun the combination lock on his locker and swung the door open, but he kept his body wedged between the door and the opening so that Mark couldn't see inside it.

Kirby unzipped his backpack. He reached his hand in, and before Mark could stop himself, he asked "Hey, what's the deal with the Pop-Tarts?"

Kirby froze, his gaze darting over to Mark even while his body remained completely motionless.

"What do you mean?" he asked. His voice was careful, measured.

Mark shifted uncomfortably. "I mean—why have you been squishing them up and leaving them in your locker? I don't get it."

Kirby stared at him. "I don't like them," he said finally.

"Well, that seems pretty—*oof.*" Someone hit Mark hard from behind, pushing him into Kirby, who stumbled.

"Sorry!" shouted the three guys who tore off down the hall like a trio of unruly puppies. *Basketball players*, Mark thought, *and they really shouldn't*—he couldn't finish the thought. The collision had left him standing directly in front of Kirby's locker. In addition to the pile of Pop-Tarts, there was a stack of magazines, a copy of *East of Eden*, a bunch of receipts taped to the back wall, and not a single thing that looked remotely related to school.

"Where do you keep all of your schoolbooks?" Mark asked.

Kirby reached in front of Mark and slammed the locker shut. "None of your business," he snapped.

Katelyn came racing up to them, completely out of breath. "Ohmygod, are you okay? Those jerks are just—*ugh*."

Mark turned to her. "No, I'm fine. Thanks." He looked back at Kirby. "You?"

Katelyn blinked in sudden recognition. "Oh, hey, you're the Pop-Tart guy! Where have you been?"

Kirby scowled.

"Oh, come on," Katelyn said, "Don't be like that."

Kirby pointed a finger at them. "You two need to mind your own fucking business."

"Hey!" Mark stepped in. "What's your problem? Normal people ask each other questions. And I don't like you talking to my girl-friend like that."

Kirby narrowed his eyes at Mark for a moment before his face went completely blank.

Katelyn tugged on Mark's arm. "Come on," she said. "Let's just go, okay? This morning is crappy enough already."

He let her tug him away from Kirby, but it still bothered him. The weird locker. The blank look. But mostly, yeah, the way he'd talked to Katelyn.

It followed him all morning—the feeling itched between his shoulder blades. Something he couldn't see, or reach, or quite get rid of.

When he got to lunch, he found Jason and flopped down across from him.

"Jaaaaaysus. What's your problem?" Jason said around a mouthful of sloppy joe. Mark shook his head. "I don't know. Maybe it's stupid. Kirby—that guy, with the locker next to mine?"

Jason nodded.

"Yeah. He pissed me off this morning and I can't shake it."

"What'd he do?" Jason asked.

Mark told him the story exactly as it had happened. It didn't make the strange feeling between his shoulder blades any better.

Jason chewed. Swallowed. Shrugged. "Is Katelyn pissed?" he asked.

Mark sat for a minute, thinking. "Not really," he said, finally. "But it's not really about that. Not for me."

Jason eyed him. "You're telling me you're pissed because he emasculated you in front of your woman?"

Mark blinked. "You know the word *emasculated*?"

Jason threw a wadded-up paper napkin at him. "I do actually pay attention in class sometimes. Plus that shit impresses the hell out of girls. Anyway, that's it, huh?"

Mark nodded grudgingly. "Yeah, more or less. I don't know. It just seems like you don't get to be all weird and then be a dick to me in front of my girlfriend for no reason."

"I guess I can see your point. But now the real question is: What're you going to do about it? I mean, you've got two choices here that I can see. One: Let it go. Two: Remasculate yourself."

"I don't think *remasculate* is a word," Mark said.

"Bro, I know it's not a word, but it means the right thing. And it doesn't change the fact that you've only got two choices."

Katelyn walked into the cafeteria just then, and Mark turned to look at her. She caught sight of him sitting with Jason and smiled, heading toward them.

Was it Mark's imagination, or was her smile just the tiniest bit smaller than it had been this morning? Was there a fraction less sparkle in her eyes?

Maybe he really only had the one choice. Even if it wasn't a word.

It took Mark a couple of days to figure out exactly how to make sure Kirby never smirked at him again. Picking a fight would be easy, but it might also get him suspended . . . or worse. He needed something different. Something better. Something that Katelyn would appreciate.

When the idea came to him, it was so perfect. A couple of blue boxes, some packing tape, and getting to school a little bit early was all it took.

Mark hovered in the chem lab door and waited for Kirby to get to school. He trudged in, head down, dragging that stupid saxophone. Mark could hear, over and over in his head, Kirby's hissing, angry insistence that he and Katelyn should "mind their own fucking business."

Kirby didn't even look up before he got to his locker. It was perfect.

When he saw the boxes of Pop-Tarts taped to the metal door of his locker, Kirby froze. His entire back went so rigid that Mark's breath caught. It occurred to Mark in that moment that it was possible he'd end up having a fight after all, but he didn't really care. It might be worth getting a suspension.

Mark watched as Kirby slowly peeled the boxes off his locker, his shoulders creeping closer to his ear with each screeching crackle of the packing tape pulling away from the metal. He opened his backpack and shoved the boxes inside, cramming them on top of each other.

People walking past noticed. There was some eye-rolling. There was some laughing. Kirby hunched even further into himself, which didn't seem entirely possible. Mark was so focused on watching Kirby that he jumped—badly—when Katelyn whispered in his ear: "What's going on?"

Mark turned and grinned at her, feeling the sort of triumph that he'd envisioned when he'd first thought of this plan. "Just contributing to Kirby's Pop-Tart supply," he said, unable to stop the grin that twitched at the corners of his mouth. He fought to get a serious expression on his face and held Katelyn's gaze. "I don't think he appreciates it, though."

It might have been the two of them talking that caught Kirby's attention, though the hall was crowded with people. Maybe it was just luck that he turned around. Whatever the reason, though, Kirby did turn. And when he did, he looked straight at Mark and Katelyn.

The victory Mark had been feeling swelled for a moment, crescendoing into a strange sort of joy. Kirby looked defeated.

No, more than that. He looked broken.

The expression in Kirby's eyes dragged Mark's joy down with it.

The last box of Pop-Tarts was still in Kirby's hand. Mark noticed that they were strawberry-flavored. He wondered if Kirby would have the balls to storm across the hall and smash them in his face. Or just flat-out punch him.

He could hear Katelyn's breath in his ear.

Kirby just dropped the box of Pop-Tarts. Someone else hurrying past kicked the box on accident, sending it skittering down the hall.

Kirby didn't watch its progress. He didn't walk toward Mark and Katelyn.

He lowered his gaze to the linoleum floor, turned, and trudged off, with his backpack full of crushed Pop-Tart boxes hanging off his shoulder.

"Whoa," said Katelyn. "That was, like, super mean," she said to Mark.

Anger flared in his chest, probably meant for Kirby but directed at Katelyn instead.

"Mean? It was just Pop-Tarts, for fuck's sake! And he was awful to us the last time we talked. Was I supposed to act like that's okay?"

"Did you see the look on his face, though? I mean, this isn't someone like Jason—someone who's gonna look at a locker covered with Pop-Tarts and laugh and offer everyone breakfast," she said.

"I didn't want him to laugh!" Mark exploded. "I didn't want him to offer everyone breakfast! I wanted him to be sorry he acted the way he did!"

Katelyn crossed her arms. "And you don't think that's mean?"

Jason walked up to them, his chemistry book in his hand. "What's mean?"

"Nothing," Mark said, at the same time that Katelyn chimed in with, "Covering Kirby's locker in boxes of Pop-Tarts."

Jason's eyes widened. "Whoa."

"Exactly," Katelyn said, her voice filled with vindication.

"That's *awesome*," Jason finished.

Katelyn made a frustrated noise. "You two don't get it, do you? Ugh. I just—ugh."

She pushed past Jason and turned down the hall toward her first-period class.

She didn't text Mark that morning.

She wasn't at lunch.

By the time the school day ended, Mark was practically panicking. Everything he'd done had been to win Katelyn's affection back after Kirby had made him lose face—this was worse than backfiring. This was . . . this was maybe even a breakup. She'd never gone this long without texting him.

She was waiting by his car, though, and when he noticed her there, he took what felt like his first real breath all day.

"Hey," he said.

"Hey."

"I'm sorry about this morning," he said. "I guess—I can see where you're coming from. But I had to do something, and the Pop-Tarts seemed better than hitting him or whatever."

Katelyn looked at him. "You really think you did a good thing? I mean, why did you have to 'do something' to begin with? You could have just walked away."

Mark just stared at her.

"Hello?" she waved a hand in front of his face. He blinked. "I mean, I don't like Kirby either, but this is . . . shitty."

"I'm sorry," Mark said. "I never thought of it that way. I really didn't mean anything by it."

Katelyn chewed on her lip for a moment. "I don't know if that makes this better or worse," she finally said. "And if you never thought about it, I think maybe you need to."

Mark blinked again. "What are you saying?"

"I'm saying you're acting like a jerk, and I don't want to hang out with a jerk."

"Are you breaking up with me?" he asked. Katelyn let out a frustrated noise. "You don't get it at all, do you?"

"No! I don't!"

"Well, call me when you do," she said tartly. Then she spun on her heel and marched away while he stood there, aching and confused.

He left her alone for a few lonely, terrible days. How could he have been so wrong about the whole thing? He'd been trying to . . . what? Impress Katelyn? Protect her? Prove himself to her, maybe. And instead, he'd ruined everything and he didn't know how to fix it.

Then on Monday, he'd looked for her before first period, but she wasn't there. He was late to third period, trying to see if she came out of the art room after her second period class, but she wasn't there either. Unable to stand it any longer, he texted her.

R U okay?

I'm home sick, she texted back.

What's wrong?

Strep throat.

He hesitated for just a moment before he sent the next text. *Can I bring you your homework?*

He held his phone too tightly, waiting for the little typing bubble to appear.

There was a long pause before she replied.

A very long pause.

Finally:

Yes. Thanks.

Everything in him lightened. His hands and feet tingled with it. It spread across his face in a grin that he couldn't stop.

His thumbs tapped against the screen of his phone. *Ok. See you after school.*

All he could think about the rest of the day was getting her homework. What else he should bring her—flowers? Popsicles? Soup?—and most of all, what he would say when he got there.

This was a second chance, and he wasn't about to blow it.

After school, he put her carefully stacked assignments in his car and drove to the grocery. Simultaneously panicked about needing to find the perfect "get well" things and also not wanting to arrive any later than absolutely necessary, Mark scurried around the store, picking things up and putting them down again.

He grabbed flowers and put them back, pulled a can of soup off the shelf and put it back, and then ice cream, and then a magazine, and then finally he put all of it in a basket and rushed through the checkout.

At Katelyn's house, he rang the doorbell and shifted from foot to foot anxiously.

In his pocket, his phone dinged, and he ignored it. Probably Jason.

No one came to the door, which seemed odd. Her parents were probably at work, but Katelyn's car was sitting in the driveway, complete with the dent in the fender where she'd backed into the corner of her house.

Mark rang the doorbell again, and his phone dinged once more. This time, he pulled it out of his pocket, juggling the grocery bags and schoolbooks to get to it.

Two texts from Katelyn.

Come in.

No really, COME IN. (This one had a smiley face after it.)

Mark opened the door and stepped into the house.

"Katelyn?" he called quietly.

"In here," she croaked.

He walked into the living room and saw her lying on the couch. She had on yoga pants and a hot-pink sweatshirt, but her face was pale and there were circles under her eyes. Her hair was pulled back into a messy bun.

She was still the most beautiful girl he'd ever seen.

"Hey," he said. He opened his mouth to tell her all the pretty things he'd been storing up to say—that she looked beautiful, that he'd be sick in a second if it meant she'd be well, did she want a Diet Coke?—but none of the words would come out. Instead he just stood there, dumbstruck, with his mouth hanging open.

She smiled at him. "Hi."

The rough sound of her voice propelled him into motion and he held out the flowers. "These are for you."

"Thanks," she said. "They're gorgeous."

"You're gorgeous," he blurted out.

Her smile deepened, and though her cheeks were still porcelain pale, there was a fresh sparkle in her eye that gave him hope.

"I brought soup and ice cream? I didn't know if they might sound good. And I have your homework!"

"Maybe some ice cream," she said.

"I'll get you a spoon," he said, starting toward the kitchen.

At the same moment, she stood, saying, "No, it's fine, I've—"

And then, without meaning to be, they were face-to-face with only a couple of inches between them. She smelled like sleep and shampoo and he closed his eyes and breathed her in.

"Mark," she said.

His eyes flew open. "I'm sorry, I didn't mean—"

"No, it's okay," she said, breathless. "I just—I don't want to get you sick."

He laughed the smallest possible laugh, not wanting to break the spell of the moment. "I don't care," he said.

He leaned in and pressed his lips against hers. Her mouth was hot with fever, but fresh with something minty and sweet, and he thought he could eat her up right there.

She wobbled on her feet and he caught her by the elbows and lowered her to the couch. "Easy," he said.

She smiled up at him. "Sorry."

"Don't apologize," he said. "Not one little bit. I'm going to get you a spoon."

He left her on the couch and walked into the kitchen. He grabbed a spoon out of the drawer and everything about being in her house felt new and familiar at the same time, which was maybe the best feeling he'd ever had in his life.

They spent the rest of the afternoon on the couch. He fed her ice cream and helped her with her trig problems. She put her feet in his lap and leaned her head against his shoulder.

The next afternoon, they did the same thing.

It has been heaven, and Mark has been thrilled and relieved. He's thought that the worst was behind them. He wants to see her every second. To spend every minute with her. He'd been so irritated when he couldn't find her before the pep rally today. So irritated that she'd been late, so that they might not be able to sit together.

He lies between the bench seats of the bleachers with his eyes squeezed shut and hopes and hopes and hopes that she isn't here. He hopes she's sick. That her car has quit. He even hopes that he's pissed her off somehow—anything that would mean that she isn't in this gym, in this moment, listening to the sound of this terror.

When he closes his eyes, he can hear his heart beating. It sounds like her name. Like a prayer.

Katelyn . . . Katelyn . . . Katelyn.

PRESUMED DESTROYED

I am not defective.

I am not malformed.

My imperfections are entirely cosmetic. A discoloration in the steel along my handle. A vein slightly lighter, mildly less tempered than the rest of me. But my barrel, my chamber, my trigger and hammer are unmarred. My action is every bit as precise as any other.

And yet I was separated from my siblings, sorted into a pile of discards.

You cannot know the misery of being deemed unworthy of one's purpose, even before knowing what that purpose might be.

I was tossed into a holding crate, doomed to be melted down—re-smelted into that angry bright liquid from which I was forged. Destined to lose my identity in the fiery melting pot. This was to be my fate—but it didn't happen that way.

Instead I was saved.

It was not out of compassion. No, nothing so selfless. I was saved out of greed. A worker in the factory, whom I did not know, and did not care to know, stole away with my crate. All of us relegated for the furnace were instead offered for sale in a dark room to a shadowy man.

"See what I've brought you? There are more than two dozen here."

"Yes, two dozen substandard pistols."

"Minor flaws, that's all."

"I have a reputation."

"So only take the best of them."

"Fine. I'll give you forty a piece."

"Seventy-five."

"Fifty. My final offer."

"Take ten of them, and you have a deal."

"Agreed."

The shadowy man was the first to hold me in his poorly manicured hand, but he never pulled my trigger. I was nothing but a commodity to him, and he was merely a middleman to my destiny.

I was smuggled on a long journey in darkness, to a place far different from where I was forged. Plenty of time to wonder what I'd be used for. I knew the possibilities were endless. I come from a family of both fame and infamy. Distant cousins fought wars, bringing both devastation and freedom. Some kept the peace in the streets of cities but were also abused by those sworn to protect. I tried to imagine the sort of hand I would fall into and what purpose that hand would have for me.

In the end, I was sold in a filthy alley—a quick, quiet cash deal— but at least I now belonged to someone.

My first owner was a man of brutal camaraderie. I never knew the name of his gang, only that he belonged to one. From the moment he held me, I knew what I was to him. A symbol. An icon of his manhood, of his pride, of his ascension from impoverished mediocrity. To him I was a ticket to greatness. He would test the speed of his draw to an empty room. He would show me to his friends, bragging. And he would keep me loaded. There was always a bullet in the gullet of my chamber, lodged there, choking and heavy, in that penultimate position, awaiting the act. My act. My one true function.

I understood him all too well. He had passion, but it left me cold, for it was a careless passion. He believed my power to be his own and he took it for granted. On the rare times he fired me it was a pointless act—such as the time he aimed me upward on New Year's Eve in a vain attempt to pierce the sky. He pulled the trigger with such random, reckless abandon, I felt only shame.

Do not misunderstand; I didn't hate him. I pitied him, though. He thought my presence in his life would bring him respect, but how could it when his own actions engendered such disrespect?

Then, in a moment of weakness, he resorted to crime. A store of convenience in the predawn hours of a violent summer storm.

The clerk seemed defiant, rather than compliant, when he saw me.

"*Calm down, kid, put that gun away. No one's gotta get hurt.*"

"*Shut the hell up, old man. Just gimme everything you got in there.*"

"*You don't want to do this. Just—*"

"*I said shut it. Do I look like I'm playin' around? Give me all the money.*"

I felt hot in his hand. His sweat conducted his nervousness like electricity, and it empowered me. I felt alive, born anew, and yet disgusted by the feeling. Was this my purpose? Was this it? So compelling, yet so ignoble. I could feel his adrenaline as if it were my own. I could feel the fear on the other side of the barrel too, but I could feel something else. Something like experience. And it was not the experience of my owner.

"Hold on a moment. . . . Just let me open the register."

"What are you doing? Stand up straight, old man!"

And just like that, the tables turned. A standoff. I could see the gun the man was holding. A Desert Eagle .50 caliber. It was a beautiful weapon that made me feel inadequate, inferior. It was as if that gun was mocking me, laughing at me. The shame of being used for a lowly heist was replaced by the embarrassment of being bested.

"Whoa, man . . . Take it easy . . ."

I could feel my owner's cowardice. It had always been there. His bravado was just a thin veneer slathered across it like cheap paint on an old revolver. He was having second thoughts about this whole thing. Was I failing him, or was he failing me? I could not provide him what he wanted. I could not bring him true respect, and he could not give me a purpose. In a moment he faltered, lowering me just a bit, and my rival, the Desert Eagle, took its cue to shame me once more, for a weapon like that is all muscle and no remorse.

The shot rang out like cannon fire and it burst into my owner's arm. He swore and cursed as he bled, but still he held me, cradled me. He ran, bursting through the door, setting off the convenience store's disturbingly cheery electronic doorbell. The clerk didn't even bother to yell at us.

We ran through the rainy streets. Cars whizzed by, people ignored the wounded man. I was shrouded in darkness as he had stuffed me in his pocket, but I could feel his broken manhood, his lost dreams. When we got home, he closed me in a toolbox like a coffin, and I sat there for months. Time faded with no way to measure the days in the darkness.

Such was my existence. And in time, I came to believe I had no purpose. No reason to be. The prospect filled me with lethargic despair.

Then, after many months—perhaps years—he opened my steel sarcophagus, reached in, and pulled me out. His wound had healed, but I sensed in him a scar of firm resolve. He had a new intention for me, but it confused me, because I also sensed that he would never fire me again.

He slipped me into a pocket filled with crumpled dollars and stray coins. Small bills and spare change speak of such shallow, trivial things: what they have been spent on, or the wallets and purses they have known. Their chatter annoyed me, and it made me wish he would spend them frivolously so I could be rid of them. As it turned out, he was far more interested in finding them companions than he was in me.

He took me out in an alley, perhaps the same one in which he purchased me, and, as he held me up to show me off, I realized the truth. I was about to change hands! The bullet that pierced my first owner's arm, in a way, tore open a new future for me—for now I would pass into another's possession. Who shall own me? I wondered. And for what purpose? Would I be used for a family's protection? Would I fire upon coyotes or other scavengers? Or would I be put on a pedestal in a collection, to be revered as a work of art?

"Okay. I got the money you asked for right here."

"Good. You came alone?"

"Yeah, of course. Just like you said."

"Good. Then take it, kid. I hope it brings you more luck than it did me."

And now, in the faint light of the familiar alley, I am thrust into the hands of my new owner, and I am reborn!

Into the life of an angry, frightened boy.

As the boy holds me in his cold, shaking hand, I know that he's different. I feel an unnamable pain in him—the kind that ricochets so quickly through one's soul, it cannot be caught, only pursued with increasing desperation. In him, I feel deeper emotions than I ever knew existed. A blinding spectrum of feelings my previous owner only scraped the surface of.

He stuffs me into his coat pocket. I couldn't be more snug if I were in a holster. The coat is snug on him as well, as if it's several years old and he has outgrown it, but no one has bothered to get him a new one. Or perhaps he's the one holding on to this thread of an earlier time—a time before he felt the need to have me in his pocket. I feel safe here, and yet not. I hear my first owner run off, and I never see him again. The boy runs in the opposite direction.

I long to comfort him—to soothe the rawness of his wounds. They are not like bullet wounds. Those are easy to see and define. Gun wounds are not subtle or deceptive, for more than anything, my kind is honest, even in dishonest hands. We speak in plain and simple terms. There is nothing ambiguous about a gun.

But the boy's wounds are of a different kind. Intangible. Hidden—even from himself. And they are deep. I'm not privy to the experiences of his life that brought him to this moment. We weapons are not blessed with a historical perspective on the lives we enter. We exist in the moment. We sense deeply the searing "now." And this boy's now is filled with mines and monsters.

I ride home in his car nestled in the glove compartment. I come to know him even more as I lie among the detritus of his life. A forgotten theme park pass. A parking violation he's afraid to show to his parents. A cherry ChapStick that melts by day and solidifies by night. A folded envelope of school pictures that he doesn't want to keep but can't bring himself to throw away. They all lie silently, for these things have nothing left to say to anyone. Here begins my deep desire to truly understand him, for only then can I hope to quell the demons that so torment him.

When the boy gets home, he takes me out again. He holds me tightly in those first few hours, extending me outward, his arm stiff, squinting one eye and pointing me at the wall. He says nothing. I hear nothing but a television from the other room. But the boy's hand feels so comforting, I relax and let him hold me. And I know in that moment that I will not be used today, but that I will be used.

He moves me from location to location, hiding place to hiding place, within his car. I am kept beneath the driver's seat. Then in a shoe box in the trunk. Then wedged in the gap beneath the spare tire.

When he does take me out, it's not to wave me in a show of bravado. It is merely to regard me. To take me in from every angle. To study me with eyes so intense, it would make me blush were I able. He shows me to no one. I am his secret.

Finally he brings me closer, deeper into his life. He moves me from the car into his sock drawer. A soft, warm place. It becomes my home. When he transfers me this time, there is something different about him. It excites me. I know that the day I will be used is near. My days pass easily now, filled with muted anticipation. Surely I am more to him than an object in a drawer.

But weeks pass. Since the day he put me in the sock drawer, I have never been out of his house. I have become a domesticated thing. A pet waiting in silence for the return of my master. Some days he ignores me, others, he feeds me with his attention. I grow warm and grateful in his grasp. Once—only once—he sleeps with me beneath his pillow, and I am proud to be a protector of his dreams.

While my first owner once practiced the speed of his draw in the mirror, the boy draws me, but in a very different way. With pencil and paper. With his door locked he leaves me perched on his desk, unloaded, always unloaded, and proceeds to sketch me. I am his model—and he captures me in that drawing—if not my weight and density, at least my personality. My striking profile. Then, to my absolute surprise, he hangs the picture on the refrigerator, like a child.

I want his mother to look deeper when she sees it—to question it. Instead, she is just annoyed.

"*I don't like it, Kirby.*"

"*It's just a drawing.*"

"*Why would you draw such a thing?*"

"*I don't know, I just felt like it.*"

She doesn't see me there, the edge of my grip sticking out of the pocket of his hoodie, like a dare. I'm still unloaded, but dangerous all the same.

"*Could you maybe draw something a little less bleak?*"

"*How about a fighter jet?*"

"Sure."

"Much more deadly than a pistol, but hey, if it makes you happy."

And if she were to see me in the moment, what then? Surely I'd be removed from the boy's presence. And although the thought brings me great sadness, and even greater anxiety, if my removal can ease his sorrow, perhaps it will be for the best. I grow guilty in these moments. I feed off of his own guilt and her worry. I feel worthless, unneeded, alone. I feel what Kirby feels.

But she doesn't see me. She doesn't even know to look. To her, a drawing is a drawing, and kids draw guns and battles and other violent things. They play games of graphic carnage and go on to lead productive, normal lives. She does not see that today a gun really is a gun.

He leaves the kitchen, returning to the disheveled sanctuary of his room, where he tears the picture to shreds and commences to draw a fighter jet blowing apart a defenseless town.

A day comes when I am once more freed from the sock drawer. Kirby handles me carefully and aims me like he did the first day he bought me. Then he stuffs me in his snug pocket, and before long we are running through the streets, just the two of us moving to the cadence of his drumming heart. I hear him racing up stairs. The cold wind brushes by, and I feel as if I am on top of a mountain. He pulls me out, and I see that in a way, it is a mountain. A corporate mountain. The mountain of the human machine. We stand on top of an office building, and he stands near the edge.

He holds me out in cold hands, just over the edge, but I know he will not drop me. There is a wild excitement in him, but behind that is that pain I feel every time he holds me. It's stronger here. Unbearable. I want to deny it and exist in his excitement, but I know I can't. The two emotions go hand in hand.

Then he kneels down and looks over the edge of the building. A supermarket is across the way, where dozens of shoppers move to and from their cars, carts rattling.

He takes aim at an old man making his way across the street. He pulls the trigger.

Click.

"Take that!"

The man continues across the street, none the wiser.

Kirby aims again—this time at a teenage employee struggling to wrangle carts.

"You're toast, asshole!"

Click.

My clip is empty. All my bullets are back in the drawer. And I am glad. I am glad that this game can ease Kirby's pain.

Next, a middle-aged man fumbling with his keys:

Click!

Three teens sneaking beer out of the market:

Click! Click! Click!

"Serves you right, shitheads."

Yes, the game eases his pain, but not enough. It's like trying to bail water from a sinking, shotgun-blasted boat. With each pull of my trigger, there's even greater longing in him. Greater need to carve some sort of retribution out of the world.

"Hey! You can't be up here!"

A security guard has come onto the roof. He doesn't see me at this angle; he only sees Kirby standing there. I feel Kirby's sudden wish that the gun was loaded. I feel his intent. I feel him cursing that he did not bring bullets, and I feel myself being quickly stuffed back into his jacket as Kirby turns around in one fluid motion.

"What's the problem? I'm just taking in the view."

"You gotta get down from here, son. You're not allowed up here."

"Screw you. My uncle works for this company."

"I don't care if he's the president. Now get the hell off this roof before I call the cops."

I feel a knot of fear in Kirby's stomach. He takes off, and soon I am home, once more nestled among white socks.

Alone again, I have time to ponder what Kirby has done with me today, what it all meant. I have been in human hands enough to glean more than just the powdery residual of right and wrong. I have grown to feel things beyond what was intended. A gun should feel a need to be fired, nothing more, and yet I find myself feeling a growing concern for the boy who wields me. If I had been loaded with bullets, would he have shot the guard? Would he have shot the shoppers? Or is it truly just a game to him? A reality game. When does reality start for him? Is it when the bullets go into my chamber? Is that when it becomes real for him, or will it still be just a game? I see in my mind's eye the security guard lying dead in a pool of blood, and Kirby standing over him, holding me to the side. I see him dropping me and running off. I do not want to be abandoned. But I also don't want to abandon him. There must be another way this can end. There must be, but I'm not wise enough to see it.

* * *

For seven days he keeps me in the back of his sock drawer, ignoring me, perhaps denying my presence. I wonder if his own actions spooked him. If he has come to terms with what had happened on the roof. I picture him growing older, keeping me as a trophy. Firing me at a shooting range. Years from now, teaching his children about me, how to use me, what I am. How dangerous I can be in the wrong hands. But even as I think about this, I know the wrong hands may be his. I bury my thoughts in a casing of denial, and when he takes me out again, I realize he's encased himself in denial as well. A denial of what happened on the roof, of his own self, his own future, and an inability to find a new one.

Today he does something he's never done before. He offers me to someone else. A girl with a boy's name. A friend. I didn't know he had any. I am relieved. I am jealous. I am ashamed of my jealousy. He would have her use me to defend herself, and I think for a moment that I will change hands once again. My destiny will rebound onto a different course. But no. She refuses. He puts me away. He takes me home.

But the following day he takes me out again, and this time he does something else he's never done before. He loads me . . .

. . . with a single bullet.

Something happened today. I don't know what it is. Something to his friend perhaps? Whatever it is, it's tipped the boy off his delicate balance. I can almost feel him falling as he loads that bullet. I know what he plans to do. There's only one reason to load a single bullet into the chamber of a handgun.

And for all the power I have, I know I cannot stop him—and for once I wish I truly were defective. That my hammer would miss the mark, or shatter before striking the shell. I am powerless within my power.

His hand is colder than it was on the day he bought me. His hand shakes. His chest heaves with sobs. *Lay me down,* I plead. *Lay me down and walk away. Call your parents to the room. Let them see me. Let them know. There is nothing ambiguous about a gun! If they see me, they will finally tear through their own denial and pull you in from this icy edge.*

But he calls no one. He just closes his eyes. Then he presses the end of my barrel to his temple. I feel the pressure on my trigger, and I try to resist even though I know I can't.

We stay like this forever.

And then he jerks my barrel from his head, the bullet still in the chamber, unfired. His breathing heavy and uneven, as if he has just come up from deep underwater. He places me down on the table, staring at me as if I've somehow betrayed him. Then he quickly puts me away. Not in the sock drawer, but in another shoe box, in the closet underneath a dozen other things. He hides me not just from others this time, but from himself.

And I am grateful.

I think it's over.

I think whatever crisis brought him to the brink has subsided, and his climb to a better place has begun. He may forget me, I think, or sell me, or save me for some nobler purpose, in a nobler time of his life. I can wait for that. Guns are notoriously patient.

But I am not forgotten.

The next day, he comes for me once more. To hold me. To ponder me, this time in an opaque sort of numbness. I cannot see through the veil of his thoughts today, but I do know that his intentions are no longer turned inward.

I sense such a weariness in his soul now when he holds me. I channel from him a hopelessness heavier than all the weapons in the world. I want to tell him that this pain will pass, as all pain does, but even if I could tell him, I know he would not believe me, and I think that perhaps I am damaged after all, for the pressure of his despair is breaking me. But I hold together for him, for if I can hold together, perhaps he can too.

Fire me, Kirby, I silently plead. *Take me to target practice. Expel that pain with my bullets, shredding a paper target. An effigy of the world you've come to despise.*

Or hurl me into the sea! Let that singular act of rejection free you. I can rest forever satisfied, even as I rust on the ocean floor, if I know you are saved. If my true purpose is to fly from your hands in an affirmation of your own life, so be it. I can accept the sacrifice.

But no. My purpose lies down a darker path, somewhere in the realm of the unthinkable. Now when he holds me, I sense a decision has been made, for he grasps me with firm resolve. He loads my full clip. He slips me into his pocket. He says no good-byes as he leaves the house this morning. He doesn't even turn back to look at it one last time.

He picks up a girl who I don't know, because he's never had me with him in her presence before. He keeps me concealed, but only inches away from her. He tells her to bring him coffee, but then he leaves her, and drives off. Now he heads for school with the single-minded determination of a torpedo. Then, parking his car, he walks toward the building with ballistic focus, his footfalls steady, measured, and relentless.

And I know beyond the shadow of any doubt, that on this day, in this place, in these hands, I will meet my destiny.

And I am terrified.

THE SECOND

Dad selects a piece of bacon from the pile on his plate and balances it on Hound Dog Griselda's nose. Griz freezes.

"Someone has to take that hellhound to the vet," says Mom.

Griselda stares at Dad. Her eyebrows crumple at the sound of the word *hound*. It is one of many words that interest her. She is concerned, but her attention doesn't waver. She doesn't drop that bacon.

"All her shots need to be up-to-date, and she needs to be licensed, and it has to happen soon. *Before* she eats one of the neighbors' cats," says Mom.

"I'll call around today," says Dad.

"Seriously, Doug. Do it this morning, *before* you go to sleep," says Mom.

My Dad is a day sleeper: nine a.m. to five p.m., the man is dead to the world. This is not the only way he is contrary.

"Cross my heart," says Dad. "Griz will be a law-abiding canine citizen by the end of the day. Won't you, Griz? Won't you just be all legal and registered? You are still going to eat a damn cat, though, aren'tcha?"

Griz hears her name. She hears the love in Dad's voice. The teasing doesn't register, though; that's for Mom. Mom is unfazed. We all know cats are Griz's weakness. If she had a choice between a fluffy kitty and skillet full of bacon, she'd go for the cat first. We put up BEWARE OF DOG signs the day we moved in, but cats don't read. Sooner or later an illiterate house cat will mosey over the backyard fence and meet the jaws of death.

"Okay, Griz," says Dad. Griz's nose flips the bacon into the air, and her teeth clack together: end of bacon; end of discussion; moving on.

"This one," says my mom, and she points to me by tipping her head over her coffee cup in my direction. "She's failing study hall." She holds up her phone, where, I'm guessing, she heard from the school.

"Technically, I'm failing Muskrat Lodge, but, yeah, it's study hall," I say.

"She's failing a class where all she has to do is show up," says Mom.

Says Dad, "That's quite an accomplishment."

I study the coffee in my cup like it is the most interesting thing in the world.

I drink the last of it before I say, "Well, yeah, I'm going to attend faithfully beginning today. I didn't know they took attendance. I thought it was more optional."

I truly did think that. I'm still getting the lay of the land at

Middleborough High School, home of the Mighty Fighting Musk-rats. Two weeks in, here's my honest opinion: On a scale of one to ten, it sucks to eleven. But there is no point in whining about it. Before we moved, my parents said they were sorry for the inconvenience. I said, "No problem. I'll handle it."

Mostly, I *am* handling it. I signed the student behavioral contract wherein I swore to avoid bullying, hate speech, and illegal substances. The insane rule forbidding yoga pants? Fine. Who gives a shit? I exercise my constitutional rights of free speech, press, and assembly in a manner that does not disrupt the educational process, which is to say, I don't exercise them. I know my opinions are uncool. I keep them to myself.

I'm a short-timer riding out the remainder of my senior-year sentence. I'm meticulous about the requirements of homework and the material covered on tests. I consume and regurgitate expectations.

But I did slip up on the Muskrat Lodge attendance matter.

It's just that my study hall is scheduled right after lunch. As a senior, I'm entitled to leave the school for lunch, so I just took advantage of that extra time. I'd walk home, raid the fridge, have a beer, play a little classic *Duck Hunt*, then return to school fortified and more able to suffer fools gladly. Those long lunches were doing wonders for my mental health. It was a great system while it lasted.

"I'm passing my actual classes," I say. "I'm going to have the credits I need at the end of the year."

"Yep," says Dad. "She's going to granulate."

Granulate. Dad's jokes are always dumb and dumber wordplays at the lowest level, but they are also always his truth-absolute.

A truth from Dad's perspective: The function of school is to grind human beings into small, uniform particles, to *granulate* them. Compulsory education is an instrument of indoctrination designed to produce docile, herd-thinking sheeple.

His opinion about public education doesn't mean I'm off the hook. Neither of my parents wants to homeschool a sheltered spelling-bee champion. I attend school. I will earn my diploma because a diploma is a handy thing to have in this imperfect world. It's like making certain Griselda has her shots and is properly licensed before she eats a cat. It just simplifies things in the long run.

"One other thing: they can't use the photo I provided for the yearbook," I say.

"I love that photo," says Mom.

Me too. That picture captured me at a golden moment.

"It's my rifle," I say. "Me holding it in the picture violates community standards. My skull mount probably does too, since it might be understood to condone animal cruelty."

"To some ways of thinking, rejecting that picture is a violation of the First Amendment and an insult to the Second," says Dad. "You plan to raise a ruckus?"

"I thought about it—considered it as a matter of principle—but no. The whole yearbook thing? I don't need it. It's meaningless." That's my truth. It would be different if the yearbook pages were going to be full of photos of friends who mattered to me. It would be different if someone looked at that book in twenty years and said: "That Reba girl? She skinned that buck's head and simmered it for hours. She dug the brains out with a bent clothes hanger." It would be different if I were back home, where guns and girls like me are normal, not weird. Back home, what I'd accomplished was understood and appreciated, but I'm pretty sure I'm the only girl in Birdland who ever peeled the face off a deer.

When I get through the doors, the announcement speakers are blaring. ". . . starting our day with a pep assembly. After attendance, proceed in homeroom groups to the gym. Go Muskrats! Go-o-o-o Muskrats! Blue and white, fight, fight, fight! Attention all students, let's get this party started!".

Damn. I suppose they announced this yesterday—probably in study hall or some other time when I was absent or not paying attention. If I'd had a clue I could have showed up late enough to avoid compulsory enthusiasm hour. Now, though, I'm caught off guard and swept up in the tide of muskrats swimming toward the gym to make merry and frolic and generally assemble in the name of pep.

From the hallway I can see that the band kids are already standing in a half-moon on the basketball court, squirming in place while they bang their drums and toot their horns. The girls who swing blue-and-white flags are flapping like butterflies. A baggy faux-fur rodent is pacing the sidelines doing weight lifter poses. What the hell goes on inside that giant costume head? What makes a person think: I want all eyes on me while I strut and grab my saggy stuffed-animal crotch?

I don't know. What I *do* know is that this is not my place and these are not my people.

It's my last chance, and I grab it. I peel away from the homeroom herd, slither sideways and into the bathroom across from the gym doors. The place is choked with muskrats. Most of them are primarily concerned with the mirrors, so a stall is open. I take it. I slide the little lock shut. I have no business to conduct. I just sit down, pull my legs up, and disappear—or good as. I settle in. I'd rather spend an hour curled up in a bathroom stall than be subjected to mandatory fun with a mob of muskrats. Is that right? Is the word for a bunch of muskrats a *mob*? I know crows travel in murders and hounds hunt in packs. Maybe it's a sog. A sog of muskrats. That sounds good—but really? I have no idea, and I doubt I'll ever care enough to find out; muskrats are varmints.

"Clear the room, students." It's a voice of authority. I ignore it, but the muskrats shuffle and snuffle and obey. I wait another minute before I put my feet on the floor.

Welcome to my fortress of solitude.

I haven't really escaped anything; the rally noise sloshes and flushes down the hall and through the walls. I lean against the side of the toilet stall. According to the scratches on the back of the door, CM+BA, Chad is a douchecanoe, molly rülez—and Suzie? Suzie is a mystery because that part is scratched out, but I'd put good money on slut.

The screaming and rumbling changes.

It's as chaotic as a flood creek, a stampede.

I look at my phone. The assembly shouldn't be over yet, but something sounds . . . broken.

"Lockdown. Shelter in place. This is not a drill. Lockdown. Shelter in place. This is not a drill." The recorded voice is calm, commanding, and loud enough to cut through the noise.

When silence comes, it comes thick.

The phone in my hand hums. It's a mass text: A baby-blue icon and the words: *WEAPON ON CAMPUS*. The phone hums again: *SHELTER IN PLACE*.

The first time I practiced for this catastrophe, I was wearing a pink ballerina tutu. We sat criss-cross applesauce with our backs against the wall. One teacher locked the door. The other teacher closed the window shade. It was hide-and-seek. We had to sit perfectly quiet to win. And we were. We were perfectly quiet while there were footsteps and voices in the hall. Perfectly quiet. Perfectly quiet. And just before we couldn't possibly be perfectly quiet anymore, one teacher clapped and said we'd won the game, and the other teacher gave us a special treat—something sweet.

So I know what to do.

I sit criss-cross applesauce on the toilet seat.

It's movement and noise that give away the game. The cat that freezes rock-still when Griz approaches? That cat lives. The cat that runs? Griz crushes its spine. The cat that tries to fight? Griz shakes it like a rag until it comes apart.

When the door to the bathroom bangs open, I flinch. I look at the flimsy latch. I look at the stall door. If there is a gun on the other side—if there is a trigger pulled—there is no shelter. I'm a sitting duck. The doors to the open stalls bang open, one by one. Each time the whole set of stalls shakes. The latch to my hiding place rattles, shiny and crackable as a plastic tiara. A piece of it hits my cheek when the door is kicked in.

I half fall off the toilet against the wall of the bathroom stall.

There are two guns pointed at me.

It's only for a second, only until the guns see I'm completely defenseless. Then a hand reaches down and helps me up. The grip on my arm isn't rough or tender. It's purely professional. It never falters as it guides me to the bathroom door.

"Shut your eyes."

I hear the words, but I don't act.

"Shut. Your. Eyes."

When I do, they lead me out. I keep my eyes closed. I'm completely in the dark. I see nothing. When I wobble, I borrow the strength of that hand on my arm.

"What's your name, hon?" It's the school secretary. She's holding a clipboard.

She doesn't know me. She gave me a schedule the day I started, and called a student to take me to my first class and explain the maze of buildings and halls. She butchered my name every time she said it.

"Reba Landrieu," I say.

She flips through the pages, makes a tick mark on a page. Then she reaches out and pats my shoulder. "Your parents are waiting. You just need to visit Jerry first; she's an EMT. She'll check you out."

Jerry is wearing blue gloves. She does a come-along-with-me wave with her fingers. "I'm just going to pat you down." She uses the backs of her hands like the agents during airport security. "Do you have any pain? Bumps or bruises? Did you fall? No? That's great. Can you sit here, please?"

I sit on the footboard of a fire truck. "I'm okay," I say.

There is a heap of brown crumpled on the parking lot asphalt.

A puddle of limp, soft stuff like an ugly bath mat. It's the mascot's pelt. Maybe there is blood on it. I think it might be blood—or not.

EMT Jerry wraps a blood pressure cuff around my arm. We are both quiet while she works.

"I'm okay," I say.

"Are you?" asks EMT Jerry.

"I am. I sheltered in place," I say.

"Good girl," says EMT Jerry. "Smart girl."

"I'm okay," I say it again. "Nothing happened."

"No. Something did happen. You are safe now. You can go home. But something did happen." Jerry hands me a sheet of paper and says, "Give this to your parents. You read it too. You don't have to be bleeding to be hurt. Go to your parents now; they're waiting over there." She points at a herd of people at the far end of the parking lot.

I do as I'm told. When I come to the sagging yellow police tape that marks the edge of the crime scene, the crowd opens for me. I duck under. Someone waves a microphone in front of me, but there's my dad pushing it out of the way and standing between me and the world. My mom has her hands on my face. We lean together and our foreheads touch. That's when she starts to cry.

We walk the couple of blocks home. Dad keeps his arm around me, pulls me under his wing. I cling to the back of his coat, the wool crumpled up in my fist. It's kind of hard to walk that way. Our paces don't match. Our steps are jolting and slow, but neither of us lets go.

Griz is waiting when we open the front door. I drop to my knees and hug her, bury my face against her stinking velvet ear.

"I'll make coffee," says Mom.

Dad walks to the living room. I hear the television, the background noise to life at home. A reporter is standing in front of the sign that says MIDDLEBOROUGH HIGH SCHOOL. She touches her ear and looks down at her handheld mic: "Sorry . . . It *is* confirmed that the shooter is dead of self-inflicted wounds. There are other casualties but no identification or details. What we know so far is that at least three students are dead; more than a dozen have been taken to local medical centers. Police are still in the process of clearing the building."

The scene changes to a doctor who says, "The next three days are going to be crucial for the patients in critical condition. At this point, those kids are still in surgery."

Then the screen shows us the school again with the emergency vehicles still parked in front. There is a crowd huddled across the street. "This is a community in shock. Grief counseling will be available tomorrow at . . ."

Dad switches to his ordinary news channel. The screen is divided into four squares, the guy in the lower-left box is talking . . .

"Gun ownership is an important life choice." Two of the other people start jabbering, but the guy stays calm and continues: "Look, I'm not here to engage in the gun-control debate. It doesn't matter how I feel or how you or your viewers *feel*. It's a fact that at least one hundred and twelve million Americans own guns—seventy-five million own them for defense. Making that choice, deciding to keep a gun for self-defense: it's an important decision. Taking a life is hard. Ongoing training is vital. It's not just target practice—it's a question of mental preparation. A panic-stricken, unprepared human being is incredibly dangerous to themselves and others . . ."

Did that kid feel like he was defending himself? Is that what made him dangerous? When he turned the gun on himself, was that part of the plan? Was it straight-up suicide? In the second when he put the gun to his own head, were all his other choices gone?

Dad clicks off the television.

Mom sits beside me on the couch and tucks my hair behind my ears. "You want some food?"

"A shower." I didn't know I wanted that until I said it, but that's what I want. I want hot water and the smell of Pure Prairie Sage Goat's Milk Soap. I want to feel like I'm starting the day over. I want to wash the smell of fear and industrial bathroom cleaner out of my hair.

I've been standing under the water for a long time when I hear a knock on my bathroom door.

"Reba? I'm going to take Griz to the vet. Daddy's staying here— with you. Or you can come, if you want . . ."

"I'm okay, Momma." I haven't called her Momma for a long, long time. "I'm okay."

I sit criss-cross on my bed with my laptop on my knees.

I have no idea what really happened.

"School shooting Middleborough," I ask the search engine.

The search engine answers, but it's no better than the television.

I don't know what happened today, even after I see a picture of that boy, the one with the silky flop of hair. It's the picture that would have been his little square in the yearbook. He's spindly and pale—a flat-ordinary, unsmiling kid. Maybe he's shy. Maybe the camera clicked when he wasn't ready. Maybe it's a mask.

I fall into the clickhole path of the search. I click from page to page. There have been school shootings in Finland, Germany, and Brazil.

I thought it was a special American problem. It isn't. Not even if the guy from Brazil says, "This is like something that happens in the United States." Does it count as a school shooting when the Taliban boards a bus and shoots three girls because they are students? Is there a big difference between shooting a six-year-old in a classroom and killing a six-year-old in a movie theater?

The texts start at about 4:15 p.m. That's how long it took for my friends back home to get out of school and hear what happened. I start responding: *I'm OK, I'm OK, I'm OK.* But then I come to the first message from someone I hardly remember. Oh yeah, Savannah B. was one of my science project partners sophomore year. I can't remember what she looks like. I stop saying I'm okay. I stop thumbing through the texts.

I've got an incoming call on my laptop. It's Brody.

Some nights since I've been here, the only thing that's mattered is that moment when I turn on the camera so Brody can see me and I can see Brody. He usually calls late at night—after I shower, when I'm ready for bed, that's when Brody calls. It's always been that way. Even when we saw each other every day, we spent hours looking at each other through our computers. The calls are the one thing that I still have.

There's Brody. I want to rub my face against his chest and breathe him: clean sweat, open water, and cold smoke on his skin. I want to smell his dirty fingers. But this call is too early, and it isn't just Brody. There are four faces crowding into the range of the camera's eye. There's his semi-jerk friend, Gord. I will never understand the appeal of that wad. Emma's there, because she is always stuck to Gord like a tick. The fourth person is Lily Pisanti. What the hell is Lily Pisanti doing sitting on Brody's bed peeking over his shoulder? She isn't our friend. She's not even in our class.

"Shit, Reba," says Brody. "Damn. Tell us."

"What?"

"We saw the news. That's your school, right? Middleborough. That's some crazy shit. What happened?"

Nothing. Nothing happened to me. That's the truth.

"I'm okay." I look at them. All of them are waiting for me to tell the story. I remember the way Brody's hair felt under my hand, but I can't touch him. I see Lily Pisanti's hand, curled like a claw on his shoulder.

The voices start rattling like talking heads arguing on the TV news. "Did you know that kid, the shooter?" No, Gord, I did not.

"Was he a creeper?" Compared to you, Lily?

"He was kind of cute, you know, with that hair . . ." WTF, Emma?

"Look," I say. "You're getting pixeled. Can you hear me? Can you hear me? Connection's bad," I say. The picture's fine. I can hear them fine. I just don't want to . . .

"Hey, hey?" Brody leans forward. If we were together, I would so let him hold me. "Later. I'll call again later," says Brody. He leans back, and I see how Lily Pisanti is still behind him.

I break the connection. I set the control to offline, because, really, my connection broke a while ago. I just didn't know it.

I hear the garage door. I hear the *clickety-tappy-tap* of Griz's toenails on the hall floor. She bumps her bone-hard head on my closed door. When I open it, she presses her face into my open hand.

I pull on some sweats.

I walk into the kitchen. The sound on the television is muted, but I can see it's the same old story. A mound of pictures and flowers and flickering candles is growing around the MIDDLEBOROUGH HIGH SCHOOL sign. That's the backdrop now for the news cameras. Then it's the doctor at the hospital podium. The crawl at the bottom of the screen says SIX CONFIRMED DEAD. Then footage from what must have been the surveillance camera in the hall outside the gym. That terrified stampede is what I heard. Then they show us his face again and then another photo of him eating a sandwich. He's just a guy eating a sandwich. These must be the pictures of the dead: round cheeks and long, wavy brown hair; a stretched, beauty-pageant smile full of Chiclet teeth; an older guy—must be a teacher. If I've seen these people before in halls or classrooms, I couldn't tell you. None of them look familiar.

Then it's the talking heads. I can guess what they are saying: No one expected this . . . There were signs . . . He was on meds . . . He should have been on meds . . . He had a gun . . . a gun . . . a gun.

"Do you want the sound up, honey?" Mom touches the clicker before I answer.

". . . an elementary school teacher has asked each child to bring a canned food item to school." The talking head holds up a can of soup. "She has the kids keep the can on their desks to give them a sense of empowerment and security. If an intruder attacks, the kids are supposed to throw the cans . . ." The talking heads erupt into argument.

I pick up a can of tomatoes that's sitting on the counter. It doesn't make me feel empowered or secure.

Mom gives me a side hug and takes the can from my hand. "Dinner soon. Venison chili," she says.

Griz puts her nose under my hand and leans against my leg.

"Want to go outside? Let's go outside." I'm doing the talking, but Griz is the one who pushes me along to the door.

The two of us step into the twilight backyard. It's overcast. Maybe it will rain later. The white vinyl fence panels shine, reflecting the porch light. I sit, criss-cross applesauce, on the empty deck. Griz squats beside me on her haunches. She leans against me. In the sky above, crows circle toward a big tree in the distance. Griz shakes. She smells better, but she hates a bath. Her new tags jangle. One says she lives at 22 Widgeon Way. Another proves she is operating within the law.

In a far corner of our yard, a black-and-white cat jumps from a shed roof to the fence post.

Under my hand, I feel the crest of tough hair rise along Griz's spine. I hook my fingers under her collar. If she decides to go for it, my spindly fingers can't hold her back.

"Shush, Griz. Griz, Griz, Griz, no." It doesn't sound like an order, but Griz hears me. She turns away from the intruder and toward me. Unless I pull the trigger, that stupid cat is safe.

"C'mon, Griz, let's go have some chow."

Griz rumples her forehead and stands. So do I. I never take my hand away from her collar. It's her job to protect me. It's my job to be in control.

ASTROTURF

Kirby Matheson stole my life.

There had to have been signs. Some warning. But I was too stupid to see it coming.

Every time I see him I remember. Like now. He's just standing there, his arms hanging at his sides like he doesn't know what to do. All I can see is how he looked when he showed up and took over the life I was supposed to have.

"Table for four?" Nicole asks, menus in hand, already leading the way to the Mathesons' usual table.

Kirby blinks twice, and then says, "Uh, no, just me. But . . ." He looks around the restaurant and then quickly away from where they usually sit. "Can I sit on that side?" he asks, pointing toward the original part of the restaurant, from when it was just a counter and a few tables.

"Sure. How about over here?" she asks, leading him to one of the smaller booths near the windows, across from the counter. "Ray will be right with you."

Technically, it's Maria's turn. But she won't care. Not for a kid by himself, and not tonight. Another night, or a family, any of the usual good tippers, and Maria would be swooping in, my station or not. Emilio says she's earned the right, having been here from week one. I think he's just afraid to argue with her. Federico isn't, but Emilio is in charge of the front of the house. Federico rules the kitchen.

Tonight Maria's leaning over the counter, flipping through a catalog, occasionally glancing up to check, and then pass on, most of the tables. She barely spares Kirby a glance.

There's a picture on Mom's dresser of me and her and Dad. It was taken at a school picnic the year before Dad left, when I was still oblivious to what was coming. Mom and I are looking at the camera, smiling. I'm holding some stupid award thing I got at the picnic. Dad's looking off to the left, like he's already plotting his escape.

And there is Kirby, lurking behind Dad, like even then he was waiting to walk in and take over my life. He's out of focus and blurry, but it's him. I only noticed he was there a few years ago—the last time Mom and I moved, when I was unpacking the odds and ends boxes—and since then, I haven't been able to get the image out of my head. Like if I had looked at it when it was taken, really looked at it, I would have had some hint of what was coming.

I remember being sure that when Dad got home from his business trip, we'd get a dog.

He'd been weird, he and Mom both. Whispering loudly in their room. Having those conversations over my head that I didn't understand. The morning he left for his trip, they stopped talking when I came into the kitchen for breakfast.

I was sure it was because they were finally getting me a dog. I'd wanted a little brother, or even a sister. When I whined for too long, Mom said they got the kid they wanted the first time. I knew even then that was bullshit, but I understood I should stop asking. They'd already gotten me a new bike. We'd gone to Disneyland when I was seven. But I was eight then, and Dad had always said we could get a dog when I was older. So it had to be a dog.

I was sure that was it. The big secret. Somehow I knew Dad wasn't really on another business trip. So he had to be picking out our dog.

When Mom started packing stuff up in my room, talking about poor kids who didn't have toys, and wouldn't it be nice to give them some of my old ones, I thought it was some kind of test to make sure I was ready for the responsibility of a dog. I put everything in the donate box and then started stacking stuff beside it, which made Mom cry. I thought she was proud, because I was being so responsible and generous and so ready for a dog.

The sign went up on the front lawn the same week Mom and Dad sat me down and explained that while they both loved me very much, they didn't love each other anymore. More Dad than Mom with the not loving, from the way Mom looked when he said it.

Dad left that night. I was even too stupid to realize he didn't take any bags or anything with him because he'd already moved all his stuff. At least all the stuff he wanted.

Mom and I would have to move soon too.

But the leaves turned and it got cold and we were still there. We unpacked some of the boxes, but Mom put them in the basement for later.

On Christmas morning we had cinnamon rolls and sausages and chocolate milk—all the things we liked and Dad didn't.

Mom got a job, we adjusted to a new schedule, the sign remained out front, and we stayed there, without Dad. It worked.

Then the sign changed, and Mom started packing for real. We were really moving this time. Dad kept promising to help with the packing and the moving, but like with promised trips and movies and treats, he never showed up. We were still moving stuff by the carload to our dinky new apartment across town when they showed up.

The Mathesons, though I didn't know their name then. I didn't know any of them then, except for Kirby.

He was eight, too, but he was in second grade, so I knew who he was but we didn't play together or anything.

I was up in Mrs. Hinkle's tree hiding from Mom. It was a better hiding spot than under our tree. She would have known to look there. Kirby hopped out of a car that looked kind of like our old car, which Dad had taken with him, and then walked over to my curb and tightrope-walked it like I always did. Then he hopped the cracks in the sidewalk, ran across the lawn, and stopped short at our tree. He walked partway around it, and then the other way, and then ducked under the branches, out of sight. He was shorter than me. He could probably still stand up under there. It would be quiet and dim, like being inside a living cave. The tree shuddered. He was pulling on the branches, or maybe ripping them. He was hurting it. But it was his tree now.

While Mom was handing over the keys, I stared at Kirby. Mom

was thanking them over and over for taking our house. I was trying to decide the best place to punch him for maximum effect. Maybe his face. Maybe his stomach. All I would have to do is take one big step and I could hit him. But then Mom's hand landed on my head, and she steered me off the porch and pointed to the car, like she'd known I was two seconds from attack.

I sat in the too-hot car that smelled like feet and laundry detergent and waited for Mom to finish hugging neighbors good-bye, watching Kirby walk into my house. He kicked the front step and then hopped up the others while his dad waited for him. I could see them through the bare windows, walking through the living room, and then into the dining room, and then I couldn't see them anymore, but I knew they'd be in the kitchen. I climbed into the front seat so I could lean forward enough to see him run to my swing set. His father was out there with him. And his little sister—she wasn't a little brother, but close enough. All that was missing was the dog I'd always wanted.

They got the dog later. It barks like crazy when I deliver their pizza.

Mom moved closer to the car, but someone kept coming over to hug her or give her something. It took so long that eventually I saw Kirby look out my bedroom window. His dad opened it and they leaned out, and I knew his dad was pointing toward the park, which you can see from my window if you lean just right and look between the houses across the street. He still has my room. If I drive by after dark, I can see him, sitting in front of the computer or sometimes on his bed, sometimes just the light bleeding around the edges of the blinds. A few years ago they threw away my swing set.

For a while I had to see Kirby a lot—at school, where his class-room was next to mine and we had to use the same door, and some-times when I went over to my old friends' houses. But then Kirby changed to St. Puke's. I didn't have to see him every day in the hall-ways, on the playground, or walking my old route home from school with the kids I used to play with. I didn't have to see his parents—his mom *and* his dad—at Parents' Night and every other school thing.

I didn't have to watch Kirby living my life, only better.

Mom worked a bunch of different temp jobs and then got one steady one. When she decided I could stay home by myself some-times, she got a second job and we left that first crappy apartment for one with two actual bedrooms. Even better, the second job was only a block away from Brothers Pizza. At least once a week she parked me at Brothers with enough money for one slice and a bottomless soda while she worked. I was supposed to do my homework, but once they got used to me, I sat at the counter and talked to Emilio and Federico—the "Brothers" themselves. Or Maria, who looked exactly the same then as now, right down to her huge pile of dyed-orange hair. Emilio would bring me extra pizza and dessert. Sometimes if Mom worked real late, I would go in back and listen to the radio and help roll silverware in the napkins.

They started letting me unofficially work there when I was twelve. One night when I was picking at my slice, trying to make it last and wishing I could have three, Emilio said, "Raimondo"—he always calls me that even though my name is just Ray—"you might as well be on the payroll, so long as you're here all the time." I swept floors, cleared tables, took out the trash, and basically did whatever Emilio told me to in exchange for several dinners a week, more cake than any kid should ever eat, and a little money of my own. It kept me fed; sometimes it kept both of us fed when Mom lost her first job and we were living on just the second one. A lot of nights Mom would have a slice or they'd give her a "to-go" bag on my "tab" when she came to pick me up.

When I turned fourteen I started working at Brothers for real.

"Ray!" Federico yells behind me, followed by the bell that Emilio said is supposed to be our more genteel signal that there's food to run. They had a huge fight—in Italian—about the bell. Emilio won, sort of. Federico rings it, but he yells first, which defeats the purpose, but Emilio won't give in and remove it.

The food is for Maria's table, but I run it over and then grab them more sodas and grated parm.

I swing by my tables on the way to Kirby's. He hasn't even opened the menu Nicole left for him. Maybe he doesn't have to after all these years.

"Are you ready to order?" I ask him. But he looks up like he's surprised to be asked. "I can come back, or . . ."

"No. I'll have a slice with sausage and mushrooms, and a Coke, no ice."

"Anything else?"

He shakes his head and hands me the menu. Nicole's standing at the counter, watching me, a weird look on her face. I walk over and put the menu away and then detour around the other end, behind the cash register, and into the back, all without looking at her.

I put the order slip into the carousel and spin it toward Federico, but he waves his hand at me instead of grabbing it.

"Slice. Sausage and mushrooms."

"One slice?" Federico asks, like it's my fault it's slow.

"One slice."

Federico starts mumbling in Italian, and Maria says, "Hey!" from the other side of the door.

"Can't hear to run the food or when she screws up an order, but her ears have no problem with the whispers," he grumbles louder.

"What'd he say?" she asks when I come back through the swinging door behind the counter.

"How happy he is you're working tonight," I say. Nicole snorts, but Maria just waves her finger at me. Whenever Emilio isn't here, she sees it as her duty to keep us all in line, most especially Federico.

She busts my ass and makes me do way more of the grunt work than I should have to, but Maria's the one who taught me what I needed to know to move from washing dishes to bussing tables, and then to waiting on them. She's the one who told Emilio she needed a break from the crap shifts, so he would let me wait tables on the slower nights and weekend days.

"Go on, kid," she said on my first night wearing a long-sleeved, button-down white shirt and clip-on bow tie (bought by Mom at Goodwill). "Regulars. Good tippers. A good first table."

The walk across the restaurant area of Brothers felt like I was walking onstage in front of a crowd.

"Hi," I think I said. "Welcome to Brothers Pizza. I'm Ray. I'll be your server." Mom had coached me, and right after I said it I could hear Emilio's barking laughter, and the others. (Brothers isn't a "server" kind of place, Maria mocked later.)

"What?" I asked, because I'd been distracted by the laughing and missed the start of the order.

The man smiled at me. "A large antipasto, no olives, extra salami, add artichoke hearts."

"I'm not sure . . ."

"It's what we always order," the woman said, leaning past him to talk closer at me. "They'll do it." She pointed to the order pad in my hand and I started to write, but I couldn't remember and looked up. "No olives," she said. I wrote it down. "Extra salami." I wrote it down, pausing over whether salami had one "l" or two, and going with one. "And add artichoke hearts. Just tell Federico it's for us."

I wrote it down, word for word, but I was afraid to ask who "us" was. I hoped Federico would know, and he wouldn't make me come back out and ask.

"Two orders of the cheese bread and two medium pies, one sausage and mushroom. The other half cheese, and half green pepper, basil, and fresh tomato. And a half bottle of the red," the man said, pointing to his chest, and then his wife. "A Coke—"

"—Diet Coke," the girl said.

The man looked at her for a beat and then said, "A Diet Coke," but he said it like the word *diet* tasted funny. "Kirby?"

Kirby was scrolling away on his phone.

"Kirby?" his father said again, and then Kirby said something but I missed whatever he said, because it was only then that I realized who they were. Who Kirby was. And they were all staring at me.

"What?"

"Chocolate milk," Kirby said slowly, and then he scowled at me, like he thought I was messing with him. Like I thought he was too old for chocolate milk.

"Great," I said, too loud. "I'll be right back with your drinks." I made a point of smiling big at all of them, especially Kirby, so they'd know I wasn't messing with anyone. Kirby just crossed his arms and slumped back against his chair.

His dad said something to him, squeezing Kirby's shoulder and dipping his head so Kirby couldn't ignore him. Kirby stopped scowling, but he wouldn't look at me when I brought the drinks. All except the wine—Emilio brought the wine since I wasn't allowed, making a big fuss over them.

When he thought no one was looking, Kirby pulled the glass of chocolate milk to him, tilted his head, turned it around until he found the angle he wanted, and then stirred the extra chocolate around in the bottom of the glass—not enough to mix it in, but just enough to make it swirl up in the milk and then settle again. Then he held the straw out of the way and took a long sip from the glass, and smiled. He drank every drop and then scraped up every smear of chocolate with the spoon.

They left me a good tip, despite the fact that I screwed up the pizza order, brought Carah regular instead of diet, twice, and almost spilled water all over Mr. Matheson.

At the end of that first shift I counted out a chunk of my tips for the hostess, busser, and dishwasher, and then stared at the bills Mr. Matheson had handed me when I tried to give him his change.

I carried them around in my wallet for a few weeks before I forgot where they came from and bought something.

I'd almost stopped thinking about them.

Then school began, and there was Kirby, looking a little uncomfortable out of uniform like all the St. Puke's kids look at first. If he knew who I was, from Brothers or from before, he never let on, and I didn't say anything. Since he was a freshman, we didn't have any classes together except gym, and I didn't really do much at school except school, but when we passed in the halls he didn't say anything or look at me.

The next time they came in, and the next, they were someone else's table.

I tried to ignore them, but it was hard. They always sat at the same table. Emilio made a fuss. Kirby's father joked around and his mother smiled, with her fancy clothes and hair, her shiny painted nails.

My phone vibrates in my pocket. Text from Mom. But before I can look at it, Federico yells, "Ray!" and then the bell dings.

"If you're gonna holler, you can skip the bell. Emilio's not here."

He glares at me, then goes back to his muttering. I hear two of Federico's three favorite curses and smile harder. Some nights getting Federico wound up is all the entertainment there is.

I slide the slice in front of Kirby, along with some napkins. "Need a refill?" I ask, even though it doesn't really look like he's touched the Coke.

"No thanks." Kirby's looking at the slice like he doesn't remember how to eat it.

"Let me know if you need anything else."

I check on my other tables, drop some checks, and then lean against the wall behind the register, where Federico can't see me, to text Mom. Yes, I dropped off the rent. No, I couldn't fix the toilet. Mr. Arneson said he'd come by when Mom got home. She asks about work and I say fine and then "g2g," which she finally learned means I can't text anymore.

Kirby and his sister always have new stuff—sneakers, iPods, phones. They often tune out and play with their phones when they're done eating, sometimes even during.

My phone is held together by duct tape, and Mom hates it when I play on it when we're sitting at the table.

The Mathesons still come in two or three times a month, but it's been less than before. Every time the same table, same order, except Kirby gets Coke now, no ice. I don't think he really likes it, because he never needs a refill. I only wait on them sometimes. Everyone wants to wait on the Mathesons.

Mr. Matheson orders for delivery whenever Mrs. Matheson is out of town for work. I can always tell because he doesn't ask for artichokes on the antipasto when she's out of town. Sometimes he only orders one pie—sausage and mushrooms for him and Kirby, veggie on half if Carah's home. Sometimes—more often, lately—he orders a side salad and a small white pizza with fresh basil, and when I deliver it he asks about school or the weather or sports, and I never know what to say. I usually just pet Pepper and nod to whatever Mr. Matheson is saying, and then take the money and leave.

He doesn't know that I can hardly stand to ring that bell and then have to be there on the porch talking to him being all nice and friendly and asking questions.

That still feels like my house and my life that someone else is living. And every time I pull out of the driveway with the empty delivery bag, there's this strange sense that somewhere, sometime, someplace else another me is coming down the stairs and into the kitchen, ready for pizza, and someone else is driving away.

Nicole's ringing up to-go orders. Even on slow nights there are a lot of carryout orders and deliveries. Her magenta-tipped ponytail bobs as she smiles and flirts with the regulars and grabs the phone in between. She can do eight things at once without missing a beat, making everyone feel she is really focused on them.

I have to make change for one of my tables and clear a few others that have turned over since the busser went home. Finally the PDA couple are done sucking face and want to leave.

"Here. Before they go for round four," I say, handing Nicole the guy's credit card and the check.

"Wish Emilio would add *that* to his No list—No solicitations. No cursing. No smoking. No guns. No swapping saliva."

I deliver the credit card receipt and start sloppily clearing the table around them so they'll leave as soon as he signs it.

Kirby's just staring at the table in front of him.

"Is it okay?" He doesn't seem to get what I'm asking, so I point to the slice he's only taken maybe three bites from.

"Yeah, fine." He takes another bite as if to prove it.

Another text from Mom. She's heading home. Good. Then Mr. Arneson can come fix the toilet and I won't have to worry about it anymore. God, it's nice not to be constantly hiding from the landlord or afraid to call him like that first place we lived.

"What's with tonight?" Nicole asks, sliding along the counter and leaning over to look past me and into the dining area. "It's dead."

Three tables eating. Two done and with their checks. None that need attention.

"Weeknights are always slower," I say, "but Thursdays are usually better than this. This is . . . yeah, totally dead."

She sniffs and her nose wrinkles. "Is that what stinks? It's so-dead-it's-decomposing night?"

"Gross." She smiles like it's a compliment. "Seriously gross." She just smiles bigger.

If it doesn't pick up soon, Maria will cash out, which is fine by me. By now I can handle a slow night by myself. Nicole will help if we get slammed. And Frank can bus tables in between deliveries. More money for me.

"You're welcome, by the way," Nicole says.

"For what?"

"I gave him to you," she says, as if it was obvious. Then she nods to the booth by the window, the only one occupied on this side.

"His dad's the big tipper, not him," I say. "Besides, they might as well all be my tables tonight." Maria isn't even pretending to pay attention anymore.

Nicole doesn't say anything, but I can feel her look. Yup, chin down, brows up.

"What?"

"You're always staring at him," she says. "Here. School." She looks toward Kirby, as if to make the point.

"Am not."

Chin lower, brows higher. And a smirk. "Maybe he's scoping you out too. You should go for it."

Huh?

"I mean, what's the worst that can happen, he shoots you down?"

"I'm not scoping him out."

"It's okay," she says. "I don't think anyone else notices. You're cool."

Kirby's just twisting the straw wrapper around his fingers, first one way and then the other. Over and over.

The wrapper is going to rip. It has to eventually. But one way and then the other, over and over around his fingers, and it doesn't rip.

The phone rings and Nicole's gone before I can tell her, again, that I don't stare at him. Except I probably do, just not for the reason she thinks.

"Federico!" she yells through the swinging door. "Phone. It's Emilio."

After a few beats I can hear Federico's end of the call, even out here, and Maria hustles in back to shut him up.

Nicole leans on the counter next to me again, dramatically, like we're both sighing over Kirby. I should have said something before. Now it's weird. She makes that stupid sighing sound again.

"I don't—"

But she's gone, grabbing menus on her way to greet the people at the door.

Kirby is still twirling the wrapper. One way and then the other. Over and over.

Maria's nowhere to be seen, so I take the new table, get them their drinks, put in their order, and then swing by to check on Kirby. He looks up.

I open my mouth but nothing comes out. The wrapper is

suspended, mid-twirl, between his fingers. This feels important. An important moment. I have no idea why.

"Anything else?" I finally ask.

"No thanks," he says, going back to his rhythmic twirling.

"A box?"

His head swings back and forth like a pendulum, not even looking at the half a slice he has left.

"Another Coke?" He doesn't respond, like he can't hear me anymore. The Coke is still three-quarters full. Like always. The wrapper twirls one way, and then the other.

"Chocolate milk?" The wrapper snaps. He looks up at me. He blinks. I don't know who is more surprised, him or me.

"Yeah," he says, smiling, like he's found something he thought he'd lost. "Chocolate milk." Like he can already taste it.

From behind the counter I watch him smile, rubbing the two pieces of the straw wrapper between his thumb and fingers in both hands. Like he's reliving something really good, something happy, a good day. Or a good memory. I stir long after all the chocolate syrup is incorporated into the milk, then add just a little bit more to pool on the bottom.

I put the glass down on the table with a fresh straw, the long-handled spoon still in the glass.

He's staring at the glass with an even bigger smile.

I put down his check and he digs into his pocket and pulls out some bills. He looks at the check and then hands me a twenty. I dig through my apron, count out his change, and put it on the table.

"If you need anything else . . ." But I don't finish saying it because he shakes his head, dismissing me.

He stares at the glass and then sits up in the booth, pulling it toward him with just his fingertips, like it's too cold or hot to touch with more of his hands.

"You see the new table?" Nicole asks. "Ray?"

I nod, waving her off.

Kirby turns the glass, looks at it from one side and then the other, and then sips his chocolate milk like it's the best damn thing he's ever tasted. One sip. Then another. Then a gulp, from the glass with the straw held out of the way. "Ray!" Federico calls, and then the damn bell.

I deliver the food to the couple in the corner and then take the order from the new table. Nothing to do now until the food is ready to be delivered.

Kirby drinks the rest of the chocolate milk, savoring each sip, and then uses the spoon to sweep the last of the chocolate syrup down into his mouth. He puts the glass down and wipes his mouth with the side of his hand. He stares out the window for a while, and then picks up the coins from his change, sorts them in his hand.

He puts all of the change back on the table except for one coin. He holds it between his thumb and finger, turns it, looks at one side and then the other, rubs his finger over it, and then holds it in his palm. The smile is gone, replaced with a strange calmness. He's not fidgeting or playing with it. Just sitting there, holding it. I've never seen him sit totally still.

"Ray!" The bell in the kitchen dings. I deliver the food.

The door opens—more customers. Nicole shows them to a table in the main area, near the windows. Three couples. Should be a decent check.

I drop off more water to the table with the food and pick up the credit card and check from the couple in the corner.

I need Nicole to ring up the credit card, but she's still talking to the new table. Smiling. Nodding.

She has a nice smile. And I like her hair, the way the magenta looks like it's climbing up her dark curls. And the soft hairs at the back of her neck when it's up in a ponytail.

I like the way she gives the table this one smile, all sweet Italian-girl charm, and how it immediately morphs into something else when she turns back to me, something sharper and more real. I like her face, the way she moves. I like her. More than I like most people.

"You got it?" she asks when I hand her the credit card to run.

"Yeah, thanks." I try to smile big so she knows I appreciate her asking.

She looks at me a little funny and I tone the smile down.

When I come back to put in the new order, Kirby's gone.

"Yeah, he left," Nicole says. "Although I think you can do better. Better than Mr. Coke-no-ice-and-never-smiles over there. I mean, he's even quieter than you are. You need someone who will carry the conversation."

"And a girl." I look at her. "I don't really care what people think, but . . ." I want *her* to know. "I like girls."

"Okay, then," she says, but I'm not sure she believes me.

After work I walk Nicole to her car. She's looking at me weird again.

Nicole turns left out of the parking lot toward her subdivision. I turn right, toward home.

Too many nights I detour through Birdland, the what-ifs nearly choking me. But tonight I turn left on Main, drive through downtown, past the office park and what passes for an "industrial park" around here, across the train tracks, through Little Mexico, and beyond until the grass dwindles and I get to the part of town no one's trying to gentrify.

There's no grass at all outside our new place. But it's a nice apartment in a good building. Mom likes her job and has some friends. She doesn't worry as much anymore. We're okay.

Especially tonight. The light is still on, all of the month's bills are paid, and Federico sent Mom carbonara, which will make her smile for real. Maybe she should just marry the old guy. The carbonara *is* that good. Then I wouldn't have to figure out what to do with my life. Waiting tables in your family's business isn't pathetic. It's family.

GROOMING HABITS

Today I narrow my list down to two boys. I write the date, January ninth, and the time, 4:45 p.m., at the top of the paper and slip it into my wallet. With the school year almost half over, it's time to make a decision. Chad was such a total disappointment. And a complete asshole. This year, I'll be more selective, more thoughtful, more mindful of what I need, not just opening my legs for any guy who wants me. No, not this year.

Caleb Graham and Kirby Matheson, my two final choices, are both in my seventh-period debate class. Even the quiet ones must talk in debate because you can't debate with sullen looks and pouty glances. Even though I like both of their pouty glances.

Two or three times a week, early in the morning, I see Kirby huddled at a table in the library pouring over a tattered copy of *East of Eden*. I've spent time quietly observing him: how he peeks through his bangs, how he contemplates the trees outside the window, how the tips of his fingers travel over the seam on his paper coffee cup.

I glance at the clock. It's later than I usually stay, and I shove my notebook in my bag, swinging it over my shoulder. I'm surprised Mom hasn't called, and when I glance at my phone I know why. It's dead.

I walk down the hall, the sound of my boots clicking hollowly, and I see it: the dented blue surface of Caleb's locker. I pause midstep, listening. In the distance a growling floor polisher grinds across tile, but the school is mostly quiet, almost empty.

Carefully I choose a strand of hair from the right side of my scalp. I twirl it around my index finger. Twirl, twirl, twirl until it's tight, cutting into my skin, and I angle the hair precisely and tug, hard. Perfect, the hair doesn't break. The root pops free. I quickly grab another and do it again as I exhale slowly, reining in my nerves.

I look up the hall, down. It's only me, a flickering fluorescent light, and posters publicizing an upcoming pep rally. The metal is cold on my fingertips, and I lean in close to locker 303, my nose hovering next to the vents, and I take in a deep breath. I recoil in disappointment. It's vinegary, musty, like sweaty socks. And probably a forgotten moldering sports cup.

Fucking jocks.

Kirby's locker is close by. This time when I inhale, I bite my lip. It smells like boy: satisfyingly musky, like an overworn sweatshirt—one worn to bed, one worn while watching a movie at midnight, one worn while reading *East of Eden* burrowed under the covers on a cool night. A scent to be left behind. A scent that could linger in my hair after a kiss. A scent I'd smell as I pull the borrowed sweatshirt over my head and hold it close, replaying his whispers in my ear over and over: *I love you. I love you.*

I back my way through the heavy side doors and into the parking lot, thinking of ways to make Kirby mine.

Because my list is down to one.

Kirby Matheson.

Smiling to myself, I let the warm afternoon cling to my skin and unlock my car. It beeps.

"Hey." A deep familiar voice purrs, and my keys drop to the asphalt.

I turn. My eyes dart around the parking lot, briefly resting on the one, two, three, four cars left. My heart pounds in my chest. I'm sure he can hear it.

"What are you doing here?" I ask.

Chad's slow grin sends quivers of anger through my limbs. He has no right to grin at me.

"You look good," he says, bending down to scoop up my keys. He takes his time standing, scanning my body with a languid inspection. I see it in his eyes as he glances at the car door behind me. He's remembering the last time we were together, alone in a desolate parking lot. The last time we leaned against this car, my naked back against the dirty window, his thick hands rucking up my skirt, his beer-laced whispers hot on my neck.

"I know." I snag the keys and hug my bag over my middle. Waning sunlight reaches over the school's flat roof, haloing his golden head and throwing his eyes into darkness. I don't need to see his eyes. I know what they hold. Lust. Arrogance. Pity. "Why aren't you at school? Didn't classes start more than a month ago?"

He shrugs. "College isn't my thing. I dropped out."

I shift, moving closer to my car. Away from him. He takes a small step forward. Light spills across his chest and the Muskrat insignia on his letterman jacket looks a little too victorious. Chad graduated last spring, yet still wears his high school football jacket. I try to ignore the sadness burdening my chest at the sight of it.

"And what do your parents have to say about that?" I ask.

"I'm eighteen. I can do what I want," he says as he steps closer. "And who I want."

"I have to go," I say, reaching behind me to open the door.

He places a hand on the window, pushing the door closed. "I want to see you," he says, and his breath feathers across my cheek.

"No," I whisper, gathering the strength to send him away. "Not after what you did."

"Come on, Abby."

"You showed all your friends."

"It's not like your face was in it." He moves forward, reaching out to touch my hip. "Only the hottest parts of you," he whispers.

That familiar burn of bile creeps in, clawing at the back of my throat. I shift away from him. "Go away, Chad." I straighten, meeting his gaze. "I've moved on."

He stiffens, stepping back. "Oh, is that why you won't return my texts or calls? The new year's fresh and you got a new guy to go along with it?"

Soon. "Yes." I open my car door with a flourish.

He shakes his head. "No, you don't."

"Yes, I do!" I sound too petulant and moody. I lengthen my

spine, trying to appear stronger than I feel. "People move on. I've moved on."

"You already found another—" he starts, but I cut him off.

"I'm done with this, Chad. Good-bye."

"Really? You're really done with this?" he asks, swirling a finger in the space between us. "You think you can replace me?"

"Yes," I say. My pounding heart skips. Kirby isn't mine . . . yet. But if I lose confidence, I lose Kirby.

"You think you can, but you can't."

I try to hide my limbs, shaking as I slip into the car. "You should go back to school," I say before closing the door.

As I start the car, he growls, "Slut. I should tell—" But I rev the engine to bury the rest of his sentence.

Our eyes meet through the glass. He shakes his head, slowly and deliberately, backing away. I hold his gaze, trying to appear undaunted, but I can barely keep tears from brimming. I throw the car into reverse and drive away, my wet face drying in the air blowing from the vents.

Kirby would never treat me like this. Kirby isn't a jock. Kirby isn't always surrounded by his dudes, isn't always first-bumping greetings and high-fiving victories. Kirby doesn't whisper dirty jokes to girls on their way to class in the hallways. Kirby has the fathomless eyes of an artist, not the vacant stare of a football lemming.

With a shaking hand, I peel off the fake lash strip from my right eye and carefully place it on my thigh. I use my index finger and thumbnails to single out the longest lash I can tweeze, and tug and tug and tug until I feel the satisfying pop of the root escaping my skin. I let out a long breath as I drop the eyelash.

I rustle through notebooks and scrabble across the bottom of my bag to fish out my phone, trying to plug it into the car charger. I narrowly miss a curb and earn a honk from the car behind me. I give my rearview mirror a shrug and a wave, swerving to pull into the Trader Joe's parking lot.

I drop my forehead onto the steering wheel, scoop up the strip of fake eyelashes, and, with practiced fingers, press it back onto my lash line. Opening the window, I take the arid evening air into my lungs, trying to shove away the panic. Chad wanted to scare me. He's jealous, and while a part of me—and not a small part—loves that he is, I've trusted him with my secrets. Secrets that could bury me alive.

After a couple of moments I lift my head, defeat hunching my shoulders so far forward I feel as if I could shrivel up like a parched flower. A car pulls into the space next to me with a tin-can exterior and beady Mardi Gras necklaces swinging from the rearview mirror. I peer through the reflections of clouds on the glass and see a waving hand, a Cheshire cat smile, and the window drops.

"Abby! Hey there!" The voice is like an unreachable itch. She comes around the front of her car, hefting an overstuffed plastic purse on one bare shoulder. "How you doing, honey?"

"Hi, Mrs. Fawnee." I force a smile. Skin stings at the corners my eyes. Too many forced smiles in one week. "I'm okay. You?"

"Oh, you know," she says, pink lipstick clinging to her front tooth. "Sometimes I wish my gun would go off while I'm cleaning it and hit Orrin in the ass." She laughs, lifting a leathery bare shoulder, but sobers quickly. "Now, Abby," she says, placing a manicured hand on my door, fingers straining beneath glittering rings. "How's your mama doing? I thought I saw an ambulance at your place the other day."

I sit back, subtly checking my shirtsleeve to make sure it's covering the bandage. "Oh, that was nothing," I say. "She's fine. Staying healthy. Active, even."

"Well, good to hear." She levers sunglasses back over her ash-colored hair. "You coming or going, sweetie?"

"Huh?"

She twitches her head at the store. "You going in?"

"No, I—" It's then, out of the corner of my eye, that I see a guy saunter through the glass doors into the store. A tremor of excitement blooms in my chest. "I mean, yeah, I am, just trying to remember what I need." Before I realize I've done it, I'm out of the car and walking beside Mrs. Fawnee toward the store. She's chattering about how gloomy Sundays are without football, but she'll always have Bud Light. I absently offer up basketball as an alternative, and she glares at me like I'd asked her what brand of sunscreen she uses.

Kirby is standing in the cereal aisle, a loaf of bread hanging from his fist. His dark hair is tousled, as if he's spent the last few minutes burrowing his fingers through it. He wears a dark blue sweatshirt and jeans, sneakers that are high-topped and, frankly, monumentally big. I suspect the sweatshirt smells wonderful. Shoppers steer carts around him as he remains motionless, staring at a box.

Mrs. Fawnee is still talking incessantly when I excuse myself. She calls after me, "Say hello to your mama!" as I grab a hand basket and hurry up the aisle parallel to Kirby's. I come out the other end and peer around the corner. Kirby scans the fronts of other cereal boxes, like he's looking for something more significant than nutritional content. I love the focus in his dark eyes. Singular. Specific. Lost to everything else except his mission. One day I'll be on the other end of that focus, and a deep chill of exhilaration passes through me.

Without warning he stalks off, stuffing the bread between cereal boxes on a shelf. I follow, still with the basket, tossing a random item or two inside. I side-glance the cereals. I can't determine which one he focused on exactly. One offers a cartoony superhero figurine inside, another a box-top sweepstakes for a coin collection.

I spot him leaving the store. I ditch my basket next to a display of browning pomegranates and try not to rush out the doors behind him. I stop short, seeing myself in the door's reflection. My hair has escaped the ponytail I so carefully constructed this morning, and I quickly reposition the clip-in extensions I added to cover the bald spot. I check myself one more time and go outside.

But he's not out front. I scan right and left but see no sign of him. Then I hear it, a busted tailpipe or maybe a broken muffler. A blue car rounds the corner, louder than it is fast, and I recognize it from the parking lot at school. Kirby.

Jittering anxiety propels me forward. I'm not thinking; I'm just moving unconsciously. As if I am watching it all play out on a video. It's not until I'm in the car, speeding through a yellow light to keep up with Kirby, that I wonder what I'm doing, wonder what I'm hoping to accomplish.

I have to be smarter about this. Boys don't like frantic, needy girls. I need to be less frantic. Less needy. More mysterious.

Desirable.

I snag my charging phone from the passenger's seat. Sixteen missed calls from Mom. The sun slips below the buildings in my rearview mirror and I realize how late it is. Chad kept me late. Mrs. Fawnee kept me later.

And Kirby. Kirby could keep me as long as he wanted.

Our house is dark when I arrive. The twilight shepherds in indigo clouds, shrouding stars above the neglected roof. I hit the button. The garage opens with its usual screech and I watch as a light pops on in the den. My stomach seizes and I breathe through it, snagging my bag from the passenger's seat. I gingerly pick my way through the cardboard box and plastic bag–riddled garage floor. Inside the house it's hot, sticky. The thick scent of stale cigarettes permeates everything: the flocked green wallpaper, the threadbare tufted sofa, the shredding vinyl chairs in the kitchen. It's in my clothes. My books. My bed. They say you get used to a smell, become scent-blind when surrounded by it for long enough. But that's not true here. Sometimes I think the smell is the only thing holding the house together.

"Abigail!" Mom calls. I stand in the dining room and dump my bag on the cluttered tabletop. As approaching wheels rumble on the kitchen linoleum, dread overtakes me. "Where the hell have you been?"

"I had to stay late," I say.

She enters the room. The rolling grumble of her wheelchair dampens on the stained Berber carpet of the dining room. "I need my pills. You didn't put my pills on the counter this morning."

"I'm sorry, I forgot."

"Is that the excuse you're going to use when I'm dead? You forgot to give me my pills?"

"I'll get them now," I say. I try to get around her wheelchair but she grabs my upper arm. Her fingers press into the stitches and I wince, slicing pain stinging my skin.

"If you want me dead, girl, all you have to do is wait." Her voice is low and gravelly and full of loathing. "It will happen in due time."

"I don't want you dead," I say through the pain, and it doesn't sound as believable as it should.

She lets go. "Uh-huh."

I look down at her as I pass. The scars map her scalp, lacy and intricate, tufts of graying blond hair on the unmarred skin. It could be beautiful in its graceful lines if it didn't mark time like a gravestone.

Mom whirls around and zooms back into the kitchen behind me. She's too strong today, like she was last week when I forgot to leave her meds on the counter. I grab the stepping stool from the pantry. The pill bottles are on the highest shelf in the Tupperware cabinet, where she can't get to them. She may be strong, but she can't get out of the chair except to hoist herself into bed or onto the toilet.

"Where's the car?" she asks, knowing damn well it's in the garage.

"Garage."

"Surprised you didn't wreck it."

"Not yet."

"You'll do it again soon enough."

The words make my chest ache. But she knows that. That's why she said them. She ensures there's a daily reminder of what I did. As if my father's absence isn't enough.

"Aunt Jinny called today," Mom says.

"Oh?" I drop one blue pill on a small bread plate, followed by one white and two green. I should know the names, but I don't. I know which pills make her sleep, though. The peach-colored ones. "What did she have to say?"

"Wanted to talk about the money again." She wheels closer. "Hurry up with those damn pills. I'm getting shaky."

I scoop them up in my palm and hold them out for her.

Mom's fingers clamp around my wrist and she pulls her face close to mine. "Jinny said she thinks someone has been siphoning money from the account. She thinks it's me, but it's not me." Her breath is sour. She hasn't eaten for hours.

"I don't have access to the account yet. You know that."

She releases my wrist, and I drop the pills into her hand. "Fix my Diet Pepsi. I'm going to watch my show." After placing the pills in her lap, she wheels through the kitchen and into the den, where she parks herself next to the coffee table and lights up a Parliament. "There's still glass in the corner," she says, jerking her head to back of the room. On the wall, a dripping stain of Diet Pepsi, and a small, almost undetectable splatter of blood.

My blood.

My arm pulses where she dug her fingers into the stitches.

The TV is loud when it flicks on. It's too loud for her to hear me take down the other bottle of pills, the only ones left on the shelf. The peach-colored ones. It's too loud for her to hear me crush them up. At first two, then I add in one more. It's too loud for her to hear me pour the Diet Pepsi and stir and stir and stir, hoping the crushed pills dissolve. It's too loud for her to hear me curse when they don't.

I scoop out half the sludge at the bottom of the plastic cup—because I'm never giving her a real glass again—and place it on a plate. The other half dissolves well enough in the Pepsi, hiding in the bubbles. I mix what's left on the plate into a spoonful of peanut butter, and hand her both.

She lifts a brow at the spoon in her hand.

"You need something in your stomach," I say, and nod to the pills nestled in her lap.

Mom sneers in my direction, kicks back the meds, and takes a long swig of her Diet Pepsi. I wait for a reaction but she only coughs, wipes her mouth, and licks the peanut butter off the spoon.

"Is this super crunchy?" she asks.

I nod. Smile. "Just how you like it." I sink down into the sofa and feign interest in her Hollywood gossip show. I examine her face in the jaundiced lamplight. Her forehead is crosshatched with ever-cracking lines and her cheeks with branching, broken capillaries. Beneath that wrinkled cage of stress and cruelty her fine features still hold symmetrical beauty. When we lived in Miami, I remember her lying by our pool, face tracking the sun like a marigold, a sweating rum and Diet Pepsi next to her. She laughed a lot back then. We always preferred her drunk, Daddy and me.

I tunnel my fingers under the hairpiece clipped to my head and snag a strand growing from my scalp. I twirl and pull. And then another. Twirl, pull, twirl, pull, twirl, pull, while I wait.

Thirty-five minutes later, she's slurring her words. The ash is long on her cigarette and perilously close to collapse. I pick it out from between her fingers, my palm catching the ash, and toss it in her empty plastic cup.

"I stopped," she mumbles. "I stopped loving you."

It doesn't shock me. I've heard it before. "I know," I say, slapping the ash off my palm. The words rush from my mouth before she says them. It's easier to hear it in my own voice. "I ruined your body. Killed your husband."

"You got out of your car seat." She tries to wheel toward me but her hands slip. "Why the hell did you get out of your car seat?"

You hit Daddy, I want to say, like I want to say every time she asks me that question, but I only tell her I don't remember why I unlatched my seat belt and dove forward. Before the accident, after one of their arguments, I overheard Mom tell Aunt Jinny that her fights with Dad were only little incidents.

I pick up the spoon she'd licked clean from its spot on the floor, snag the cup from her lap, and take them to the kitchen. By the time I return she's snoring, head hanging and mouth drooling. As I drape the granny-square afghan on her lap, she snorts awake and mumbles, "I should have aborted you when I had the chance."

Ah, there it is. The statement that finally pierces me, like she's been throwing darts at me all night, and bull's-fucking-eye. Finally this one strikes me in the chest. I let the afghan slip to the floor and leave.

Kirby lives on a quiet street in Birdland, a neighborhood Grandma loved when she was alive. She wanted to buy a house there when she and Granddad moved to Middleborough. Not the concrete, louver-windowed house Mom and I live in now, aged beyond its years by nicotine and hostility.

I roll my car into the darkness of a broken streetlight across from Kirby's house. The address wasn't difficult to find. They're the only Mathesons in town.

Their driveway is empty. No cars are parked out front. The house is dark. I crack the window and sink down in my seat, leaving my phone facedown in the cupholder so the cold bright screen doesn't highlight my face in the night. I peel off the fake eyelash and pluck a few of the real ones left while I wait. A couple of houses down, a person drags a trash can to the curb, the rumble of its wheels the only noise besides a barking dog.

My eyes drift closed.

I allow myself to think of Kirby, because I need to think of him. I imagine what we'd talk about, how he'd touch me. I'd show him all I know about my body and what I know about his. Where to kiss, stroke, lick. He'd be impressed by my experience, excited by my willingness, eager to explore whenever we could steal away from school. From our homes. From my home.

I pop awake when the busted muffler reverberates around the corner. The thrill of it shoots me straight in my seat, only to slump back down as the headlights sweep across my windshield, then highlight the facade of the Matheson house and finally flick off as he parks in the driveway.

Kirby swings the door open and ducks out of the car. He's wearing the same sweatshirt, same jeans, sneakers, a backpack draped over his shoulder. I love his height, a tallness that will eclipse my own frame, and his gait is long and apathetic, as if the world should be in a hurry to get to him and not the other way around. Unlike his rush to leave the grocery store earlier.

Another car pulls up to the front of the house.

"Kirb," a man calls through the passenger's-side window. "Out of the driveway!"

Kirby turns from the front door and sneers back at the man. He dumps his backpack on the front steps and stomps back to his car. The two exchange parking spots. As the man approaches the front door I realize it must be his father. His build is lanky like Kirby's but he's taller, skinnier, with a hunched back and haphazard hair.

His father sweeps an open palm to the front door while peering into Kirby's car.

Kirby doesn't move from his place behind the wheel. The bones of his face are lit from below, the sterile light of a phone blinding him to his father's frustrated invitation. His father gives up, goes inside, the door thudding closed behind him.

Kirby is close, parked catty-cornered to me, so I slip lower, my eyes at the horizon of the car window. He shakes his head at whatever he sees on the phone. Raising his head, his face goes slack, staring off into the middle-distance. I jerk back when he explodes. One punch into the dashboard, two, three. I can't hear what he yells—it's too muffled by the glass and steel surrounding him—but I know with the deepest part of me that I can help.

He's in pain and I'm in pain. He'll see when we're together that we can save each other. All I need is the chance to coax him into understanding this.

Kirby storms out of the car and into the house. A light turns on in a room on the side of the house. I don't debate it in my head long because the desire to see him in his environment lures me deep into the shadows of the side yard.

Through the parted curtains, one shaded lamp throws off a sallow glow. I creep closer, peer in through the sandy dirt smeared on the glass. His room is small, perhaps depressingly typical. A neatly made bed. Posters on the walls. His abandoned backpack slumps on a desk chair. Spare and monklike, it's a cloistered, solitary room. I think back to his doodle-laced notebook in debate class, his scattered counterpoints, and his muddled arguments. Ah. So this room is an ordered place for a cluttered mind.

That's information I can use.

I duck against the wall as he comes back into the room. He throws the window open and I shrink back. I sense he's motionless, standing before the window, staring out at the nothingness. He murmurs a soft curse.

I want to take a few steps and stand before him, gently caress his face. Tell him we'll both be all right if we're together.

Thick rain drops thud on the ground, fluttering leaves above me. I wait for what seems like fifteen minutes for him to turn away from the window, and then I dash back to the car, rivulets of water snaking down my arms and legs. I flip wet bangs from my eyes and back the car up until I have a better view of his bedroom window.

I strip the fake lashes away and resist fingernail-tweezing the tiny hairs left on my lids. I rub my eyes, but the compulsion to pick is too strong. I find a single strand of hair on the left side of my head, where I've allowed the hair to grow back into short tufts, and twirl and pull—the pop of the root escaping the skin calming me.

It's time, I decide. And without further thought—because there's no need for it—I get my phone and send the e-mail.

It's before sunrise when I wake, the clock in the dash reading well after six thirty a.m. I push myself upright, stretch my neck to the right, to the left, and drive away from Kirby's house. The headlights pick up the swirling fog on the asphalt as I speed home. In the den, the lamp still burns in the window. The garage screeches open and I run inside.

Even though I'd rather get right in the shower, I check on Mom. She's still slumped over in her wheelchair in the den, the afghan resting unused at her feet. I approach slowly. Quietly.

"Mom?" I whisper.

No answer.

"Mom?" I say again, this time more loudly, and wait for a reaction.

Nothing.

I reach out and nudge her shoulder. It's warm. A begrudged relief.

Her head tilts back, forward again.

"Mom!" I shout. When she lets out a wet snore and a curse, I know she's fine.

I'm too excited when I arrive at the library forty-five minutes later. But Kirby isn't there. I drag myself along with the day, searching for Kirby in the halls at school, in the cafeteria, even trying to inconspicuously walk by his locker a number of times, but I don't see him. When he slumps into his chair in seventh-period debate, calm overtakes me and I know the two of us will be okay.

I stay behind after school, a notebook open on the desk in front of me, and I stare at the line of cars filing out of the parking lot outside. The waiting is excruciating, and I wonder why I keep doing this to myself. Hold out the carrot for the donkey and hope it bites.

I grab a strand of hair to keep my shaking hand busy and twirl. Pop. Twirl. Pop. And another. And another. And another until I exhale a long, slow breath through my pursed lips. I'm calm. Ready.

I replace the hairpiece on the side of my head and focus on the open notebook, strewn with a latticework of hair.

There's a knock on the classroom door.

"Ms. Leeland?" Kirby says.

I look up. Smile warmly. Close the notebook. "Hi, Kirby," I say.

"Hey," he says. "Got your e-mail. You wanted to see me?"

"Yes, come in," I say, gesturing to the chair on the other side of my desk. "And will you please close the door behind you?"

HYPOTHETICAL TIME TRAVEL

The walls in this house are thin—thinner than at home—so I can hear my parents clearly in the next bedroom. During my fifteen years of life, I've made it a policy to tune out when they argue, but this time, I need to hear. I point the remote at the small TV on the antique dresser and turn the volume way down.

"I can't do this!" Mom sounds nearly hysterical. "And I won't. So stop asking!"

I'm sitting propped against a pile of lace-edged pillows in a guest room where the walls are covered with paintings of flowers in vases, Victorian tea sets, and fluffy cats. At my feet, Pepper, my dog, opens his eyes and jerks his head up. I pat the lumpy mattress a few times until he crawls up the length of the quilt to lie beside me.

"I know it's hard," Dad says. "But we have to figure it out."

"*We* don't have to figure out anything. I already told you. This is up to you. Make your decision and leave me out of it!"

There's silence for a moment, and then the sound of their door gently closing. Dad's voice comes through the wall beside me just as loud as it was before. "Grace, please!"

If my brother were here, this would have been the point when we'd roll our eyes at each other. I'd have whispered something like, "For two otherwise intelligent people, you'd think they'd know that closing a door won't make it soundproof while they're *yelling*."

He'd have responded with, "Intelligent? Them?"

Then I'd have gotten annoyed because, really, they're very smart—Mom's a crash reconstruction engineer and Dad was a computer programmer before he started writing gadget reviews from home three years ago—but Kirby never gave them any credit or cut them any slack.

Of course the fact that my brother isn't here to criticize them, and never will be again, is exactly why my parents are so wrecked. They have decisions to make: Should he be buried or cremated? Now that they've found a minister willing to perform a memorial service, should we go ahead and have one for our family? If yes, now or later? And how much later?

"I understand what you're feeling," Dad tells Mom, "because I'm feeling it too. Believe me. But Kirby was our son, and despite how things ended, we've spent over sixteen years loving that kid. Making these decisions and going through this process together is going to help us get some closure—"

"And remind us that he spent all those years not loving us back?"

"I don't . . ." Dad pauses for several seconds. When he speaks again, his voice is quieter. "I don't think that's true."

"I do. Because a person who loves their family"—Mom is gasping between words, like she's fighting to keep from crying—"who has *empathy*, who isn't evil, they don't get a gun and start firing. They . . . they wouldn't be capable of it. But he did. He *was*." Her voice breaks. "So that's how I know he didn't love us."

There's a creaking noise, and I imagine that my father must be sitting beside Mom on their borrowed bed. I rub Pepper's ears as I strain to hear Dad's next words.

"Honey, that wasn't our son. You know as well as I do that when people are going through something, they can lose themselves—"

"Jack, *don't*." Mom's words come out hard. "This isn't like what happened to your brother. Or like when you lost your job."

"I know. But in a way—"

"No! Roger only wanted to hurt himself, and you didn't get around to hurting anyone. But Kirby planned this. He wounded kids. He murdered them! And he did it in front of Carah. I can't ever forgive that. Any of it."

"I'm not asking you to forgive," Dad says. "I'm *asking*— Oh, God."

At that, my dad starts weeping. Mom joins in, and their combined sobs are too much. As tears stream down my face, I hug Pepper closer and turn the TV up again.

Two hours and two and a half episodes of *Gilmore Girls* later, there's a knock on the door.

"Yeah?" I say.

Kirby always said Dad looks like a tall, bald-headed scarecrow, and that description has never been more fitting than now. As he steps inside, his eyes droop with sadness behind his thick glasses, and his long arms flop at his sides as if he's too exhausted to ever use them again.

Only five days ago, my parents and I had no idea that everything in our lives was about to be turned inside out, upside down, and backward. Back then we weren't in constant contact with police officers, attorneys, and funeral homes. We hadn't exiled ourselves to the home of family friends to avoid the media vans outside our own house. And we didn't wish every day that we could find a way to wake up from this nightmare.

Only five days ago, my parents and I weren't yet the closest relatives of someone who had spent his final minutes of life terrorizing, hurting, and killing his classmates before committing suicide. Because Kirby wasn't yet a dead murderer.

Dad glances down at me, at the TV, back at me. "This isn't happening today, Carah." His tone is firm but not mean. He makes his way over and takes the remote from the nightstand, pointing it at the screen. "Not for the entire day, at least. Okay?"

Fear ignites somewhere between my heart and my stomach. I sit still, staring at the nothingness on-screen while my eyes sting with tears. I pet the soft, black hair on Pepper's head, trying to calm myself, trying to breathe deeply enough to extinguish the mini fire my dad's words have sparked inside me. But I guess oxygen fuels the flames.

What does he want me to do? Leave with him to discuss Kirby's dead body with some stranger? Because I'm with Mom on that particular subject: I can't and I won't.

Dad rattles the leash he brought in with him, and the noise causes an explosion of doggy joy beside me. Giving a quick bark,

Pepper scrambles over my legs. As he races a circle around my dad in the center of the room, his tags clink together.

"Looks like someone is in the mood for a visit to the dog park this morning," Dad says, smiling at me.

I frown in response. By getting Pepper all excited about his leash—which Dad knew would happen—he's pretty much given me no choice.

My best ways of coping have included keeping my phone turned off, staying away from the Internet, steering clear of all forms of news, and watching feel-good television in bed all day. I'm not anywhere near ready to face the real world outside, where people hate my parents and me because of my asshole brother.

"Carah, do you *see* this?" Dad pats Pepper's head. "This is a Labrador retriever right here. And he has a serious need to get some *retrieving* out of his system. Don't you, boy? Don't you?"

My dad isn't good at the forced enthusiasm, but since this type of thing would usually be Mom's job, it isn't like he has a lot of practice, either. Anyway, it's Pepper, looking at me with his golden-brown eyes, who does the convincing; I know I have to get up. For him.

"All right." I let out a loud sigh. "I'll do it."

Dad leaves so I can get dressed. I dig through my splayed-open suitcase and put on clean yoga pants, a big sweatshirt, and running shoes. Avoiding looking at myself in the vanity mirror, I pull my long brown hair into ponytail. It feels bumpy, but I don't care.

In the living room, Dad hands me my phone. Without turning it on, I drop it into my pocket, along with a few doggy cleanup bags and treats that I already grabbed. It's possible that I have messages waiting for me—the type of messages I'd really love to see. But I'm terrified I'll find the other type instead, so I don't look.

Pepper wheezes with excitement as I leash him, and Dad follows us out the front door with his car keys in hand. He tells me to avoid walking anywhere near Birdland, that he'll meet me at the dog park when he's done at the funeral home—maybe in an hour or two—and to be careful. Pepper and I start down on the sidewalk and I wave as Dad backs out of the driveway.

Seeing him like this, as the parent in charge, the one holding things together, is strange; not long ago, I wouldn't have believed it possible. In fact, the last meaningful conversation between Kirby and me happened as a result of Dad's unreliability.

On a Thursday night almost two weeks before today and exactly eight days before the shooting, I was one of the few people still at school almost five hours after the final bell had rung. The second big deadline for the yearbook was coming up and we were behind as usual. Things weren't so serious that Ms. Naman was trying to pull us out of our other classes, but still bad enough that we were all showing up an hour or two before school and then staying much longer afterward. During the weekend, some of us had been plugging away on it until midnight.

"I'm done with this!" Vincent announced, sliding his chair back and hopping to his feet. "For the night, I mean. Obviously, I'm not *done* done because, *impossible*. See you all tomorrow. Don't work too hard."

Without waiting for a response from the rest of us, Vincent rushed from the yearbook room—the smallest classroom in the entire school—leaving the door wide open behind him.

Sitting across the table from Gwen and me, Jolie, our head editor, rolled her eyes. "And it's down to just us three once again. The three who are always caught up on our own stuff, who have to help the slack staffers."

"We should probably stop being so awesome," I said.

"For sure," Gwen said. "Just think of the amazing lives we could be living outside this room."

We said things like that all the time, but it was a joke and we knew it. There was nowhere else we'd rather be and nothing else we'd rather be doing. This was Gwen's and my second year on yearbook and Jolie's fourth. We were addicted to this massive project, where each of us got to be a photographer, journalist, designer, and marketer all at once.

Jolie said, "I'm feeling like maybe if the boys in this class didn't spend all their time talking about movies and *Doctor Who* and how they'd use a time machine, they could finish their own spreads before deadline."

Stretching my arms, I glanced over my shoulder at the wall clock. Seven exactly. I still had another thirty minutes before Dad would be coming to pick me up—if he didn't forget again. I'd left my phone in my locker by mistake, so I hadn't checked in with him to make sure. "Let's get our own time machine. We can go back and use creative motivation methods on the others."

"Oh, I've got some *real* creative motivation in mind." Jolie mimed punching the air a few times, and then strangulation using both hands.

"FYI," Gwen said. "I'm not on board with time traveling for class purposes. The only way I'm flying away to some other year is if it's, oh, around twenty-five A.D."

"You mean so you can hook up with your Lord and Savior?" I asked.

She pushed her blond bangs out of her eyes. "If by 'hook up with,' you mean, '*hang out with* all the time,' then yes, Carah, that is my plan."

"We know you better than that," Jolie teased. "And that foot-washing prostitute had better watch her ass if you ever get a time machine."

Gwen said, "It'd be no contest. Pretty sure Mary Magdalene wasn't even J. C.'s type."

I laughed. Before I started hanging out with Gwen freshman year, I'd never known anyone who refused to go out with boys from school because of a mad crush on Jesus.

"We might as well wrap up for the night," Jolie said. "I'm having a hard time focusing, which does me no good for copyediting."

While she and Gwen went around checking that all of the computers had been turned off, I saved my changes and logged off my own machine.

Jolie pressed the power button on Vincent's monitor. "Today in U.S. History, I was seriously thinking about what I'd do if I could go back in time. When I'm old and done caring about whether or not I might accidentally expunge my own existence, I think I'd want to change the world in a big way. Like by keeping Christopher Columbus from getting funding. Or killing Hitler before he came into power."

"*Every* time!" I slapped my hand on the table. "It never fails. Whenever we talk about time machines, someone always wants to go back and kill someone. Why can't we have hypothetical time travel without becoming hypothetical murderers?"

"Okay, fine." Jolie shrugged. "I'll go back and make sure Baby Hitler is never born. Better?"

"Much."

"But how would you pull that off?" Gwen asked. "Find Hitler's mom nine months before his birthday, give her some condoms, and say, 'Make your husband use these. Trust me on this'?"

Before Jolie or I could answer, a familiar voice from near the door chimed in: "That's what *I'd* do to make sure my sister was never born."

I turned my head, and sure enough, there was Kirby, leaning against the filing cabinet like it was no big deal, like I hadn't told him the last time he'd shown up here out of the blue that he couldn't step foot in this room.

It seemed like a lot of kids at school didn't even realize he was my brother—he usually avoided me, so I did the same—but Jolie and Gwen knew; they were the ones I complained to about his moodiness.

Crossing her arms over her chest, Jolie said, "Kirby, we'd never let you get away with erasing Carah. And you'd better start being nicer to her, or she'll find a way to go back and make sure she grows up as an only child. How would you feel about that?"

His back went straight and he narrowed his eyes. Both of us inherited dark circles under our eyes from Mom. I'd been covering mine with makeup since fifth grade, but Kirby didn't really have that option. His had been looking extra purple in recent weeks, which made him look extra tired and extra mean. "How would you feel," he spoke in a bland tone, "about me making sure Carah never starts hanging out with you bitches in the first place?"

At that, I stood. "Kirby, just get out! You know you're not allowed in here."

"Find your own ride home, then," he yelled as he stalked back to the hallway. "Dad isn't coming for you."

I pushed my chair in. "I'm so sorry about him, you guys."

"Not your fault," Jolie said. "Anyway, I've been called far worse things."

Gwen nodded. "Me too. Just the other day, my brother told me I was a mediocre photographer. For real. Mediocre!"

"Brothers are the worst. See you two tomorrow." I ran after Kirby, and found him scuffing his rubber soles against the waxy floor to make screeching noises as he walked. "What happened?" I asked, coming up beside him. "Why are you here instead of Dad?"

Kirby glanced over. "Why do you think? Mom's flight home was *supposedly* delayed until morning. Dad's off the rails and told me to come get you. Of course, J Building's locked up and you're not answering your texts, so I had a great time waiting at the door until that Vincent guy finally came outside. Thanks for wasting my time, by the way."

My defensiveness was far overshadowed by worry; January had become our father's worst month. Uncle Roger jumped to his death two weeks after Christmas back when Kirby was in eighth grade and I was in seventh. "Kirby, what's wrong with Dad?"

"An excellent question, and one I ask myself every day. I swear to God, that man is useless. No wonder Mom's screwing her coworker."

I glared at him.

For months after his older brother's suicide, Dad had washed his antidepressants down with alcohol and drank all day, every day.

When his manager finally confronted him over it, Dad drunkenly threatened to kill him and his family. No one called the cops—even though they probably should have—but he did get fired over it.

Gradually, things got better again at home, but hearing Dad was "off the rails" was enough to put me in a panic—especially since Kirby had told me a few weeks before that he thought Mom might be having an affair. I got along with Mom much better than Kirby did, and I didn't think it was true, but I couldn't completely rule it out, either.

"I'm serious. Is Dad drinking? Did he forget to take his meds? *What?*"

Kirby shrugged. "Both? Neither? I don't know. He didn't want to leave the house. Do you have to be so dramatic about it?"

"Yeah, *I'm* the dramatic one."

"You are." He pursed his lips. "And so are your friends who can't take a joke."

I started toward the sophomore hallway, and Kirby followed. "Yeah, speaking of my friends, you don't get to call Jolie and Gwen 'bitches.' And you can't just barge into the yearbook room like that. If our teacher had been there, I could have been kicked out of the class for it."

"Give me a break. What's the big deal about your precious yearbook room, anyway?"

"The big deal," I said, "is that only yearbook students are allowed to see which photos we're using, or know the theme, or see what the cover looks like. That's how we keep it a surprise for everyone at the end of the year."

Kirby hurried to get ahead of me and then started walking backward. "Do you think there's one single person—aside from you so-called yerds—who gives the slightest shit about the theme? Come on. There has to be some other reason for the extreme threat of kicking you out of the stupid class."

I think back to Mrs. Naman's rule sheet from the start of the year. "Well, we do have our equipment. Cameras. Computers. And we have to protect our work. If someone got in there and—"

"Sabotage!" Kirby punched a locker as he yelled the word. "Now, *that's* a reason I buy. Your teacher wants to make sure no one sneaks inappropriate words or pictures into the book, right? Because that would get her fired. So she tries to make you feel like you're in this exclusive club." He put on a high-pitched voice. "'Okay, children. Now, remember. You must protect our secret theme. Or else!'"

I hated the way he put his cynical spin on everything. A year and a half in yearbook class, and I'd never thought of it like that. My footsteps echoed as we continued in the direction of my locker without speaking. Kirby had gone back to dragging his feet, which caused me to grit my teeth.

"It's better when no one's here," he announced. "Peaceful. Like a place I'd actually want to spend my time."

I always found it creepy being here after hours, and Kirby, with his extra-annoying shoe sounds, was making it worse. I truly didn't get why he thought our school was so awful. I hung out with my friends and made sure to avoid the jerks as much as possible. It wasn't hard. "Maybe if you survive the apocalypse, you can claim the school as your new home," I said. "Until then, I guess you're stuck with the rest of us."

I stopped at lockers 203 and 204, turning the combination and popping open the top one first, and then the bottom.

"Why do you suddenly have two lockers?" Kirby asked.

Only juniors and seniors were assigned full-length lockers at our school, so those of us with half lockers sometimes had to get creative. After over four months of me crawling underneath Bobby Avalos between every class, he came up with the idea that we should keep our coats and bags in mine and our books and pencils and stuff in his. "Bobby and I are sharing now."

"Ah. Bobby Avalos," Kirby said. "The football player."

"Soccer player," I said, sliding on my coat.

"Right. But did you know that in every other country in the world, soccer is called *football*?"

I draped my bag over my shoulder and stared at my textbooks, trying to remember which ones I needed. "I don't hear Bobby and his teammates calling themselves *football players*, though. Sometimes they say *footballers*."

"Fun fact: Guys who call themselves *ballers* are twenty times more likely to give you chlamydia." He reached into Bobby's locker and pulled out my stuffed black Lab. "What's with the Pepper replica?"

I snatched it away from him, and then tucked my geometry book into my bag. "It's mine. From Bobby."

Kirby snorted. "A stuffed animal. Such an original gift."

"Who said it needs to be original? He takes his puppy to the same park I take Pepper to, so he knew it would be meaningful. In fact, that's how he asked me to winter formal. He put this dog and a card in my locker for me to find one morning."

"Typical."

"If you ever had the guts to ask someone, I doubt you'd come up with something better."

"Maybe not, but I wouldn't go for the biggest cliché of all time." Kirby leaned his back against the locker next to Bobby's and slid down slowly, until he was sitting by my feet. "You and your footballer sound like a couple of single parents in a rom-com. Meeting at the park with your kids. Moving in together." He gestured at our lockers. "How positively adorable you are."

"Oh, shut up." Simultaneously I used my hand to slam Bobby's locker and my foot to kick mine shut. Then I raced for the exit.

I'd made it all the way out the door, down the dark walkway, and almost to Kirby's car in the empty student parking lot before he caught up. "I'm thinking of asking someone to the dance," he said.

Kirby never, ever said "I'm sorry" or admitted when he'd been trying to get a reaction out of me. Instead he softened his tone and offered something—usually a compliment or a confession—to smooth things over until he was in a bad mood again.

He stepped forward to unlock the passenger door, and then he even opened it for me. Another unspoken apology.

I sat down and placed my bag on the cleanest floor mat in the history of floor mats. The outside of Kirby's car was filthy, but you could seriously eat off any part of the inside. "You realize that the dance is happening in, like, a week, right?"

"I know. I'll ask tomorrow. A footballer, so I can be like you."

With the parking lot lights shining on his black hair, he smiled down at me, watching my face as if he expected an ecstatic reaction to his announcement.

Mom and I sometimes talked about Kirby never having girlfriends, and discussed possibilities of where he went when he disappeared from his room at night. He was always so secretive, like he had another life and we weren't allowed to know about it. Mom had a theory, and I'd been sure she was wrong. Now I wasn't so certain.

Kirby made his way around the car. Once he was sitting beside me and had started the engine, I turned the radio all the way down, so I could make sure I did this the right way. "Are you telling me you're going to ask . . . a boy to winter formal? Because I think that's really cool and—"

"What?" He stared at me. "No! Haven't you heard of girl soccer players?"

"Of course." My face was hot and getting hotter by the second. So much for Mom's theory, then. "You just said *footballer* and I thought, 'Well, girls aren't really *ballers*, are they?' And—"

"Carah, stop," Kirby said, calmly. "Thinking about that, I mean."

"Okay. Sorry."

He steered us out of the parking lot and onto the main road. In the darkness, I turned to check if he was annoyed. At that same moment, he looked over and, with a smirk, shook his head at me very slowly. I covered my hand over my mouth to keep a giggle from escaping.

"And now for a completely different subject." Kirby gave my arm a light punch. "If Bobby Avalos giving you that stuffed dog was *so* thoughtful, how great would you think I was if I gave you a real dog?"

I'd wanted to have this conversation since forever, but now I was afraid to get my hopes up. "Do you have a particular dog in mind?" I asked, trying to sound casual.

"We all know Pepper has liked you better than me from day one.

It's been over three years since Dad brought him home, so maybe it's time we made it official."

My mouth fell open. "Is this real life? You're giving me your dog?"

He chuckled. "Yeah. *My* dog that was supposed to be the consolation prize when our parents forced me to go back to public school. *My* dog that sleeps in your room and that you walk and feed every day."

"What's the catch?"

"No catch. I just don't have time these days to do that stuff, and it would be nice if our parents didn't have this one extra thing to guilt-trip me over."

They did love saying things like, "Why don't you go and spend some time with your dog, Kirby?" and "Why did we even get you a dog when you make your sister take care of him?"

Both of us wanted them to keep their mouths shut about it, but for very different reasons, obviously.

"What do you want in exchange?" I asked.

"I don't know. How about . . . do you have any quarters in your bag?"

I scoffed. "You'd sell Pepper for quarters?"

"Just one quarter. That's all I need. Remember how a couple of days before Uncle Roger died, he stopped by and gave me that coin collection? Some of the state quarters were missing, but I've found all of them now—*except* for freaking New Hampshire."

I hadn't known Kirby was finishing the collection. The last time we'd seen Uncle Roger, he'd given me something too: a skinny gold ring with a diamond in the center. I never took it out of my jewelry box or reminded anyone that I had it; I was unsure whether I'd be expected to hand it over to my cousin Lucy—it was the wedding ring her mom had worn back when she was still married to Roger many years ago—or if I'd be allowed to keep it because it was the last gift I ever received from my favorite uncle.

I turned on the interior light and poked through my change purse. "I have one bicentennial quarter and the rest have eagles on the back. But I'll check my room when we get home. Or I can for sure get what you need online if I don't have it."

Kirby shook his head. "That's cheating. I'd rather find it myself than have you order it. Eventually, one will turn up."

"Okay. Just so we're clear, then. You're still giving me Pepper even if I don't give you New Hampshire?"

"He's yours. As of right now."

A grin spread across my face. "And if some random stranger says, 'Hey, you! Who does that dog belong to?' what will you say?"

"I'll say, 'Hey, Random Stranger. That's Carah's dog.'"

"You know what?" I put out my right hand. "I like the sound of that very much."

Kirby took his hand off the steering wheel for a moment, grinning back at me as we shook on the deal. "I kind of thought you would."

My dog and I are almost to the park. His tail is swinging side to side and his tongue is hanging out of his mouth as he struts down the sidewalk, pulling me along. I, however, haven't been quite so upbeat about taking this walk.

I'm relieved to be upright and outside. I'm glad the whole world hasn't changed like I'd expected it to five days ago. But I feel guilty for having the nerve to experience relief or gladness about anything. I'm waiting for someone to recognize me, waiting for them to say to my face the type of things they said online after the shooting:

Kirby Matheson was a fucking loser. Why couldn't he have just hanged himself?

At least we can be glad knowing this piece of shit is burning in hell.

People need to stop saying he "snapped." He didn't. This was premeditated murder.

In cases like this, you can be 99.9% sure it's the parents' fault. Not trying to make excuses for a killer, but I feel no pity for the two assholes who raised him either.

His parents need to be prosecuted in his place.

Everyone in his family HAD to know he was capable of this. They just LET it happen.

I hope his family members are haunted every day for the rest of their lives, knowing they are responsible for ruining so many lives.

This kid's family should be executed in the same way he executed his classmates.

These are the gist of some of the comments on news articles, and they could have been written by people from anywhere in the country. Anywhere in the world, really. Or it could have been people from Middleborough, where I've lived all my life, who posted those things. Regardless, because of what I read that first day after the shootings, I know there are some who say that because we shared a home and DNA with Kirby, my parents and I deserve to be arrested, tortured, or even killed.

At the park's entrance, I toss Pepper's poop bags into the trash can while he tries to drag me away. I have to jog to keep up as he leads me to the off-leash area. "We're here now," I say, unclipping him and setting him free. "What's your rush?"

That's when I spot Bobby in his Middleborough High letter jacket. His back is to us, and he's about to toss a Frisbee for his chocolate Lab, Coco, who's staring right at Pepper. Bobby lets the Frisbee go, but instead of chasing after her toy, Coco bolts toward us. Bobby turns, confused for a moment until his eyes lock on me.

My first thought is that I should have taken the time to brush my hair and dab on some under-eye concealer.

My second is that, under the circumstances, I couldn't have had a more idiotic first thought.

My third is: *I have to get away from here! Now!*

It's too late, though. Coco and Pepper are brown and black streaks as they run circles together. Bobby is rushing toward me, and memories of the last time I saw him are flooding my brain.

That day. Bobby drove me to school. We sat high in the bleachers at the pep rally. We held hands for the first time and my heart was beating so fast. Then . . . there were gunshots. Screams. Bobby pushed me down and we lay under the bench together. Frozen. Waiting. Trying not to make a sound. More screams. More gunshots. Screams. Gunshots. Crying, crying, crying.

When it was over, Bobby kept his arms around me. He held his sweatshirt against my face to block my view as we stumbled down the steps and out of the gym.

Outside, we were told that the horror inside was my brother's fault.

Kirby had been the shooter.

Kirby had shot himself.

People were dead.

Kirby was dead.

I collapsed to the ground. I shook uncontrollably. Sounds came out of my mouth that I'd never heard before and that I never want to hear again. I howled and sobbed and wailed, and Bobby stayed with me. He stayed until someone in the crowd pointed me out to the police. Until the police led me away and drove me to meet my parents at the station.

The location of our lockers was the reason Bobby and I started talking in the first place, but it was at this park where we got to know each other. In front of us now, our dogs are playing as if nothing's changed, and while nothing could be further from the truth, maybe the fact that Bobby came here means that he doesn't agree with the comments on the news articles.

Maybe.

"Coco missed him like crazy," Bobby says. "I've been bringing her here a few times a day, hoping you'd show up. And here you are."

"Here we are."

He kicks at a dead leaf on the grass. "I called you a bunch of times. It always went right to voice mail."

"I'm sorry. I got my phone back from the cops the other day, but I haven't been brave enough to turn it on yet."

"Oh, no," he blurts out. "You don't have to apologize. I'm just letting you know you're going to have a ton of messages from me when you do turn it on. I was trying to keep you updated. They're saying school will reopen on Monday. But maybe you already knew about that?"

I shake my head. "I don't know about anything. There's so much craziness, and we're staying with friends. My dad's the only one who's even been by our house, and that was just to pick up the dog and pack some clothes."

Pepper runs up to us with Coco's Frisbee in his mouth, which Bobby takes and throws. As both dogs dash after it, he turns and looks right into my eyes. "Carah, how have you been holding up? Really."

"Really, I never knew anything could be so horrible." I have to focus on my feet to keep him from seeing my tears forming. "All night long, I have bad dreams. All day, I think about what he did. To those kids. To their families. To our family. Why would he do it? *Why?*"

"I don't know," he says quietly.

He doesn't tack on that I, of all people, should have known; he doesn't even seem to be thinking it. But I hate that I wasn't able to stop this, and that I never saw it coming.

"I've been going to all the candlelight vigils," Bobby tells me. "And I was at the hospital with some of the guys to see Morgan yesterday. She's looking better. I also saw a lot of your yearbook friends visiting Vincent after surgery. He's all right too."

Morgan Castro and Vincent Long. Just two of Kirby's victims.

Two of the luckier ones.

Pepper comes back with the Frisbee again while Coco trails

behind. This time I grab it and throw it right to Coco. Pepper rushes to wrestle her for it, and I tell Bobby, "If it had been anyone else's brother, I'd go with you. To the vigils and the hospital. I want to see Vincent. And Morgan too. But since it was my brother, I feel like I should stay away, so I won't make anyone feel worse."

"You wouldn't. Everyone saw you that day. They all know that you were totally caught off guard and as freaked out as the rest of us."

"I don't think *everyone* knows. I went online to read about the shooting—"

"And you read the comments, right? I read them too, and those people, they don't have a clue. Your friends. My friends. Me. All the people who do know you, we know you aren't to blame. I mean, the fact that you were there was proof enough. You were Kirby's *sister*, and he didn't even warn you or try to keep you away."

My hands fly up to cover my mouth, but I'm already crying.

I can't do this. I can't be here.

Not knowing or caring where I'm going, I hurry to get away. Before I've made it ten feet, I'm sinking to my knees on damp grass.

Do you have to be so dramatic about it?

That's how Kirby would have responded.

But as Bobby hunches over me, what he says is, "I'm sorry. I shouldn't have said that."

I choke out, "You're right, though. It's the truth."

My brother knew without question that I'd be in the gym that morning, but it didn't stop him from walking in there and shooting a whole bunch of people, including himself. Mom's right; he never cared about any of us. Me, least of all.

In the distance, someone shouts, "Carah!"

Bobby straightens up. Standing, I wipe my eyes with my sleeve and I follow his gaze to my dad, who's hurrying toward us.

"What's going on here?" Stopping next to me and placing his hand on my shoulder, Dad scowls at Bobby. "Carah, is this guy bothering you?"

"What?" And that's when I realize what this must have looked like to him—me standing here crying while talking with some boy he's never seen before. "No, no. I'm fine, Dad. This is Bobby. I've told you about him. Remember? He has a Lab too." I nod toward the dogs. "Bobby, this is my dad. Jack Matheson."

"Nice to meet you," Bobby says. "I'm really sorry for . . . what you're all going through."

He puts out his hand. Dad lets go of me to shake it, and his face relaxes as he does so.

If the shooting hadn't happened, Bobby would have picked me up at our house for the dance. This introduction would have happened under such different circumstances.

Beside me, my Dad's energy is all kinds of impatient, so I tell Bobby, "We have to go now."

"Okay."

He looks like he wants to hug me, but he isn't sure the moment is right with my father hovering like this. I lunge forward and throw my arms around him anyway. "Thanks for bringing Coco. And yourself."

"Of course. I'm around if you want to meet up. Just text or call me." Bobby reaches into his pocket and pulls out a pale yellow envelope with my name written on the front in Jolie's tiny handwriting. "I almost forgot. Jolie asked me to give this to you if I saw you."

I take it and then Dad helps me collect Pepper, who's nowhere near ready to stop playing. We basically have to drag him away from Coco.

"I'm sorry," Dad says, as we walk to the car. "I thought it would be good for you to get outside, but then I drove across town, realized what an idiot I was, and felt terrible. I shouldn't have forced you to go out alone like that."

"I wasn't alone."

Dad unlocks the doors and I help Pepper into the backseat. Once I'm in the front beside Dad, I turn over Jolie's card and smile at the two Band-Aids sealing it shut. Jolie will do anything to avoid licking envelopes; I once watched her dip her fingers in Pepsi to moisten the seal when she had to mail a hard-copy receipt to an advertiser for last year's yearbook.

"So the funeral home didn't take as long as you were expecting?" I ask.

"I couldn't do it." Dad rests his forehead against the steering wheel. "I didn't go."

"Dad, you have to take care of this."

"I know. I know I do." He lifts his head. "Carah, there's something I need you to tell you. It's okay if you're angry with him like Mom is. If you . . . hate him. But it's also okay to still love him."

"Dad—"

"Just let me finish," he says, holding up his hand. "My older brother let me down too. When I found out Roger had killed himself, I was so angry. So lost. I felt like he'd done it to punish me. And like it negated everything that had come before. I thought my memories of fun camping trips in Montana or good times at Thanksgiving were all lies because it must have meant nothing to Roger. It took me a while—too long, really—but I finally came to realize that a person's death isn't their whole life. And I know it isn't the same situation because of what your brother did at the end—"

"No, it *isn't* the same. Kirby ruined so many lives. He ruined *us*! The people we used to be don't even exist anymore. You and Mom are now the parents of a murderer. I'm the sister of a murderer. That's how everyone is going to see us from now on."

"Is that how Bobby sees you?"

"I don't know. How could he not?"

Dad lets out a loud breath. "What Kirby did. It changed you. But it changed everyone else, too."

"Exactly. And you know who doesn't have to suffer for it? Kirby. Even if he was sorry, he's made it so he can never apologize. Meanwhile I'll be apologizing for him as long as I live."

"I know. Me too. But you were always more than just our daughter and his sister. You're creative and driven and kind, and you're going to do so much with your life. Your brother has taken a lot, but he can't take that. And I do believe there were times when he helped people, when he made things better. He was part of our family, and we weren't wrong for loving him."

Part of me wants to yell at Dad that Kirby never deserved our love, but another part of me wants to believe he's right. The brother who mocked me for being a yearbook nerd, called my friends "bitches," and did everything he could to keep his life separate from mine for the past few years was the same brother who played with me when we were little, comforted me during our parents' many arguments, and gave me the best gift ever—Pepper.

I don't know how to respond to my dad right now, so I rip open Jolie's card instead. On the front it says IN DEEPEST SYMPATHY, and inside there are a bunch of signatures, along with a few short notes. From what I can tell, Jolie rounded up everyone from yearbook class to write inside this card for me.

Everyone, including Vincent.

Thinking of you during this difficult time.

Praying for you and your family. xoxoxoxo

If you need someone to talk to, I'm here.

Wishing you peace and comfort.

I'm so sorry for your loss, Carah.

Lots of love to you, girl.

Carah, we all love you. Don't ever forget that.

My tears blur their words.

If time machines were real, I'd be figuring out exactly which moment I'd have to travel to in order to prevent Kirby from doing what he did. But time travel doesn't exist and it never will. Not in my lifetime, at least. I know this because I would have already gone back if I could; I wouldn't have hesitated to do whatever it took to stop the shootings.

All I have now is the knowledge that my brother did some good things and some monstrous things in his life. I can't change any of it. But I can stop letting his actions define me. I can turn on my phone and let my friends know I'm going to find a way to be okay, and that I want to make sure they will be too. I can help my dad make decisions that, to him, feel impossible right now.

I pull open the glove box and sift through it until I find some leftover McDonald's napkins. I hand one to Dad and keep one for myself. "If you're ready," I say, wiping my eyes while he blows his nose, "we should head to the funeral home. Do you think they allow dogs in there?"

ALL'S WELL

Mom stands guard on the same kitchen tile where I left her, studying the TV mounted under the cabinets. Did she sleep? I heard her come up the stairs last night. I heard the water in the shower this morning.

On-screen, an overly manicured blonde is reporting live. "Tell me," Carolee at Channel 6 prompts, "How do you feel about returning to school? Have you been forever changed by the shooting?"

My classmate Gillian Marie sweeps her newly ginger curls to one side. "We've all learned a lot about fear and personal strength and conviction. For example, I always wanted to be a redhead because they're so witchy and cool. But I never would've actually dyed my hair if I hadn't almost died. You know, dyed. Died. Or nearly died. It changes a person. And so does a new hair color."

And we've officially run out of things to talk about. I peek inside my brown lunch bag—a green apple, a wedge of Swiss cheese, and a mini bag of Cheetos, to offset the otherwise obnoxious healthiness. Then I grab the remote and turn off the television.

"Hey!" Mom exclaims. "I was watching that!" She absentmindedly takes a bite of bagel. "Ruben, you don't have to go today, you know. I could call in sick and we—"

"I am going to school." She has a little problem with anxiety.

"There's no shame in admitting you're not ready." She's been on meds since the divorce. "Or waiting to make sure the new safety protocols are effective in—"

"I am going to school." I get it: I'm all she's got. But if I don't go today and come home safe, she may never let me out of the apartment again.

The good-bye hug lasts for four Mississippis. "You'll check in between classes, right?"

The thing is, she's not much better on days when we haven't just had a school shooting.

Kirby's name leads the chorus. Billie, Mia, Tyler—the names of the dead, the wounded, the heroes—they make up the verse. The song rages in the parking lot. Alongside the bike rack, it's whispered through tears.

I know what you're thinking. That's Ruben being dramatic again, mentally sketching a scene for his latest graphic novel. Too bad he never finishes one. Too bad he can't draw worth a damn.

Well, screw you. I've got Mrs. Johansen for first-period English, and she called me A Real Writer last week. She said my imagination is a wonder, and it's too bad that I've been strangled by the testing-obsessed education system. She said I should find an illustrator to team up with. I've got somebody in mind already.

Mom has already texted me twice, spooling me back into her stress web. I'm trying to be patient, but I'm desperate to think about something, anything else.

"Hey, kid!" a voice calls, shoving a handheld camera in my face. "Just one question!" The asshat jostles through the crowd in front of me. "Where were you when Kirby started shooting?"

I wonder if he's pro media or indie. He's not playing by the rules.

I tug my hood tighter, trying to escape into the crowd.

"Kid!" The guy tries again, grabbing my arm. "Where were you?"

"Taking a goddamn piss, all right?" I shout, jostling myself free. "I was holding on to my . . ."

Oh, crap. Where is my brain? Now, I'll be *that* guy on the Internet forever.

Mom will see the video. We'll have to talk about anger management and how my future college admissions counselor and every prospective employer will turn me down because I almost mentioned my dick, and the video will live online forever.

I blame Dad. Kirby may have killed people, but Dad ruined lives. Sure, I get that Mom is exhausting. She frets over every little thing. But the more he lied about where his time and money were going, the worse she got. Besides, dumping your high-maintenance, now-ex-wife on your sixteen-year-old kid is bullshit. I mean, really? I get that the associate at his law firm is hot. But it's not like being married stopped him before. He couldn't wait two lousy years until I bailed for college?

I shove past a couple of girls carrying instruments and that brings me back to myself again. I'm surrounded by people hugging, crying. I feel like an ingrate, a whiny idiot. Lots of parents get divorced.

None of my best friends died. None of my best friends are hooked up to tubes in the ICU.

Then again, I don't have much in the way of best friends.

I missed the whole thing, thank God. I heard the shots and stayed put until it was over.

Today I wore my long black coat and hoodie to hide my face and body from the cameras, trying to stay low on adult radar. I've had my fill of sympathetic *cluck-cluck* noises. They don't know what went wrong. They can't promise it won't happen again.

There's a rumor going around that Kirby may have had an accomplice who chickened out, who might set out to finish the job. It's bullshit, I'm sure. I'm pretty sure. Mom is obsessed with the idea.

She kept asking me if I was in classes with any of his friends.

What did I know about Kirby? Not much. Come opening weekend, he was at every superhero, sci-fi, horror, and fantasy flick. I'd see him at the theater, always fourth row. Close enough that he was in the thick of battle, far enough away that his neck didn't get sore. I'd turn and nod to him from up front.

I thought about asking Kirby to come with me sometime. But then I saw him out with John and Meiko and figured . . . eh. Why make the effort? Apparently, I was wrong. Or at least something inside him was wrong. What if I'd gotten off my ass and gone to sit beside him, offered to split a tub of popcorn? Would that have made a difference somehow?

"Where've you been?" My stepcousin Logan's voice is intense as he scolds me in the sophomore hall.

It's a werewolf-y name, Logan. Wolverine's name. Where were

the X-Men when we needed them? The Avengers? Wouldn't it have been something if I were a mutant? If Ruben Chase was just my secret identity, and I was in the restroom, changing into my black leather and cape? I could've flown through the halls and flung out my hand and melted the bullets and . . .

"Sorry, man," I say. "I was running late." We're supposed to stick together today. I don't want to bitch to him about Mom. Or at least I don't want him telling his mom I bitched about mine and have her pass that on. "I couldn't decide what to wear."

His laugh is too sharp, and everybody stares. Up ahead, Amber Delaney drops her books.

"Karl Andrews hyperventilated in the parking lot," Logan informs me. "He's in the nurse's office."

Post-traumatic lung implosion. Poor guy. It's about a third less crowded in the hall than usual.

"You better hang that coat up in your locker," Logan advises. "People will wonder what you're hiding under there." His tone catches me off guard. He says it like *he's* wondering.

I feel better with the trench on, like Nick Fury. Give me an eye patch and I'll be all set.

Logan and I have been cousins for less than a year. He's the new stepson of my aunt Jill. When my mom and I moved here, he was the first person from school who I met.

We could've hit it off. We didn't. He could've taken me under his wing. He didn't.

Doesn't matter. I've got better things to do than talk sports with the superficial people.

I scan the crowd for Misty Chen. She does all the posters for the

Thespians' Club. I spotted her last week at the Joss Whedon movie marathon. I wonder if she's at school today.

Me, Misty, and Kirby were all in that theater for hours. Together but not together. Weird, huh?

When the bell rings, I take my time wandering into English class. On the way, I text my mom.

Not dead. She won't think that's funny. I backspace until it disappears. *All's well.*

Lots of vacant chairs; one in five students are absent today. No, make that one in four.

Most important, there's no Mrs. Johansen. The bright spot of the day I'd been hoping for dims. I poured my soul into my extra-credit crossroads demon/possessed Impala/witch-hunting story. (Okay, it technically might have started as *Supernatural* fan fic, but I changed the names.)

"Good morning, class," begins the sub, whose name (according to the chalkboard) is Mr. Gomez. "Mrs. Johansen sends her thoughts and prayers. She has decided to take her maternity leave starting immediately." Maternity leave? I didn't realize she was pregnant.

If she's pregnant, she must've had sex. I knew she was married, but sex? That's disgusting. She's at least thirty years old. You should never have to think about teachers having sex.

Gomez is hypersensitive to any mention of violence. He stumbles all over talking to us about Dickens's *A Tale of Two Cities* without mentioning the guillotine. Next up on the syllabus is *Hamlet*, though, so he's basically screwed.

God, I miss Mrs. Johansen already. My algebra teacher, Mrs. Russell, worked up until the day she delivered. People were taking bets as to whether she was going to pop out the kid in class.

I'm spacing out when there's a knock on the door. It's Misty Chen, in full artsy glory. Gomez looks relieved to take a quick break. He excuses himself, they speak in low tones, and then he turns to motion to me. "Ruben, you're needed in the office."

"I didn't do anything wrong." Why did I say that?

"You know what this is about?" I ask Misty as we head past a long row of lockers. I've never seen the hall this empty. There's always a student running in late or a janitor carrying a mop.

"You don't?" she replies. "I'm an office assistant, first period. Except the day of the . . . when Kirby . . . I . . ." She was there.

"I was in the john," I admit.

Misty smirks. "I know. Everybody knows."

The Internet. "Great."

She takes pity on me. "I like your coat."

I'm actually getting kind of warm. I consider stashing it in my locker, but I don't because she said that. Misty is a fashionista. On a day that everyone else is in almost uniform jeans and T-shirts, she's got on a flouncy turquoise-and-white dress with silver shoes. There's a pink streak on the left side of her bangs. She's nothing like Amber. It's like Misty's trying to prove that what happened won't change her, except . . . "What happened to your leg?"

The bruise is bigger than my hand and covers most of her knee, bleeding into the shin. She could've worn jeans to hide it. "I fell," she says.

I imagine the chaos—people pushing, shoving. She can't weigh more than 105 pounds.

Wait. "Is it my mom?" I ask, reaching for my phone. She works in the city. She could've gotten in a car wreck. It's not like the rest of the world no longer exists. This isn't the only place where bad things happen. No reply. We turn the corner. The office is only steps away. "Did my—"

Misty reaches for my free hand and gives it a gentle squeeze. "Nothing like that. "

I'm shocked enough to come to a halt in front of the library. "You're holding my hand."

Thank you, Captain Obvious. The world has changed. We're all closer somehow because of what we lived through, because we survived. I should say something now about my graphic novels and how I'd like her to do the art for me and how it would be fun to hang out. Or not fun. More like two kindred souls . . . no, dear God, not that. She's still holding my hand.

Her showing up to fetch me, it's not a coincidence. It's a sign. A sign—could that sound any flakier? Any more like something Mom would say?

I'm a writer. I need a pen and paper. A keyboard. My phone.

Misty gives my fingers another squeeze and then gestures across the hall at the counselor's office. "Ms. Washington is waiting for you."

Not the principal's office. This must be some kind of random psych check on the student body, which is fine, I guess. It's at least potentially less boring than listening to the sub's lecture.

The cinder-block walls of Ms. Washington's office have been covered in a textured wood paneling, painted a soft yellow. The barrel-shaped chairs are deep and soft leather. The walls are adorned with motivational posters: a photograph of a bald eagle labeled SOAR. A photograph of otters floating on their backs, holding each other's paws—FRIENDSHIP. The wall calendar theme is kittens, and a collection of little crystal angels gleams under the brass reading lamp.

Ms. Washington invites me to have a seat and leans forward in her chair, folding her hands on the cluttered desk. "Ruben," she says. "It's not uncommon in the wake of a tragedy to find yourself grappling with mood swings or intense emotions. Feelings like sorrow or anger."

Great, she watched me tell off the reporter on YouTube.

"Sometimes, we may even find ourselves tempted to lash out at those who're trying to help."

I did unleash a bit. "Look, I may have lost it for a minute there, but—"

"Lost what?" Now she's retreating, leaning back in the chair.

"My temper," I admit. "But that could've happened to anybody. You're just in the moment, you know? And it feels right."

"Do you think that's how Kirby felt?" she asks, head cocked. "Lost in the moment? Did you feel a connection to him?"

I have no idea how Kirby felt. I barely knew the guy, except . . . "We liked the same movies."

I overheard similar conversations in the hall. "Kirby was in my gym class." "Kirby almost rear-ended my car once." Kirby, Kirby, Kirby.

"You went to the movies together?" Now Ms. Washington's right eyebrow is cocked too.

"No," I assure her. "I saw him at the theater a lot, though. We were both into geeky stuff. Sci-fi, fantasy, superheroes, horror."

"Vicarious thrills." She opens a manila folder on the desk. "Horror like this?" She shows me my latest extra-credit story for Mrs. Johansen.

"Sure." I can't resist asking. "Did you read it?" Wait. "Why do you have that?"

Ms. Washington skims the text. "Mrs. Johansen said that a lot of your writing is violent."

"Mrs. Johansen said?" Hang on . . . Oh, hell. "Look, no, I barely knew . . . I thought you meant this morning in front of the school. That guy with the camera. He touched me." That sounded worse. "I mean, he took hold of my arm. I was trying to get away from him. I didn't want to answer his questions. I'm sick of the media vultures, so I told him to back off. I thought you'd seen the video."

"There's a video?" Ms. Washington returns my story to her file. Then she excuses herself and leaves the office for forty-two minutes. Forty-two minutes.

The end-of-first-period bell rings.

The start-of-second-period bell rings.

I text Mom: *All's well.*

I'm starting to think Ms. Washington's forgotten about me when she returns with a tight smile, reaches for a pen, and begins scribbling. "Kir—I mean, Ruben." She takes a breath. "Kirby is on everybody's mind. Ruben, you live down the street. I don't think there's much substantial academic achievement happening in this place today. Why don't you take the rest of the day off and come in with your mother tomorrow? I'll give her a call."

No, no, no, no. "This is all a mistake," I say. "Uh, Mom has been under a lot of pressure, and . . ."

Stop talking. Nothing I can say to Ms. Washington is going to help. She barely knows me.

I need to talk to Mrs. Johansen. I'm her star student, her "little Stephen King." I know she didn't mean for this to happen. If I could just talk to her in person, everything'll be fine again.

Her house is on my way home.

Mrs. Johansen lives in a green cottage with blue trim located between the high school and my house. I've seen her out there, raking leaves as I walked home. I stopped to talk to her and her husband. I wonder if she'll return to teaching after her baby is born.

I pause at the fence, and a white Shih Tzu appears in the picture-frame window, barking its furry head off. The lace curtains flutter. I spot another face peeking through. Mrs. Johansen?

I unlatch the front gate and take a couple of steps up the walk to Mrs. Johansen's door. I'm imagining ringing her doorbell and her answering. When she sees me, she laughs and apologizes and says the shootings have made all of us crazy.

The barking trails off, as though the dog has been carried away from the front of the house. I ring the doorbell and wait. And wait. I ring it again and wait some more.

Mrs. Johansen opens the door. She's got her phone in her hand. "Ruben, what are you doing here? You're supposed to be in school."

"They sent me home," I tell her. "They think I'm . . ." Like Kirby. "They're—Ms. Washington—is worried about that last story I wrote for your class. For extra credit. Did you read it?"

Of course she did. She's the one who gave it to Ms. Washington.

"Yes. It was . . . very imaginative." Last week my imagination was a great thing. Today, staring at me on her front step, standing on the monogrammed doormat, she sounds unsure of herself.

"Look," I begin. "This is all a misunderstanding. You know me, right? You get that I understand the difference between fantasy and reality and that because I fantasize about killing demons on the page doesn't mean that I would ever shoot a human being in real life." The dog suddenly appears at her feet, yipping at me. "Or, for that matter, a Shih Tzu."

But she's not paying attention. She's looking over my shoulder. I turn to find out at what as the police cruiser pulls along the side of the road and two uniformed cops get out.

I cannot freaking believe this. I glance back at Mrs. Johansen as she's pulling the dog back by its red rhinestone-studded collar and closing the door. Closing the door in my face.

My instincts scream at me to run, even though I haven't done a damn thing wrong. But cops can shoot you for running, right? They can shoot you for standing still. I raise my hands.

They could shoot me anyway. Why are people wasting time being scared of me? If I hadn't had to take a piss, Kirby could've killed me. If I make a wrong move—or even if I don't—I could die on my favorite teacher's doorstep. Nowhere is safe.

No wonder my mom has an anxiety disorder.

I call Dad from the police station for all of the obvious reasons. He's a lawyer. I wasn't a truant. Mrs. Johansen didn't want to press charges for trespassing. Writing a horror story isn't an admission of state of mind, and even if it was, having a state of mind isn't illegal.

Since there was no reason for me to be there, I was on my way home in Dad's Mercedes within an hour. "I have a lot going on at work today," he informs me. "I had to cancel my four o'clock. Did you call your mother?"

"I texted her." All's well.

I'm impressed that he came to rescue me himself. That he didn't send an associate to handle it for him. Maybe he was embarrassed that his kid was in trouble. Maybe he cares.

Dad swings into the drive-through at McDonald's and we order some McNuggets and Cokes. He doesn't send his support checks on time. He's always a day late. Not so late that it gets him in trouble, just late enough to make a point. Mom tells me about it, every month the same conversation.

As we pull into my apartment complex parking lot, Dad says, "I read your story. The school faxed a copy of it to the police station." He looks at me sideways. "I thought you wanted to be an artist."

"I want to write," I say. "I'm going to find an artist to do the illustrations for me."

"For your comic books?"

Graphic novels. "Yeah."

He ruffles my hair like he did when I was a little kid. "You've got genuine talent. You scared a bunch of grown-ups into thinking you're really dangerous. That's kick-ass writing, right?"

I hadn't looked at it that way. But I can see where a lawyer would. "I guess."

He ruffles my hair again. "Hang in there, son."

Huh. Dad thinks I'm a kick-ass writer. I shut the front passenger door feeling better than I have all day and take the stairs to my front door two at a time.

My phone buzzes in my pocket and I expect it to be Mom. Or maybe Logan, wondering what happened to me. I forgot that we were supposed to walk home together.

Instead, it's Misty. She writes: *Mrs. J called Ms. W, said she's sorry she flagged you.*

That's something, I guess. I write back: *Thx. Lunch tomorrow?*

I hit send before I can take it back.

Misty again: *Sure. C U then.*

I reach for the doorknob, but right then Mom opens it from the inside. "Why didn't you tell me you had been arrested?"

"I wasn't arrested," I say. "It was all a misunderstanding. You can ask my counselor at school. You can ask Dad."

But Mom's not listening. The TV is on in the kitchen, just like it was this morning. Just like it was last night. There's a screen grab of me shouting at this morning's video reporter on YouTube. Meanwhile, Channel 6's Carolee is saying, ". . . unconfirmed reports that sixteen-year-old Ruben Chase may have been a coconspirator in the school shooting that left—"

I grab the remote and punch the off button. "You were right," I admit to my mom, surrendering. "I never should've gone to school today. I never should've gotten out of bed today." I slip off the long coat, realizing that I can call Dad and he'll make the station back off. Maybe even apologize, but it's already out there. "Misty's parents are going to see that and—"

"Misty." My mom's shoulders relax. A smile tugs at her lips. "You have a girlfriend."

"A *friend* friend," I say. "A *maybe* friend friend."

This time I don't mind when Mom hugs me for four Mississippis.

I ask, "You're not afraid of me?" She's afraid of everything else.

"I've never been afraid of you," my mother explains. "I'm afraid *for* you. It's called being a parent. Someday you'll understand."

I disengage without pushing her away. "If you say so."

Mom tightens her grip on my arms. "Just don't get her pregnant. Or catch a disease."

Just like that we're back to normal . . . or at least the new normal. All's well.

BURNING EFFIGIES

When Kirby Matheson shot up the Middleborough High School gym, it had nothing to do with them.

They'd been in Dalton's SUV, crammed six in the back with Carly sitting bitch between Dalton and Cranmer. By chance Alice saw Kirby walking through the lot. She'd watched him through a puff of smoke, rolling her eyes. When the shots started, she didn't recognize them as gunshots. None of them did. They didn't know anything had happened until the school began to empty and the cops arrived with sirens blasting. Then they pressed together and pushed their fingers against the glass.

After it was over, the parking lot swarmed with reporters for days. There were many recollections of Kirby on the news, quotes online breaking down his whys and his pain. Mics were shoved into every flushed, tear-streaked face that wandered too close to the news vans. Except for theirs. Freshmen, seniors, teachers, and cafeteria workers—hell, even friends of teachers and cafeteria workers. But not them. None of the reporters asked what they saw. What could they have seen, doped-up kids cutting class? Only Kirby, walking through the lot before it all began. It had happened at their school. It had happened to them, and not to them at all.

Kirby hadn't shot anyone they particularly cared about. Billie Palermo, maybe. The new kid. The transgender transfer. She might have become one of theirs if she'd had more time and a little less sweetness about her. A little less big-boned softness. A little less of an obvious desire to fit in.

But she didn't, and none of theirs would have been caught dead at that stupid first-period pep rally, listening to the cheer-morons try to rhyme while flashing their poms, their asses, and their bleached-white teeth. Go, Middleborough Muskrats. Go. Go fuck yourselves.

It was all too easy to slide out the side doors and into the parking lot, ignoring any teacher who called their names, and once they were beside Dalton's dented maroon Explorer, draped across the hood with their boots kicking the tires, none of the chickenshits had balls enough to order them back inside.

How those teachers must have run when the shooting started. How they must have screamed.

"Only two news vans today," Cranmer says, walking Alice down the hall. "By next week there'll be none. How soon they forget." He shakes a smoke from his pack and pops it between his teeth. As long as he doesn't light it, faculty keeps their mouths shut. Too many unanswered notes sent home. Too many missed parent-teacher meetings. And Cranmer has gotten too fast at chewing and swallowing the evidence.

"How fast we'd forget," says Alice, "if it weren't for shit like that."

She nods at the main entrance as they pass, where techs are installing new metal detectors while a freshly appointed and very stern-looking security guard stands supervising. Alice swipes the smoke from between his teeth and sucks air through the filter.

"They're making it harder on us," she says. "Harder to ditch to the lot."

"Allie. Don't be a pessimist. They only hired one guy, and he probably finished his gun training two days ago." Cranmer throws his arm around her skinny shoulders. He calls her "Allie" now, and his fingers press into the skin where her sweater has slid down. She doesn't know when they became Alice and Cranmer instead of Alice and Cranmer and everyone else, but they have. Jaime thinks it's a brilliant idea, and Carly says she's not jealous. Alice thinks it will be all right. Charlie Cranmer isn't always just a stoner goof. Sometimes he's sweet.

"It's stupid, though," Cranmer says, "the way they think. Like someone else is going to come in here with another gun and do the exact same thing. No way. Next time it'll be a mass poisoning. Or a fucking crossbow. How sick would that be?"

"There won't be a next time," Alice says, and shrugs out from under his arm. "What school has more than one massacre? They'd shut us down."

"What a loss."

They stop at the crossway and Cranmer lingers. His blue eyes flit around. He has a nice jawline and nice lips, and he looks at Alice like he loves her.

"Jesus, Cranmer, are you going to ask me to prom or something?"

He raises an eyebrow.

"You want to go to prom?"

"Shut up." She holds the cigarette up between two fingers. "I'll meet you and Jaime at lunch to smoke this."

"Okay," he says, and backs away. "Have fun in Spanish. Learn some swear words."

Have fun in English, she thinks. Learn anything.

Jaime's taken to wearing her hair weird. It's up in a high clip and stiff tips stick out the top like sprouts. The style makes her look perkier than she is, and since she's still growing out the last round of green dye, it also makes her resemble a sarcastic turnip.

They're sitting in Jaime's car, Jaime and her boyfriend, David, in the front and Alice and Cranmer in the back, smoking cigarettes out of Cranmer's pack that isn't really Cranmer's pack because they all kicked in for it. They're close to the school, not far back in the lot, testing the limits of the new security guard's glare. He glares and glares but does nothing. Not even when Dalton jumps onto the hood and Jaime flips him off and yells for him to get the fuck in the back. The guard thinks they're trouble. Everyone thinks they're trouble. But Kirby Matheson never hung with them; it wasn't one of them who shot up the pep rally. So there.

Alice blows smoke against the window and watches it roll and swim lazily for the roof. Through the gray haze, most of fourth-period lunch seems to have migrated outside. The cattle think it's safer there, where they aren't boxed in. Not locked down. They think it will be easier to run and scatter should the need arise.

Don't forget to zig, she almost says aloud, when you should zag.

Ten feet from the school doors, a group of girls has gathered. They stand closer to one another, closer than the rest of the groups. They stand in a circle, in rings like a tree or a sticky, stupid cinnamon roll, the least important riding the crust and the most important frosting the center. Directly in the middle is Elsa Loring. Tyler Bower's perfect blond girlfriend.

"Christ, Elsa looks like shit," Jaime says, reading Alice's mind in that way that best friends can. "Her eyes are so red they might actually bleed."

"She's probably been crying a lot," says Alice.

"Well you know it's not from smoking weed," Cranmer says.

"Don't be so sure," David adds, and both boys laugh.

"Well, whatever it's from," Jaime says, and ashes out the window, "you know she's got to be loving all the attention."

They stare at Elsa for a few moments. Her shoulders are pulled in tight and her hair is tied back in a simple elastic band.

"It does make me want to spit in her face a little less, though." Jaime sighs.

Alice sucks her cigarette hard. She stares at pretty, perfect Elsa Loring, who doesn't seem to be enjoying any of the extra attention. But then she wouldn't need to. She had plenty of it to begin with.

They say that Tyler was shot twice. They say that he died right away and didn't suffer. Alice heard whispers that you could see the blood and brains fly out of the back of his head, and when she thinks of that, her stomach clenches like a fist.

Elsa would have been near him when it happened. The players were always near the cheerleaders, Alice remembered that from the rallies she'd endured as a freshman. She wonders if they ran together.

If he pushed through people to get to her. If Elsa had been holding his hand. She wonders if Tyler was holding her tight, and then suddenly not at all.

Alice stares at Elsa and, for a minute through the smoky glass, it almost looks like Elsa is staring back. But then someone touches Elsa's shoulder and she drops her face into her hands.

Elsa Loring might have been the last person to be with Tyler when he was alive. He would have tried to protect her when he saw the gun. He was like that no matter what Dalton and David and Alice's other friends said when they cut down the jocks.

At night in her bed, Alice whispers into her pillow as if she is whispering into his grave. As if she might hear him whisper back.

"Did you die for her, Tyler?"

"Would you ever, ever have died for me?"

Someone has the idea to toast Birdland. Alice isn't sure who. She thinks it was Dalton, because it was his bottle, lifted from the back of his parents' liquor cabinet. It doesn't matter now. They're on the corner of Heron, at the edge of the neighborhood where all the streets are named for birds. Birdland, where Kirby Matheson used to live before he blew his own head off.

"Here's to Birdland," Dalton says, and raises his bottle of soda. They all raise them, Coke and Sprite and Dr Pepper, with as much whiskey mixed in as they can stand.

"To Birdland."

"And all your nests of vipers," Alice says, and drinks long and hard, carbonation burn and sickly alcohol sting, and everyone laughs and looks at her like she's said something clever.

They leave the cars, and for a few blocks Dalton takes them on a haunted tour, making up stupid shit about things buried in backyards and murders committed in ramblers. He's full of wind, like he always is, and it doesn't take long for Cranmer to join him, filling in the gaps of fake stories and glancing back at Alice so often that it's embarrassing. He and Dalton are grand-gesturing fools even when they're not drinking, and now they're so loud some pissed homeowner is going to call the cops. She wishes she hadn't worn her heavy boots. When the red-and-blue lights hit they'll have to dart into yards, try to double back to the Explorer, and hope they don't come up against a fence they can't jump.

"Does anyone know," Alice asks, "where Kirby lived?"

In the lead, Dalton and Cranmer slow.

"I don't," Cranmer says.

"Me neither," says Jaime.

"I do."

Alice turns to David.

"How do you know where he lived?" Jaime asks. Her words slur a little. Jaime always drinks too fast. Before they go much farther she'll have to pee, and Alice will have to stand guard by whatever shrub she chooses. Fifteen minutes after that she'll have to do it again.

"My parents used to know his parents," David says. "But they're not there now. My mom says they're staying with family or something."

"Take us there," Alice says.

For a few moments they look unsure. Hesitant. But then they palm their bottles tighter and grin. Their faces under the streetlights are gaunt and orange.

On the way they whisper and giggle. They make jokes about Kirby. How the idiot had no school spirit or he would have aimed for faculty. How he should have shot his parents, too, for giving him such a stupid name. In the days immediately following the shooting, it seemed like everyone wanted to remember Kirby. To break him into pieces like a disassembled watch. People who never spoke to him at all had sudden recollections of foreboding eye contact. Even among Alice and her friends, they told what stories they had, giving in to the urge to be involved in something that seemed so important to everyone else.

But eventually they ran out of pieces of Kirby to analyze. The shock and the mourning and the brief period of head-hanging gave way to ridicule. Laughter and shouts of "Too soon!" that were only followed by more laughter.

Some in town said that Kirby was in hell, but Alice hoped he wasn't. She hoped he was right there beside them, listening to every insult. She hoped he knew what a joke he still was. That the biggest joke of all was he thought he could kill himself and escape it.

"That's it," David says, and points. It isn't much. An average house, and in the dark and the shadows of trees it could be white or beige or blue. They stand for a minute where they are, a few houses down on Egret Lane. No one asks Alice why she wanted to come. Perhaps they don't remember that it was her idea.

"Let's go," Jaime says after a while. "There are probably cops watching, and I have to pee."

"We haven't even gone that close yet," says Dalton, but he doesn't sound eager.

"So what? It's just a house. I'm bored. And I'm out of drink. Let's go back to the gas station and get more Coke."

"Yeah," David says. "Then we can sit around a fire at Carly's place."

Carly's place. No more than two miles away. Her friends shuffle off, jeans and scuffed boots, but Alice doesn't move. No one notices but Cranmer, and he doesn't turn until they're a good distance down the block.

"Hey, Allie," he calls softly, and Alice darts forward, toward Kirby's house, into the dark.

Alice doesn't really know how long it took to get things done at Kirby's and make her way to Carly's backyard, but everyone is still there. No one has passed out yet, and no one is particularly worried about her absence. Such friends I've got, she thinks, but she won't waste much of her disgust on them. Not when she has Kirby tucked underneath her arm.

"Alice!" Jaime half shouts. "Where did you go? I turned around and you were gone."

"I went to get these."

She holds up the clothes. A pair of jeans and a T-shirt with long sleeves.

"They're his."

It takes them a few seconds. Then their eyes light up. They crow and jump and make Christ-poses in her honor. Cranmer slides against her like a snake.

"You broke into his house?" He grins. "You are a bad girl, Allie. You are a bad, bad girl."

She wasn't. Not ever before. She smoked and drank, blew weed and ate a little molly, but she was never bad. She was good. She went to school and didn't fail classes and in her wildest fantasies, one day not so far away, Tyler would have looked at her and said her name like he knew her.

Alice throws the clothes at Dalton and David, and they toss them in the air. Dalton dances with Kirby's shirt, mocking it like a joke date to homecoming. She lets them do it for a while, lets everyone get their digs in, before she takes the clothes back and strings them up on the wire clothesline, the shirt on top and the jeans pinned to the bottom of the shirt. A flat, empty Kirby.

Even rifling through his dresser in the dark she managed to find a shirt that he wore to school often, so the ghost hanging there looks familiar. She can almost see his face rising over the line.

No one has to tell them what to do. As if they've had it in their minds the whole time too. They spit on it and laugh. They shout insults. They shake up their precious whiskey sodas and spray it all over the jeans until flat Kirby looks like he pissed himself. They piss on him for real. They don't need secret, murdered loves to hate Kirby Matheson. They hate him plenty, just for what he did. Lifting himself up over other peoples' lives. Making himself the center of the universe. And for the fear that none of them admit to, that it could have been them, had they waved their hands in the parking lot.

"That's enough," says Alice. "Where's the lighter fluid?"

She lets Cranmer douse him with it, but she's the one who lights the match.

"Burn, motherfucker," she says, and it goes up in a rush, flames licking up the legs and onto the chest, down the arms that flap weakly. Almost as if they're trying to defend themselves.

Tyler Bower was almost perfect. Perfect dark brown hair. Perfect warm brown eyes. He knew Alice's name. He'd used it when he asked her what the reading assignment was in sophomore English. He sat two feet away for an entire semester.

Alice has replayed their handful of moments many times. Now she sits on Jaime's bedroom floor and replays them again, pretending to listen to Jaime complain about what a shitty anniversary present David got her. It *was* shitty. It was socks. Cool striped ones that Jaime liked, but not as an anniversary gift.

"Who gets their girlfriend socks?"

"David, apparently," Alice says.

"I blew so much money on those shoes for him," Jaime says. "And I get ten-dollar socks."

Alice would like to tell Jaime about Tyler. But she's never even hinted. Every time she watched him messing around on the football field and every time she left class hoping to catch a glimpse of him in the halls, it had been her secret. Once in a while he would smile at her. Alice never managed to smile back fast enough.

She would never have told him how she felt. But now that he's gone, it will always feel like they were the next words out of her mouth.

Alice thinks about Kirby a lot now too. She thinks about him rotting in the ground, in that secret place his parents buried him so no one could piss in the dirt and crack his headstone like he deserves. Burning his clothes felt good. Breaking into his space felt good. She wants to do more things like that. Things that Kirby wouldn't like. Maybe she'll beat his sister black and blue. Maybe she'll run down his parents. Sometimes she wants to stop, she wants to forget him, obliterate him, to make sure he doesn't matter. But she can't stop thinking about Kirby any more than she can stop thinking about Tyler.

Tyler isn't Alice's only secret anymore.

The jocks are throwing a party. For once everyone is invited. They pass out flyers on bright yellow paper like joiner college kids recruiting freshmen for rush week, and the address of the big, expensive house it's being held in is right there in bold. They mean it. In the wake of slaughter, all are welcome. The yellow of the paper is like a new day. Alice crumples it in her fist and it sits there, a beaten little sun.

Cranmer comes by to take her out the night of the party, and her mom doesn't ask where. She even sort of smiles at Cranmer, the same Cranmer she once told Alice looked like a coatrack covered in dirty laundry.

"Try to have some fun," her mom says. "Try to cheer up."

Nothing about curfews and no cautions. Whatever Alice gets up to, it can't be worse than having the back of her head blown off.

For a while they just drive around. Cranmer pulls into the park and turns the music up. He rolls a joint that a gentleman would have had rolled already, but Cranmer never thinks ahead. Cranmer never thinks.

"What are we doing?" Alice asks.

"I don't know. What do you want to do?"

Alice shrugs. Cranmer lights the joint and passes it to her. They smoke without speaking until it's short and wet with resin and spit and she waves it away.

"We could go to a movie," he says.

"What?"

"A movie."

Alice stares at him and he laughs. The joint hit her hard and she's almost anesthetized; she almost feels okay. It's a chore to lift her arm and a chore to breathe and that feels about right.

"Earth to Allie. What do you want to do?"

Alice rolls her head against the seat.

"Let's go to that party."

Cranmer's smile starts slow, but it spreads all the way up his cheeks. Stoned as she is it looks near cartoonish, that cat from Wonderland or like someone carved up his face like the Joker in *The Dark Knight*. She laughs. She laughs until her belly hurts, and Cranmer has to cover her mouth so he can speak the address into his GPS.

When they pull onto the street they don't have to wonder which house it is. It's the biggest house on a block full of big houses. It's the whitest one, with pale shutters and a long driveway packed with cars, a line of cars that spills down the sidewalk.

"It's so bright," Alice says, watching the silhouettes of bodies talking and throwing their heads back. There must be two dozen windows, all lit up with people crammed inside.

And on the lawn, too. Eight boys playing a screaming game of football, posturing like apes. They hit each other too hard for friends, and Alice suddenly wants to play. It looks like rage. Destruction. Grief with no place to go. It looks like fun.

"Maybe we shouldn't be here," says Cranmer.

"You got a flyer, didn't you?"

"Yeah."

"Well, so did I."

Alice opens her door and gets out. She walks up the driveway and doesn't know or care if Cranmer is behind her until he bumps into her back once they're inside.

The house is big, but it's still hot as she walks through the rooms. The people they pass are drunk to the last, obliterated, and it's barely ten thirty. Cranmer taps her arm and hands her a cup of something. It tastes a little like fruit punch and a lot like vodka. When she drains it, he grins and fetches her another.

"If any of us ever had a house party this loud," he yells into her ear, "it'd have been busted up two hours ago."

Alice watches the disgusted, irritated way Cranmer looks at the people around them. They own things that he doesn't. They get away with things that he won't. And this is how they grieve.

Elsa is standing outside on the back patio. She's done her hair, but her cheeks are red from whatever she's drinking and she stares down into her cup. She looks strange, all alone.

"Why'd you want to come here?" Cranmer shouts.

"I don't know," Alice says.

He waits for her to say more, but she doesn't, and he swipes a bottle from the kitchen counter and drags her back out to the car.

"It was good for this at least," he says, and takes a drink.

Alice stares up at the lights. At the shadows. They all belong to Tyler's friends. Tyler's girlfriend. Up on that hill, loud and sad, is Tyler's life without him in it.

"Just don't drive anywhere," she says.

"Why not?"

"Just don't."

She takes the bottle and drinks it down. More vodka, this time flavored like marshmallows.

"Whatever you say." Cranmer shakes his head. "You're getting really weird, you know that?"

It doesn't take long for the alcohol to make her slow, and the weed is still stuffed into her head, soft as cotton. The house twinkles up on its hill. Sometimes it screams.

"Do you think that was Elsa screaming?" Alice mutters as Cranmer's hand slides underneath her shirt. Her seat lurches back and the world tilts.

"I don't know." His mouth is close to her ear. His lips are dry. She thinks she can feel his teeth once in a while. He climbs over the center console and lowers down on top of her. She doesn't look at his face and her mother's words flicker through her memory—a coatrack piled with dirty laundry. She laughs once, and Cranmer smiles.

"Maybe it was Jackson."

"Screaming like a girl?"

"Maybe. Ow."

His hands twist up under her bra. It pinches and he's heavier than he looks.

"I can't get this off," he says, and abandons it to go after her jeans. He kisses her a little, but never on the mouth, and she hasn't looked at him once. In her mind she's up on that hill, under the lights, and Tyler is there. He would see her and think she was brave for coming. He would nod like they shared some great secret.

In the car there is only cold plastic on the door handles and glove box, the stale smell of smoke sunk into the upholstery, and Cranmer's breathing, heavy and excited. The tug of her jeans down her legs.

"I used to have a crush on him, you know," she says.

"Who?" Cranmer asks without stopping.

"Tyler Bower. Ever since I saw him on the first day of school."

"Yeah? That's weird," Cranmer says, and unbuckles his belt.

"He had brown eyes. Brown hair. He moved like nobody else on that field. I watched everything. I saw everything." Her shoulders bounce. Her hips bounce from being pulled on.

"He moved like . . ." She can see him in her mind even though her eyes are open. Even though she's still staring at the house full of his friends. She can see him, but the drink in her blood hides what she wants to say. "He moved like . . ."

"Christ, Allie, will you shut up?"

She does. She lies still underneath Cranmer and thinks about Tyler, lying still in a box underground in the cemetery. She thinks about Elsa Loring. She thinks about the dark, broken space of Kirby Matheson's bedroom, and the dead smell of it. But mostly she stares up at the house, all of that sparkling yellow light, and thinks about how all of this is real. All of this is permanent, and none of it will ever go away.

HOLES

Let me just clear this up.

I don't go to Middleborough High. I go to Ashton, forty-six miles away (I looked it up). Too far to hear gunshots or sirens. We watched all the news coverage that night, and for days and days after, and everyone had a cousin or a friend of the family or an old babysitter who lived sort of close, but no one with any connections to my school was hurt. Someone who used to teach algebra here and transferred over there, like, ten years ago, but he was halfway across the school from the pep rally and is totally fine. That's the most direct connection we have.

Except, you know. Me.

At least everyone else seems to think I'm a direct connection.

I think if the boy in that picture they plastered all over the news didn't have the same blankness in his eyes, the kind of hollowness I've never seen in any smile before or since, I wouldn't even have recognized Kirby Matheson.

But, you know. That's just me. What I think on this matter isn't important.

I'm not being snarky, here.

I would just really like everyone to understand that what I think on this matter isn't important.

It was the Monday after the shooting when people started approaching me. I'd spent the whole weekend listening to my mom murmur about how she should call Mrs. Matheson when we all knew she wouldn't, and putting on headphones to drown out the sounds of my stepsister crying as if this had anything to do with her. Our parents hadn't even met back when my mom and I lived on Egret Lane.

I don't know how people at school found out. My guess is that my mom mentioned it to some parent and everyone gossiped about it until it got back to someone's kid. *You know Laura? The assistant Features editor for the* Ashton Gazette? *The tall girl on the swim team? Yeah, you know her. Right, that one. Sure, she's nice enough. I never think about her much. She kind of keeps to herself.*

She lived next door to that guy who shot up Middleborough.

Isn't that interesting?

And maybe this next part is in my head, but when I sat down in homeroom on Monday and everyone was looking at me and elbowing the people next to them and somehow convincing themselves I couldn't hear them whispering, I swear I felt them thinking, *Hey, didn't that guy kind of keep to himself too?*

It was Nicole who actually came up to me first. She's the editor-in-chief, a senior, so she's four years older than me. She once told me that if I were two years older I'd absolutely be her pick to take over when she graduated. I never thought she really liked me much, and since she said that I've had this pathological fear of doing something stupid in front of her, which means that I'm constantly doing stupid things in front of her.

Like dropping all my books all over both our feet when she sidled up to me at my locker. See, stupid things. It doesn't help that she's seriously pretty and has been the subject of more than one confusing dream. I don't know why I'm telling you this.

She crouched down to help me pick them up. "How are you doing?" she said.

"I'm fine."

"I wanted to talk to you about a possible feature," she said.

"Sure, okay."

She stood up and tucked a strand of hair behind her ear. I was still on the floor, looking up at her. "We were wondering if you'd feel comfortable writing . . . something about Middleborough."

"Some kind of follow-up to Anya's piece?" Anya, our photo editor, called up the families and friends of people over in Middleborough and did this really gorgeous special edition of the *Gazette* that was just a bunch of pictures of all of the victims as little kids or with their friends or dressed up for homecoming, with some quotes about them from their friends—funny stuff and heartbreaking stuff and everything in between. It was seriously beautiful.

I didn't really think there needed to be a follow-up.

She said, "Actually we were wondering if . . . I mean, if you would feel comfortable . . . writing about . . . you know. Kirby."

She was the first person I'd heard refer to him by just his first name—on the news it was always Kirbymatheson, like it was one word—and for some reason that really pissed me off. Maybe because it seemed like she was trying to imply some familiarity, like I didn't even need a last name to know who Kirby was, which of course was incredibly stupid since it's A) not exactly a common name and B) not exactly a name anyone with a pulse wouldn't recognize now.

So maybe being bothered by that was just me being stupid in front of Nicole like usual.

"Okay," I said.

"Really?"

"Yeah, I can do some research into profiles of people who do this, maybe talk about warning signs and copycat crimes and stuff like that. That would get us a lot of reads and piss off the school board, which is always fun."

"No, I . . . I was thinking more that you'd want to write about what you knew about him already, not like a research piece. You know, kind of . . . revealing him in a way, what kind of things might have influenced him, what he was really like."

I remember staring at her. "So you want me to memorialize a guy who just shot up a school."

I said that right to Nicole Kramer.

Like I said. Stupid things in front of her.

She squirmed her purse higher up on her shoulder and said, "Leo said you could just talk to him if you wanted. Tell him some anecdotes or whatever, and he'll actually put the piece together. If you don't want to write it, if that would be too hard, we'd understand."

"I lived next to him when I was younger," I said. "He was just some kid and I was just some kid. We weren't even friends."

297

She was quiet for a moment, then said, "That's not what your mom said to Tasha's mom."

"Who talked to your mom, I'm guessing."

"Talked to Stephanie's mom, who talked to Rashid's mom, who talked to my dad."

The bell rang. "My mom wants to be closer to a tragedy," I said. "Doesn't everyone?"

"Look, if you don't want to do it, don't do it," she said. But in her eyes I could see her ticking down a list. Moving me down lower. No longer sticking me right at the top of the list of people she'd want to take over for her if they could.

I freed my chemistry textbook from the wreckage of my locker. "I guess I could do the interview," I said.

She reached out and squeezed my arm. *Nicole Kramer touched me.* "You're so brave," she said. And then she said, "Um . . . Laura? I'm really sorry for . . . you know. Your loss. Eesh, we're going to be late."

She galloped off to class, and she probably couldn't hear me by the time I found my voice to say, "I didn't lose anything."

At lunch, my best friend Priya and I lay on top of some unidentified senior's car, like we always do, to eat our carrot sticks and crappy cafeteria pizza and something they were calling chocolate mousse. She had big sunglasses on that made her look like an Eastern-Eyed Click Beetle and was tilting her face up to meet the sun.

"I'm way too pale," she said. "If people can't tell the second they look at me that I'm gonna get skin cancer, what's the point of living?"

"I ask myself that every day," I said. I was wearing a big floppy hat because even fake redheads can burn like crazy, it turns out.

She nodded toward the end of the parking lot. "They've still got those security guards," she says.

"Yeah."

"Like, what, do they think what'shisname's gonna waltz into campus and start blowing people up? Pretty sure that's against the laws of physics."

"Biology."

"Whatever."

"They want me to write about him," I said.

"Who does, the Gazettacult?"

"Yeah."

"Why?"

I broke a carrot stick in half and shoved a piece of it in her mouth so she wouldn't be able to speak right away. "I lived next door to him when we were kids."

She chewed slowly and swallowed. "Wild."

"I guess."

"Did you, like, know him?"

I shrugged.

"But you didn't, like, know he was going to do this."

"Are you joking? I haven't talked to him in, what, five years? We weren't exactly Facebook friends."

"Why not? I'm Facebook friends with this bitch who used to pull my hair in kindergarten."

"*Why?*"

"I dunno. I'm Facebook friends with everyone."

"But not Kirby Matheson."

She laughed a little. "No, I was not Facebook friends with Kirby Matheson."

"You still probably know as much about him as I do," I said.

I watched some seniors come out of the front door, shoving each other around. They say they're going to put metal detectors up by the front doors, but I still don't know if that's just a rumor.

"So what do they want you to write?" she said. "Something about what a sweet kid he was, how could he have done something like this?"

"They said I could do an interview if it's too *emotionally difficult* for me to write about it myself."

"Woe is Laura."

"They want me to humanize him," I said. "Talk about how he was as much a victim as everyone else."

"A victim of what?"

"I don't know. The system."

"Well, he was, like, mentally ill, right?" she said.

"You gotta assume, but, like, I'm on antidepressants and I'm not going to mow down a school, and it's thanks to people like him that everyone thinks I might."

She lay on the windshield and stretched her arm behind her head, shirt riding up to reveal the two piercings on the top and bottom of her belly button. "I guess it's important to talk about this shit from both sides. Feeling sorry for the victims, feeling sorry for him."

"Yeah. Sympathizing with him."

"He *was* a person."

"Why do people keep saying that like it means something?"

"Who said that?"

"Nicole. You."

"Wow, that's, like, a whole army."

"That's not even why they want me to write about him," I said. "They don't want me to write about him because they actually feel some kind of empathy for the guy. They want me to do it because they think it's such an edgy thing for the school to write about, that everyone will think we're so ahead of the times to be able to write about this guy as a fully developed whatever so soon after it happened. We'll have that kind of impartiality my sister's college counselor's always telling her she needs to try for her essays. You know what she tells her? That if they want an essay about who was the best president and why, you don't write about Roosevelt or JFK or Lincoln or Jefferson, because everyone's going to do those. You have to pick William Henry Harrison. You pick Chester K. Arthur. You pick *Nixon*. It doesn't matter who you have to defend as long as it isn't boring."

"So the newspaper doesn't want you to be boring. It'll be a nice change from bake sale announcements."

"But . . . once you decide you're going to find every little bit of anything good in absolutely everyone, or once you decide that it's important to *recognize* every single bit of good in absolutely everyone . . . I mean, don't you think that's potentially extremely fucked up? You're going to turn into one of those people who buys Hitler's paintings because you think they're proving some kind of point, when really the pictures aren't all that good and, oh right, he was Hitler. But good for you for being able to see past genocide! Look how enlightened you are!"

Priya said, "All right, Tiger, calm down. Matheson wasn't Hitler."

"Okay, so I'll give some interview about how he wasn't Hitler."

"I'm pretty sure it was Chester A. Arthur."

"That's what I said."

"Liar."

"Shut up."

"Just talk about something nice that happened when you were kids," she said. "You don't have to go and spell out, like, look at this poor troubled lad who deserves our forgiveness. Just talk about a time you hammered croquet brackets into the ground to pretend you were doing slave labor."

"What?"

"That's what I did with my next-door neighbor. But she died."

My throat felt tight all of a sudden. "In the shooting?"

She looked at me, sunglasses slipping down her nose. "What? No, she just, like . . . died. Last year or two years ago or something. I only know from Facebook. Her profile's still up with this extremely unfortunate photo. I want to send her family some anonymous offer to Photoshop the zits out."

"Okay, see, *she's* dead and you're not talking about her like she's some angel."

"Well, I'm a cold, heartless bitch—we know this." She pushed her sunglasses back up. "You're not."

"He wasn't my friend," I said.

She singsongs, "*I don't believe youuu.* Give me the rest of your pizza."

"No. I hate everything."

"I know, dear."

"What am I supposed to do?"

"Just tell a story," she said. "You're good at telling stories."

The newspaper office was bustling, mostly because we had a dance the next week and there were a lot of advertisements from our sponsors that needed to be arranged and printed perfectly. That was what everyone cared about at this point. This girl in the corner was sniffling into a tissue, but I think I remembered her having allergies.

Leo opened up a new document on his computer. "Okay, I'm just gonna take some notes, is that cool?"

"Yeah."

"You sure you don't want to write this yourself?"

"Uh-huh."

"Okay. Whenever you're ready."

I started with the facts, like a good reporter. "I lived next door to Kirby Matheson on Egret Lane from the time I was, I think, six to when I was nine. We were the only kids on the block, other than his sister, so I knew him pretty well. His mom and my mom were sort of friends. Like if they were both in the yard they'd stop and talk for a while, but it's not like they were going out to lunch with each other all the time."

Leo nodded, typing.

"We went to each other's birthday parties for at least a few years in a row. We used to play out in my backyard and he'd come in, you know, for apple slices or whatever when I was going in."

"What was he like?" Leo said.

And it was time to start storytelling.

"Nice enough," I said. "He was, you know, quiet. All that

stereotypical stuff people always say. He seemed so normal, never would have thought, et cetera."

"Did your parents like him?" he said.

"Parent. Just my mom."

"Right, sorry."

I didn't know why he was apologizing. There was no reason he should have known. "And yeah, sure, I guess."

"Did you ever think he'd do something like this?"

"What, you mean when I was eight?"

"Or since then, if you ever thought back to him."

"I didn't think back to him."

"Never?"

"Do you think about kids you knew when you were little?"

"My friends? Yeah, sometimes."

"Well . . . I didn't."

"Okay," he said. "So when you were a kid, then. You never thought he'd do something like this."

I said, "I still can't imagine anyone doing something like this."

"I don't know if we can use that," Leo said.

"Why?"

"I don't know . . ." He typed for a while. "It's just kind of obvious, I guess. That's what everyone says, you know. Unfathomable tragedy."

"Maybe that's because it's unfathomable."

"We're journalists," he said. "We have to dissect this stuff, it's our job. We can't just say something's too horrific to talk about. How about that rugby team that ate each other in the Andes? There are, like, four movies about those guys."

"So we're trying to make a movie, then?"

"Don't mince words, Laura."

I couldn't believe I used to have a crush on this guy.

"Okay," he said. "Why don't you tell me a story about him? It would make a good opener."

"Okay."

"Yeah, you got one?"

"Yeah."

He smiled a little at his screen. "Awesome."

"Okay, so one time . . . I was about six, maybe, and he was eight. I was in my yard catching all these fireflies in a jar; it was probably August. One of those sticky nights. Mosquitos. So I'm running around kind of scooping up as many as I can and trapping them in there, and then he comes out."

"Kirby."

"Yeah. And he says, 'Hey, gimme that.' So I give him my jar."

"Because he was your friend."

"What?"

"I'm just clarifying, you know, he asked you for something and you willingly gave it to him."

"Does that matter?"

"It's about filling in the holes, that's all. Making him make sense."

"So he took the jar," I said.

"You said you gave it to him."

"Okay, fine, I gave it to him. And he takes it and he pokes holes in the top of the lid so the fireflies don't die. I'd totally forgotten to do it."

"What did he poke the holes with?"

"What?"

"For the holes in the jar. What did he use? I'm guessing he didn't just have a pocketknife on him."

"So he ran inside and got a knife, I guess."

"That's interesting," Leo said. "You know, him having a weapon already."

"That's not . . . Maybe it was scissors."

"Scissors can be a weapon."

"This is so fucking stupid," I said plainly.

"No," he said. "This is actually really good. We can do a whole thing, like, juxtaposing how he felt about life. Saving a bunch of fireflies and . . . you know."

"And murdering a bunch of people," I said.

"Yeah."

"You're a journalist," I said. "You're not supposed to talk around stuff."

"Yeah, yeah."

"Don't mince words, Leo."

He hit ctrl-S on his keyboard. "Anything else?"

"I don't think so."

"Okay. Thanks, Laura. This will run in two weeks, probably. We don't want to put it in the dance issue. Seems kind of tacky. Thanks for doing this. It was really brave."

"Yeah."

Here we go. One night only.

You want to hear a story?

I was about six. I was in my yard catching fireflies, scooping them up into a jar. It was August, probably. One of those sticky nights. Mosquitos.

And the boy next door, the one who laughed that time I skinned my knee, the one who bit me, the one who used to ask me whenever I was crying if it was because I wanted my dead father—

He came outside and grabbed for my jar and said, "Hey, gimme that."

And he took it from me.

And he shook it until they were all dead.

I'd forgotten to put holes in it.

They couldn't get out.

HISTORY LESSONS

"Is that Matheson?" I ask. "What the fuck is he doing?"

Jackson half turns, following my gaze. He frowns.

"What's he got in his—"

When the bullet tears into Jackson, his brain misfires, sending frantic, confused messages through his body. It gets everything all tangled up. He doesn't know what's happening. He's dying faster than he can process it, dying faster than he can take in Kirby Matheson and the gun and where all the blood is coming from and why can't he get up because he wants to get up. *It's not happening, man, sorry*, I think, but what's coming out of my mouth is something else entirely, all of it animal, none of it words. Jackson's in my lap and he's heavy, heavier the more of himself he loses, his teeth stained red, his arms flapping uselessly against the ground like a bird with wings too broken to fly. Matheson looms over Jackson and me, his gun half poised, and I remember the three of us when we were young and how Kirby

was, and how I knew then—*I knew*—and how sorry they made me
for it and how sorry they'll all be now. I want to tell them both but
by the time I find the words, Jackson's dead and gunfire is echoing
in the distance.

"Mrs. Parker is drinking again. I could smell it on her."

"You're lying," Katy says from the front steps.

I dribble the basketball against the driveway.

"Why the hell would I lie about something like that?"

I'm not lying. Jackson's mom is drinking again. Bet she started
up as soon as she got the call. I always thought Mrs. Parker was looking for a reason to get back in the habit and what better one than
your son's death, right?

Not like you can tell a childless parent they haven't earned a shot
or seven.

"Remember when he told us she was getting help? Knew it
wouldn't last." I toss the basketball, the arms of my black suit jacket
straining against the reach. Suit doesn't fit. Last time I wore it was at
my cousin Lissa's wedding a year ago, but hell if I was going to buy a
new one for a funeral. "Just thought he'd be alive to see it."

The ball bounces off the rim of the basket attached to the garage.
It rolls down the driveway and out onto the street. I expect Katy to
chase after it for me like she always does, but she just sits there on the
front steps of my house, picking at her shoes. Her eyes are red and
watery and the skin of her nose is peeling from the constant leaking
and blowing ever since Matheson shot up the school. But I guess sex
appeal must transcend tragedy because every part of her that's right
is louder than everything that's wrong. Blond hair, bright blue eyes,

perkiest tits in town, and hey, all must not be lost if I can still appreciate the beauty that's in the world. My parents aren't home—they'll be consoling the Parkers for a while—so I decide I'm going to fuck Katy today, because if anything'd raise Jackson from the dead, it'd be that. He loved her, poor bastard, and the closest he ever got to nailing her was hearing about it from me.

"You know, you try to picture Matheson now and he'll only ever have a gun in his hands, but the thing is, he only ever *had* a gun in his hands. Just weren't looking closely enough." I scratch the back of my neck. Jacket's too small and the dress shirt I'm wearing is itchy, or maybe it's the T-shirt underneath. "Most of us, anyway."

I wait for it, wait for Katy to tell me how *I* was looking, how I knew, because it's the least I deserve to hear from someone else, but when I glance at her, she's not listening to me. I know she's not because she gets this little wrinkle right in the middle of her forehead when that happens.

"It's gonna be weird when we go back," I say, trying to bring her round to me again. "No Billie Palermo hanging around, staring at your rack."

That gets through. She winces.

"Shut up, Nate," she says, and then she surprises me: "And don't talk about her like that."

I raise my hands in mock-surrender because I don't know what else to do.

"Get me the ball."

She finally looks up to squint at it. The basketball ended up in a puddle across the street and drifts there stupidly like it doesn't know it's not meant for water. Jackson gave it to me for my birthday last year. I already had—well, a few. But to be honest, there's not much I don't have, so the thought's gotta count. I made sure every game of Twenty-one he lost to me—Katy cheering us on like we were saving the world—he lost playing with that ball.

"Get it yourself," she says.

I don't. I sit beside her, feeling the heat coming off her through the black dress she's wearing. It's a little small for her, so tight it rounds out her hips and hugs her ass. Who wears something like that to a funeral? Not that anyone really noticed. Jackson's funeral was the kind of thing he hates—hated: a production. The Parkers had to keep pushing it back to accommodate the number of rubberneckers who wanted to see the show. News crews, even. He's probably on television right now, his face a backdrop for a voice-over about a community in shock in a world that isn't.

I nudge Katy.

"Come on," I say, like it's as good as a heartrending speech about all the bullshit we've found ourselves living through. It's not, but it's the best I can do. Jackson was the one who was good with words and I'm better at stuff like this, I guess. I put my hands against her cheeks until she looks at me. I feel the makeup she's wearing, heavy and cakey, covering flaws she's sworn to never let me see, which makes me wonder why I like her if what I'm looking at isn't real. Then again, I don't really want to see what's underneath if she thinks it's that bad. Her lip trembles, all dry and flakey too.

"Should we talk about it?" she asks. "It's got to be eating you alive."

I let go of her face but suddenly some part of me wants to push my palm against her cheek and keep pushing until she falls off the steps.

"Nothing to talk about," I say instead, getting to my feet. "I'm going upstairs."

She follows me like I knew she would, and then we're in my bedroom and she's on top of me, her head tilted back, her long hair cascading over her shoulders, past her bare, milk-white chest. She unzipped her dress but didn't take it all the way off, so it sits around her middle and over my hips. I only took off my pants. She digs her fingernails into my scratchy black shirt, pretending to be into this, even though she's not. It doesn't matter. I don't really need her to be.

I'm no better anyway, if I'm being honest. I keep thinking about history class last fall. Ms. Leeland teaching us about Kennedy's assassination. She played it on the television and we watched, all of us leaning forward and holding our breaths, waiting for that moment the president went down. Leeland turned it off just before it happened, said we didn't need to see it. There was a tiny uproar and I was part of it, pissed enough to call the whole thing a tease. Leeland didn't like that, judging by the look she gave me for it. But I YouTubed it later, like I figure everyone else did. I'll never forget that spray of blood from Kennedy's head or Jackie flailing in her pink dress, desperate to make it all end differently somehow. I couldn't imagine what that was like, having someone die in front of you in that way. Now I know. What's really fucked up is they still have that bloody dress locked away somewhere, preserving the gore.

I didn't understand it then, why someone would do that, but I understand it now. It actually makes less sense to throw something like that away, the last part of someone you have.

Katy gets off me and I let my gaze drift out the window beside the bed. At first there's nothing out there, just my reflection faint in the glass, and then I blink and there's something, someone—this wiry thirteen-year-old boy materializes out of nowhere on the sidewalk.

I know you, I think, and as soon as I think it, my heart flattens out and goes still.

The boy's back is to me, his head tilted toward the basketball still floating in the puddle where we left it. The basketball Jackson gave me. I sit up and that dead feeling in the center of my chest gets worse. *I know you.*

"You were so mean to him," Katy whispers.

"What?" I turn back to her. She hasn't pulled her dress on. "Katy, what the hell did you just say to me?"

"Nothing."

Her eyes are fixed on a point beyond me, some point through me. I don't know. I look back out the window and the kid has disappeared. So has the basketball.

After Katy's gone, I hit the shower and then I hit the fridge, and then I hit the couch because the cold leftover spaghetti I finished off isn't sitting right. I stare at the blank TV screen and think about all the television Jackson isn't watching, will never watch, which is stupid because he likely wouldn't be watching it anyway, the fucking bookworm. *I'd* be watching it with my phone in one hand while he told me all about whatever book he was reading because I'm so *tragically under-read.* Which I guess is true. But the thing is, Jackson didn't know what it was like to stare at pages and have to untangle the letters on them into words, and by the time you've got the words to make a story, you're exhausted. It drove me nuts, him and Matheson going over all the old *Goosebumps* books Matheson's mom stockpiled from thrift stores. A whole world of killer dummies and scarecrows they never let me in on. I can read, even though it's hard. Hell, I even like doing it. I just choose what I read carefully because it takes me a while and there's plenty else I can fill that time with, and with more of it too. Jackson acted like it was his God-given duty to catch me up on the world of books, and he wasn't too bad at it either. I could tell you everything about *Game of Thrones* before it hit the small screen.

I wonder who's going to catch me up now.

"*Nate.* Wanna play?"

I blink and Ian's there, waving one hand in front of my face and holding an Xbox controller in the other. I can't believe I didn't hear him because he stomps around the house most days like someone's paying him to do it. He reminds me of Jackson when he was young, kind of. You get the sense the boy he is isn't too far off from the man he's going to become. I tell him to *fuck off* because *I'm busy* and then I sink deeper into the couch. He scowls.

"Fuck you," he snaps back, but the vehemence is lost in how shrill his voice gets, how it splits right over the *fuck*. He turns beet red and faces the television. Puberty's not been so kind to my baby brother. He's going through this stage where he reminds me of the Xenomorph in *Alien*, and by that I mean he looks like a weirdly elongated dick most of the time.

I close my eyes for a while until Ian curses and then I open them to check his progress. I'm a better player than he is. He's in an alleyway, cornered by zombies, which is how it usually ends up happening in this game. Melee is his preferred method of combat, usually, but when there's this much of a horde, the only thing you can do is shoot your way out. He pushes a button and his baseball bat disappears, swapped out for an assault rifle, and then zombie heads are exploding everywhere, a massacre. He works his way through and then he heals himself from what little damage he took before moving on, a pile of corpses in his wake. A cold sweat breaks out on the back of my neck.

Is that Matheson?

Ian's character slowly moves down an alleyway, a telltale sound cue alerting him to a special infected nearby. He crouches and then creeps his way to a weapons cache and finds a sniper rifle. He looks through the scope and everything seems to recede, the living room disappearing itself for a different place, a different time.

What the fuck is he doing?

What's he got in his—

Crack. Ian fires the gun. The bullet meets its target. The weirdly soft *thud* of its body follows, falling from the top of a building onto the ground.

JacksonJacksonJacksonnomanpleaseno—

I lean back into the couch, swallowing hard and breathing heavily. Too heavily. That must be what gets Ian's attention because next thing I know, his small hands are on my shoulders, a tight, yet somehow still weak grip. He says, "Nate." And he sounds just scared enough that it clears the fog in my head. He stares down at me and I want to tell him he's a baby, but not in the way I would to piss him off. Just that he's fucking young is all, and his hands are so tiny. He relaxes a bit when I finally register him and says, "You went, like—weird."

"I'm fine."

"I'm supposed to tell Mom and Dad if you act weird."

I glare at him, daring him to do it, to carve out a spot for him-self on my shit list. He knows better than anyone else that that's the worst place in the world to be. But he doesn't crack, the little pissant, so he just might risk it. I push him away.

"Don't be a fucking dick," I tell him. "And get lost for real this time."

He turns the game off and stomps out of the room. I smirk after him, but as soon as he's gone, that goes too and I'm sorry for all the silence that's left behind. Ian's not so bad, really. It's just—something's bugging me. I mean more than everything else that's bugging me. I walk over to the window and stare out of it, my gaze skimming the street, but it's empty.

When we were kids, I used to dream about Matheson. The same dream, over and over. And the weirdest part is he never did anything to me in it. He was just there, like I didn't want him to be.

When my parents come home, I'm still on the couch flipping through the channels, and the strange thing is, I don't remember getting up. At all. I don't remember Ian signing off for the night, but he must've. I just feel like I've been sitting and my index finger has been pushing the channel button for a while before the front door opens and the couch cushions on either side of me depress. Dad claps a hand on my shoulder but he doesn't leave it there, would never leave it there because he doesn't really know how to dad. Also, he's got to make room for Mom, who has to put both her arms around me, no matter how awkward a position she forces us all in to do it. She's so bony the comfort she thinks she offers feels more like a punishment.

"How are the Parkers?" My voice crackles. How long has it been since I used it? My eyes drift to the clock on the wall. After midnight. Jesus.

"Not too good," my dad says, just as useless as he always is when it comes to the more human stuff. Maybe his lack of being able to say the right thing is where I get it from. I'm sure Mom did all the Parker-consoling while he just sat there. "Not too good at all."

"How are you?" Mom asks. I shrug. Part of me wants to throw Dad's words back in their faces—*not too good, not too good at all*—so they could hear how absurd they really sound, but I won't. Mom's hand skims my hair. "Tell us what you need."

"Nothing," I say. "I'm fine."

"You're not fine, Nate," Mom says, which doesn't really leave me much to follow up with. I shrug again and she persists. "Tell us what's on your mind. Don't bottle it up. You know what happens when you do that."

"I don't know." But they're not satisfied with that. I keep my eyes on the television, some infomercial about a fancy blender. I clear my throat. "I was thinking about—about when we were kids. Me and Matheson. Remember that?"

Like they would ever forget. I feel the two of them look at each other over the top of my head. I lean back a little, waiting, because somebody owes me an apology, I think, and I would be okay to start with them. *We're sorry we doubted you, Nate. We're sorry we didn't understand what you were trying to tell us at the time. You were right all along. You knew.*

"You can't blame yourself," Mom tells me.

But that's not what I meant at all.

I open my eyes to Ian bitching about how *I liked Jackson too, so why don't I get to stay home?* He shouts it in the hall right outside my room just to wake me up. I guess that means no one's going to force me to go to school. I don't know how many days you get off after your best friend's insides end up all over your outsides, but I'm pretty sure I'm going to take them all.

I roll onto my side and close my eyes but sleep doesn't find me again, so I wait until I'm sure Mom and Dad have left for work and then I crawl downstairs. My stomach's too uneasy for something solid, so I grab one of Mom's protein shakes. My mother is obsessed with her weight; she can't trust herself to eat a meal, so she drinks them all. I down it in two swigs and it's chalky. If this is what she's living on, no wonder she's so fucking sad-looking all the time.

I lean against the kitchen counter and stare out the window. It's gray. It's been gray a lot lately, the weather in some weird synchronicity with everything going on. I move from counter to kitchen table, sifting through the mail. I get cards just about every day. Lots of them are from people I don't even know, all of them telling me how brave I am because I had a body on top of me and a gun pointed at my face. *Sorry, sorry your best friend is dead.* My mom's keeping them all, like these are the kind of mementos you want to look back on. I don't know. Maybe they would be, if they said the thing I really want to hear. I wonder what kind of cards Jackson's parents are getting. Matheson's.

I pace the kitchen until I spot an open letter next to the phone. I don't think anything of it until I see the signature on the bottom.

Miri Howard. It makes me feel something like—not nostalgia, but a turning inside out. Like my body is smaller than it actually is. Some fucked-up mental reversion into a previous self.

Dr. Howard.

This is how I remember Miri Howard: dumpy and middle-aged. So she's got to be even dumpier than that now. Definitely older. I was only thirteen when I saw her, and even then I couldn't understand why she was in such a rush to be so damn geriatric. How can you trust somebody like that enough to tell them whatever's in your heart? That's what she said to me that first day. *Tell me what's in your heart.* I was hungry because I hadn't eaten lunch yet—my parents promised me McDonald's after the therapy session was over—and my knuckles hadn't healed up, is what I think I said. Dr. Howard didn't like that at all.

You really hurt that boy, Nate. Aren't you sorry?

I pick up the letter—it's dated last week—and skim over it because what the fuck does Dr. Howard want with any of this. *Extend my condolences. . . . Given our history, I thought I'd let you know I'm here for Nate. . . . After a trauma like this, if he needs to address anything he's feeling—fear, depression, guilt. . . .* Guilt?

I laugh and it echoes hollowly around the room.

"I didn't kill anybody," I say to no one.

She closes out her condolences with *Call if you need anything.*

Her letter next to the phone.

Goddamn it.

Time for some recon. At lunch, I get in my BMW and I drive over to the middle school. I sit in the car and stare at the building. How do you trust a box like that now? Pressure cooker of kids, all of them hating or loving each other too much. And then those special few, the Kirby kids. Just give me five minutes, and I could weed 'em out. I know I could. Because I knew Kirby Matheson before *he* knew he was Kirby Matheson.

And I really hurt that boy.

It's fifteen minutes before I drag my feet out of the car and walk them into the school. When I push through the front doors, the smell is—all schools smell the same, I think. Sweat and cleaner and paper. It turns my stomach enough I'm afraid that if I take one wrong step, I'll vomit. I swallow hard, tugging at the collar of my over-shirt, pulling it away from my neck and adjusting the collar of the T-shirt underneath it. For a second I think I smell blood. I breathe in through my nose and out through my mouth—all that stuff they tell you to do that's supposed to help you when you're panicking but doesn't really help at all. A locker slams shut and the sharp, surprising cut of sound makes me flinch like a pussy.

When I find my feet again, sweet-talking the faculty is easy. Maybe easier now because of Jackson. I don't have to work so hard at charming; all I've got to do is make them feel like their worthless condolences mean something to me. I tell them *I'm here for Ian* and *Didn't my parents call, let you know I was picking him up? They were supposed to call. This whole thing with Jackson, it's just thrown them, I guess. . . .*

It works but it kind of feels like something I should apologize to Jackson for. Then again, I hope if I were the one who bit it, he'd use my name to open as many doors as he could for himself because he needed all the help he could get. All the help I could give him. Sometimes I wonder if I hadn't picked him whether or not he'd have been next to Matheson in the school that day, a gun in his own hands.

Sometimes I think I saved him.

I stand in front of the open doors to the cafeteria, trying to hear myself think over the swell of voices—the talking, laughing, shouting, shrieking—of mouths chewing, bodies navigating the spaces between each other. The clatter of trays and cutlery hitting the tables. My feet are stuck again, don't seem to want to direct me forward. I search the room for my brother but at first, it's like everyone looks alike. Moving targets.

Ian and I catch sight of each other at the exact same moment. His eyes widen in disbelief and his pimply face gets all flushed. I nod and he stumbles over to me with all the grace of someone who's only just discovered they've got feet and they're thinking too hard about how to use them. As soon as he reaches me, he says, "What's wrong? What happened? Are Mom and Dad okay?" Ian's like that. Doesn't see the point in having one thought at a time when he could have a million.

"Jesus, relax," I tell him. "You were bitching so much about having to come here today, I'm busting you out. Get your shit and let's go."

His eyes get even wider. "Where?"

"Does it matter?" Jackson and I used to bail and do whatever all the time. The point is, you're not in school. But Ian starts making this bitch-face, like school is the only place he ever wanted to be when he got up this morning. I roll my eyes. "You gotta come with me, man. Your teachers thinks this is a Mom and Dad–sanctioned field trip. You don't go, they'll start asking questions. If you blow this for me, I'll make you live to regret it."

"But," Ian whines, and his voice somehow manages to break over one syllable. Impressive. Before I can drag him out by his freakishly large ears, this girl sidles up, like a girl-version of my brother. All legs and arms and pasty skin, interrupted by swathes of irritated white-heads. There's something familiar about her I can't totally place. She says, "Ian, I'm saving your seat. Are you coming back . . . ?"

She notices me then and I smile at her, that winning smile Katy always tells me she likes because it gives her all sorts of dirty thoughts. The girl—whoever she is—turns red, her eyes growing as wide as Ian's. She steps back. That's all Ian needs. Next thing, he's practically dragging *me* out of the school.

"You asshole," he mutters.

I glance back at the cafeteria just to wave at her and piss him off, but I stop dead in my tracks because he's there again. In the corner. That kid from yesterday, the one who took my basketball. That flash thought—*I know you*—is in my head again, and when I blink, he's gone and all that's left is the unsettling question of whether or not he was there at all. I know I didn't see a ghost. I didn't see a ghost of a ghost. Didn't see that boy I knew years ago, didn't see his scrawny arms and legs and baby face before he grew up into a killer.

I didn't see Kirby Matheson.

I ask Ian when the last time he got drunk was and he tells me he's never been drunk and that settles that. I drive us down to the Hyland River's edge and take out the two six-packs in my trunk and it makes me feel depressed as hell because this was for celebrating.

This was for Jackson and the presentation he was supposed to make in English Lit, what was it, a week after he died? About some book that was so boring he didn't even think it was worth telling me about, and he could usually find something good in anything or anyone. (Like Matheson. *Stop it.*) He always got nervous when it came to that shit, talking in front of people, convincing them he was worth listening to.

Ian and I stretch out on the grass. I pick at the tab on my beer can. Ian's already had a taste and said he didn't like it, and I called him a prissy princess who didn't appreciate the manlier things in life, so now we're adequately annoyed with each other. He pouts while I drink. It's four beers before I feel like talking and four more before I wonder who's going to drive us home.

"So who's the girl?" I ask.

He turns red. "Don't want to talk about it."

"At least tell me her name, man."

He fights it for a long time, torn between wanting me to know— every guy wants to share when they've found someone worth jerking off to—and knowing nothing truly good can come from me having the information. Just more big-brother ammunition.

"Susanna," he finally says. "Susanna Byrd."

"Byron Byrd's little sister?"

"Yeah. Remember, you wrecked her scooter?"

I shrug like it doesn't matter to me one way or another. Ian makes a disgusted face. I remember. Of course I remember it now. Me and Jackson, holding her arms. Rick Harris pretending like he was going to run her over. But Rick was the one who smashed the scooter against the monkey bars, not me. He was the kind of guy the world answered to. So fucking cool. I wanted to be that guy. When he moved a couple of months after that, I was.

Christ. I haven't thought of him in a long time.

"Huh," I finally say. "Susanna Byrd."

"What?" A challenge.

I shrug. "She could do worse and you could do better."

Mom and Dad are not fans of the Byrds. The Byrds are a little too outside of our income bracket. My parents come from the good old school of never trusting people with less than what you have, because they're looking for ways to take it from you. It's an ugly philosophy, sure, but that doesn't mean it's wrong. They never liked the Mathesons, either, and look how that turned out.

"I never said I *liked* her," Ian snaps, because he never really gets when I'm giving him a compliment.

"Sure, right."

"Fuck off," he grumbles.

I like the way he hates me. It's familiar. Nice.

"Ian," I say after a minute. "Can I ask you something?"

"What?" He sounds wary.

"You tell Mom and Dad I was acting weird?" As soon as it's out of my mouth, he tenses and I'm not so buzzed that I can't see it. I angle myself up on my elbows. *"Really?"*

"I didn't tell them you were acting weird," he says.

"You sure about that? Because I found a letter from Dr. Howard by the phone today. Did you know about it?" He looks even more uncomfortable. "Oh, fuck. Seriously, Ian? And you didn't tell *me?*"

"They were only talking about it," he says defensively. I groan, lie back, and cover my face with my hands. "They've *been* talking about it. Maybe more since they got the letter last week. You can't blame them, I mean . . . you saw Jackson *die*, man. Right in front of you. And it was Matheson who did it, of all people. Come on. What makes you think they *wouldn't* want to send you to a shrink?"

"*A* shrink. *A* shrink is one thing," I say. "But Dr. Howard? What the fuck do they need to call her haggard ass for? Just because she saw me one summer, she thinks she knows me? That she's an expert on what went down with Matheson?"

"They didn't say they were going to send you to her specifically," he says, which isn't what I want him to say. He's supposed to say what a couple of idiots our parents are, thinking I can't handle this. He's supposed to side with me on this one, just grunt the affirmative if words escape him, but he doesn't. God, he sucks.

"If they set up an appointment behind my back," I say, "you gotta tell me." He still doesn't say anything. I kick him in the leg, hard. *"Ian."*

He sighs. "Yeah, sure."

"That's real convincing, man. I don't fucking believe you."

I finish off the beer in my hand and crack open a new one. It's warm but I don't care. Doesn't have to be cold to get you drunk. And I think I'm pretty much there because being pissed at Ian already feels not that important.

"First time I got wasted was out here," I tell him, and he looks slightly relieved that I'm changing the subject. "Me and Jackson. And we were exactly your age too. Summer we were thirteen."

"Jackson did that with you?" he asks. "That doesn't sound like Jackson."

"Well, it was." Jackson had a million reasons not to do things but he only needed one to change his mind, and I could usually provide it. I smile thinking about it, that day. It was good, like—just simple. It was simple when everything else that summer wasn't. "We stole some peach schnapps from his mom's liquor cabinet and just—"

"*Peach schnapps?* Who's the prissy princess now?" Ian demands, and I laugh because every time he's funny, I'm never expecting it. I know he's smart but I never really think of him as clever.

"Anyway, we liked it so much we did it again." Because that first time was amazing. Magic. Exactly the right amount of alcohol between us. We soared on it for a while, came home bright-eyed and red-faced, but our parents didn't notice a thing. The second time, well. Not so much. We thought we could only feel *more* amazing on more booze. Gross miscalculation. We were beyond seeing straight that day. Stumbling all over each other and freaking because we had no cover. That's when Matheson found us and helped us out, made sure we didn't drown in the river, called home for us, made our excuses, pretended we were all friends. And then Jackson got it into his dumb fucking skull that there was no reason we couldn't be.

He didn't know about Kirby like I did.

Ian clears his throat. "Can I ask *you* something?"

"Shoot." Bad choice of word.

"Kirby," Ian says. I stare at the sky and the sky is still gray. He says, "You're the one who beat him bloody."

"Yeah." I crumple up my now-empty can and toss it in the river, and something sparks in me a little, because I think if anyone's going to get it, it's Ian. He's smart. He'll tell me about my amazing foresight.

"So why wasn't it you? Why didn't he kill you?"

I stare at the moving water until it seems to stop.

"What the fuck, Ian?" I ask. "Why the fuck would you say that to me?"

Ian looks to the water and shrugs.

I'm in Katy's car and I mostly remember getting there. My head is against the cold window and my eyes are open and it feels like they've been open for a while, but they only just now decided to start seeing. I'm still drunk, I think, or else I'd be in a world of pain—I am *not* looking forward to this hangover. I listen to the wheels on the road, an aimless drive through town. The first signs of life I give her, she asks if I'm going to puke. I shake my head. My chin and neck are wet, which means I've been drooling on myself. Great.

"Where's Ian?" I ask thickly.

"After he helped me drag your ass into the car, I dropped him off at your place."

"Where's my car?"

"Where you left it."

"Okay." I close my eyes again and drift for a while until another question floats to my head and I can't seem to not ask it out loud. "What've I got to be sorry for?"

"What?"

"Nothing. Forget it."

"Baby." She reaches over and squeezes my shoulder. "What'd you say?"

I shift away from her touch as much as I can in the small space. "Everyone acts like I've got something to be sorry for. You. My mom. She told me I can't blame myself for it. Blame myself for what? I didn't do anything. You know what Ian said to me?"

"What?"

"He wanted to know why Matheson didn't kill me." I open my eyes and turn my head to her, give her a lazy grin. "I think my brother wants me dead. But I guess that's the way it's supposed to be." She doesn't return the smile. "It was a joke."

"It's not funny," she says.

I straighten. The seat belt's a little tight on me. "Oh, what? What the fuck, you think he should've killed me too?"

"That's a pretty big leap you just made there."

"And that's not an answer."

"You beat the shit out of Kirby when you were thirteen," she says, and it's true, I did. Bloodied my knuckles on his face. It felt good. "And then you never let him forget it—"

"Oh, and you're some saint, huh?" I demand. Her eyes stay on the road. "Hey, Katy, tell me what the last thing you said to Billie Palermo was."

Silence, just like I knew there would be.

"I keep thinking about her," she says after a while.

"Gross," I say, and it's meant to make her laugh, but it doesn't.

"We were total assholes to her."

"We were kidding around." I don't like thinking about Billie Palermo. It's one of those things that has become bigger now that she's dead than it was at the time. "And you didn't answer my question. You think he should've killed me?"

"Jesus, Nate. *No,*" she says. "It just means you gave Kirby Matheson a lot of shit, and when he came to school he had a shot at you and he didn't take it. That's all."

She takes her eyes off the road long enough to give me one of those looks that made me like her. That no-bullshit, this-girl-could-finish-my-insults look. Katy's a lot smarter than she lets people in on, and she says it's because the way she looks, no one's going to take her seriously anyway. But for just this second, I wish she were as dumb as she pretended to be, because between Ian and her, I got this thought in my head and it's that I gave Kirby Matheson shit and he had a shot at me and he didn't take it.

When she's sure I'm sober enough, Katy drops me back off at the river. I thank her for the ride. After she's gone, I sit on the hood of my car, the taste of her still on my lips. That's something I usually like, but now it just feels wrong.

I listen to the cars on the street, a little ways away, some group of people laughing. It's a startling sound. I feel like I've been living in a bubble where nobody laughs anymore, and if they do, they don't really mean it. I miss Jackson's laugh, stupid as that sounds. It was easy to make him laugh, and it's hard not to feel good about that kind of shit. I rest my arm over my eyes because my eyes are burning. Last thing I'm going to do is cry like a bitch next to the river, so I bump my head against the windshield until it's the only thing I feel. I don't want to go home, so I doze for a while, until the sun goes down and the streetlights turn on.

Until I hear this noise somewhere on the street behind me.

It takes me a moment to place it; the rubbery rhythm of a basketball hitting the ground. It draws my arm away from my eyes and makes me sit up.

The sound gets closer.

I slide off my car and face the street.

I see him.

A shadow on the sidewalk. I can't make out his face, but I know the shape of him, that gangly, awkward body. And there it is again: *I know you.* He's got that basketball—*my* basketball—in his hands, dribbling it against the pavement, and I say, "Hey!" before I really know what I'm doing or if I want to be doing it. He turns. A car goes by, washing his face in light, and it's like getting sucker punched because that's Matheson, somehow, I swear. It has to be because there can't be two of him, can't be more of him . . .

"Where'd you get that basketball?" I ask.

Of all the fucking things I could say.

And like that he drops the ball and tears off running, and before I know it, I'm after him, scrambling up the grass. My feet hit the pavement hard. He's halfway across the street by the time I'm where he was, but I can catch him. He's only a kid now. I can catch him.

I bridge the gap between us, getting so close. I reach out and my fingers nearly grasp his shirt, but he slips away, twisting between two cars parked on the curb. I maneuver my way between them, catching my shirt on the grille of one, hearing the material tear. I run into the road at the same time a car rounds the corner and clips me in the side—

—and the impact sprawls me across its hood. The sudden stop of the car hurls me to the ground. I land on my side, the wind knocked out of me so bad I'm afraid it'll kill me, the inability to get air back into my lungs. But after an agonizing moment, it happens, and once I can breathe, there's room enough inside me to feel all the rest of it. My aching shoulder and ribs. Jesus Christ. *Fuck.* Somebody says something about calling an ambulance even though I'm not any-where close to dead. Jackson's dead and I'm so far from it. I clutch my stomach as the crowd grows and grows around me and all I see are legs, and through them I see him again, hovering just outside the scene before he disappears.

I got bruised ribs, a bruised hip, but no broken bones, which in my opinion means I faced off with a car and won. Except my parents think this is a sign of something, think I threw myself in front of an oncoming vehicle in a fit of grief. So that's how I find myself in Miri Howard's office a week later while my mom waits outside in the car, as close to the front door as she can possibly get just in case I decide to take off.

Miri Howard talks to kids as young as six and as old as nine-teen. Her office is a mess of plastic toys and teenybopper magazines I wouldn't want any six-year-old reading. I sit in a hard plastic chair, staring at a pile of tiny metal cars that have been shoved into an empty room in an old Barbie Dreamhouse. After a while Miri's sil-houette fills out the frosted glass door to her office, and if that's any-thing to go by, she's gotten dumpier. The door swings open and I'm right. There she is, as grandmotherly as she's always aspired to be, her hair all silvered, more wrinkles than seem necessary lining her face. She smiles at me like we're old friends.

"Nate, why don't you come in?"

I get to my feet, sort of at a loss for how I should commandeer this. Throw one of those panty-dropping smiles her way so I can get mine? I shudder.

"You got tall," she says as I pass her.

"It happens," I reply. She closes the door behind me and I take a seat across from her desk in an even more uncomfortable chair than the one that was in the waiting room. It's hell on my beat-up body. She settles in her chair, pushing some papers aside to smooth her hands across the polished wooden surface in front of her. She meets my eyes.

"I'm so very sorry for your loss," she says, and she really sounds it and sometimes it's hard to know what to do about that. It's hard not to feel every part of Jackson's absence in that kind of sincerity.

"Thank you."

"I hear you got in a fight with a car. How'd that go for you?"

"I'm sitting in your office, aren't I?" I ask, and she smiles and it's freaky, the ease of this. I shrug and look at the dying fern in the corner. "Drunk boys will be drunk boys."

"I see," she says. "And how are your parents doing?"

I hesitate, not sure what she means by the question. The summer I was here because of the thing with Matheson, my dad had walked out. Temporarily. Left us for this walking, talking, midlife crisis named Grace until Grace realized how pathetic he really was. Before he came back, my mom spent most of her time locked in her bedroom while I had to look after Ian. If Matheson hadn't happened, that summer's highlights would have only been those moments of escape by the river with my best friend.

"Smooth sailing" is what I finally settle on.

"That's good."

An uncomfortable silence follows, and I wonder if she remembers how I don't do well with it, how there are only, like, two people I can stand to be quiet around and one of them's dead. I dig my fingers into the arms of the chair and I resist opening my mouth until I can't anymore.

"I knew," I say.

"What's that?"

"About Matheson. I knew."

She leans forward, just slightly.

"You knew he'd—did he tell you his plans to—"

"No, no, no," I say quickly, shaking my head. "Nothing like that. Just. I knew there was something fucked up about him, since we were kids. I tried to tell you guys. You didn't get it. But I knew what he was capable of then. I did."

Her gaze gets just a little too intense and makes me squirm. "You thought then that he was capable of something like this?"

"That's what I said." I hate this. Everything feels like—it's getting smaller, or something. My clothes feel tight. I swallow. "He died in my arms, you know."

"I know. I'm very sorry. That must have been unbelievably hard." Her voice is kitten-soft. I don't trust a voice like that. "Nate, do you think about that often? About when you were kids and what happened between you and Kirby?" I don't say anything, just shrug. "Why do you think that is, that you're focused on that?"

"You guys thought *I* was the fuckup. You thought I was *dangerous* for kicking his ass—everyone got so scared I'd do something like that again—but I didn't and I was *right* about Matheson because look at what happened—"

"You have some excellent hindsight," she says.

"Yeah, and I'm still not the one who brought the fucking gun to school." I glare at her. "Everyone wants to know why but I've always known the answer. Kirby Matheson has always had a gun in his hands. You just weren't looking closely enough. I was."

"Have you considered the possibility that this is your defense against what happened, Nate?" she asks. "A little revisionist history? Because I don't—"

"Why am I the revisionist?" I ask. "Maybe it's the rest of you."

"Okay, fair enough. Tell me about what Jackson was like back then," she says, and I blink. It's not what I was expecting her to say at all.

"Jackson?" I can't help the smile that kind of lands on my face when I think of Jackson. "He was like Ian is now. You know. Scrawny. Shy. Bit of a loser, before me." And she laughs at that. "He was a good kid. Thank God I fixed him."

"Okay," she says. "And you. What do you think of yourself during that time, Nate?"

"What?"

"What do you remember about yourself?"

"I don't know what you mean." I shift in the chair again. "I was just me."

"You want to know how I remember you?" she asks, and I open up my arms like *Go for it.* "Shorter. A smart aleck." I smirk but she doesn't stop there. "But I also remember a boy who felt like there were a lot of things out of his control. Your dad walking out on you, your mom not handling it so well, and then Kirby Matheson—"

"And then Matheson comes along and tries to steal the last good thing I got left," I say before she can keep going, and I am acutely aware of how right out of the pages of some thirteen-year-old girl's diary I sound. But it's true. There's no better way to put it. Matheson tried to take Jackson from me when I needed him more. I chew on my thumbnail. "You know, he didn't just *find* me and Jackson at the river. He followed us there, just looking for a space he could fit himself in. He wasn't even trying to hide it. Who the fuck does that?"

"Someone who wants a friend," Miri says.

"No . . ." I stop, laugh. "Okay."

"Okay what?"

"That's your lead-in, right? You're trying to make me guilty."

"Why would you think that?" she asks.

"Because that's what everyone's doing." I start ticking it off on my fingers. "Katy thinks I should feel guilty. She thinks this should be eating me alive. My mom thinks I should be blaming myself; my little brother thinks Kirby should've killed me. And now you, you're sitting here trying to make me feel bad because you think Matheson wanted to be my friend? And what, he went on a shooting spree because I told him to fuck off?"

"No, Nate, that's not it at all," she says, but I'm not buying it, because otherwise people wouldn't keep saying this shit to me. "After a violent tragedy like this, it's not uncommon for people to be determined to make sense of it. You've got a loaded history with Kirby Matheson and you seem fixated on it—"

"Not more than anyone else."

"It's not quite the same." She pauses. "You're focused on the past, but not in a productive way." She stares at me, and I make myself stare right back. "You see, I don't think you knew Kirby was capable of what he did, and Kirby's not around to tell us why he killed his classmates. It's nobody's fault, but it's important that when we have these opportunities to look inward, we do. To realize it's not really about Kirby now, it's about what's left." She leans back in her chair, surveys me. "And if you don't deal with it, it's going to deal with you."

"So how was it?" Katy asks me from the front step.

"Pointless," I say. "My mom asked me when I think I'll be ready to go back to school this morning. Yours bugging you yet?"

"No," she says. "What do you think it's going to be like?"

I dribble the basketball against the driveway. Even this little movement bugs the sore parts of my body, but I grit my teeth against it. Pretend it doesn't hurt until it goes away.

"I don't know. I haven't really thought about it."

I've thought about it a lot. About what it's going to be like to take those first steps inside, to find the place so changed. Katy said there's been talk about building some kind of memorial, because it's not like you can pretend it never happened, and no one's going to tear the school down to forget it. We'll just live with our dead until we join them.

"What if something happens?" she asks. "What if someone—"

"No one took a shot at you," I tell her. "The only person who might have is dead. You've got nothing to be afraid of, Katy."

I toss the basketball and watch it bounce off the basket. One of our spare balls. It rolls down the driveway, out onto the street. I turn to Katy. Our eyes meet. She gets to her feet and jogs after it, manages to reach it before it finds its way into the road. She tosses it to me.

"Let's go upstairs," I tell her.

"Okay."

I watch her head in. As soon as the door is closed behind her, I roll the basketball down the driveway and watch it reach a new puddle across the street. When I go inside, Katy is talking to Ian at the kitchen table. He's working out some math problems and she's helping him because, like I said, my girl's smart. Katy scruffs up his hair and then she laces her fingers through mine.

"Stay down here for an hour or so," I tell him. He doesn't answer. I smack him on the back with my free hand and get a grunt of acknowledgment. "Dick."

"Fuck off," he grumbles.

In the bedroom, Katy takes off her pants while I take off mine.

"How do you think Mrs. Parker is doing?" she asks me.

"Not too good," I say. "Not too good at all."

I toss my pants on the floor and watch her take off her shirt, because I always like to watch that part. She catches me, turns pink, and even smiles a little while I admire her, and for a minute it's like everything's how it was. This is me and her, like it always is, and Jackson's downstairs, sitting on the couch, maybe playing video games with Ian and silently lamenting the fact he's never the one who's getting laid. And Matheson—Matheson's just this brief moment in time that never amounted to anything.

Jackson's just downstairs. . . .

I'm so lost in it that I grab the edge of my overshirt and pull it a little upward before I realize what I'm doing, and then it all hits me at once. I let it go before Katy can see what's underneath. My arms hang uselessly at my sides. The moment is over, except that's not true—it never really existed.

"What?" she asks.

"Can I ask you a question?"

"You can ask me anything," she says.

The quiet stretches between us, and in that quiet I think of Jackson and the bullet, his body in my arms. I think of Kirby Matheson and the gun he always had even when we couldn't see it. I think of my fist against his face when my hands were no bigger than Ian's. I think of Jackson's blood. How I was covered in it. It seeped through my clothes, stained my skin red. I took a shower that same night, peeled out of my shirt, and I'll never forget the tacky feeling of it separating from me. After I washed myself off, I remembered Kennedy and the pink dress and how it's been kept safe, and I couldn't throw my shirt away or wash it out. I feel it now, settled against me, the blood long since dried, the deep red turned rusty brown. That's never coming out, what's left.

What if it's my fault he's dead?

"Nate?" Katy tilts her head. "What is it?"

"Nothing. Never mind." I clear my throat. "I'm, uh—I'm going to leave the shirt on."

She takes my hand and hers is warm.

"Come on," she says.

Katy gets off of me and I let my gaze drift out the window beside the bed. The basketball sits in the puddle where I left it. After a moment the boy is there too.

My reflection, faint in the glass.

ABOUT THE AUTHORS

"Miss Susie" by Steve Brezenoff
Steve Brezenoff is the author of the young adult novels *Guy in Real Life*; *The Absolute Value of -1*; and *Brooklyn, Burning*, as well as dozens of chapter books for younger readers. He grew up on Long Island, spent his twenties in Brooklyn, and now lives in Minneapolis with his wife, Beth, who is also a writer for children, and their children, Sam and Etta.

"Violent Beginnings" by Beth Revis
Beth Revis is the *New York Times* bestselling author of the Across the Universe trilogy and the companion novel, *The Body Electric*, as well as numerous short stories. She's currently working on several new YA novels in her rural North Carolina home with her family and dogs.

"Survival Instinct" by Tom Leveen
Tom Leveen is the author of several YA novels, including *Party*, *Sick*, *Random*, and *Shackled*. His novel *Zero* was a YALSA Best Book of 2013. Tom has twenty-two years of theater experience as an actor and director, and frequently teaches and speaks at high schools,

universities, and conferences. One of his goals in life is to help people know and believe that their words, written or spoken, can make the world a pretty awesome place. So? What d'you say? He's on Facebook, Twitter, and at tomleveen.com.

"The Greenest Grass" by Delilah S. Dawson
Delilah S. Dawson is the author of *Hit*, *Servants of the Storm*, and the Blud series, including *Wicked as They Come*, *Wicked After Midnight*, and *Wicked as She Wants*, winner of the RT Book Reviews Steampunk Book of the Year and May Seal of Excellence for 2013. She has short stories in the *Carniepunk*, *Unbound*, and *Three Slices* anthologies in addition to novellas and comics. Her next book is *Wake of Vultures*, written as Lila Bowen. Delilah lives in the north Georgia mountains with her husband, two kids, a floppy mutt named Merle, and a Tennessee Walking Horse named Polly. Delilah dealt with bullying and depression in high school and tried to take her own life. She's glad she failed, because it really did get better. (www.whimsydark.com)

"Feet First" by Margie Gelbwasser
Margie Gelbwasser has written for many magazines including *SELF*, *Ladies' Home Journal*, *Parents*, *New Jersey Monthly*, and *Girls' Life*. She's had two YA novels published by Flux. *Inconvenient* (2010) was named a 2011 Sydney Taylor Notable Book for Teens, and *Kirkus* called *Pieces of Us* (2012) "suspenseful, disturbing, and emotionally fraught." She also writes middle-grade books under the name Margaret Gurevich. *Chloe by Design: Making the Cut* (Capstone, 2014) her first middle-grade novel, is billed as a "Project Runway for Teens," and received praise from *School Library Journal*, *VOYA*, *Booklist*, and

Kirkus. The sequel, *Balancing Act*, will be published by Capstone in September 2015. She lives in New Jersey with her math-wiz husband and superhero-loving son.

"The Perfect Shot" by Shaun David Hutchinson
Shaun David Hutchinson is the author of *The Deathday Letter*, *fml*, and *The Five Stages of Andrew Brawley*. His fourth novel, *We Are the Ants*, is set to rule the world in spring 2016. He lives with his partner and dog in South Florida and watches way too much *Doctor Who*.

"The Girl Who Said No" by Trish Doller
Trish Doller is the author of *The Devil You Know*; *Where the Stars Still Shine*, an Indie Next List Pick; and *Something Like Normal*, which was a finalist for NPR's Best Teen Books of All Time, among many other accolades. She has been a newspaper reporter, radio personality, and bookseller, and lives in Fort Myers, Florida, with a relentlessly optimistic Border collie and a pirate.

"Pop" by Christine Johnson
Christine Johnson grew up in, moved away from, and finally came home to Indianapolis, Indiana. She lives there with her two kids. She likes all kinds of things, but making things up and writing them down is her favorite. Follow her on Twitter—@cjohnsonbooks.

"Presumed Destroyed" by Neal Shusterman and Brendan Shusterman
Neal Shusterman is the *New York Times* bestselling and award-winning author of *Bruiser*, which was a Cooperative Children's Books Center (CBCC) choice, a YALSA Popular Paperbacks for Young Adults pick,

and on twelve state lists; *The Schwa Was Here*; and the Unwind dystology, among many other books. He lives in California with his four children.

Brendan Shusterman, whose artwork inspired many elements of *Challenger Deep*, is a budding artist and author—not just following in his father's footsteps, but blazing trails of his own.

"The Second" by Blythe Woolston
Blythe Woolston lives and writes in Montana. Her first novel, *The Freak Observer*, earned the William C. Morris award. She followed with *Catch & Release* and *Black Helicopters*, which was shortlisted for the Montana Book Award and won the High Plains Book Award for YA. Her fourth novel, *MARTians*, lands in October 2015.

"Astroturf" by E. M. Kokie
E. M. Kokie writes about teens, particularly those on the cusp of life-changing moments. Her debut novel, *Personal Effects* (Candlewick Press, 2012), was a YALSA Best Fiction for Young Adults and Amazing Audiobooks for Young Adults Top Ten title, a Lambda Literary Award Finalist, and a 2013 IRA Young Adult Honor Book. A lawyer by training, she loves a good story and a good debate, even better if she can have the last word. She can be found online at www.emkokie.com, tweets as @EMKokie, and blogs at www.thepiratetree.com, a collective of children's and young adult writers interested in literature for adolescent readers and social justice issues.

"Grooming Habits" by Elisa Nader
Hi. I'm Elisa. I like cheese and reading and binge-watching TV shows. Writing is scary, but not as scary as, say, Civil War amputations. My

debut novel, *Escape from Eden*, was released in 2013 and received a *Kirkus* star by a (possibly drunk and very kind) reviewer. I'm an Aquarius. Uh . . . let's see . . . I'm not very good at writing my own biography. Or autobiography. I guess this is reading more like a slightly incoherent personal ad.

"Hypothetical Time Travel" by Mindi Scott
Mindi Scott is the author of *Live Through This* and *Freefall*. She lives near Seattle, Washington, with her drummer husband.

"All's Well" by Cynthia Leitich Smith
Cynthia Leitich Smith is the critically acclaimed, *New York Times* bestselling author of the Tantalize-Feral universe series YA novels. Her titles have been honored among Oklahoma Book Award finalists, NEA Choices, CCBC Choices, Bank Street Choices, YALSA Popular Paperbacks, Writers' League of Texas Book Award winners, and more.

She was named the first Spirit of Texas young adult author by the Young Adult Round Table of the Texas Library Association and the first young adult author to be honored with the Illumine Award by the Austin Public Library Friends Foundation.

Cynthia is a popular writing teacher, serving on the faculty of the Vermont College of Fine Arts MFA program in Writing for Children and Young Adults. Find her at www.cynthialeitichsmith.com.

"Burning Effigies" by Kendare Blake
Kendare Blake is the author of six novels, including *Anna Dressed in Blood*, *Antigoddess*, and *Ungodly*. Her writing is generally dark, violent, and full of doomed love and cursing. When she's not writing,

she enjoys travel, eating, and eating while traveling, especially if the food is weird or French and drowning in sauce. She lives in Kent, Washington, with her two cat sons, her baby dog son, and her husband. Contact her at her website: kendareblake.com.

"Holes" by Hannah Moskowitz
Hannah Moskowitz is the author of *Break*; *Invincible Summer*; *Gone, Gone, Gone*; *Teeth*; *A History of Glitter and Blood*; and the middle-grade novels *Zombie Tag* and *Marco Impossible*. Her novels have received starred reviews, landed a spot on the ALA's Rainbow Book List, and received a Stonewall Honor. She currently lives in New York City. Visit her at hannahmoskowitz.com.

"History Lessons" by Courtney Summers
Courtney Summers lives and writes in Canada. She is the author of several YA novels, including *Cracked Up to Be*, *This Is Not a Test*, and *All the Rage*. Visit her online at http://courtneysummers.ca.

HERE'S A LOOK AT A POWERFUL NEW NOVEL
FROM ONE OF THE AUTHORS OF *VIOLENT ENDS*,
SHAUN DAVID HUTCHINSON:

15,000,000,000 LY

I SAT BESIDE THE WINDOW PRETENDING TO READ PLATO'S *Republic* as the rest of the passengers boarding Flight 1184 zombie-walked to their seats. The woman next to me refused to lower her armrest, and the chemical sweetness of her perfume coated my tongue and the back of my throat. I considered both acts of war.

In the aisle seat a middle-aged frat bro babbled on his phone, shamelessly describing every horrifying detail of his previous night's date, including how drunk he'd gotten the girl he'd taken home. And he ended each sentence with "like, awesome, right?"

It sounded less, *like, awesome*, and more like date rape.

"Flying alone?" asked the perfume terrorist. She had a Chihuahua face—all bulging eyes and tiny teeth—and wore her hair in a helmet of brassy curls.

"Yeah," I said. "I'm searching for someone."

"And they're in Seattle?"

"I don't know," I said. "Which is why I'm searching for him rather than meeting him." I wasn't exactly *trying* to be rude, but I hated flying. I understood the mechanics, knew my risk of dying in a car was far greater than in a plane, but cramming a couple hundred sweaty, obnoxious people into a metal tube that cruised through the air at five hundred and fifty miles per hour short-circuited my rational brain and loosed the primal, terrified aspect that didn't grasp science and assumed flying the unholy product of black magic. Reading and not having to make small talk kept me calmish. Not that my oblivious seatmate had noticed.

The woman tapped my book with a well-manicured fingernail. "It's nice to see a young man reading instead of staring at a phone."

"Let me tell you about cell phones," I said. "They're two-way communication devices designed to slurp up your private personal information through their cameras and microphones and myriad sensors, then blast that data into the air for any determined creep to snatch and paw through. You believe no one is watching because it helps you sleep at night, but someone is *always* watching. And listening and collecting your GPS coordinates, from which they can extrapolate that you swing by Starbucks every morning on your drive to work, except on Fridays when you take the long way so you can grab a tasty breakfast sandwich. Phones are doors into our lives, and the government keeps copies of all the keys."

The woman smiled, her coral lips taut, and lowered the armrest. Finally.

But I hadn't really spoken to anyone in so long that instead of returning to my book, I kept talking.

"My boyfriend disappeared," I said. I peered over the seats at a gangly flight attendant near the cockpit who was facing the exit, gesturing at someone with his hands.

"Thomas Ross. He's who I'm hoping to find in Seattle." The flight attendant glanced over his shoulder, his hawkish nose a compass needle pointing directly at me.

"Interesting," the woman said, though her tone said otherwise. I kept babbling anyway.

"Tommy vanished two months ago. I'm the only person looking for him. Not the police or our friends. Not even his parents. He disappeared and they've stitched closed the hole in their lives; continued attending their everyone-wins-a-trophy soccer games and forced family suppers, because to them, he never existed."

The flight attendant slid into the galley to allow a red-faced sheriff's deputy wearing a hunter-green uniform onto the plane. A burnished gold star hung over his left breast pocket, and he carried a gun clipped to a belt strapped around his waist.

The sheriff's officer floated down the aisle, his shiny shaved head swiveling from side to side, scanning each traveler like he possessed a Heads-Up Display feeding him their names and personal details.

"Tommy'd earned a 3.98 GPA," I said. "He worked as the assistant editor for the Cloud Lake High *Tribune*, kicked ass on the debate team. And I'm certain he loved me. It's the only thing I'm certain of. He wouldn't have just left."

The woman, and everyone else on the plane, watched the cop shamble in my direction.

"Teenagers often make rash decisions," the woman said. "Your *friend* will turn up."

Turn up. Like a missing sock or the Batman action figure my older brother had hidden from me when we were younger. Like Tommy wasn't missing but had simply been misplaced.

"Also," I said, "the universe is shrinking."

The sheriff's officer stopped at my row and faced me. His name tag read BANEGAS. "Oswald Pinkerton? I need you to come with me."

"No Oswald Pinkerton here," I said. "Maybe he's on a different flight."

The cop puffed out his chest, trying to conjure the illusion that he was tough, but his arms looked like the only thing they were used to lifting was a television remote. "Don't be difficult, kid."

"Perhaps you should do as he asks," the woman said. She tucked her legs under the seat so I could, what, crawl over her?

"Let's go, Oswald." Officer Banegas moved aside to allow my seatmates to shuffle into the aisle and clear me a path.

So close. One flight, with a layover in Atlanta, from finding Tommy. Or from crossing off another place he wasn't and further crushing my remaining hope of ever seeing my boyfriend again. If Palm Beach County's Least Competent had stopped for coffee or taken a detour to the toilet to feed the sewer gators, the flight attendant would've shut the doors, the pilot would've taxied to the runway, and I'd have escaped. But maybe this was better. If I'd gone and hadn't found Tommy, I might have been forced to entertain the possibility that he'd vanished for good. This way, I could continue believing I'd find him.

I sighed, grabbed my backpack, tossed the *Republic* inside, and followed the deputy off the plane.

Banegas clapped his hand on my shoulder, leaving me no choice but to accept my temporary defeat. The hatch clunked shut, and I resisted the urge to turn around. My feet weighed a hundred pounds each. Clearly, God had cranked up the gravity.

The terminal—with its gaudy, outdated palm-tree-and-pastel Florida decor—greeted us as we exited the jet bridge. Deputy Banegas guided me to a seat in front of the windows with a view of the runway.

"Wait here," Banegas said. He moved off to the side and mumbled into his shoulder radio.

My plane backed away from the terminal to begin its journey. *My plane.*

I'd planned my getaway perfectly. I'd convinced my parents that Lua, Dustin, and I were road-tripping to Universal Studios for the weekend, and I'd begged Lua to cover for me even though I wouldn't tell her where I was going. She'd reluctantly agreed after extracting a promise that I'd explain everything when I returned.

I'd paid for the plane ticket using a prepaid credit card and found a place to crash using HouseStay to avoid having to deal with a front-desk clerk who might question my age. I'd even downloaded Seattle public transportation apps and devised an efficient search pattern that would have allowed me to best utilize my time.

But despite my planning, my plane was flying away without me, and my parents were definitely going to ground me, probably forever.

My life's pathetic theme song repeated in my head. *You failed. You failed. You're a loser and you failed. Dada da doo dee.*

Lua could've written better lyrics, but the beat didn't suck.

Officer Banegas loomed over me. "Come on," he said. "We'll wait for your parents in the security office."

"Can I watch my plane take off at least?" I asked. "Please?"

"Whatever, Oswald."

"Ozzie," I said. "Only people who hate me call me Oswald."

"Fine," Banegas said, annoyed or bored or wishing he'd called in sick. Then he smirked and added, "Oswald."

I walked to the window. My breath fogged the glass as the last feeble rays of the day lit the sky to the west with the colors of orange-and-pink swirled sorbet. I tracked my plane as it turned at the end of the runway. The wing flaps extended. I'd always wondered at their purpose, but never enough to bother looking it up. I considered asking Deputy Banegas, but he struck me as the type who'd cheated his way through college and had only joined the police force because he thought carrying a gun would be cool, then had been disappointed to discover the job consisted mostly of filling out paperwork and offered depressingly few opportunities to actually shoot people.

"How'd my parents find me?"

"Hell if I know," Officer Banegas said.

"Oh."

My plane's twin engines roared. I couldn't hear them inside the terminal, but I imagined their growl as the blades spun madly, faster and faster, struggling to reach critical speed before the road ended. I imagined myself still buckled into my seat, gripping the armrests, trying to ignore my seatmate's fragrance offensive and banal chatter.

The front wheels lifted as the nose pitched up. The air pressure over the top of the wings decreased, allowing my plane to defy gravity. It soared into the sky while I remained rooted to the earth.

Deputy Banegas tapped my shoulder. "Come on, kid."

"Sure." I retrieved my backpack and followed Banegas. We'd reached the lone shop in the center of the terminal when the shouting began. People ran to the windows. I ran to the windows.

Banegas yelled after me, cussing and huffing. I ignored him.

I pressed my face to the glass, crowded on both sides by travelers and airport personnel, and watched my plane tumble from the sky and crash into Southern Boulevard on the far side of the fence separating the runway from the road.

I didn't think about the individuals who died—the perfume bomber, the frat-bro date rapist, the passengers who'd watched Officer Banegas perp-walk me off the plane—only that they burned beautifully.

Then the floor shook; the windows rattled.

Someone screamed, breaking the held-breath paralysis that felt like it had stretched across infinite days though had lasted but the length of a frantic heartbeat.

Officer Banegas's radio squawked. He stood to my right, his arms limp, his eyes wide, watching the nightmare through the glass like it was a TV screen rather than a window.

"Holy shit," he said.

Panic spread like a plague. Rumple-suited businessmen with phones permanently attached to their ears, weary parents and hyper children, heartsick halves of couples desperate to reunite with their missed loved ones, usually ornery ticket agents, and every spectrum of humanity between. None were immune. They screamed and huddled under rows of seats and ran and cried, their actions ineffectual. Their tears inadequate to douse my plane's beautiful fire.

I didn't cry.

Not me.

I laughed.

And laughed and laughed and laughed.

It took two paramedics and a shot of something "for my nerves" to dam my laughter, but far more effort to finally quench the flames.

14,575,000,000 LY

DR. TAYLOR DAWSON REMINDED ME OF BEAKER FROM
The Muppet Show—all lanky with wild red hair and bulbous, para-
noid eyes. How the hell was I supposed to take a man who looked
like a Muppet seriously? Meep meep, motherfucker.

"Do you know why you're here, Ozzie?" Dr. Dawson sat in a spa-
cious flannel chair with a legal pad balanced on his knee. He was the
first of my many therapists to favor paper over a touch-screen tablet.

The therapists my parents forced me to see always wanted to
know why I thought I was there. Sometimes I claimed my parents
had too much money and an overwhelming sense of suburban
guilt. Other times I said it was because my brother had freaked
out when I'd boarded my windows and taped cardboard over the
air vents to keep government spies from spraying me with poison.
I most enjoyed informing them they were nothing but the next
name on a list; an alphabetical convenience. Everyone deserved to

understand their place in the universe, including two-hundred-dollar-per-hour psychologists with tacky, generic paintings hanging on their walls.

Which is exactly what I told him. "You were the next name on the list of psychologists approved by my parents' insurance. After Conklin, but before Dewey."

Dr. Dawson scribbled a note on his pad. "I see you have a healthy sense of humor."

"I don't find this funny," I said. "I'm missing work to waste my time talking to you."

"You believe this session a waste of time?"

"Of course."

"Why?"

I cleared my throat. "This is a waste of time because we're going to spend the next"—I checked the time on my phone—"twenty-nine minutes discussing my parents and my brother and possibly the crash of Flight 1184, because everyone seems to want to know about *that*, after which I'll tell my parents you're a quack or that you leered at me or wore cologne that gave me a headache, and they'll schedule an appointment with the next doctor on the list, who will ask me the same stupid questions as you, and to whom I'll give the same stupid answers."

Dr. Dawson's face remained impassively goofy. "Therapy only works if you participate."

"Is that so?"

"It is," Dawson said.

I raised my hands over my head. "Then let's make with the healing, Doc."

Dr. Dawson wrote another note. *Dear Diary, patient is combative and entirely too chatty. I recommend intensive electroshock treatments and a full frontal lobotomy.*

"Why don't we start with your parents?" he said.

"Fantastic."

"Do you get along with them?"

"Meh . . . ," I said. "The *real* problem is they don't get along with each other. Which is why they're getting a divorce."

Dr. Dawson nodded along. "Does that upset you?"

"Why should it? I'm leaving for college after graduation—probably—and Renny's shipping out for basic training in a month."

"Renny is . . . ?"

"My brother Warren, but everyone calls him Renny."

"Are you two close?"

"I have this recurring dream where I'm sailing a boat on a chocolate pudding sea. Renny flies overhead on a missile equipped with a saddle and stirrups, toward a village inhabited by man-sized, flesh-eating emus. He yells that he really loves scrambled eggs before the missile strikes the emu village and explodes."

"Are you worried about your brother joining the military?"

"I'm worried he's going to shoot his foot off," I said. "I'm worried he's going to be the guy everyone hates and who winds up eating his gun from shame. I'm worried the army is going to strip away the things that make him my brother and return him to us as a hollowed-out shell of a human being."

Dr. Dawson's eyebrow twitched, but he refrained from writing down what I'd said, though it probably killed him a little. "It's clear you have complex feelings regarding your brother, and I'd like to unpack those during our next session, but right now I'd like to discuss Thomas Ross."

"Or we could talk about something else." I wriggled in the leather Judas chair I'd been forced to endure, trying to find a comfortable spot. "For instance, were you aware Maya Angelou worked briefly as both a madam and a prostitute? Or that D. H. Lawrence climbed trees in the nude to combat writer's block? I've never had writer's block—not that I write, I'm more of a reader—but I doubt buck-naked tree climbing would help if I did. I should give it a try."

Dr. Dawson nodded appreciatively. "Why do you believe you're the only person who remembers Thomas Ross?" Clearly my non sequitur had failed to deter Dawson. It had worked on Dr. Askari, though it honestly hadn't taken great effort to derail her thought train.

"I'm not crazy," I said.

"No one is suggesting you are."

"Aren't you though? Isn't that why I'm here? Parents of perfectly sane kids don't send them to therapy."

Dr. Dawson frowned. "Of course they do. Therapy helps people sort through complex thoughts and emotions. Think of therapy as an antibiotic for the mind."

"So you're saying I'm diseased? That I've got a mental infection?"

"That's not what I'm saying at all," Dr. Dawson said. "And I think you're smart enough to know that." He moved his legal pad to the side table, giving me his full attention. "Now, why don't you tell me about Thomas Ross."

Dawson wasn't the first persistent therapist I'd encountered. Dr. Butte had evaded my attempts to dodge her questions too. I'd had to resort to asking her how often was too often for someone my age to masturbate in one day to fluster her.

"What's to know? I met Tommy in second grade. He kissed me in eighth. He was my boyfriend and best friend. July third, he existed; July fourth, he didn't. Not even his parents remember him."

"Why do you?"

"Because God has a warped sense of humor? How should I know?"

"Do you have a theory?"

"I have a lot of theories."

"Tell me one."

As therapists went, I kind of admired Dr. Dawson's tenacity, but he wanted to know about Tommy. He'd probably ask about Flight 1184 before our hour was up, which necessitated this being our one and only session. It also meant it couldn't hurt to indulge him a little.

"Have you ever heard of a false vacuum?" I asked.

"I have not."

"The scientific explanation, which I have to admit I probably don't understand as well as I should, describes the stability of our universe as the result of resting in the lowest possible energy state. A false vacuum is one in which it only appears we're in the lowest energy state, until a vacuum metastability event occurs, knocking us into an even lower state." It'd taken me a long time to wrap my brain around the science, and I figured it probably didn't make much sense to Dr. Dawson either. Which he confirmed.

"I'm not sure I understand," he said.

"Imagine the universe is a pot of nearly boiling water. The bubbles on the bottom of the pot are other universes that appear real and stable to their inhabitants, but which, in reality, are not. Eventually, those bubbles rise to the surface and pop. That's a false vacuum."

Dr. Dawson's hand twitched. "And you believe we're living in a bubble on the verge of bursting?"

"It's a theory."

"But how does that account for Thomas Ross's disappearance?"

I'd said more than I'd meant to, but I'd already decided to tell my parents Dr. Dawson fell asleep during our session as my excuse for not wanting to see him again, so it didn't matter.

"If our universe is a false vacuum, then it stands to reason we're part of a larger universe. What if the people living in the real universe are trying to warn me?"

Dr. Dawson uncrossed his legs and recrossed them, resting his hands in his lap. "So your theory is that the inhabitants of the true universe have stolen your boyfriend and left you the sole custodian of his memories in order to send you a message?"

"Like I said, it's one possibility. Besides, there are other weird events."

"Flight 1184?"

Shit. I'd walked right into that one. "Sure."

"Do you feel up to discussing it?"

"Why not? I'll always remember those long, meaningful talks I had with the FAA investigators as the highlight of my nearly brief life."

Dawson retrieved his notepad. I swear he actually looked relieved to hold it again. "The police report states you were laughing after the plane went down."

"Went down." I shook my head. "Why does everyone go to such

ludicrous lengths to avoid saying 'crash'? They say the plane 'went down' or 'fell' or, my personal favorite, 'attempted an uncontrolled emergency landing.' But the fact is the plane crashed. It crashed into the ground killing a hundred and sixty-seven people. A hundred and fifty-five in the plane, and twelve on the road it crashed into. If Renny hadn't snooped on my computer and ratted me out to my parents, the death toll would've been one sixty-eight."

"Why were you laughing, Ozzie?"

The FAA investigators had asked me the same question a hundred different ways. I think they believed my laughter was an indication I'd caused the crash or been involved in some way, but they hadn't found a speck of evidence I'd been responsible. After they released me, my friends and parents constantly told me how lucky I was fate had plucked me from my uncomfortable seat on the express flight to a fiery death. But I didn't feel lucky.

Dawson patiently waited for my answer. Less than ten minutes of our session remained, and I had nothing to lose.

So I said, "You want to know why I was laughing?"

He nodded. "I do."

"Because I went looking for Tommy and the universe killed a plane full of people to suggest I stay in Cloud Lake. Don't you think that's funny?"

Dr. Dawson glanced at his notepad, then at me. "No, Ozzie, I don't."

"Well, I think it's hilarious," I said. "Especially if it's true."